Transformed . . .

The cats prodded and nipped at me. They wanted me to do something, but what?

"What do you want?" I whispered. "I don't understand!"

They only continued till I drew back in alarm, about to strike back at these who had been my only friends. But there was something else growing in me, more than fear, stronger than anger, something burning up and blazing free—

Magic. My magic. I had no idea how I did it, but I was suddenly a cat among cats, and slipping easily with them through the narrow window out into the free world outside. I was an odd, pale cat, rough-furred and not particularly pretty, but it was so amazing to have this shift in senses, this sharpening of scent and sound, this change in how I moved, to have a tail to lash and whiskers to twitch—oh, I cared not how I looked in that first wild moment.

But I was a human as well as a cat, and the two natures were too overwhelmingly curious. I *had* to know what Aunt Dorcas had been planning to do with me. And then, with my altered sense, I could smell the foulness, and with my human mind I knew: Aunt Dorcas was working in the Black Arts.

—From *Cat-Friend* by Josepha Sherman

D0048491

MAGIC
TAILS

Edited by
Martin H. Greenberg
and Janet Pack

DAW BOOKS, INC.
DONALD A. WOLLHEIM, FOUNDER
375 Hudson Street, New York, NY 10014

**ELIZABETH R. WOLLHEIM
SHEILA E. GILBERT
PUBLISHERS**
http://www.dawbooks.com

Copyright © 2005 by Tekno Books and Janet Pack

All Rights Reserved.

DAW Book Collectors No. 1340.

DAW Books is distributed by Penguin Group (USA).

All characters and events in this book are fictitious.
Any resemblance to persons living or dead is coincidental.

If you purchase this book without a cover you should be aware that this book
may have been stolen property and reported as "unsold and destroyed" to
the publisher. In such case neither the author nor the publisher has received
any payment for this "stripped book."

The scanning, uploading and distribution of this book via the Internet or any
other means without the permission of the publisher is illegal, and punishable
by law. Please purchase only authorized electronic editions, and do not
participate in or encourage the electronic piracy of copyrighted materials.
Your support of the author's rights is appreciated.

First Printing, September 2005
1 2 3 4 5 6 7 8 9

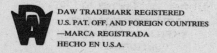

DAW TRADEMARK REGISTERED
U.S. PAT. OFF. AND FOREIGN COUNTRIES
—MARCA REGISTRADA
HECHO EN U.S.A.

PRINTED IN THE U.S.A.

ACKNOWLEDGMENTS

Introduction copyright © 2005 by Janet Deaver-Pack

"Ali Babette," copyright © 2005 by Thranx, Inc.

"Cat Among the Pigeons," copyright © 2005 by Elizabeth Ann Scarborough

"Dark Eyes, Faith, and Devotion," copyright © 2005 by Charles de Lint

"Sleeping Beauties," copyright © 2005 by Jody Lynn Nye

"The Snow Queen," copyright © 2005 by Michelle West and Debbie Ridpath Ohi

"The Devil's Bridge," copyright © 2005 by Edward Carmien

"Pharaoh's Cat," copyright © 2005 by Lisanne Norman

"Cat-Friend," copyright © 2005 by Josepha Sherman

"The Bedtime Story," copyright © 2005 by Edward Serken

"Bargains," copyright © 2005 by Richard Lee Byers

"All the Pigs' Houses," copyright © 2005 by Mickey Zucker Reichert

"Ever So Much," copyright © 2005 by Bruce Holland Rogers

"Suede This Time," copyright © 2005 by Jean Rabe

"The Cobwebbed Princess," copyright © 2005 by Andre Norton

CONTENTS

INTRODUCTION

Janet Pack

"Dogs think they're human. Cats *know* they are." Those of us who are fortunate enough to share our lives with cats understand very well that this quote is not quite true.

Obviously, cats are quite different from humans. They are thoroughly mythological, and at least half magical. Their very attitudes suggest the veracity of this statement. Finding them in odd places (or just trying to find them sometimes) hints at their ability to disappear. Reaching up walls toward doors or windows invisible to two-legged associates is common. Cats watch things in midair, perhaps in other dimensions. Their talents to get what they want when they want it are fundamentals of cat psyche. And their abilities to sense when we need solace, protection, or cheering up are legendary. They also have an excellent network for adopting us as companions, using animal shelters as their locus operandi. And they've all been quite proud since human medical research has proven that cats can help reduce hypertension, worry, and loneliness.

I came out of the closet a few years ago about being cat-dependent. That was a shock, but one I embraced wholeheartedly after a hard look at my past. A beautiful longhaired gray-and-white lady named Star adopted me around age 5. Her son Prince used to help me with my homework. My next four-legged partner was Ari Mithral Shannonn, a 16-pound, turquoise-eyed, red-nosed Siamese-tabby. He thought himself my protector as well as my playmate until complications from diabetes conquered him. Bastjun Amaranth and Canth Starshadow padded after in his enormous pawprints. Now I'm urged to say that I share my life with two black cats named Tabirika Onyx and Syrannis Moonstone, and a large rare mist cat longhair who deigns to answer to Baron Figaro de Shannivere. All of them were (and are) different, all treasures of their species.

Here are thirteen new stories for felineophiles, featuring all aspects of cat machinations without a hairball among them. From leading children into dark and uncommon paths, to outsmarting the devil, to solving mysteries and protecting their human charges to the end of their nine lives, all these stories revolve around the wit, the uncommon abilities, and the intriguing natures of cats.

So pull up your favorite pillow, keep the scratching post nearby, and have your designated human light the fire. A walk through imagination with cats is never dull. Good reading! After all,

"A cat's a cat for all that."

Janet Pack
Tabirika Onyx
Syrannis Moonstone
Baron Figaro de Shannivere
Williams Bay, Wisconsin,
June 2002

ALI BABETTE

Alan Dean Foster

Alan Dean Foster was born in New York City and raised in Los Angeles. He has a bachelor's degree in Political Science and a Master of Fine Arts in Cinema from UCLA. He has traveled extensively around the world, from Australia to Papua, New Guinea. He has also written fiction in just about every genre and is known for his excellent movie novelizations. Currently, he lives in Prescott, Arizona, with his wife, assorted dogs, cats, fish, javelina and other animals, where he is working on several new novels and media projects.

Soda was glad she didn't have to close up. Even without being stuck with the responsibility of securing the place, Monday nights sucked. True, a less-than-grand total of four customers since nine o'clock made for no fights, no arguments over who had the next game on the one slightly tilted pool table, and reasonably clean johns, but it also meant next to nothing in the way of tips. When you were young, single, and tending bar in greater New York (actually it was Hoboken, but greater New York sounded so much better), you needed every buck from every jerk. She bid good night to Dave, who would handle the closing, and left.

Only one fool hassled her on the bus on the way home. It was too late and too cold outside even for most muggers. Glancing left and right before getting off the bus, she assured herself no one was lurking in the shadows waiting to jump her. Concluding the brief reconnaissance, she knew she was luckier than many. Her building was only a block from the bus stop.

It was dark, it was freezing (hey, it was Jersey in January), and she was drained. The weekend had gone pretty good, but now she needed rest. She had the next three days off, and she intended to use every one of them to catch up on her sleep and Those Things What Needed Doing. Maybe Gerry would call. Stax was sharp, looked great, dressed fine, but he was a lazy narcisstic bum. Bit of a raging male chauvinist, too. By contrast, Gerry didn't look like much; but he was pleasant enough and made good money working for the Port Authority and was occasionally nice to her. After five years working steady behind the bar at the DEW DROP INN on Clancy Avenue, and after as many failed relationships, she was ready to sacrifice muscles for money and compliments for kindness. Her mother called it maturing. Soda called it growing tired.

Being moderately attractive, she had discovered soon after graduating from Carver High, didn't automatically guarantee you the hand of a Prince Charming. It didn't even guarantee you a chance with the Evil Grand Vizer. Most of the guys who wandered in and out of the DEW DROP INN were little more than testosterone-powered lumps of clay.

Not that she was in desperate need of permanent male companionship. She was used to being on her own. But—it *would* be nice to have someone warm to curl up next to at night. Someone to confide in, someone you could talk to secure in the knowledge that your words wouldn't be taken the wrong way, wouldn't be twisted into something nasty and hurtful.

She'd had her fill of that.

The pillow caught her eye because of the way it reflected the light that was bolted over the entrance to the apartment building. It caused her to pause below the landing. More than a dozen heavy cardboard boxes had been dumped beside the stone steps, next to the regular garbage bin. They were pregnant with junk, the refuse of lives too busy to bother with their contents. Most of what she could see in the dim light looked just like that: junk. But the pillow was different.

Nobody was peeking out any of the first-floor windows, watching her. The panes of the old brownstone were dark. No one else in the building that she knew of worked her late hours. Moseying over to the pile of cardboard, she peered closer at the corner of the pillow that was protruding from one. The material looked like silk, or maybe satin. It did not appear to be stained. Either way, it was a cut above what she had tossed on the secondhand couch in her tiny living room.

After a brief struggle with the box sitting above it, she pulled it free. It was a throw pillow of normal size. Gold tassels decorated the four corners and gold fringe, apparently intact, lined the seam. The material itself was silvery. Her couch was a patterned forest green, but the potential contrast didn't concern her. *Architectural Digest* was unlikely to come calling to do a story on her place any time soon. Intricate embroidery in a script she didn't recognize decorated both sides of the shimmering material. Under her gentle ministrations it fluffed up quite nicely. Finding it almost made up for the lousy night at the bar.

It looked good, snugged in a corner of her couch, resting up against one rolled arm. Setting aside the mug of instant hot cocoa she'd brewed, she reached down to carefully smooth out the fabric so the elegant gold embroidery would show clearly, rubbing her open palm from one corner of the pillow to the other.

On the third hand pass, the pillow exploded.

Well, didn't actually explode. Smoke and haze erupted from it, but the only sound was a soft underlying hissing. Fearful that it might contain some harmful substance, she put her hand over her nose and mouth and stumbled backward toward the kitchen. She was hunting for the phone to call 911 when, through the rapidly dissipating vapor, she found herself staring at—a cat.

Sitting on the couch atop the inexplicably reconstituted pillow, the cat stared back.

This in itself was nothing remarkable. Staring was a common attitude of cats. What *was* extraordinary was the cat's attire. In fact, she mused as she forgot all about the telephone, calling 911, and everything else, *any* cat attire was extraordinary. Cats came clad in fur; long or short. They did not dress in diaphanous silk pantaloons, jewel-encrusted turbans, miniature vests of gold-and-silver thread, and small boots of crimson silk boasting upturned toes. When they visited apartments in northern New Jersey, they tended to arrive via cracked doors or half-open windows, not exploding pillows. Otherwise, the interloper appeared to be a perfectly ordinary gray-and-black housecat.

That was a very big Otherwise, however.

Clutching her robe closed, she swallowed hard. Before she could pause to reflect on the absurdity of it, she found herself asking, "How did you get in here?"

Perhaps not surprisingly, the cat rose to stand on its hind legs, crossed its front paws over its chest, and replied, "Thrice you rubbed the enchanted Pillow of Sitting and Sleeping. I came at your command."

"It wasn't a command," she protested, remembering to add, "You can talk."

"Verily, fifty-five languages and one hundred and sixty-two dialects can I speak, plus the languages of the djinn that no human can understand."

"Djinn? You mean, you're a genie?" Aware that she was speaking nasally, she removed her hand from her nose and mouth. If it hadn't hurt the cat, the smoke and mist that had heralded its improbable arrival was probably harmless to her as well. She was tired and bewildered, but otherwise felt all right.

"I am the djinn Asami el-Razar el-Babesthi the Magnificent, of the line of Al-Bintetta the Stupendous, of the djinn of fabled Samarkand. The great and ancient Samarkand of trade and legend, not the sorry Central Asian pit stop it is now."

"How—how did you get here?"

"Air courier. I was a gift that was not appreciated, and was peremptorily cast out without the vessel wherein I dwell being properly caressed." Burning bright yellow eyes regarded her thoughtfully. "You have released me from the Pillow. Thereby am I commanded by the Great and Almighty Turazin, ruler of all the feline djinn, to grant, whosoever caresses my container appropriately, three wishes."

"Three wishes!" This wasn't happening, she told herself. But then, why not? This was Jersey. Anything and everything could happen in North Jersey, and often did. Visions of riches vast enough to embarrass the Lotto began to swim in her head. Or at least, they did until the djinn spoke again.

"Alas, there seems to be a problem."

A catch. There was always a catch. That was Jersey, too. "What problem?"

"You are not a cat. I am not a djinn of the human kind. I am a djinn of the Felidae. I am empowered to grant cat wishes to cats. That is one reason why I was not released earlier from the Pillow. The one who dwells high above you and who received me does not associate with cats."

"That's pretty dumb of them. Me, even though I've never been able to afford one, I've always really liked cats. Sometimes I'll feed one or two of the neighborhood strays, but they never stick around."

"Very sensible attitude."

"If you don't mind, I think I'll have to call you Razar. Your full name is a bit of a mouthful for me."

Dropping back down to all fours, the djinn looked around the apartment. "Speaking of mouthfuls, I'm been asleep for two hundred and twenty years, and I'm famished. You wouldn't happen to have any cream around, would you? Or a dead mouse?"

"Sorry. Fresh out. Although it shouldn't take long to find rats in this neighborhood. How about some milk?"

Long whiskers and pink nose screwed up disdainfully. "I prefer thick cream. But no djinn can choose its place of releasing. Milk will do."

She sipped her cocoa and watched the cat as it sat contentedly on her kitchen table and lapped milk from a saucer. "About those three wishes, now. You're sure they have to be cat wishes?"

Sitting back on his haunches, Razar daintily licked his right paw and used it to clean his milk-stained whiskers. "I very much fear that is the way of things. While I cannot conjure mouse or milk for my own meal, I could for example provide my new Master with an unending supply."

"Hey, no way! Remember what I told you about the neighborhood rats. If that's what I wanted, I wouldn't need to wish for it."

Razar the Magnificent belched softly, in most stealthy feline fashion. "Not bad milk. I prefer that which comes from the dromedary, but this was most eminently satisfactory. I confess that beyond my customary bindings I find myself favorably disposed to you—to you—"

"Soda," she replied quickly. "That's not my real

name, of course. My real name's Emmaline Ray Coarseguth. From Waco, originally."

"I can see why you prefer the other." The cat turned thoughtful. "As I say, I quite like you, Soda. But the Law is the Law, and I cannot break it. What can I do to favor you within the strictures that are imposed upon me? How about a charmed scratching post that will never wear out?"

"No thanks." She brightened, crossing one leg over the other. Part of her robe fell to one side. "Could you make it, say, an eighteenth-century ivory-and-precious-stone-inlaid French marquetry cabinet with a scratchable leg?"

Protruding through small slits in the top of the golden turban, fuzzy ears dipped forward. "Alas, it is not within my power to manifest such transparent circumventions. The wishes I grant must be those any true cat would long for."

This wasn't going as well as she hoped. "How about a lifetime supply of canned tuna?"

Razar brightened and stood up on his hind legs. In that posture he looked terribly cute, she decided, in his admirable miniature genie outfit. "Now that is something I may easily obtain for you! Your first wish?"

"No, no." She waved him off and he dropped back to all fours. "I'm just trying to establish some parameters here, that's all. Actually, I'm not real fond of tuna."

"You have no taste." The cat was clearly disappointed. One paw rose to indicate the rest of the modest apartment. "But your dwelling confirms that."

"Look, I didn't wish for criticism either. This is nothing that a small bejeweled palace swarming with servants wouldn't fix." She waited a long moment before adding, "I suppose that's out of the question, too?"

Whiskers bobbed as Razar nodded gravely. "No

solid gold cat boxes either. Gold means nothing to a real cat."

Then what would, she pondered? If she was a cat, what would she wish for that would also prove of some value to a human? The djinn had mentioned cat boxes. She doubted wishing for one filled with small diamonds instead of clay litter would fulfill the requirement of asking for something a cat would also want. For that matter, a cat would probably disdain diamonds in its litter box, gemstones being decidedly nonabsorptive.

She might be able to wangle a nice bed out of The Magnificent, but she already had a bed. Dammit, this wasn't fair! She had recovered the pillow and freed its somnolent occupant. Didn't she deserve a proper reward? So she was taller and had less hair than a Siamese or Calico, so what?

That line of reasoning would gain her nothing but frustration, she realized. It wasn't Razar's fault. He seemed more than willing to please. But it appeared that rules were rules, even for feline djinn. Just like she couldn't serve anyone under eighteen, and sometimes had to cut off regulars who'd imbibed too much.

No matter how hard she tried, she couldn't think of anything that would appeal to a cat as well as herself. Then it came to her. Setting her empty mug aside, she drew her robe tighter around her. Outside, the cold depth of night still chilled the city.

"Cats love strong smells, right? I want a vial—no, make that a gallon. Yes, that's it. A gallon of the finest perfume."

"Ashelemak—so it shall be." Rising again onto his hind legs, Razar brought his front paws together in— well, not a clap. They were cat's paws, after all. It was more like a soft *pouf*. From within the pouf, an exquisite decanter appeared, filled to the brim with a bright golden liquid. Delighted, she reached excitedly for the stopper. Removing it, she brought the inner tip toward her nose.

It never got close. Hurriedly, she restoppered the gallon decanter.

"What the hell is *that*? It smells awful!"

"To a human, perhaps." Razar was unapologetic. "To a cat, it is the essence of aromatic beauty."

"But I wanted perfume suitable for a human!" she protested.

Front paws spread wide and the djinn shrugged soft, furry shoulders. "You wished for perfume. I am compelled to bring only that which is intended to satisfy cats, not humans."

She nodded slowly and sat back in the chair. This was going to be harder than she'd imagined. At least the fine crystal decanter was salvageable—provided she could ever get that hideous smell out of it. And she'd wasted her first wish. She wouldn't make that mistake again. She couldn't afford to. Perhaps she should try to be as realistic as possible about the situation, scale back her wants.

"What about a lifetime credit at the Fulton Fish Market?" Visions of endless lobster dinners sallied through her head.

"Your second wish?"

She shrugged. She was dead beat, and the conundrum she faced seemed insurmountable. "Hey, why not?"

"Arelemoku!" Paws traced a rapid pattern in the air. By now she was used to the smoke and vapor. It seemed unnecessarily theatrical.

A square piece of parchment appeared on the water-stained coffee table in front of her. Frowning, she leaned forward to get a better look at it. "This isn't a card granting credit."

"Of course not." Razar shook his head slowly. "Did you think a cat would carry a credit card, or any kind of human document?" One paw tapped the parchment. "You must memorize this. As soon as you have done so, it will vanish."

"What is it?" she asked dubiously.

"A detailed map of the market to which you wish unrestricted entrance, showing every entryway and exit plus the times of day and night when they are never watched. During those times, you may slip freely into each booth and secure whatever seafood you desire. This ability will now be with you forever."

"I can't steal fish! That isn't what I wanted. Even if I could, I can't spend that kind of time away from work."

Razar the Magnificent shrugged again. "A cat could. Any cat would be thrilled to be granted this kind of access."

Two wishes gone. She absolutely, positively, could not waste the third and last. "You said that you liked me. But you're not being very helpful."

"I'm sorry. Truly I am." He sounded sincere. "Don't you see, Soda? The enormity of the problem facing you has defeated many, many humans down through the ages." He sighed. "It is ever the same when I am accidentally called forth by a human instead of by a cat. Humans and cats simply want different things. There is no way around it." He met her eyes evenly. "You might as well spare yourself the mental agony and just wish for something simple to get this over with. A toy play mouse, perhaps, or a ball of string. And could I have some more of that milk, please?"

While she poured him another saucer full, she ruminated on the unfairness of it all. A real genie, three genuine wishes—and all three of them apparently useless to her. She could think of many things to wish for: all of them priceless to a cat and far less so to a human.

She could wish for a lifetime of good health, and

probably receive it—provided she was willing to see veterinarians for the rest of her life. She could ask to never go hungry again, and probably wouldn't—provided she was willing to eat cat food. Face it: cats' wants were simple and straightforward. It seemed they did not, did not ever, coincide with those of human beings.

Except perhaps . . .

She straightened in the kitchen chair. It was hard and cold against her back. Like so many of the things in her life. "Here is my third wish, Razar."

He stopped lapping and rose one more time onto his hind legs. "Are you certain, Soda? I truly feel for you. But believe me when I say that you have been preceded in your frustrations. I hope that I may grant you something a little useful, at least, before I must leave you."

Having given the matter considerable thought and come to a resolution, she nudged the saucer closer to him. This time, she was reasonably certain what she was going to ask for would be understood by any cat. Or at least, by any female cat.

"My third wish is for a male companion for the rest of my life. One who is forever kind, thoughtful, and considerate. One who won't abuse me, or curse me, or steal my paycheck. One who won't spend all his time watching television, or complaining about my cooking, or the way I look when I wake up in the morning. One who'll sleep beside me in bed, and help to keep me warm, and whose love will be undying, no matter where I live or if I put on a little weight when I grow old."

The djinn nodded understandingly. Reaching toward the ceiling with both hands, he hissed the command "Asenarelt!"

There was a sizable *pouf* of mist. When it cleared, he was still there. Only now his fine raiment had gone, turban and slippers and vest and pantaloons and all,

down to the last gleaming jewel. Only he remained.
Reaching out as he contentedly resumed sipping his
milk, Soda slowly stroked the head and back and tail
of Razar the Magnificent, late of glorious and splendid
ancient Samarkand. Glancing up from the milk, he
winked at her. Then he began to purr.

Unsurprisingly, she was quite content.

CAT AMONG THE PIGEONS

Elizabeth Ann Scarborough

Elizabeth Anne Scarborough is a Vietnam Army Nurse Corps veteran and author of numerous short stories and 25 novels, including the 1989 Nebula award-winning *Healer's War*. She has been collaborating with Anne McCaffrey on the Acorna series. Her most recent solo novel is *Channeling Cleopatra*.

I never expected to see Sarge after his escape and yet, one day I was awakened by the familiar but half-forgotten sound of his voice.

Sarge and I first met in a prisoner-of-war camp, where he saved my life and I saved his. Our services to each other at that time are of no particular consequence to the tale at hand, so suffice it to say that he prevented his fellow prisoners from making a meal, a hat, and fiddle strings from my person. He was rather surprised when I reciprocated by keeping him well supplied with the fat carcasses of the rats and occasional birds I caught in my capacity as guardian of the prison's granary. In doing so I helped him gain strength for his escape, in which I also assisted.

As I escorted him out the back way from the prison's storehouses, he saluted me with a last scrub of my ears and disappeared into the woods.

After the war, I found lodgings with an elderly woman and her equally elderly cat, Willow, in their cottage beside the forest road. I was thunderstruck when Sarge came to our door bearing a deer for dinner. He remembered me as well as I remembered him.

"Well, bless my soul! It's my old mate Captain Shadow from the prisoner of war camp at Castle Keep," he said. "This *is* a fine surprise! Here now, Captain, look at the fine big rat I've brought *you*."

That night we feasted, and afterward Sarge and Dame Agatha exchanged stories. In the process she disclosed something I had never known, that she had once served the queen, first as a chambermaid and then as a nurse to the twelve princesses. In particular, she had many stories about the mischievous and resourceful eldest princess, Marni.

She also told Sarge of the strange goings on at the palace, and the king's offer to give any man who could discover how the princesses came to ruin a new pair of dance slippers every night for the last six weeks the princess of his choice and half the kingdom.

Several princes had already tried to find out what the girls did at night to wear out their shoes, but had had no success and now languished in the royal prison.

Sarge laughed. "What a problem! I fear I can't take it too seriously after the rest of what the country's been through. Sounds to me like bored, rich, spoiled young ladies trying to amuse themselves. Couldn't be too hard to solve, eh, Captain Shadow?" I was seated on his shoulder and rubbed my face against his grizzled cheek.

"Well, then, why don't you try?" Dame Agatha asked.

"Me?"

"Yes. The nobility hasn't been able to outsmart the princesses, which is why the king has said that any *man* who could solve the riddle could claim the reward."

Sarge grinned. "That sounds like fun, but I doubt the king would be willing to give *me* such a great field promotion. And I confess it seems to me to be a lot of fuss over nothing. I don't see why the king hasn't simply had a woman stay with them at night.

"He tried that, but all of them claimed the girls slept soundly through the night. I think the women set to guard them fell asleep themselves and didn't like to confess it. No, simple it may seem to you, but the princesses have fooled everyone, and the king is in a proper tizzy about it."

Sarge said, "I suppose any father would be, if his daughters had such a secret and wouldn't confide in him. And for a king, people might decide if he couldn't control his own daughters, he wasn't fit to rule."

"I suppose that's why if they fail, the princes have been tossed into prison. So they can't carry more tales home to their fathers, who might try to take advantage of the situation."

Sarge shrugged and scratched my cheek thoughtfully. "I've been in prison and faced death all these years with no hope of reward—not even my back pay. This sounds easy by comparison, eh, Captain Shadow? Shall we have a go at it?"

He slept that night curled in quilts by the fire and I slept beside him, my tail on the floor and my front paws and chin on his shoulder, for it did not suit my purpose that he should slip away without me. If he stirred, I would know it. Old Willow sauntered up to me after he and Dame Agatha were asleep.

"I suppose you'll be going with this man, Captain Shadow?"

"He'll need someone to get him out of prison again if he fails," I told her. "I've done it before."

"Very well," Willow said. "Since you've been kind

to me, I will give you some advice. Princess Marni
was not as young as Dame Agatha implied when we
left service at the palace. She was fully twelve years
old, and had helped care for her ten sisters. The ninth
weakened her mother so that she was constantly ill.
The tenth sent our gracious queen to her bed, and the
eleventh was too much for her. She died soon after.
The point of this being that Marni, anxious to help
Dame Agatha and the other servants with her mother
and to calm her little sisters, became well acquainted
with the use of a sleeping draught,"

I thanked her.

The next day we set out with a good lunch packed
for us by Dame Agatha and the old cloak I liked to
sleep in to keep Sarge warm, for he had none of his
own. I slept in the hood when I didn't feel like walking, though most of the time I patrolled the woods
beside the path, staying alert for possible food or
danger.

And so we reached the palace in fine shape. The
gate guards were no problem, for one of them was
another comrade of Sarge's, and though he laughed
when Sarge told him our business with the king, he
let us pass.

The king was arguing with two suitors and a half-
dozen princesses when we entered the audience
chamber.

By unspoken mutual consent, we distanced ourselves from each other so that he strode in alone and
I slipped in after, concealed by the swirl of his cloak.
I hid myself near a convenient pillar and watched
the audience.

The herald didn't know what to make of Sarge. He
assumed Sarge had entered carrying a message, and
they whispered together for a moment.

Meanwhile, the princes were being marched away
by the guards. The king and the princesses set at each

other jaws that would have marked them as relatives
if their crowns and coronets had not.

"You see what you ungrateful girls have brought
me to?" the king cried. "Now the parents of these
lads will, no doubt, make war on our country and we
will be forced to further bankrupt the treasury and
beggar the people to supply yet another army. I should
imprison you instead of them until you tire of this
nonsense."

Princess Marni, for the tallest girl of the lot had to
be she, flipped a fawn braid over her shoulder and
fixed a brown eye with an amazing amount of flint in
it upon her father. "We might as well be in prison
already," she said, growling, not whining. "You never
let us have any fun at all. You complain about us
buying so many shoes, but if we were going to the
normal number of dances and balls and parties for
girls our ages, we would be having shoes and gowns
made all the time, and jewelry, too, and you'd be paying for the parties. You're getting a bargain when you
think of it."

The king turned several interesting shades of color
and then pointedly ignored her as the herald caught
his eye.

"What is it, Herald?" he asked.

"This person, Your Majesty—this common person—"

"Soldier," Sarge corrected gravely.

"This common soldier wishes to accept Your Majesty's challenge."

"Does he? Well, then, come forward, fellow, and
let us have a look at you."

Sarge stepped forward and the girls giggled among
themselves, all but Princess Marni, who glowered at
him as if about to challenge him to a duel.

"Here to accept my offer, are you?" the king asked.
"What is your name?"

"Obviously, Daddy, if he is a prince, he is incognito,

so telling us his name won't do any good because he'd have to lie," Marni said sarcastically.

"No prince, incognito or otherwise, Your Highness," Sarge said with only a slight bow to the princess and her sisters. "I am Allistair of Oxenbridge, a former master sergeant from Your Majesty's forty-second regiment, and I served during the recent belligerence between Your Majesty's realm and the Gromulvian Alliance. I fought at Finn's Field and Timmons Wood, helped defend Castle Cairndrum and Cairndrum town, where I was wounded and taken prisoner. I escaped and returned to my regiment. After a few skirmishes too insignificant for your exalted attention, the war ended and I was released from duty. As Your Majesty may be aware, Oxenbridge was destroyed by the enemy and so I am now—uh—seeking my fortune I believe is the term."

"Unemployed, I believe, is the more correct term," the princess said.

"Fortunately for the realm, no longer at war, I am," Sarge admitted. He graciously did not mention the back pay the Crown still owed him.

"So, looking to marry money perhaps?" the king inquired without sounding as if he thought that was in any way a bad thing to do.

"Not if the young lady attached to the money doesn't wish to marry me, Your Majesty. I simply heard of your domestic difficulty and thought perhaps I could be of service once more to my king." He bowed very grandly this time.

"You know my terms?" the king asked. Sarge nodded.

"But Daddy, he's OLD!" squeaked a princess who looked as if she was too young as yet to have caught her first mouse. Sarge was no youth, but neither was he elderly. He had a few years on Princess Marni, as well as I can tell such things about humans, but his experiences had grayed him before his time and gave him at times the aspect of one far older.

"That's to his credit," the king told the daughter. "You lot need a firm hand and are obviously able to get around the young noblemen who may die for the sake of your silliness. I only hope the sergeant here outwits you and then I wish it were our custom that he could marry the lot of you and take you off my hands."

"I couldn't marry them, sire, but possibly I could train them up into a pretty decent palace guard," Sarge said with a twinkle in his eye.

"Could you teach me to fire and load cannons and muskets?" asked a lanky teenaged princess with slightly protruding front teeth and a tendency to bounce up and down.

Sarge smiled, "Certainly, Your Highness. If I am permitted the liberty of the armory and the palace artillery, we could start now."

"Ye gods, no!" the king cried in protest. "For heaven's sakes, don't arm them. They're enough trouble as they are. And at least until the three nights are over with, I will have a well-qualified babysitter for them during the day. A veteran of training raw recruits and many battles—why didn't I think of that?"

"Because you wanted us to marry kings and princes," said a dainty princess with fluffy yellow hair and a big-eyed, small-chinned face that resembled that of a kitten, without the whiskers and fur, of course.

"If he marries you and wins half the kingdom, he'll get an automatic promotion," the king said. "Very well, sergeant, you may commence your duties by accompanying my daughters everywhere."

"All of them, sire?"

"It's not as hard as it sounds. They are confined to their quarters until they stop being disobedient and willful and tell me why their dancing shoes are destroyed every night."

"It's not our fault you won't believe the work of the cobbler is under an evil spell," sniffed a princess with knee-length dark-brown tresses. She might have been three years younger than Princess Marni.

"So during the day my daughters will entertain you in their suite, and at night you shall sit outside the only unbolted door giving access to the quarters. This will go on for three days, starting today, and three nights."

"I understand, Your Majesty. I was wondering if I might take a look at the evidence."

"Eh?"

"The offending footwear, sire."

While Sarge was doing that, I decided to do a little reconnaisance of my own. I therefore sought out the kitchens. The cook's cat, a youthful lady with a soft gray coat of a serviceable length, neither too long nor too short, and large golden eyes, hissed at me until she heard I'd brought tidings of Willow who was, luckily for me, her great-grandmother. After that, we got along famously. I am not, despite my ear, a badlooking fellow and although the lady had royal connections, I was a cat of the world, a brave defender of her very home, and had led a life filled with interesting adventures. Or so I felt when she looked at me.

I groomed her face and ears to gain her confidence, and allowed her to do mine. After all, I needed her help and I didn't wish to arouse her suspicions, did I?

Fortunately, this lady had an overabundance of the curiousity which is a characteristic of many of our kind, and thought nothing of it that I was similarly endowed. She had learned much of the castle's history and folklore and something of its structure and knew the cellars and attics, towers and closed-off wings as hunting grounds. The castle was built upon ancient foundations which were built on even more ancient ones whose origins harkened back to more magical times, when fairies, who seemed to be from her description a cross between mankind and catkind, roamed freely aboveground.

I thanked her for the information and asked the way to the princesses'chambers.

"Oooh, are you going up there, then?" my new friend inquired. "You'll have a lovely time. The princesses like our kind, especially Marni."

I remarked that from what I had seen of her highness, Marni was less kittenish and more of a sourpuss than anything.

"She's only like that around the king and especially over this suitor thing. The girls are very close and want to stay together, not be bartered off like prizes at a fair. The king has been very strict indeed with them since their mother died, and Marni, being the eldest, took it hardest. She was twelve at the time and more aware than the others."

I gave my new friend a lick on the nose and let her know I would bear that in mind, then set off to see what I might.

Sarge sat in the corridor outside an open door holding a pair of shoes so thoroughly ravaged that I wondered if perhaps the princesses were concealing a puppy in their room—or a whole pack of puppies. I put my paw on one of the shoes and gave it a good all over sniff but couldn't detect a hint of canine. There was, however, a wild scent there unlike anything I had ever smelled before. I would call it a smell of greenery and water. Not what I'd expect of a ballroom.

Princess Marni appeared at the door. "If you want to inspect our quarters, sergeant, then I suggest you do it soon. We are about to retire. Oh! Where did you come from, my lovely fellow?" she asked, no longer speaking to Sarge but bending down to stroke my head. Her honest appreciation of my considerable charm and beauty raised her in my estimation. I decided not to claw her, but instead purred under her hand. "Is he yours?" she asked Sarge with a sudden childish eagerness much more attractive than any other attitude she had displayed thus far.

"No, my lady. He is his own creature. I suspect he followed me into the palace seeking daintier scraps or fatter rodents than he is used to. He seems to like you." Sarge added cannily as I emoted for all I was worth.

The princess suddenly scooped me up, and carried me inside the door, just as I had hoped she might. "Oh, sisters, look what I've found! He came with the sergeant. Isn't he lovely?"

The youngest ones squealed. "Oh, can we keep him? He is so beautiful. Like black velvet."

"And those eyes!" exclaimed another.

"And such a loving fellow. Listen to that purr!"

And they all petted me and passed me around among them.

Princess Marni said to her sisters, me, and Sarge, "Well, this calls for a celebration. We usually have cocoa before we retire. Perhaps you would care for a cup, sergeant? Obviously you must be a nice man to be in such good company."

"Oh, I am," Sarge agreed readily. "And he is a very nice cat to be with, likewise."

"Please, sergeant, may we keep him in here with us?" asked one of the princesses.

This played into my paws nicely and Sarge was wise enough to realize it. "I'm sure he'll be happier to be spending the night with lovely ladies and soft beds than out here with me."

Things were looking up. When the kitchen brought the cups and cocoa pots, the princesses didn't pour until the servant fetched a saucer and milk for me, too. The new friendliness of the princesses cheered both Sarge and me after such a long and tiring day. I found the milk they offered quite refreshing and Sarge toasted them all, each with a cup of cocoa, before, after many good nights and shy "byes" from the younger princesses, the door was firmly shut between him and us. Too late Willow's words about Princess Marni's knowledge of sleeping draughts came back to me along with a vision of how her back was between us and the tray with the refreshments.

The beds were in two rows along the outer walls, the wardrobes on the shorter walls at the ends of the room. I kept opening a heavy eyelid thinking to see the princesses pulling nightdresses over their heads before slipping under the coverlets. Instead, they donned frothy dresses and the new dance shoes, still smelling of dye and fresh leather soles.

And then—I fell heavily asleep, my chin dropping to my front paws even as my eyelids fell like draperies and I knew nothing more. When I finally awoke, the stars were growing pale outside the mullioned windows. Across the room there was a sound like giant mice in the wall. Then a wardrobe door popped open and twittering princesses poured into the room. Each quickly removed her ballgown and ruined dance shoes, tugged on her nightdress, and crawled into bed.

Princess Marni petted me as she slipped into bed and asked, "Did you guard our room from intruders while we were gone, brave cat?" She kissed the top of my head. "Shhh, this must stay our secret."

But when they were settled, I rose and stretched and padded to the door, scratching to try to awaken Sarge. The door was locked. I yowled and jumped onto the bed of the nearest princess, the youngest. I patted her face with my paw and meowed piteously until she roused and ran barefoot to the door. She unfastened the latch and I bolted for the hallway.

Sarge awoke to my careful insertion of claws into his chest. He stretched and yawned.

"I must have been more tired from our journey than

I realized, Captain. I am not in the habit of sleeping on guard duty," he told me, scratching my head. "You should court-martial me here and now."

I made a reassuring sound and butted his hand. We still had two nights left, but something had to be done about the cocoa drinking and door locking. The cocoa tray sat outside the door. I slapped one of the cups.

"Aha, so you think there was something other than chocolate in the chocolate, too?" he said, rising and stretching. "I should have been more careful. We won't be doing that again. I hope you were more watchful than I was."

In two more hours Princess Marni, dressed in a becoming gown of mint-green silk, unlocked the door and held out a dozen ruined dancing slippers, their ribbons tied together in a bunch. Sarge accepted them with a bow and a rueful grin to answer her challenging one. Marni had a fetching dimple at one side of her mouth. "More evidence, sergeant?"

"Your Highness is too kind," he replied with a bow.

I sauntered through the open door and twined around first Marni's ankles and then the ankles of the other ladies, making myself agreeable.

Marni simply stood aside and waved him into the room.

He turned back to her and said, "I'd like to know something, my lady."

"You may ask all the questions you wish, since that is why you are here, but I can't say how the shoes got ruined."

"That was not my question."

She had preceded him into the room, her back to him, and now she whirled with a swish of skirts and a look of surprise and asked, "What is it, then?"

"I simply wanted to know why, if your father objects to the cost of your cobbler bill, he doesn't simply refuse to pay for new slippers. If you need them to do whatever it is you do that ruins them, it seems to me the easiest way for him to solve the problem."

"*He* doesn't pay for them," said the fluffy-haired blonde princess.

"But it was implied that your shoe bills are burdening the treasury."

"That is simply royal paternalist propaganda," said another princess, close to Marni's age but with quite a serious air. Her brown hair was already pulled severely back and very thick spectacles covered her eyes. "The money for our shoes and our clothing allowance, indeed for many of our expenses, comes from the funds our mother left us. Papa fears we will spend it all before time for our weddings, which he says will beggar the kingdom."

"Ahh," Sarge said sagely, pursing his lips and nodding his head in the general direction of his boot toe, as if deeply pondering her words.

"Which is hardly fair since, except for offering one of us as a prize for whoever betrays our secret, he means to marry us off each to the highest bidder for political or financial gain," the serious princess continued. "So he will certainly profit from us in the end."

"Even if we're *not* boys," said the youngest, picking me up by wrapping both arms around my middle.

"You see, sergeant," Marni said, "Even before the shoes, our father has considered us an unnecessary expense. Our real crime—and that of our mother—is that we're all girls. None of us is the son he really wanted."

"That is why we are so many," said the princess who wanted to learn to fire a musket. "Because they—kept trying until Mama got it right."

"Only she never did and she died," the youngest said sadly, burying her face in my neck ruff. I purred and nuzzled her.

"And so far he has not found a new wife willing to

take on the task of bearing a son against such over-whelming odds, and helping to raise twelve daughters besides," Marni said. "So at least we haven't had to put up with a wicked stepmother. However, to cut expenses, he dismissed all of our servants as soon as everyone was out of diapers. He claims that although our funds may pay the salaries of our staff, he would have to pay for their upkeep."

"But we don't care," the youngest said. "We look after each other. Like this morning, Siggy brushed my hair, Cressa brushed Siggy's, Lilia brushed Cressa's, Suzelle brushed Lilia's, Minda brushed Suzelle's, Amalee brushed Minda's, Jenet brushed Amalee's, Caro brushed Jenet's, Flida brushed Caro's, Dahlia brushed Flida's and Marni brushed Dahlia's. Marni does her own. She knows how to do everything."

"Hush, Petti. You're chattering," said Dahlia, the fluffy-haired one in a yellow silk gown cut the same as Marni's mint green.

"Oops," Petti said, and squeezed me while bringing both hands to cover her mouth.

"One of our mother's maids stayed to take care of us after mama died," Marni continued, clearly needing to air her father's parental deficiencies. "Petti needed a nurse, and Dame Agatha had lost both husband and unborn child in a coach accident. She had nowhere to go. But as soon as Petti was—um—able to find the privy tower alone—Father said Dame Agatha *had* to go. *And* Willow, the little cat Mama gave me for my third birthday." Marni's eyes glistened and her voice caught. I leaped from Petti's arms to Marni's shoulder, purring consolingly in her ear. She reached up dainty fingers and twined them in my coat, then turned her face to bury it in my side, using me to wipe her tears. Then she sniffed and with her head high and haughty again continued, "That was all right, of course. We gave Dame Agatha a pension and Willow and have been on our own ever since."

Sarge had been silent through all of this, but now he looked into Marni's eyes and said, "I think if your father had been as much surrounded by young men as I have been, he would have learned to value you more. We men may fight for our homes, but without ladies there is no home, no family, no civilization, to fight for."

"And yet, sergeant, *you* have no wife or daughter," Marni said. "or you would be proposing bigamy to try your hand at father's challenge."

He dismissed that with a wave of his hand. "I was a lad of sixteen when I enlisted to serve your father, lady, but I had a mother to knit me hat and mittens for the first cold winter, and two sisters, one older and married who had already made me uncle to a niece, and one younger, my dearest companion, who cried inconsolably when I marched away and wrote to me faithfully until . . ."

He examined his boot toe again.

"Until what?" Marni asked softly.

"Until I was captured and news came to me from another prisoner that Oxenbridge had been destroyed by the enemy. The inhabitants were put to the sword."

Each princess gasped and several buried their faces in their hands. Petti ran to Sarge and clasped him around the waist and hugged him. Marni stretched out a hand and laid it upon his. "I am so sorry. You do not deserve to be caught up in our little squabbles after losing so much, but . . ."

He looked into her face and was able to smile, for his grief was an old scar by now, rather than a bleeding wound. "But the battle is joined and the rules of engagement, if you'll pardon the wordplay, my lady, must be respected. We soldiers understand these things."

At that point, pretending to chase something, I scampered across the room and leaped to the top of the wardrobe from which I had seen the girls emerge.

I then pretended to bathe, but first I caught Sarge's eye and saw that he understood that I was presenting him with a clue.

Which came in handy when the king came, bearing brunch. During the course of the meal (I lay under the portable table and enjoyed scraps of ham, bacon, and seafood mixed with egg), the king inquired if Sarge had solved the riddle.

Sarge smiled and said, "I have a few leads. The princesses' quarters have been thoroughly searched, I presume?"

The princesses groaned and their father said, "Many times."

"Well, then, we can dispense with that."

This pleased the princesses, and for the entire rest of the day he did no investigating except to ask them questions, tell them stories of his travels and listen to their own stories. So charming was he that by evening the princesses who weren't making moon eyes at him were stealing peeks from under their lashes.

Princess Marni alone kept her poise and teased, as she handed him a cup of cocoa, "And what would you say of us if you told our story?"

Sarge shook his head and smiled into her eyes, "That, my lady, would be a *real* challenge. It would need to be full of magic."

"What sort of magic?" she asked.

"The kind that fairy tales are made of," he said. "Where the beautiful princess falls in love and lives happily ever after. Of course, there are twelve of you, so it would have to be an uncommonly long fairy tale. He lifted the chocolate to his lips. Marni opened her mouth, then closed it, but looked troubled. I don't think Sarge was going to drink the chocolate after my warning but just to be safe, I bumped his cup with my head and some of it spilled down his front. The princesses competed to wipe it away.

Once Sarge had been locked outside, the ladies

dressed, changing their day gowns for evening and their everyday shoes for the new dance slippers. As they set off, I hid in the rustling lavender skirts of Princess Petti and followed her through the wardrobe door.

No wonder a search had never revealed how the ladies left their chamber. Marni knocked on the back of the wardrobe, and it magically opened out onto a long spiraling flight of stone stairs. Lit only by the candle Marni carried, the princesses descended. I didn't bother to conceal myself. The light was fine for my cat eyes but too dim for anyone to spot a shadow-colored, pussy-footing cat.

At the foot of the stairs was a peculiar looking forest, with leaves of strange unleafy pinks, purples, and blues that shone in the dark. At the end of the tree-lined path was a silvery lake. There the princesses were met by twelve of the best-dressed sailors I have ever seen, all in evening garb. I hopped aboard the last boat as it pulled away from shore. In a short time, it landed on an island that was actually an open-air floating ballroom. Pillars twined with vines of gold and silver supported a brilliant multicolored canopy piped with gold. The dance floor was a mosaic of variously colored stone in a pretty pattern. I admired it, but it was wasted on the princesses, who couldn't see it for their sailing skirts as they were whirled around and around.

Delectable snacks adorned tables between the pillars. I snagged some and watched the girls wear out their shoes. The night faded, and we climbed back in the boats. As the princesses disembarked, I jumped out, too and pitter-patted past them down the forest lane. I bounded up the stairs ahead of them, pushed open the wardrobe door, and ran to Marni's bed. When the girls arrived, their faces shining and their shoes in tatters, I looked up sleepily and yawned.

At the first opportunity, I left Sarge to continue

charming the princesses while I visited the cook's cat, whose name, I learned, was Flo.

"These fairies you were talking about," I said, referring to her tale of the castle's origins. "They look like regular people, right?"

"Except some say their ears are a bit pointed, like ours," she said.

So *that* was what had seemed so odd about my princesses' dance partners! "Are they harmful creatures or good?"

She flicked her tail uneasily. "Why are you asking that, Shadow? Are our princesses meeting fairies?"

"I think so. They're meeting twelve men with pointed ears. Do you think they'd *hurt* the princesses?"

She licked her paw thoughtfully. "All I know about fairies is they play tricks." She told me about some of the tricks and the more she told me, the more worried both of us became.

"We must stop them for their own sakes, as well as Sarge's. He must see this for himself tonight."

"But how can he when the door is locked?" Flo asked.

That *was* the problem, but surely it wasn't insurmountable?

All day I considered the problem. If only Sarge were a cat, he would find a way to get in, I thought. We cats can always find a way to get in or out as we wish. And of course, there I had my solution.

This called for expert timing. That night, I waited until the girls disappeared through the wardrobe door, all except Princess Petti. Then I ran to the chamber door and began yowling my head off, scratching and alternating yowls with piteous cries. Princess Petti ran back out the wardrobe door and to me. "What's the matter, kitty, are you hurt?"

"Yeeeeowwwwt!" I demanded.

"Kitty, I can't! I have to go now or I'll lose my sisters. I—"

"Yeeeeowwwt!" I screeched again, as if I didn't understand a word she was saying.

"Shhhhhhhhhh, someone will hear you. You'll wake up the sergeant, though none of them ever DO wake up, no matter what, after they have the cocoa."

"Yeeeeeowwwwwt!" I repeated, clawing at her dress.

"Oh, very well," she whispered and lifted the bolt to the door. I went out. Sarge was standing, alert, ready to save me from whoever was skinning me alive, but I gave him a look. For a human, he was very smart. He pretended to be sleeping, even managing a convincing snore.

As soon as Petti closed the door, before she could bolt it again, I screamed, "Rrrrrrow!" demanding to be let back in. I heard footsteps scampering, then the door cracked and she said, "Silly kitty. Come on, but be quick. Marni will be so cross if I miss the boat."

I was fully prepared to repeat everything again, but Petti, bless her, was young and careless. She bolted for the wardrobe, but the door she left *un*bolted. I mewed softly and Sarge crept in. I quickly led him to the wardrobe.

He clomped behind me in his soldier's boots. Rats. The girls would hear him for sure. I did the only thing I could think of. I backed up to him suddenly and thoroughly sprayed the boots.

He started to curse at me, but suddenly understood, and sat down long enough to peel them off. Then he padded after me into the wardrobe.

The girls, except for Petti, who was halfway down the last flight, had come to the foot of the staircase. I took the stairs several at a time, Sarge following quickly. As I caught up to the last skirt, he ducked behind the trees.

The princesses' chattering concealed the noise of our movements.

When the boats arrived, I hopped aboard without being seen and hid in the folds of a skirt, but Sarge was stuck behind the last pink-leafed tree, frowning at the water. I heard only the faintest gurgle as he slid into the lake.

The boat slowed appreciably and Princess Lilia, who was the occupant, looked around. "Peculiar current here tonight," she said to the man paddling the little craft.

He smiled. He had pointed ears and teeth like mine, but not as adorable. I didn't actually care for them on a two-legged being. And now that I studied him, I saw that his clothing, for all of its elegance, was made of paper. It crinkled when he moved. With that one discovery, everything changed, though I alone seemed to notice.

The little island, no longer a pavilion with golden pillars and a colorful canopy, was simply a flower-strewn glade within a circle of mossy trees. A fairy ring. I checked the table. The offerings were not nearly as dainty, though more suited to my feline taste than the princesses', being composed of raw fish, insects, bird eggs, and turtles on the halfshell.

With my customary perspicacity, I recognized that the place was under what Flo had called a glamor. The princesses saw the illusion the fairy men spun for them and on my first visit, I viewed the place the same way. Once I knew about the trick, however, and was concentrating on helping Sarge, I saw the place as it was, without the veil more suited to human wishes than feline.

Each fairy locked eyes with each princess as he whirled her around the floor to music that was really nothing but a rather chilly wind. The girls didn't seem to notice their own goosebumps.

Sarge crawled out of the lake to join me.

His face fell as he watched the dance, as if he saw that he was vastly outnumbered in a battle. He petted me, murmuring, "If they've such elegant suitors to claim them here, who am I to stop them, Captain? Better to keep their secret and take whatever the king has in store for my failure."

I heard him with my right ear. With my left ear I heard the fairy squiring Princess Marni saying, "After tonight you need never climb the stairs again, love. You and your sisters will come with us to our own kingdom and be our brides."

And as if she didn't have a brain in her pretty head, Marni smiled idiotically and said, "How nice."

That was too much for me. I raced in among those high stepping feet and began shredding paper pants, not minding a bit if I took some fairy skin in the process.

The fairies yelled, the princesses shrieked, but nobody saw me. It was as if, in order to maintain their spell, the fairy princes had to concentrate too hard to allow themselves to see anything as earthly as a cat. Then one of them stepped on my tail. I yowled and clawed my way up one side of him and down the other.

He screamed, trying to shake me loose. The dance stopped as his brother fairies grabbed for me and struck at me, and snatched at my tail as I dodged between their legs.

"Don't do that! You'll hurt him!" Marni cried, and elbowed fairy princes aside to scoop me safely into her arms. "Captain Shadow, you poor kitty. Are you hurt?" I mewed as pitifully as possible. The other princesses closed in around us, cooing sympathetically at me.

Princess Flida looked up, intending to give her partner a piece of her mind about molesting helpless cats. Her mouth fell open in shock. "Where is my prince?"

Princess Amalee asked, "What happened to the pillars?"

Then the rest of them began discovering the true nature of their trysting place. I had broken the spell!

The fairy princes began hopping into boats and paddling away, and would have left us stranded.

Sarge chose that moment to make himself known, however. Plucking a departing fairy prince from his craft by the scruff of the neck, Sarge dropped him into the water and commandeered the boat. Another boat rescued the soaked prince.

"Here, my ladies," Sarge said. "It's only one little rowboat," which it indeed was and not a very seaworthy-looking one at that. "But we'll make do. The trip to shore isn't long. I'll take you across one at a time."

Princess Marni was the last to cross. She lamented to Sarge as they hurried down the path, "How could I have been so foolish? I'm the eldest. I should have known better."

"Nonsense, my lady. The fairies wove their deception from the unhappiness of you and your sisters, who missed all the parties and courting pretty young girls should have. They probably meant no harm and sought only to fill your need."

What nonsense! Twelve healthy young females in the human equivalent of estrus? Those fairies must have smelled them from clear across the lake and determined to lure them.

"Then you don't think they meant us harm?" Marni asked.

"Well, *they* probably didn't think what they had in mind would harm you," Sarge grunted. He hustled the girls up the stairs and through the wardrobe door. I sprang in behind them, just as the door to the fairy world closed behind us.

Sarge turned and pushed at it, but it was sealed shut. Marni tried knocking, as she always had knocked, but it would not open again. The door to fairyland was closed forever.

When the king came to brunch that morning, Sarge surprised him by telling him that he had learned the princesses' secret. When he told the king where the princesses had gone to ruin their shoes, the king laughed.

"Fairyland! Now that is a likely story. Can you prove it?"

Triumphantly, Sarge drew forth the jeweled leaves he'd plucked to prove where he'd been. But as with the other fine things, the leaves had turned ordinary and were now dried bits of moss."

"No, sire. I guess not," he said.

This would not do! The other princesses muttered, but Marni did not speak. I crawled out from under the tablecloth and climbed into her lap, then reached up and patted her lips with my paw. I couldn't be any clearer than that.

The king heaved a resigned sigh and raised his hand to signal the guards. "I thought better of you than to lie, sergeant. You are the first to try to tell me such a wild tale."

"It may be a wild tale, Father, but it's not a lie!" Marni blurted out. "It's all true. He followed us and discovered our secret, then saved us from being carried off to fairyland by our dancing partners." Now the other princesses chimed in with agreement and explanations and exclamations.

"Silence!" the king roared. "If you all confess that the soldier is telling the truth that you never would tell me, then I must accept it. I will reward him as promised. Or perhaps, after getting to know my daughters, you would prefer prison?"

"Hardly, Your Majesty. I have become fond of all of them, but I choose Princess Marni, if she will have me."

Marni, uncharacteristically speechless again, gazed into his eyes, gulped, and nodded.

"Hmph," the king said. "Very well. But before I

plan the wedding and give you half my kingdom, since you can't prove to me *what* they were doing, can you at least tell me how you learned it when men of higher rank could not?"

Princess Petti giggled and piped up, raising her hand and waving it excitedly. "I know, I know, it was the kitty, wasn't it? He made me unlock the door for him."

But she seemed so pleased I had to wonder how much I had fooled her.

Sarge reached over to scratch my whiskers. "Yes indeed, little princess, you've discovered my secret weapon. Your Majesty, may I present my accomplice, Captain Shadow, the cat among your pigeons."

The princesses cooed, very much like pigeons, or maybe turtledoves. It was too much for me. Leaving them all to their happily ever afters, I jumped down, zipped out the door, and raced for the kitchen. A cat may look at a king, it's true, but on the whole, he'd much rather see another cat.

DARK EYES, FAITH,
AND DEVOTION

Charles de Lint

Charles de Lint is a full-time writer and musician who presently makes his home in Ottawa, Canada, with his wife MaryAnn Harris, an artist and musician. His latest novel is *The Blue Girl*. He also has the latest volume of Newford stories published as well. For more information about his work, visit his Web site at www.charlesdelint.com.

I've just finished cleaning the vomit my last fare left in the back seat—his idea of a tip, I guess, since he actually shortchanged me a couple of bucks—and I'm back cruising when the woman flags me down on Gracie Street, outside one of those girl-on-girl clubs. I'll tell you, I'm as open-minded as the next guy, but it breaks my heart when I see a looker like this playing for the other team. She's enough to give me sweet dreams for the rest of the week, and this is only Monday night.

She's about five-seven or five-eight and dark-skinned—Hispanic, maybe, or Indian. I can't tell. I just know she's gorgeous. Jet-black hair hanging straight down her back and she's all decked out in net stockings, spike heels, and a short black dress that looks like it's been sprayed on and glistens like satin. Somehow she manages to pull it off without looking like a hooker. It's got to be her babydoll face—made up to a T, but so innocent all you want to do is keep her safe and take care of her. After you've slept with her, mind.

I watch her in the rearview mirror as she gets into the backseat—showing plenty of leg with that short dress of hers and not shy about my seeing it. We both know that's all I'm getting and I'm lucky to get that much. She wrinkles her nose and I can't tell if it's some linger of l'eau de puke or the Lysol I sprayed on the seat after I cleaned up the mess my last fare left behind.

Hell, maybe it's me.

"What can I do for you, ma'am?" I ask.

She's got these big dark eyes and they fix on mine in the rearview mirror, just holding onto my gaze like we're the only two people in the world.

"How far are you willing to go?" she asks.

Dressed like she is, you'd be forgiven for thinking it was a come-on. Hell, that was my first thought anyway, doesn't matter she's playing on that other team. But there's that cherub innocence thing she's got going for her and, well, take a look at a pug like me and you know the one thing that isn't going to happen is some pretty girl's going to make a play for me from the back seat of my cab.

"I can take you any place you need to go," I tell her, playing it safe.

"And if I need something else?" she asks.

I shake my head. "I don't deal with anything that might put me inside."

I almost said "back inside," but that's not something she needs to know. Though maybe she already does. Maybe, when I pulled over, she saw the prison tattoos on my arms—you know, you put them on with a pin

and the ink from a ballpoint so they always come out
looking kind of scratchy and blue.

"Someone has stolen my cat," she says. "I was hoping you might help me get her back."

I turn right around in my seat to look at her straight
on. I decide she's Hispanic from her accent. I like the
Spanish warmth it puts on her words.

"Your cat," I say. "You mean like a pet?"

"Something like that. I really do need someone to
help me steal her back."

I laugh. I can't help it.

"So, what, you flag down the first cab you see and
figure whoever's driving it'll take a short break from
cruising for fares to help you creep some joint?"

"Creep?" she asks.

"Break in. But quietly, you know, because you're
hoping you won't get caught."

She shakes her head.

"No," she says. "I just thought *you* might."

"And that would be because . . . ?"

"You've got kind eyes."

People have said a lot of things about me over the
years, but that's something I've never heard before.
It's like telling a wolf he's got a nice smile. I've been
told I've got dead eyes, or a hard stare, but no one's
ever had anything nice to say about them before. I
don't know if it's because of that, or if it's because of
that innocence she carries that just makes you want
to take care of her, but I find myself nodding.

"Sure," I tell her. "Why not? It's a slow night.
Where can we find this cat of yours?"

"First I need to go home and get changed," she
says. "I can't go—what was the word you used?" She
smiles. "Creep a house wearing this."

Well, she could, I think, and it would sure make it
interesting for me if I was hoisting her up to a window,
but I just nod again.

"No problem," I tell her. "Where do you live?"

*   *   *

This whole situation would drive Hank crazy.

We did time together a while back—we'd each pulled a stretch and they ran in tandem for a few years. It's all gangs inside now and since we weren't either of us black or Indian or Hispanic, and we sure as hell weren't going to run with the Aryans, we ended up passing a lot of the time with each other. He told me to look him up when I got out and he'd fix me up. A lot of guys say that, but they don't mean it. You're trying to do good and you want some hardcase showing up at your home or place of employment? I don't think so.

So I wouldn't have bothered, but Hank never said something unless he meant it, and since I really did want to take a shot at walking the straight and narrow this time out, I took him up on it.

He hooked me up with this guy named Moth who runs a Gypsy cab company out of a junkyard—you know, the wheels aren't licensed, but so long as no one looks too hard at the piece of bureaucratic paper stuck on the back of the driver's seat, it's the kind of thing you can get away with. You just make a point of cruising for fares in the parts of town that the legit cabbies prefer to stay out of.

So Hank gave me the break to make good, and Moth laid one piece of advice on me—"Don't get involved with your fares"—and I've been doing okay, keeping my nose clean, making enough to pay for a room in a boarding house, even stashing a little extra cash away on the side.

Funny thing is I like this gig. I'm not scared to take the rough fares and I'm big enough that the freaks don't mess with me. Occasionally, I even get someone like the woman I picked up on Gracie Street.

None of which explains why I'm parked outside a house across town on Marett Street, getting ready to bust in and rescue a cat.

My partner-in-crime is sitting in the front with me now. Her name's Luisa Jaramillo. She's changed into a tight black T-shirt with a pair of faded baggy jean overalls, black hightops on her feet. Most of her make-up's gone and her hair's hidden under a baseball cap turned backward. She still looks gorgeous. Maybe more than she did before.

"What's your cat's name?" I ask.

"Patience."

I shrug. "That's okay. You don't have to tell me."

"No, that's her name," Luisa says. "Patience."

"And this guy that stole her is . . . ?"

"My ex-boyfriend. My very recent ex-boyfriend."

That's what I get for jumping to conclusions, I think. Hell, *I* was cruising Gracie Street. That doesn't automatically put me on the other team either. Only don't get me wrong. I'm not getting my hopes up or anything. I know I'm just a pug and all she's doing is using me for this gig because I'm handy and I said I'd do it. There's not going to be any fairy tale reward once we get kitty back from her ex. I'll be lucky to get a handshake.

So why am I doing it?

I'll lay it out straight: I'm bored. I've got a head that never stops working. I'm always considering the percentages, making plans. When I said I'd come to enjoy driving a cab, I was telling the truth. I do. But you're talking to a guy who's spent the better part of his life working out deals, and when the deals didn't pan out, he just went in and took what he needed. That's what put me inside.

They don't put a whole lot of innocent people in jail. I'm not saying they aren't biased toward what most people think of as the dregs of society—the homeboys and Indians and white trash I was raised to be—but most of us doing our time, we did the crime.

Creeping some stranger's house gives me a buzz like a junkie getting a fix. I don't get the shakes when I go cold turkey like I've been doing these past couple of months, but the jones is still there. Tonight I'm just cozying it up with a sugar coating of doing the shiny white knight bit, that's all.

I never even stopped to ask her why we were stealing a cat. I just thought, let's do it. But when you think about it, who steals cats? You lose your cat, you just go get another one. We never had pets when I was a kid, so maybe that's why I don't get it. In our house the kids were the pets, only we weren't so well-treated as I guess Luisa's cat is. Somebody ever took one of us, the only thing Ma'd regret is the cut in her check from Social Services.

You want another reason? I don't often get a chance to hang out with a pretty girl like this.

"So what's the plan?" I ask.

"The man who lives in that house is very powerful," Luisa says.

"Your ex."

She nods.

"So he's what? A politician? A lawyer? A drug dealer?"

"No, no. Much more powerful than that. He's a brujo—a witch man. That is not a wrong thing in itself, but his medicine is very bad. He is an evil man."

I give her the same blank look I'm guessing anybody would.

"I can see you don't believe me," she says.

"It's more like I don't understand," I tell her.

"It doesn't matter. I tell you this only so that you won't look into his eyes. No matter what, do not meet his gaze with your own."

"Or what? He'll turn me into a pumpkin?"

"Something worse," she says in all seriousness.

She gets out of the car before I can press her on it, but I'm not about to let it go. I get out my side and join her on the sidewalk. She takes my hand and leads me quickly into the shadows cast by a tall hedge that runs the length of the property, separating her ex's house from its neighbors. I like the feel of her skin against mine. She lets go all too soon.

"What's really going on here?" I ask her. "I mean, I pick you up outside a girl bar on Gracie Street where you're dressed like a hooker, and now we're about to creep some magic guy's house to get your cat back. None of this is making a whole lot of sense."

"And yet you are here."

I give her a slow nod. "Maybe I should never have looked in your eyes," I say.

I'm joking, but she's still all seriousness when she answers.

"I would never do such a thing to another human being," she tells me. "Yes, I went out looking the way I did in hopes of attracting a man such as you, but there was no magic involved."

I focus on the "a man such as you," not sure I like what it says about what she thinks of me. I may not look like much, which translates into a lot of nights spent on my own, but I've never paid for it.

"You looked like a prostitute, trying to pick up a john or some freak."

She actually smiles, her teeth flashing in the shadows, white against her dark skin.

"No, I was searching for a man who would desire me enough to want to be close to me, but who had the heart to listen to my story and the compassion to want to help once he knew the trouble I was in."

"I think you've got the wrong guy," I tell her. "Neither of those are things I'm particularly known for."

"And yet you are here," she says again. "And you shouldn't sell yourself short. Sometimes we don't fulfill our potential only because there is no one in our life to believe in us."

I've got an idea where she's going with that—Hank and Moth have talked about that kind of thing some nights when we're sitting around a campfire in the junkyard, not to mention every damn social worker who's actually trying to do their job—but I don't want to go there with her anymore than I do with them. It's a nice theory, but I've never bought it. Your life doesn't go a certain way just because other people think that's the way it will.

"You were taking a big chance," I say instead. "You could've picked up some freak with a knife who wasn't going to stop to listen."

She shakes her head. "No one would have troubled me."

"But you need my help with your ex."

"That is different. I have looked in his eyes. He has sewn black threads in my soul and without a champion at my side, I'm afraid he would pull me back under his influence."

This I understand. I've helped a couple of women get out of a bad relationship by pounding a little sense into their ex-boyfriend's head. It's amazing how the threat of more of the same is so much more effective than a restraining order.

"So you're looking for some muscle to pound on your ex."

"I'm hoping that won't be necessary. You wouldn't want him for an enemy."

"Some people say you're judged by your enemies."

"Then you would be considered a powerful man, too," she says.

"So the getup you had on was like a costume."

She nods, but even in the shadows I can see the bitter look that comes into her eyes.

"I have many 'costumes' such as that," she says. "My boyfriend insists I wear them in order to appear attractive. He likes it that men would desire me but could not have me."

"Boy, what planet is he from?" I say. "You could wear a burlap sack and you'd still be drop-dead gorgeous."

"You did not like the dress?"

I shrug. "What can I say? I'm a guy. Of course I liked it. I'm just saying you don't need it."

"You are very sweet."

Again with the making nice. Funny thing is, I don't want to argue it with her anymore. I find I like the idea that someone'd say these kinds of things to me. But I don't pretend there's a hope in hell that it'll ever go past this. Instead, I focus on the holes in her story. There are things she isn't telling me and I say as much, but while she can't help but look a little guilty, she doesn't share them either.

"Look," I tell her. "It doesn't matter what they are. I just need to know, are they going to get in the way of our getting the job done?"

"I don't think so."

I wait a moment but she's still playing those cards pretty much as close to her vest as she can. I wonder how many of them are wild.

"Okay," I say. "So we'll just do it. But we need to make a slight detour first. Do you think your cat can hold out for another hour or so?"

She nods.

She doesn't ask any questions when I pull up behind a plant nursery over on East Kelly Street. I jimmy the lock on the back door like it's not even there—hey, it's what I do, or at least used to do—and slip inside. It takes me a moment to track down what I'm looking for, using the beam of a cheap key ring flashlight to read labels. Finally, I find the shelf I need.

I cut a hole in a small bag of diatomaceous earth and carefully pour a bit of it into each of my jacket's pockets. When I replace the bag, I leave a five-spot on the shelf beside it as payment. See, I'm learning. Guys back in prison would be laughing their asses off if they ever heard about this, but I don't care. I may still bust into some guy's house to help his ex-girlfriend steal back her cat, but I'm done with taking what I haven't earned.

"You figure he's home?" I ask when we pull back up outside the house on Marett.

She nods. "He would not leave her alone—not so soon after stealing her from me."

"You know where his bedroom is?"

"At the back of the house, on the second floor. He is a light sleeper."

Of course he would be.

"And your cat," I say. "Would she have the run of the house, or would he keep her in a cage?"

"He would have . . . other methods of keeping her docile."

"The magic eyes business."

"His power is not a joking matter," she says.

"I'm taking it seriously," I tell her.

Though I'm drawing the line at magic. Thing is, I know guys who can do things with their eyes. You see it in prison all the time—whole conversations taking place without a word being exchanged. It's all in the eyes. Some guys are like a snake, mesmerizing its prey. The eyes lock onto you and before you know what's going on, he's stuck a shiv in your gut and you're down on the floor, trying to keep your life from leaking out of you, your own blood pouring over your hands.

But I'm pretty good with the thousand-yard stare myself.

I get out of the car and we head for the side door in the carport. I'd have had Luisa stay behind in the cab, except I figure her cat's going to be a lot more docile if she's there to carry it back out again.

I give the door a visual check for an alarm. There's nothing obvious, but that doesn't mean anything, so I ask Luisa about it.

"A man such as he does not need a security system," she tells me.

"The magic thing again."

When she nods, I shrug and take a couple of pairs of surgical gloves out of my back pocket. I hand her one pair and put the other on, then get out my picks.

This door takes a little longer than the one behind the nursery did. For a guy who's got all these magic chops, he's still sprung for a decent lock. That makes me feel a little better. I'm not saying that Luisa's gullible or anything, but with guys like this—doesn't matter what scam they're running, magic mumbo jumbo's not a whole lot different from the threat of a beating—it's the fear factor that keeps people in line. All you need is for your victim to believe that you can do what you say you'll do if they don't toe the line. You don't actually need magic.

The lock gives up with a soft click. I put my picks away and take out a small can of W-30, spraying each of the hinges before I let the door swing open. Then I lean close to Luisa, my mouth almost touching her ear.

"Where should we start looking?" I say.

My voice is so soft you wouldn't hear me a few steps away. She replies as quietly, her breath warm against my ear. This close to her I realize that a woman like her smells just as good as she looks. That's something I just never had the opportunity to learn before.

"The basement," Luisa says. "If she is not hiding from him there, then he will have her in his bedroom with him. There is a door leading downstairs, just past that cupboard."

I nod and start for the door she pointed to, my sneakers silent on the tiled floor. Luisa whispers along behind me. I do the hinges on this door, too, and I'm cautious on the steps going down, putting my feet close to the sides of the risers where they're less liable to wake a creak.

There was a light switch at the top of the stairs. Once I get to the bottom, I stand silent, listening. There's nothing. I feel along the wall and come across the other switch I was expecting to find.

"Close your eyes," I tell Luisa.

I do the same thing and flick the switch. There's a blast of light behind my closed lids. I crack them slightly and take a quick look around. The basement is furnished, casually, like an upscale rec room. There's an entertainment center against one wall, a wet bar against another. Nice couch set up in front of the TV. I count three doors, all of them slightly ajar. I'm not sure what they lead to. Furnace room, laundry room, workshop. Who knows?

By the time I'm finished looking around, my eyes have adjusted to the light. The one thing I don't see is a cat.

"You want to try calling her?" I ask.

Luisa shakes her head. "I can feel her. She is hiding in there." She points to one of the mystery doors. "In the storage room."

I let her go ahead of me, following after. Better the cat see her first than my ugly mug.

We're halfway across the room when someone speaks from behind us.

<I knew you would return,> a man's voice says, speaking Spanish. <And look what you have brought me. A peace offering.>

I turn slowly, not letting on that I know what he's said. I picked up a lot of Spanish on the street, more in jail. So I just look surprised, which isn't a stretch. I can't believe I didn't feel him approach. When I'm creeping a joint, I carry a sixth sense inside me that stretches out throughout the place, letting me know when there's a change in the air.

Hell, I should at least have heard him on the stairs.

"I have brought you nothing," Luisa says, speaking English for my benefit, I guess.

<And yet I will have you and your champion. I will make you watch as I strip away his flesh and sharpen my claws on his bones.>

"Please. I ask only for our freedom."

<You can never be free from me.>

I have to admit he's a handsome devil. Same dark hair and complexion as Luisa, but there's no warmth in his eyes.

Oh, I know what Luisa said. Don't look in his eyes. But the thing is, I don't play that game. You learn pretty quickly when you're inside that the one thing you don't do is back down. Show even a hint of weakness and your fellow inmates will be on you like piranha.

So I just put a hand in the pocket of my jacket and look him straight in the eye, give him my best convict stare.

He smiles. "You are a big one, aren't you?" he says. "But your size means nothing in this game we will play."

You ever get into a staring contest? I can see that starting up here, except dark eyes figures he's going to mesmerize me in seconds, he's so confident. The funny thing is, I can feel a pull in that gaze of his. His pupils seem to completely fill my sight. I hear a strange whispering in the back of my head and can feel that thousand-yard stare of mine already starting to fray at the edges.

So maybe he's got some kind of magical power. I don't know and I don't care. I take my hand out of my pocket and I'm holding a handful of that diatomaceous earth I picked up earlier in the nursery.

Truth is, I never thought I'd use it. I picked it up as a backup, nothing more. Like insurance just in case, crazy as it sounded, Luisa really knew what she was talking about. I mean, you hear stories about every damn thing you can think of. I never believed most of what I heard, but a computer's like magic to someone who's never seen one before—you know what I'm saying? The world's big enough and strange enough that pretty much anything can be out there in it, somewhere.

So I've got that diatomaceous earth in my hand and I throw it right in his face, because I'm panicking a little at the way those eyes of his are getting right into my head and starting to shut me down inside.

You know anything about that stuff? It's made of ground-up shells and bones that are sharp as glass. Gardeners use it to make barriers for various kinds of insects. The bug crawls over it and gets cut to pieces. It's incredibly fine—so much so that it doesn't come through the latex of my gloves—but eyes don't have that kind of protection.

Imagine what it would do if it got in them.

Tall, dark, and broody over there doesn't have to use his imagination. He lifts his hand as the cloud comes at him, but he's too late. Too late to wave it away. Too late to close his eyes like I've done as I back away from any contact with the stuff.

His eyelids instinctively do what they're supposed to do in a situation like this—they blink rapidly and the pressure cuts his eyes all to hell and back again.

It doesn't help when he reaches up with his hands to try to wipe the crap away.

He starts to make this horrible mewling sound and falls to his knees.

I'm over by the wall now, well out of range of the rapidly settling cloud. Looking at him, I start to feel a little queasy, thinking I did an overkill on this. I don't know what went on between him and Luisa— how bad it got, what kind of punishment he deserves—but I think maybe I crossed a line here that I really shouldn't have.

He lifts his bloodied face, sightless eyes pointed in our direction, and manages to say something else. This time he's talking in some language I never heard before, ending with some Spanish that I do understand.

<Be so forever,> he cries.

I'm turning to Luisa just then, so I see what happens. Well, I see it, but it doesn't register as real. One moment there's this beautiful dark-haired woman standing there, then she vanishes and there's only the heap of her clothes left lying on the carpet. I'm still staring slack-jawed when the clothing moves and a sleek black cat wriggles out from under the overalls and darts into the room where Luisa said *her* cat was.

As I take a step after her, the man starts in with something else in that unrecognizable language. I don't know if it's still aimed at Luisa, or if he's planning to turn me into something, too—hell, I'm a dyed-in-the-wool believer at this point—but I don't take any chances. I take a few quick steps in his direction and give him a kick in the side of the head. When that doesn't completely stop him, I give him a couple more.

He finally goes down and stays down.

I turn back to go after Luisa, but before I can, that black cat comes soft-stepping out of the room once more, this time carrying a kitten in its mouth.

"Luisa?" I find myself saying.

I swear, even with that kitten in its mouth, the cat nods. But I don't even need to see that. I only have to look into her eyes. The cat has Luisa's eyes, there's no question in my mind about that.

"Is this . . . permanent?" I ask.

The cat's response is to trot by me, giving her unconscious ex's body a wide berth as she heads for the stairs.

I stand there, looking at the damage I've done to her ex for a long, unhappy moment, then I follow her up the stairs. She's sitting by the door with the kitten, but I can't leave it like this. I look around the kitchen, not ready to leave yet.

The cat makes a querulous sound, but I ask her to wait and go prowling through the house. I don't know what I'm looking for, something to justify what I did downstairs, I guess. I don't find anything, not really. There are spooky masks and icons and other weird magical-looking artifacts scattered throughout the house, but he's not going to be the first guy that likes to collect that kind of thing. Nothing explains why he needed to have this hold over Luisa and her—I'm not thinking of the kitten as a cat anymore. After what I saw downstairs, I'm sure it's her kid.

I go upstairs and poke through his office, his bedroom. Still nothing. But then it's often like that. Too often the guy you'd never suspect of having a bad thought turns out to be beating on his family, or goes postal where he works, or some damn crazy thing.

It really makes you wonder—especially with a guy like Luisa's ex. You find yourself with power like he's got, why wouldn't you use it to put something good into the world?

I know, I know. Look who's talking. But I'm telling you straight, I might have robbed a lot of people, but I never hurt them. Not intentionally. And never a woman or a kid.

I go back downstairs and find the cat still waiting by the kitchen door for me. She's got a paw on the kitten, holding it in place.

"Let's go," I say.

I haven't even started to think about how a woman can be changed into a cat, or when and if and how she'll change back again. I can only deal with one thing at a time.

My first impulse is to burn the place to the ground with him in it, but playing the cowboy like that's just going to put me back inside and it won't prove anything. I figure I've done enough damage and it's not like he's going to call the cops. But the first thing I'm going to do when I get home is change the plates on the cab and dig out the spare set of registration papers that Moth provides for all his vehicles.

For now I follow the cats down the driveway. I open the passenger door to the cab. The mama cat grabs her kitten by the skin at the nape of her neck and jumps in. I close the door and walk around to the driver's side.

I take a last look at the house, remembering the feel of the guy's eyes inside my head, the relief I felt when the diatomaceous earth got in his eyes and cut them all to hell. There was a lot of blood, but I don't know how permanent the damage'll be. Maybe he'll come after us, but I doubt it. Nine out of ten times, a guy like that just folds his hand when someone stands up to him.

Besides, the city's so big, he's never going to find us, even if he does come looking. It's not like we run in the same circles or anything.

So I get in the cab, say something that I hope sounds calming to the cats, and we drive away.

I've got a different place now, a one-bedroom, ground-floor apartment which gives me access to a backyard. It's not much, just a jungle of weeds and flowers gone wild, but the cats seem to like it.

I sit on the back steps sometimes and watch them romp around like . . . well, like the cats they are, I guess. I know I hurt the man who had them under his power, hurt him bad. And I know I walked into his house with a woman and came out with a cat. But it still feels like a dream.

It's true the cat seems to understand everything I say, and acts smarter than I think a cat would normally act, but what do I know? I never had a pet before. And anybody I talk to seems to think the same thing about their own cat or dog.

I haven't told anybody about any of this, though I did come at it from a different angle, sitting around the fire in the junkyard with Hank one night. There were a half-dozen of us. Moth, Hank's girlfriend Lily, and some of the others from their extended family of choice. The junkyard's in the middle of the city, but it backs onto the Tombs and it gets dark out there. As we sit in deck chairs, nursing beers and coffees, we watch the sparks flicker above the flames in the cut-down steel barrel Moth uses for his fires.

"Did you ever hear any stories about people that can turn into animals?" I ask during a lull in the conversation.

We have those kinds of talks. We can go from carbs and engine torques to what's wrong with Social Services or the best kind of herbal tea for nausea. That'd be ginger tea.

"You mean like a werewolf?" Moth says.

Sitting beside him, Paris grins. She's as dark-haired as Luisa was and her skin's pretty much covered with tattoos that seem to move on their own in the flickering light.

"Nah," she says. "Billy Joe's just looking for a way to turn himself into a raccoon or a monkey so he can get into houses again but without getting caught."

"I gave that up," I tell her.

She smiles at me, eyes still teasing. "I know that. But I still like the picture it puts in my head."

"There are all kinds of stories," Hank says, "and we know one or two. The way they go, the animal people were here first and some of them are still living among us, not looking any different from you or me."

They tell a few then—Hank and Lily and Katy, this pretty red-haired girl who lives on her own in a schoolbus not far from the junkyard. They all tell the stories like they've actually met the people they're talking about, but Katy's are the best. She's got the real storyteller's gift, makes you hang onto every word until she's done.

"But what about if someone's put a spell on someone?" I say after a few of their stories, because they're mostly about people who were born that way, part-animal, part-human, changing their skins as they please. "You know any stories like that? How it works? How they get changed back?"

I've got a lot of people looking at me after I come out with that.

Nobody has an answer.

Moth gives me a look—but it's curious, not demanding "Why are you asking?" he says.

I just shrug. I don't know that it's my story to tell. But as the weeks go by, I bring it up again and this time I tell them what happened, or at least what I think happened. Funny thing is, they just take me at my word. They start looking into it for me, but nobody comes up with an answer.

Maybe there isn't one.

So I just drive my cab and spend time with these new families of mine—both the one in the junkyard and the cats I've got back home. I find it gets easier to walk the straight-and-narrow, the longer you do it. Gets so that doing the right thing, the honest thing, comes like second nature to me.

But I never stop wondering about what happened that night. I don't even know if they're really cats who were pretending to be human, or humans that got turned into cats. I guess I'm always going to be waiting to see if they'll change back.

But I don't think about it twenty-four/seven. Mostly I just figure it's my job to make a home for them and keep them safe. And you know what? Turns out I'm pretty good at doing that.

SLEEPING BEAUTIES

Jody Lynn Nye

Jody Lynn Nye lists her main career activity as "spoiling cats." She lives northwest of Chicago with two of the above and her husband, author and packager Bill Fawcett. She has written twenty-two books, including four contemporary fantasies, three SF novels, four novels in collaboration with Anne McCaffrey, including *The Ship Who Won*, a humorous anthology about mothers, *Don't Forget Your Spacesuit, Dear!*, and over sixty short stories. Recent books are *The Grand Tour*, third in her new fantasy epic series, *The Dreamland*, and *Applied Mythology*, an omnibus of the Mythology 101 series.

"Too haughty," the black-and-white cat said. Marco swished his fluffy tail as prince after royal prince paraded along the flagstone path past the Princess Briar Rose's blue silk pavilion in the shadow of her father's castle, bowing and smirking. "Hmph! A dandy, with not a brain in his head! Oh, look, a barbarian! I can smell the horse's blood on his spurs from here."

Briar Rose, sixteen and beautiful as the flower of her name, sighed at the multitude of handsome men in silks and leather and gold coronets. With lips as red as rose petals and eyes as blue as the sky, Briar Rose had poets getting into fistfights to recite poetry about her glorious attributes. Her knee-length, barley-gold hair fell in silken waves around her molded cheeks, soft white neck, and creamy bosom. She leaned forward and put her pretty chin on her palm, gazing dreamily, and stroked the cat in her lap with her free hand. "But surely one of them would be a worthy husband."

Marco turned his round green eyes up to the girl's face. "Not worthy of you, my dear. Not one. Daffodil, Lavinia, and Nocila would strike me blind if I let you choose any of these wretches."

Briar Rose appealed to Bruno and Humberto. "What about you?" The brown hound and the gray mouse shook their heads.

"They don't smell trustworthy," Bruno said, putting one big paw on her lap.

"They admire themselves in the polished shields of the guards before they show themselves to you," Humberto said. "They're all as vain as Marco."

The cat's eyes narrowed, but he controlled himself. Briar Rose's three fairy godmothers had placed him in charge of her well-being.

"A man, even a prince, worthy of marrying you," he said, "must have all of the finest qualities. He must be brave, loving, trustworthy, loyal, kind, curious, resourceful and respectful as well as handsome."

"Why, then," Briar Rose laughed, lifting the cat and kissing him on the top of the head, "I'd end up marrying you!"

A large, black-haired man in red leather came to a halt at the door of the pavilion and scowled as he heard the princess speak. His expression quickly changed to a simpering smile as Briar Rose put the cat down on her lap and looked up. Marco growled a word of disapproval at his hypocrisy. Briar Rose gave the man a polite smile but no word of encouragement. With an angry look, the prince stalked away.

"Not a genuine prospect in the whole litter," Marco said, and settled in, folding his white paws under his snowy white breast.

Briar Rose just stroked him and gazed out at the file of suitors. She could understand the speech of animals as a gift from her godmothers. The king and queen thought it was a fancy on her part, that she could speak to her companions, but they never believed in it. Bruno was hurt by their disbelief, but Marco had assured him it was better if they didn't. Animals would only tell the king and queen the truth about what they thought, and royal personages cannot stomach the truth. Briar Rose only listened to them because she had been taught to listen by her guardians, the fairy godmothers who had protected her from the day of her christening, sixteen years before, and the three animals who lived in the forest cottage with them.

Marco well remembered the day the three good fairies had brought the infant princess home. Marco had been three then, and wise beyond his years. He'd watched with concern as Daffodil, Lavinia, and Nocila had warded the house with their strongest spells. They had asked the three animals to help care for her, and they had accepted the task with love. Bruno, a large friendly puppy, had grown up to be her loyal protector, though he was not as well-furnished in the brain department as Marco. Humberto was clever with his small paws, helping the little princess to learn embroidery and fine thread work, though she was forbidden to spin. They had explained that a curse had been laid on her at birth by the Black Fairy, Desdemona, that Briar Rose was not to touch a spinning wheel or she would die. With all her other activities the girl scarcely missed spinning, so full was her life The godmothers had taught her to sing and read and dance, to cook and bake and brew, to garden and ride and swim, and simply to enjoy life. Briar Rose had been happy and well.

As all things come to an end, so did their peaceful years in the forest. Three weeks before her sixteenth birthday, the long-awaited summons had arrived from the king and queen of Cadmonia. Two heralds and six men-at-arms had come to escort the Princess Briar Rose and her godmothers to the castle for the girl's coming-of-age celebration. To the amazement of the men, Marco and his two companions went with them.

The king and queen welcomed their daughter's strange entourage, and gave each of the animals a warm silk cushion on the floor in her chambers. Marco never occupied his. He slept, as he always had, on the princess' own pillow beside her head, with one paw touching her hair.

The three animals found life in the castle as puzzling as the occupants must have found them. They did not like it that mice there were considered to be prey to cats and dogs alike. It was far better when the fairy godmothers' animals organized the mice to keep down the bugs that were eating the tapestries and grain, and making the humans miserable in their beds. The cats turned to hunting garden pests instead of the household rodents. In no time, all was running in harmony. The king had to admit that things had improved greatly since the arrival of the princess' odd guardians.

Preparations for the coming-of-age party seemed also to be going smoothly. Invitations had gone out six months in advance to every one of the 24 other kingdoms on the continent, inviting every prince over the age of twelve to attend. Now that she was a grown woman, Briar Rose was expected to choose a husband. Since she was an only child, the prince who married her would be ruler of Cadmonia after her father's death. There were no refusals. By seven days before the party, elegible suitors were pouring over the narrow isthmus of land that separated the peninsula on which Cadmonia sat from the rest of its neighbors.

The king and queen were determined not to repeat the mistake of the christening celebration. A special invitation had been sent out to all the kingdom's fairies, but most especially to Desdemona. The miserable page who'd drawn the short straw of delivering hers returned much the worse for wear bearing a scorched piece of parchment with her acceptance. He hadn't been able to speak since, and had been assigned a quiet chamber to himself high up in one of the distant towers of the castle.

The last of the princes paraded himself past the silk tent, then retired.

"Highness?" Daffodil asked, fluttering to the girl's right shoulder. Fairies were smaller and usually plumper than ordinary humans and had wings on their shoulders. The yellow-clad godmother touched the girl on the hand. "The promenade of welcome is over. Come and change into your feast dress."

Briar Rose picked up Marco in her arms and followed her godmother with alacrity into the White Tower where her chambers lay. Bruno and Humberto trotted along behind. "I've never seen such beautiful things, nor had so many dresses to wear. I hardly know what to do."

"People will always tell you what to do," Marco said, nestling close to her sweet-smelling hair. "It's knowing what is proper for you to do that is difficult."

"So what is proper for me?" Briar Rose asked, as violet-clad Lavinia and blue-clad Nocila helped her out of her cream-colored day dress and into the deep-red feast gown.

"You are to marry a prince, and live happily ever after," Marco said, playing with the laces of her bodice before Daffodil snatched them out of his claws and pulled them tight around the girl's waist. The fairy godmothers finished fastening her dress and laid a crown of gold on her gleaming hair. Bruno looked up at her adoringly.

"You are so beautiful," he said.

"Every detail perfect," Humberto squeaked. "This will be your night of nights."

Briar Rose knelt and impulsively gathered her three furry friends into her arms. "If anything were to happen tonight to change our friendship, I would die," she cried.

On a flurry of trumpet blares, Briar Rose sailed into the great hall. Everyone at the open square of long trestle tables rose and bowed as she passed. The girl's eyes shone as she beheld the brightly colored tapestries and hangings depending from the rafters. Bunches, garlands, and swags of roses decorated every table. Sweet scents and delicious aromas filled the air. Two gigantic sugarwork subtleties showing the princess as a flower nymph and as a queen enthroned in glory stood at the high table. Her father the king, whose long oval face and sweet, noble expression she had inherited, stood to the left of an empty chair with a high, carved back. Her mother, whose golden hair and large blue eyes were echoed so faithfully in her lovely daughter, stood to the right.

The three godmothers flitted along just above the floor to the head table. Their fellow fairies were seated in tall gilded chairs to the left of the king and his courtiers. Briar Rose curtsied to each one in turn. Marco saw the gaunt Black Fairy, Desdemona, her ebony cloak spread out around her like a filmy shadow. Briar Rose paid her an obeisance as she had to all the others. Marco went on guard as soon as he saw Desdemona. She paid him no mind, having as little respect for animals as she had for humans.

"Your Majesties!" Daffodil announced as they

came to the center of the grand table, her high voice pitched to reach every corner. "We are pleased to present your daughter, the Princess Briar Rose!"

The room burst into cheers and applause. The king and queen stretched out their hands. Blushing, the girl circled the table to take the seat of honor. As soon as she sat down, the room quieted.

"Let the feast begin!" the king announced.

Jesters and jugglers bounded out of the side halls to begin their capers in the empty square at the center of the room. Servers pushed in, carrying heavy platters of the finest meats and breads, pies and vegetables, fruits and salads. As soon as they'd stuffed a few chunks of meat in their mouths, Briar Rose's suitors made excuses to come up and speak to her. A few, Marco observed, were rude enough to try to offer proposals of marriage on the spot. The king looked like thunder, but the girl had been well prepared by her guardians.

"I am honored by your offer," Briar Rose said to each, with cool sweetness, "but I must say no at this time. You must give me time to get to know you before I decide."

Some of the princes took the refusals like gentlemen, but others glared openly at her. Marco noted who might be trouble later on. He kept close watch, vowing that nothing bad would happen to her while he watched.

But fate and physiology intervened. Even princesses occasionally have to use the necessary.

Humberto had been enjoying a bite of cheese when Briar Rose asked to be excused for a moment. Marco, seeing that the Black Fairy remained in her place, thought that all would be well. He nodded to the mouse to accompany the girl. Bruno looked up from the bone he was enjoying. When he saw Marco nod toward the Black Fairy, he went back to his gnawing.

* * *

"Are you sure this is the way?" Briar Rose asked Humberto, as he gave her directions through the endless stone corridors lit by torches and hanging lanterns.

"Oh, yes," Humberto squeaked, clinging to the ermine trim of her gown. "The palace mice taught me every inch of the place. It's just through here, my dear." He pointed a tiny handpaw toward an arched doorway where a pair of maidservants were waiting with linen towels and bowls of rosewater.

"Oh, what's that?" Briar Rose asked. Humberto turned to look. A golden ball of light about the size of his body was bounding toward them in the dim hallway.

"I know not," he said. "Best to ignore it."

But the girl's eyes suddenly gleamed with the golden light. "I must follow it."

Humberto, lacking human speech, could not call out to the maidservants for help, nor could he turn her back by himself. Briar Rose had acquired many of the traits of her animal friends, among them the curiosity of Marco. She followed the bounding light through the twists and turns of the passageways, up into a narrow spiral staircase festooned with cobwebs. At the top was a locked door.

"Open it," she said.

"My dear Briar Rose!"

"Open it!" Her voice sounded distant, and not her own. Shrugging, Humberto reached into the keyhole to turn the wards of the lock until it opened with a creak and a thump. Briar Rose passed through the door in a trance. Beyond the small attic room was empty, except for one strange object made of wood. A spinning wheel. She moved toward it, her hand outstretched.

"No, Briar Rose!"

Marco's eyes were slitted as he watched the Black Fairy eating her supper. She was enjoying herself so much it ruined his appetite. Something was making her very happy. But what? She was here, under his eye, not harming his precious princess.

He suddenly became aware of a frantic squeaking from the floor. He turned his moonlike eyes downward to see Humberto scrambling up the chair leg, his whiskers askew.

"Come quickly," he cried.

At the terrible news everyone burst out talking, crying and running around frantically. Shouting for quiet, the king ordered everyone to stop where he was.

"Anyone who knows anything about this matter, come forward," he commanded. "Otherwise, all guests must leave the castle by noon!" Marco sprang onto the table, searching for Desdemona, but she was gone. Daffodil picked him up under her arm. Lavinia had Humberto in her hands. They went to the princess' chambers. Briar Rose had been laid upon her bed, a soft coverlet laid over her. Her face was like that of a waxen image, beautiful and still.

"This is all my fault!" the mouse wailed over and over again.

"Is she dead?" the queen asked again, sitting beside the princess as dawn cast its pale light through the window. Tears ran down her face. "Her hand is cold."

"She only sleeps," Nocila promised them. Whimpering. Bruno rested his big head against her leg.

"Then wake her," the king ordered.

"We cannot," Daffodil said. "Only true love's kiss can break the spell."

"Call back the princes," the queen begged her husband. He set his jaw.

"Our daughter turned them all away. Obviously, she is not in love with any of them. It is no use. Her true love does not exist."

"I cannot bear this," said the queen. She clutched

her husband's hand. "To have her return to us, only to lose her again. I cannot bear it!"

Marco jumped up on the bed and began to lick Briar Rose's face again and again. "I must wake her! No one loves her as much as I do!"

Daffodil picked him up and cuddled his head under her chin. "I know, my friend, but her true love must be of her own species." She turned to the king. "Your love and ours prevented her from dying. Only love's first kiss may awaken her. All the kingdom shall sleep until that day. You shall have peace." The fairies all put their right hands together. A scented smoke rose from their joined fingers, filling the air. The king and queen sighed and turned, trancelike, toward the door.

"I think I will go to bed," said the queen, in a distant voice.

"So shall I," said the king.

Marco looked out of the window. The smoke poured down the tower wall and across the courtyard. Courtiers sagged to the ground where they stood. Men-at-arms leaned heavily over their shields and spears. Even the animals fell asleep.

All but the three guardians.

"What about us?" Marco asked. He hung his head. "You put me in charge, and I failed you."

Daffodil clicked her tongue. "The dark one has had centuries to hone her cunning, and sixteen years to polish her grudge," she said, her round green eyes glinting like the cat's. "You can and shall put this terrible wrong right."

"Can't you act?" Humberto asked the three wise women.

Nocila shook her head. "We can only watch and guard. What kept the curse from coming true for sixteen years was inaccessibility. Briar Rose never saw spinning wheels, so she did not touch one. Desdemona planted that single one here many years ago for just this moment. The lock should have foiled her, but Humberto opened it."

The mouse was mortified. Marco glared at him. "Maybe the palace cats have the right idea about mice." He looked up at the fairies. "I shall go in search of Briar Rose's true love," he vowed. "If you say there is one who loves her more than we do, I will find him."

"I shall sit by her side," Bruno said. "None shall approach, I swear it by my heart."

"I will wind the room round with a trap of threads so dense that all may see but none may touch her," promised Humberto. "I will not fail again."

"We give you one more gift," Lavinia said, "the gift of long life. You will need it in your tasks. We wish you all good luck. For now, we must search out Desdemona and try to persuade her to break her spell, though I hold out no hope she will relent."

"Good luck, my little friend," Daffodil said, setting Marco on his feet. "Keep your standards high. Farewell."

Before their eyes the three little women faded into bright streaks of light, and were gone.

"Well," Marco said, steeling himself. "The task won't improve for the waiting. Farewell."

The dog and mouse nuzzled him fondly. "We shall think of you every day."

"Don't think of me," Marco said, peeved but pleased. "Think of her. Guard our Briar Rose."

"We shall," said Humberto.

Marco nodded. With one long backward look at the princess, lying so still on the bed, he turned and trotted down the tower steps.

But where to begin? The princess had already seen every elegible prince on the continent. Yet the fairy godmothers had assured him that a prince was out there waiting for her. Perhaps Marco had overlooked some good qualities in the men who had come to woo her. Perhaps they were different in their home settings. Perhaps pigs flew, and he could find one to transport him across the wide world.

Instead, he had to rely upon his four small feet to carry him on his mission. The gift of long life from the godmothers didn't help at all against cold, hunger, or sore pads. It was a long, long way from the capital of Cadmonia to its nearest neighbor, Hawellia. Marco left the palace in the spring. It was not until late summer that he arrived at the castle.

The stronghold was in terrible disarray. Marco could tell from the moment he arrived that the rulers did not care for their people or their possessions. Rats ruled in the cellars, the stables, and the grain storage.

He crept in, posing as an ordinary pest-catcher. Following the smell of rotten food and the sound of drunken voices raised in raucous song, Marco found his way to the great hall.

The floor cloths in the huge room hadn't been changed in years. Hordes of overfed dogs snored in front of the fire. Men in hunting clothes lounged all over the benches and chairs around the tables. Marco spotted the prince right away. He was the horse-beating barbarian who had proposed to Briar Rose first at the dinner table. If he was a day under thirty, Marco wouldn't believe it. He crept closer, wanting to give the man every chance.

Unluckily, the prince spotted him. He drew back the flagon from which he had been drinking, and flung it straight at the cat.

Marco leaped to one side. He was footsore from his long journey, but he seemed to grow wings on his feet as he fled. He dived into one of the huge rat holes in the wall just as a wineskin struck beside him, splattering him in sour wine. He spent one night in the

stables before departing. His pads were so tender they
bled, but he was eager to put this horrible place behind him. Briar Rose's true love lay elsewhere.

From kingdom to kingdom Marco traveled, seeking
the worthy prince who would break the dark fairy's
deadly spell. Most, as he remembered them from the
feast, were rough-and-tumble men of the field. A few
were learned in the gentle arts, but were cruel to
women and animals. In the fourth kingdom Marco just
missed being skewered by an arrow launched by one
of these who was out reciting poetry he had written
to a woman. It did kill an innocent pigeon who was
sitting on a branch. Marco crossed Prince Dysart of
Olmbenia off the list, but dragged the dead pigeon
into the underbrush as soon as Dysart was out of sight.
No wind blew only ill. At least Marco would get a
meal to make up for his fright. But he would not trust
this man. He wished he could warn the girl.

The same sad scenario repeated itself again and
again. The princes were the same ones he had seen.
The only difference was that they were growing older.
By the time he reached them, many had married and
had children. A few were already going gray.

Marco fell into despair as he entered the last realm,
Greenaway. Footsore and hungry, he trudged toward
the castle whose pennant-topped turrets he could see
in the distance. This was his last chance. He remembered this prince: Golther was big, burly, and smelly.
If he truly was the princess' love, it was because he
had changed after all these years. But Marco doubted
it. He wondered if he could take ship from here to
another continent.

The well-worn road was blocked by a cluster of men
lounging around the steps to a small traveler's inn.
Marco crept into the undergrowth. Some men sat on
horses with hawks on their wrists. Others held leashed
dogs, who scented Marco and strained toward him.

One tall man with red-gold hair addressed a slender, dark man who was sitting on a stump with one boot off. Beside him was the body of a huge stag. Marco's stomach gurgled. If only he could have a piece of venison. He was so hungry!

"Gave you quite a run," said the redhead. The seated man pulled a cluster of leaves out of his boot and pulled it back on.

"Indeed he did, the big old fellow," he said, patting his prey on the neck. "He gave us an honorable chase. We were only victors because we outnumbered him so greatly." He tossed away the leaves, which landed on Marco. Marco jumped.

The seated man's eyes widened. "Why, I'm sorry, puss! Come here and let me make it up to you." He rubbed his fingers together. Marco edged forward with great care. The prince in the seventeenth kingdom had sought to entice him in exactly the same way, then tried to run him through with a dagger. "Come on, do."

"He's just a stray, Your Highness."

Highness! Marco looked at the young man. He resembled Prince Golther, but he was smaller and slighter. Why had he not come to the princess' ball? Every royal male over 12 had been invited. Then Marco calculated in his mind the length of his travels. It had been *nine years* since the disastrous celebration party. This lad was no more than twenty. He would have been a child. But now he was grown to manhood, and what a handsome fellow he was, with soft black hair and hazel-colored eyes! Marco came to his outstretched hand and sniffed. The hand shifted and came down on his head. Stroked. Rose from his hindquarters and stroked again. Marco stood stock-still out of astonishment.

"There, you see? Why, you're down to skin and bones, you poor fellow. Here." The prince took out his dagger. Marco started back, but the prince reached

to his side and cut a slice of flesh from the belly of
the stag. "Have a bite. The cooks will never miss it."
Marco seized it and retreated to a safe distance to eat.

"Sire!" the companion scolded him. Marco paid no
attention, as the prince did not. Obviously, this young
man made his own decisions. He was kind. He was
respectful to his fallen foe. He was generous to those
less fortunate than himself. He was handsome enough,
as humans went. And he must indeed be brave, because the stag was a 12-pointer, not a beast to be
brought down by a white-livered hunter. He could be
the man Marco had been looking for.

But was he curious enough? When his meal was
through, Marco rubbed against the prince's leg and
went a few feet away. He looked hard at the young
man.

"What do you want, puss?" he asked. Marco came
up, rubbed again, then danced a short distance away,
his eyes fixed on the prince's face, and waited. The
prince stood up, stomped his boot to seat his heel
again, and came up beside Marco. Marco, his heart
racing with hope, trotted a few more feet. The prince
followed. "Where are you trying to lead me?"

"Prince Reynard, where are you going?"

"On a quest," the prince said, his eyes alight. "If
you do not wish to come, then run and tell my brother
where I am going. He'll be happy to see the back of
me. There's nothing so useless as an extra prince."

Marco's callused pads were as sore as ever he remembered them, but his heart was light. The prince
ran back for his horse. Several of Prince Reynard's
friends followed. Marco waited, then began to lead
them. The horses overshot his fastest trot in a matter
of seconds. Reynard leaned down from the saddle and
scooped him up to the horse's neck.

"Point where you wish us to go, puss," the prince
said. "Tell me when to change direction. Otherwise

we shall ride straight and true." Marco nodded. "He understands me!"

"How can he, sire? He's just a cat."

"I don't know, but he does," Reynard said. "It is a wonder."

"Where are we going, Highness?" the redhead asked. Reynard smiled.

"I do not know, Theo, but it's an adventure! Ride on!"

Marco clung to the saddle cloth, his heart racing. This must be the man. He must!

It took months to ride along the coast back to Cadmonia. Marco slept at night on the prince's blanket, one paw touching his shoulder or arm, just to make sure he didn't disappear in the night. He must not lose this man.

He need not have feared. A few of the companions dropped back, not interested, thinking the prince mad or the cat a witch in disguise, but the prince persevered. Marco thought of his friends, but above all the princess. She must not sleep forever. Reynard was his best hope.

They broke through the trees, now higher and thicker, that marked the end of Hawellia. Marco looked ahead toward the isthmus. It was blocked by a tangle of dense black thorns.

Theo frowned. "This is where your brother came to see the princess who grievously insulted him."

"How did she insult him?"

"She refused to marry him, sire."

Reynard snorted. "So would I. Well, this is where you wish us to go, puss. But how do we get in?"

"This mess is impenetrable," complained Theo.

But Marco spotted a hole in the tangle. He jumped off the horse's neck and crawled into a niche that only he saw. Inside was a tunnel large enough for a man to crawl. He went back to lead Reynard to it. Theo scoffed, but Reynard followed, trusting.

"You can't go in there, sire!" Marco gave Theo a disgusted look. He would never win a princess or a kingdom with a quitter's attitude like that. Reynard seemed equally fed up.

"If you won't come, then hold my horse and guard my back! Come on, friend puss. Show me what you've brought me here to see."

With the aid of Reynard's sword they chopped through the thorns and emerged on the road to the capital. Inside, it felt as though the very air was asleep. Not an insect buzzed, nor a bird sang. Now Marco could see the castle. He trotted toward it with Reynard beside him.

Just outside the walls Marco smelled sulfur. He stopped, on guard. Reynard wrinkled his nose.

"Let's go in. It stinks out here." He made for the drawbridge, and a black shape rose out of the moat. It roared, baring hundreds of white fangs. The prince drew his sword. "A dragon!"

Desdemona! Marco threw himself at her neck, clawing and biting. Her big head swung around to bite him. Reynard recovered his wits and dove into the fray.

Together they slashed at the scaly hide. Desdemona must have been hiding here all these years to prevent Briar Rose's rescue. She raked at Reynard's arm, but only drew blood. In spite of her size she was not as swift as Marco, and Reynard's sword thrusts were weakening her. She knocked Marco sprawling with a backhanded swipe and snapped at the prince's head. He jumped away and chopped down on her neck. She shuddered, her shape collapsing into a smaller beast: a manticore. Reynard was surprised, but only for a moment. He redoubled his attack, striking again and again, ignoring the pain in his arm. The manticore shrank to a leopard, then to a fox, and finally to a mouse racing for the safety of the black tangled thorns.

Marco sprang after her and grabbed her by the neck. With one shake, he broke her neck. Dangling the corpse from his mouth, he trotted back to the prince. When he passed the midden heap, he dropped Desdemona's body on it.

"Why, you're as brave as a man," Reynard said, following him into the castle environs.

Marco gave him a look. The prince was covered with dust and blood. He must not go up to the princess like that! Marco led him up to the well in the center of the silent courtyard, sat down on the cobbles and began to wash himself with his tongue.

"I see!" The prince laughed. "Wherever you are taking me, you wish me to clean up first. Well," he said, wrinkling his nose," I do smell like I've traveled a thousand leagues." He threw the bucket down the well. The sound of the winch as it hauled the full bucket to the top was the first homely sound heard there in ten years.

Once they were both washed, Marco led him to the White Tower. The guards at the door still slept.

At the top of the stairs, a fantastic web of thread barred their way. It was a thing of beauty, but also of danger. Skeletons of monsters were tangled in it, as well as the bones of a man or two, like flies caught in lace. Reynard pushed at the fine netting, and it enveloped his hand. He tried to pull free, to no avail.

"What is this, friend? A trap? Help me!" Scrabbling in the walls made Reynard grab his sword out of his scabbard. Marco turned his big eyes to look for the source of the sound.

"Who is there?" a high-pitched voice squeaked.

"It is I, Humberto!" Marco called in his own language.

"Marco!" The mouse scrambled out of a hole near

the floor. He came out to embrace the cat, and looked up at the man. "My goodness, he's big. Is he the one?"

"I hope so."

Reynard had stopped struggling to stare at them. "Now I have seen a further wonder: a mouse embracing a cat. What other miracles will I see?"

"He is properly respectful," Marco said to Humberto. "Set him free."

The mouse clambered up the shining mesh to the very top. With his tiny pink hands he selected a thread, lifted it to his mouth, and chewed through it. The net collapsed in coils around Reynard's feet.

"There," Humberto said.

Rubbing his wrist, Reynard followed Marco to the princess' door. Marco pawed, and Reynard opened the latch.

Barking, hoarse at first, erupted from the room. A dusty brown beast charged toward them out of the shadows, only to skid to a halt at the cat's feet.

"Marco!" Bruno cried, with a howl that shook the rafters. He sniffed Reynard all over. "He smells good! You have found a good one! She will like him."

"Is she well?" Marco asked. "Bring us to him."

"She sleeps," Bruno said simply. "I have not left this place in ten long years. Humberto has fed and cared for me." He trotted ahead of the prince, who had been struck silent by yet another miracle.

But Marco knew the greatest was about to come.

As the heavy wooden portal swung aside, they could see a single shaft of sunlight falling through the window onto the bed. Exactly as Marco had left her, the Princess Briar Rose lay upon her bed, blue silk velvet coverlet drawn up to her breast, a single red rose caught in her fingertips. Her golden hair was outspread upon the white silk pillow, and her thick-lashed eyelids were closed above pale, alabaster cheeks. Reynard stood and adored her.

"How beautiful," he whispered. "She is a dryad. An angel. A goddess!" But he did not move.

"Push him," Marco ordered. He and Bruno applied their noses to the back of Reynard's knees. The prince nearly fell over, but he stumbled forward. He halted again at the bedside.

"Very well, friend puss," he said to Marco. "You have led me here. What must I do to awaken this sleeping beauty?"

"Humans!" Marco said scornfully. He leaped up onto the princess' pillow. The little hollow where he had always slept was still indented. Marco's heart pined a moment for that soft recess. If this man married his adored Briar Rose, he could be relegated to the floor, or worse yet, the stables! But she must not sleep on into eternity. She must arise and marry and fulfill her promised life of happiness. He had sworn faithfully to the fairy godmothers that he would bring back a prince worthy of her. He must not hesitate now. Humbly, but with love, he leaned down and licked Briar Rose on the cheek. Then he turned and looked meaningfully at Reynard.

The prince smiled. "I see. I hope I can give as much of myself to her as you have, to trot all the way across the land to me on your four feet. Give me room, my brave friend."

Marco made way for Reynard as the prince leaned over and touched her lips very gently with his own. The gold-lashed eyes fluttered open, and Briar Rose smiled up at her own true love.

As if a thick door had suddenly been opened onto a room where a party was going on, sounds erupted outside. Men shouted, animals bellowed, birds sang. He heard the joyful voices of the fairy godmothers and the king and queen. The prince lifted Marco up to show him to Briar Rose.

"Your valiant little friend led me here to you. I am Reynard, second son of the king of Greenaway. Since

I've been so bold as to kiss you, may I ask you to marry me?"

"Yes!" Briar Rose said. She sat up to embrace Reynard, squeezing Marco between them until he emitted a squawk of protest.

"I am sorry, O brave one," Reynard said, laughing. "Here." He reached down for a silk cushion from the floor and plumped Marco down onto it on the foot of the bed. "So long as you live, you shall have a place of honor here, in token of our thanks to you. Your brave friends shall stay here as well."

"Well, that's as it should be," Marco said, curling himself up gratefully. At last, a suitor—nay, a fiancé, who had the proper respect for Briar Rose, and for him! "I'm relieved everyone is awake at last. I can at last take up the task that is right for me, that I've neglected for almost ten years."

"And what is that?" Briar Rose asked, stroking his black and white fur.

"Sleeping," Marco said, with a yawn. "Men slay dragons. Women inspire poetry. But if there's any sleeping to be done around here, *I* will do it. Wake me in time for the wedding, will you?"

He buried his nose under his paw, and closed his eyes.

THE SNOW QUEEN

Michelle West and Debbie Ridpath Ohi

Michelle West's novels include *Hunter's Oath, Hunter's Death, The Broken Crown, The Uncrowned King, The Shining Court, Sea of Sorrows,* and *Sun Sword,* all published by DAW; she also writes a book review column for *The Magazine of Fantasy & Science Fiction.* As Michelle Sagara, she is the author of *Into the Dark Lands, Children of the Blood, Lady of Mercy,* and *Chains of Darkness, Chains of Light.* She has also written under the name of Michelle Sagara West, and has published over forty pieces of short fiction. She lives with her family in Toronto, Canada.

Debbie Ridpath Ohi is a Toronto-based freelance writer and editor. Author of *The Writers' Online Marketplace* (Writer's Digest Books, Jan/2001), she has also published short fiction and nonfiction in various print and online publications, and has a literary agent at Curtis Brown, Ltd. As creator of Inkspot, her newsletter for writers reached nearly 50,000 subscribers. She is currently working on a novel for young people. In her spare time, Debbie publishes an online comic strip, performs with her filk group, and goes camping in Northern Ontario with her husband Jeff. For more information, please see her

Web site at http://www.electricpenguin.com, or send
e-mail to her at ohi@electricpenguin.com.

There have always been stories about mirrors.
    Magic mirrors; speaking mirrors; mirrors that
lead to strange and dangerous lands; mirrors that dis-
tort and reflect a parody of the truth. Stories start with
mirrors. Stories like "once upon a time."

There is closure implied by beginning, be it of silvered surface, of unmarred length of broken glass.

Once.

Once upon a time.

There are mirrors in the house. Mirrors on the side
of the great, loud metal beast that slumbers there.
Mirrors in the long hall. Mirrors in the water room.

Cat is aware of all these. Cat has placed paws upon
the surfaces that can be reached: dainty paws, claws
retracted, forearms stretched. Cat has gazed at yellow
unblinking eyes in the round of white-furred face. Cat
understands mirrors.

But there is a special mirror, in the boy's house.
And when the boy is absent, the woman sometimes
goes to the mirror in search of the truth. She takes
off her clothing, piece by piece, eyes darting away
from the shining surface until she is finished.

Today, she is crying. When she looks at the mirror,
she does not see tears; she sees some self that cat
doesn't see. She is . . . angry today. She is afraid. She
stares and stares and then she turns away, speaking
of things that have no meaning for cat: Money. Fear.
Men.

But cat understands what happens next, is even prepared for it. She picks up a book that sleeps by her
bedside, and she throws it.

The mirror shatters. Long shards of glass, ragged
chunks of polished, glinting surface, fall from its frame
like icicles in sunlight; what clings to oiled wood are

the gaping jaws of a wounded beast. Cat avoids the carpet for days, because some broken things are too dangerous.

But cat has no words; no words to tell the boy when the boy comes home from the big, crowded place. The boy calls his mother when he opens the door, and when he hears no answer, his face freezes.

Boy is afraid. Boy is smart, to be afraid. But not so smart as cat: He climbs the stairs, walking in search of the mirror room. When he is at the top of the hall, cat tangles himself in boy's feet.

Boy bends, boy's hands scratch the back of cat's neck, but his hands are shaking and his thought is elsewhere. Cat mewls. Cat tries to drag him down the stairs, away from the mirror room.

But the woman is weeping, and the boy still has a heart. His hands stop. They are cold now; not even cat's fur can make them warm again.

"Mom?"

Boy rises. Cat rises, too, or cat's hair does. Cat catches boy's hand in his paws, extending the claws like anchors. But the boy is not afraid that cat will claw or scratch. He pulls his hand away, and because cat knows that pain waits, cat pulls claws in.

Boy's hair is gold, boy's face is white; boy's blue eyes are the wrong color. He walks to the door that is almost closed, and pushes it open. "Mom?"

The woman's crying stops. "Kay? What are you doing home so early?"

Boy's face changes again. Cat knows he is not home early, but cats can't speak, and boy doesn't. Instead, boy walks into the room, and cat shadows the swing of his slender legs, the fall of his feet.

He takes his shoes off and leaves them on the mat by the door; those are the woman's rules. There is nothing to protect his feet. Nothing to protect him. Cat's claws catch the cuff of his pants, but the boy keeps walking; cat has to let go, or cat will be cut. Boy doesn't notice. He sees his mother slumped beside the bed, and his breath cuts.

"Mom. Mom, it's okay. I'm here now."

The woman looks up. Her tears are black. "I've got good news," she tells him, as if the mirror weren't broken. As if she couldn't see herself in the large flat chunks that crush the carpet pile.

Later, boy will take the bottle away. He would take it now, but her face is wild, and he knows what that means. He walks toward her, and the shards of the shattered mirror cut the thinning undersides of his socks.

But he doesn't see the blood.

He sees the woman.

"What good news, Mom?" boy asks gently, as he sits down beside her.

"I'm getting married."

The room smells of blood, bottle, and fear.

The girl comes in the morning.

If she had come in the night, she could have talked to the boy; the boy doesn't sleep. If the boy had a mirror, it, too, would be shattered. But this is a story, and the splinters have already done their work, and the truth of that work will unfold, trapped inside him.

Instead, his drawers are pulled from his dresser and his clothing is strewn across the floor. Books and comic books are scattered face-down on top of the piles; his shelf is bare.

His clock makes an angry buzz.

The woman will not wake this morning. The boy has gathered her bottles, and his tears are not black, but he cries them. He hides the bottles in a new place. He hears the girl knock at the door, and he almost ignores it. But it is early yet, and the boy has not learned to be cold.

*   *   *

Gerta stood on the welcome mat. She had knocked twice, and twice was a rule in Kay's house. His mother wasn't well, and she needed a lot of sleep.

But the numbers on the watch kept changing, and the school bell never waited for anyone, good excuse or no. Her hand hovered above the door as she waited, but before she could knock it again, it opened.

Kay stood in the crack between door frame and door. His eyes were dark and his hair was a flyaway mess.

"Are you coming to school today?"

He nodded. "Give me a sec."

The door closed again.

She was used to this. Sometimes he invited her in, and sometimes he shut her out. She never asked why. Others had, and she'd learned from their mistakes. Kay didn't have a lot of friends anymore, and he didn't seem to need them.

Maybe that was why she liked him.

Maybe that was why she could stand on the doormat, waiting while the principal's office crept closer by the perfectly measured second. Or maybe it was just because she'd always waited for Kay.

When she'd gone to visit Kay's father in the hospital three years ago, he had become a tiny man. Something about the machines, the doctors, the pale cream walls of the halls and the rooms, had sucked the size out of him; he lay in a small, bent bed, his head between a wall of pillows. Even his hands were wizened and shrunk, but they were still much larger than hers.

"Kay'll be back soon," he'd said, his voice a wheeze of harsh air, stale breath.

She'd taken his hand, as he meant her to, and when he pulled her close, she went without demur.

"I love my wife," he'd said, and that had confused her—of course he loved his wife. All husbands loved their wives. "I love her, but she's not very strong. And Kay's a boy. A good boy, but a boy. He'll try to look after her."

She nodded, watching the green lines of the monitor banks to the left of the bed. She could see her reflection in them, if she tried real hard.

"She'll let him. But there'll be no one to look after Kay. Try to imagine what that's like, Gerta. No one for Kay."

If she could have pulled away, she would have.

He knew. He coughed as he tried to sit up, tried to regain the height that had been taken from him.

She nodded. She was uneasy. She wanted Kay to come back. She was afraid of his father now, although she'd never been afraid of him when he was bigger. She didn't know what he would ask of her.

"Watch out for him. He'll need a friend, Gerta. Be his friend."

She felt her hand relax in his. She straightened up and met his ferocious glare. "I'll always be his friend."

"Promise me."

She nodded. All her fear had gone. "I promise. I will *always* be Kay's friend."

Promises last forever. Promises last.

Standing in front of the principal's office for the third time that month, Gerta tried to remember this. She glance at Kay furtively; his eyes were fixed on the door.

"Kay—"

He turned to her, his face contorted in smile. In something like one; it was a stranger's expression. He shrugged. "Don't be so worried."

"But this is the third time. They'll send a letter home—"

"They'll give *us* a letter to send home. What are we, postmen?" He shrugged again, but the smile slid off his face; his eyes were narrow as his chin fell.

"Look, what's the worst thing they can do to us? They can't throw us in jail. They can't hit us. They can't even swear."

"Kay—"

"What?"

"They can suspend us."

"Like they'll suspend you." There again, the foreign expression. "And anyway, it's only for a couple of days. It's not like it'll hurt your grades any."

It was true. "But my parents—"

"Your parents won't get angry." He closed his eyes. Closing them was like opening a window. "Kay—"

"I'm sorry," he told her. "Look, it might be better if you just stopped waiting for me, okay?"

But she couldn't. She would wait for him just as she waited now, at the door of the principal's office.

It didn't get easier.

The next month, she was late, late, late. The principal's office was like a second home, and it wasn't a home she wanted to spend much time at. She lost the ability to speak when she entered his cavernous room; spent the time watching muted flashing lights on the phone on his desk: he put calls on hold while he dealt with "his" children.

But he was a distant figure; far worse was when Mrs. Morgan asked her to stay after school. Gerta watched her friends leave in ones and twos, speaking among themselves and casting backward glances in her direction, until the room was empty. Words would have echoed here, if she could say any.

"Gerta," Mrs. Morgan said, coming out from behind the desk that swallowed the northeast corner of the large room, "I asked you to stay because I wanted a chance to speak with you."

Gerta nodded.

"Is there anything going on at home that you want to tell me about?"

"At home?"

Mrs. Morgan smiled. Gerta had always liked her. But after today, she would be a little bit afraid of her. Kay's fault.

"No, Mrs. Morgan. Everything at home is okay."

But it wasn't.

When Gerta got home from school, her mother *and* father were waiting for her. Which meant that her father had left work early. Which meant trouble.

"Gerta, we had a call from school today."

Gerta felt her shoulders begin their downward slump. She said nothing.

"You've been late six times this month. Three times a month each month before that. Why?"

She wanted to tell them. But she couldn't. Because if she did, they'd tell her to stop seeing Kay.

And promises were forever.

But it wasn't just being late in the morning. The afternoons followed. Long ones, cold ones, hours spent waiting by the side of the school until Kay finally came out of the doors closest to the office.

He was never happy to see her anymore, but he was never surprised. He would begin the long walk through the thin felt of snow, the bright sheen of ice that had escaped salt and dirt, and she would follow.

She had asked him, the first time, why he had been given a detention. Only the first time. The things he said to her then were things that would have melted snow; her cheeks flushed when she thought of them, and she thought of them often.

Are you stupid or something? Great, start sniveling. It makes you look so attractive.

Her throat had frozen; she couldn't swallow. She had let him leave her there, by the curb, and had watched his back get smaller and smaller in the blur of those hated tears.

*   *   *

The house is full of glass. Glass blossoms upon table top, nestles between the surface of carpet and the underside of table; glass rests in the boxes in the kitchen, row upon row. Not all of it is clear; some is dark, and some the color of flawed emerald, cracked and broken. Glass holds the ashes of something too dim to be fire; the smell of the house has changed.

It is the season of thunder, the season before true winter. Cat waits in the space between curtain and window, watching the road.

Road yields boy, distant, his steps close to ground. Gold is the color of head bent against wind.

It is almost time.

Boy no longer hides the bottles. In the beginning, he tried, but the man is here, and when the man cannot find them, he is terrible.

Boy's house has dwindled to one room, one small room. It is littered with old books, old comics, old clothing. The bed is unmade, the laundry undone. One by one, he has let go of the things that were his.

But sometimes when the man is gone, he will go to the mirror room, and he will sit with the woman.

When he stops even this, he will be ready.

Kay.

"Gerta, sometimes when boys get older, they . . . they need to find male friends. You've been close for a long time, but . . ."

Gerta looked up. She knew, by heart, the way the wood grain traveled the length of the kitchen table. Knew it almost as well as this conversation.

Except that it wasn't a conversation; she never spoke.

"Gerta, don't make that face."

If she hoped for rescue from her father, it wasn't coming any time soon. Her head hurt; her throat was thick with unsaid words. She wanted to talk.

But talking—here—meant listening.

She pushed the chair away from the table and stood up.

"Gertie, where are you going?"

"I'm going to visit Grandma."

Her father snorted. "Gert, I love my mother almost as much as I love you, but that old woman is a scurrilous gossip. You don't need to see her. You don't need to speak to her. If you do, half the town will know your business before you get to school in the morning."

"I am going to visit Grandma," Gerta said, putting a pause between each word. Daring her father to say no. Daring her mother to speak.

But they didn't, because they knew the other half of the sentence: *And if you don't let me, I'll tell her that you didn't want me to visit.*

And then her grandmother would phone four times a day for the next two months. Gerta was always happy to hear from her, but sometimes her parents weren't. She wondered if she would ever understand why.

Gerta's grandmother lived down the street, around the corner, and over the hill. As a child, she had loved the sound of the words, said over and over again, like a rhyme. But she didn't feel like a child. Wondered if all the old things would seem stupid as she got older.

Like Kay.

But her grandmother didn't change. She had always been old, and would always be old; her hair was silver and white, and her eyes were clear blue in a mass of intricate wrinkles.

"Gertie!" she said, as she opened the door and opened her arms for a hug almost at the same time.

She smelled like powder and flowers. Her house smelled like baking. It was as if she had captured all those scents and made them as changeless as she herself was.

"Come in, come in. Have you eaten?"

It never mattered what the answer was. Gerta smiled.

"Here, here, that's not much of a smile, is it?" She pulled Gerta into the house, leading her to the kitchen. It was her grandmother's favorite room. Not for her the parlor and the tea rooms; she liked her baking, she liked to bustle. Cupboard to counter, she moved as she spoke.

Gerta took the chair with her name on it. She had painted it when she was five, and her grandmother had never changed it.

"Definitely not much of a smile. What's wrong, Gertie?"

"Have you—has Kay come by lately?"

For just a moment, her grandmother stopped moving. Back to Gerta, she placed her hands on the countertop. When she started to move again, she was quiet.

"It's such a pity," her grandmother finally said. "Karen was always such a frail girl."

Karen. Karen. It took a moment before Gerta realized that Grandma was talking about Kay's mother.

"That fool husband of hers," grandma continued. "Always coddling her. Never letting her grow up." She shook her head. "Ever since high school. Karen was the girl. Harry was the man." She shook her head. "He was a good man," she added. "Sometimes good men are stupid."

"Grandma—"

"Now, that husband of hers—that new one—he's not much good for anything." Dishes hit the counter, one after the other, clattering and clanging like a small storm. "He lost his job, you know. He hasn't been looking too hard for another one." She turned. "Be a dear, Gertie. Get me the cheese from the fridge. Oh, and the tomatoes."

Gerta did as bid.

"The two of them—that no good husband and Karen—they're living like teenagers again." Grandma snorted. "There's a reason people grow up when they have children."

"Kay doesn't talk about them much."

"I know, dear." Her grandmother put a large pot to boil on the stove, wiping her hands on her apron. "Talking won't do him much good."

"Then what will?"

"Oh, Gertie," her grandmother said, coming to sit down in the chair in front of Gerta. "You listen to me. If Kay had only known that—that great oaf Karen married half a year ago, you'd never have been friends. But Harry loved his son, and Karen—she loved him, too. But hers is a love that doesn't survive fear well. She thinks she *needs* a man, any man. She's afraid of being alone. Oh, what was I saying?"

"She's afraid. Of being alone."

"That's right. And you are, too. So am I, Gertie." Her smile was very strange. "We're people; people were meant to be together. But sometimes the wrong people find each other, and they don't know how to let go. They're together without ever understanding what the word means. You know what's more lonely than being alone? Being lonely while you're with another person." She shook her head. "Kay's not a bad boy."

"He's always in the office now."

Grandma was quiet.

"And he doesn't do his homework. He doesn't do anything in school. He quit the cross country team; he doesn't even want to run anymore. And he *loved* running."

"I think," Grandma said quietly, "that running

means something different to Kay now." She took a deep breath.

"But, Grandma—we used to do everything together. Now he—he's always angry. He never speaks to me. He doesn't read anymore, and he doesn't even care—"

"Hush. Hush, Gertie. Let me tell you a story."

"What story?" She didn't want to hear stories. And she did. For just a minute, she wanted to be the five-year-old girl who had painted her name in big, awkward letters on the back of her grandmother's chair.

"When I was a little girl—well, older than you, but we were young then—I had a friend, like Kay. A girl, though. She was smart, and everyone said she was lovely; she had a kind heart. Her father and mother loved her very much, but her father wasn't well, and he died when she was ten.

"Her mother had no job. Back in those days, there *were* no jobs. Not for women of her class. Her family tried to help out, but she had no money, and her husband had always handled the household finances. You understand what that means?"

"He paid the bills?"

"Yes, love, he paid the bills.

"Well, after he died, she had no one to pay the bills. And she had two children, two growing children. She sewed for them, and she tried to take jobs sewing for the other mothers in the neighborhood. People tried to find work for her—but in the 1920s, there wasn't a lot of money, there just wasn't a lot of work.

"She saw that her children were wearing threadbare clothing; that they were becoming gaunt and skinny. So she found herself another husband, a man of the community. Oh, listen to me. That doesn't mean much now either. But back then, it did.

"But he was a mean man. A small man. He wanted his wife, but he hated her children, because they were proof that she had once belonged to another man." Grandma wiped her eyes with the back of her hand. "He was cruel, to them. When he was in his black mood, he hit them."

Gerta's eyes grew round with shock. "Did they call the police?"

And Grandma's eyes were round with something else. "It wouldn't have helped, Gerta. I know that's hard for you to understand."

"But—but what did they do?"

"They endured. The older daughter was strong; she remembered her first father, and she knew that not all men were like the one in her mother's house. But her little brother wasn't so strong; he could barely remember their real father; all he knew was the second one. He swallowed all the mean words, and they worked their way into his heart, like slivers of glass.

"One day, he disappeared. When he was cold and tough, when he hated the world enough. He just disappeared."

"And what did she do, Grandma? The big sister. What did she do?"

"She left home, Gertie. She left home the very next day, and she went to find him. It wasn't easy. In fact, it was the hardest thing she had ever had to do—and she had bruises and cuts from the beatings she endured.

"But she knew that if she didn't find her brother, he would be lost forever."

"Lost where?"

Grandma's face was very still. Something about it made Gerta ask a question no five-year-old would ever have asked.

"Grandma—were you that girl?"

"Oh, Gertie, you're growing up. You're growing up so quickly." She hugged Gerta; hugged her too tightly. She hung her head for a while.

Gerta went pale. "But—but—"

"Go ahead, Gertie. Ask. I've been waiting a long time to tell this story."

"But you were an only child. Dad said so."

"I wasn't an only child. I had a baby brother."

"What happened?"

"I was too old, when I went to look for him. I waited too long. And I was too hurt by him, by all the changes in him. He saw me as our mother. He saw me as just another person who couldn't—ever—protect him, or keep him safe. He said awful things, and I took them to heart, and I cried. I thought he didn't want me. I thought—"

She shook her head.

"He was just so *cold*. But I learned something important, when I had my own children."

"Tell me."

"I learned that children are like—like my kitchen. They're like rooms, some small and some so big you put whole airplanes in them and still have room for parties. And I learned that if you make a place in a child's heart for love, they remember it. They may forget where it *is,* but some part of them knows it's still there. You can say mean things—we all do, and we regret it—but if that place was made, and it was made strong, it's still there when everything else about the room collapses.

"It's like when mines collapse, dearest. There are places where there's still air, and if you know how to look, you'll find them."

"How?"

"I don't know, Gertie."

Gerta closed her eyes.

"But I know this. I should have believed that he loved me. I should have understood that all those mean words, all those terrible, terrible things, were just a way of telling me how bad the pain was. Like a storm. Like a cold, cold blizzard. I should have waited.

"Because snow doesn't last forever. If there's sun,

if there's warmth—even if it's from a great distance, snow melts; blizzards stop."

"Grandma, how do you tell someone you love them when they don't want to listen?"

"That's not the right question, Gertie."

Gerta thought for a long time. Then, as if this were one of Mrs. Morgan's math problems, she said, "How do you make them understand that you love them?"

"*That,* love, is the right question. It's hard. People have to think of themselves, and they have to protect themselves against the elements. But they have to be true to other things as well.

"Believe it yourself," she replied gently. "Because it's your belief that counts. Try not to see your pain," she told her granddaughter gently, stroking her hair. "Try to see his."

"But he's not in pain—"

Grandma shook her silver-white hair; her hair, color of snow in the fading sunlight of the kitchen windows.

"What happened to your brother?"

"He went," her grandmother said quietly, "where lost children go. And I couldn't follow him, because I didn't know how to be lost anymore." She got up from her chair and shook her head. "Now look at me—the water's boiling. You wait here, Gertie."

The girl knocks.

The door opens and noise spills out with boy. Cat follows, crossing the threshold into winter light. Boy closes the door quickly behind him, his face in shadows.

The girl carries food.

Cat winds around her legs as she knocks on the door, waits on the steps.

Shouting from inside. The girl takes a step back, hesitates.

"Hi," girl says.

Boy does not look at her. "What do you want?" Cat butts dark head against the boy's legs, mewls.

The girl hesitates, then holds out the dish. "This is for you, from Grandma."

"What?"

"It's for—it's for your family."

"We don't need charity." Boy does not take the dish. Cat mewls again. The boy softens, kneeling beside cat. Scratches cat behind the ears.

"It's not charity. She made way too much lasagna today. Kay—you know Grandma. She *always* makes too much food. And she misses you." Girl sets the dish on the steps and sits down. She hugs her knees, rocking back and forth as she watches the boy with cat. Cat purrs, arching back against boy's hand.

The door is closed. What escapes wood and brass is like a ghost: wordless thunder, followed by the woman's cry. Boy's face doesn't change; it is cold and stiff.

"Kay?" the girl whispers.

But boy says nothing, head lowered. Cat shifts beneath boy's still hand. Lifts body upon hindlegs, paws outstretched as if to touch mirror, touch wall—something hard and cool.

Paws bat at the hair hanging in front of boy's eyes, pushing it one side. For a moment, the boy's face is in the light.

As is the bruise, blossoming beneath one eye like a dark flower, terrible in its beauty.

The bruise left its scar. Gerta could not touch it. Could not ask about it. It was there so briefly, she could pretend—when she wanted to—that she had never seen it at all. If Kay were being hit, if that man were hurting him—wouldn't he say something?

She waited for the words, but they didn't come.

Days passed. Weeks passed. She waited, outside Kay's door.

Instead, she heard voices, raised voices; she heard ugly words; she heard the thumping of heavy feet— all from the outside. He never invited her in anymore.

She was afraid. She wasn't sure she wanted to be asked in.

But she was afraid of other things. Of being alone. No, she thought. She wouldn't give up. She wouldn't give up on him.

She met him every morning. She endured the late slips and the increasingly angry questions they caused. She waited for him after school. She tried to find words that would make him happy.

Once, once upon a time, she had always been able to make him happy.

Gerta visited Kay's house several times during the spring break, but he wasn't home.

"He's out with friends," Kay's mother would tell her from the shadow of the doorway. "I don't know where."

Gerta walked the neighborhood, looking for him. Coming out of a movie theater with her grandmother, she thought she saw him once. He was crossing the far end of the street with some other children, kids she didn't recognize. Gerta had called out to him, waving. The figure she thought was Kay seemed to hesitate, but then kept walking.

Her grandmother reached out for Gerta's hand and squeezed it gently. But she said nothing.

It couldn't have been him, she told herself afterward. He would have stopped.

Wouldn't he?

Gerta planned to ask Kay about it on the way to school the first day back, but Kay wasn't home when she went to his house to wait for him.

He wasn't there on the morning of the second day

either, nor did he show up for any classes. His mother shrugged when Gerta asked where Kay was, and suggested she try Menlo Park.

Menlo Park was *not* a place that she wanted to try.

But when Kay did not show up for school a third day in a row, Gerta tucked a map into her pocket and set off to find him. It took her an hour and a half and the map was folded and creased in all the wrong places when she'd finished reading it, but she finally found herself on the winding path through a small park whose grass was littered with cigarette butts and crumpled newspaper. A man in tattered clothing was poking through a garbage can with a long stick, mumbling to himself.

Gerta's steps slowed. She glanced behind her nervously. Long shadows stretched across the path in the late afternoon sun; it was getting dark; the sun didn't break through the rows of townhomes that lined it; nor did it peer through the apartments that towered across its west side.

The man with the stick looked up.

Gerta swallowed hard. Avoiding the man's gaze, she stopped, turned, and began walking back the way she came. After only a few steps, a hand fell heavily on her shoulder. The air turned sour.

"Are you lost, dearie?" It was the old man, grinning. His front teeth were missing, and there was spittle on his cheek. "C'mon, lovely. Let old Sammy help you."

"N–No, thank you," Gerta said, her eyes widening. She felt hollow, light, unable to move.

"And you have such pretty hair. It looks so soft. Here, let me—"

"Leave her alone, Sammy."

Gerta turned and found herself pinned by the fierce gaze of a short girl in paint-splattered jeans and an oversized tie-dye shirt that fell to her knees, the sleeves rolled up to her thin shoulders. Several others stood behind her, all boys. One of them looked familiar.

"Kay!" cried Gerta. She took a step forward, then stopped. Kay had turned his head away, purposefully avoiding her gaze.

The old man was pouting. "Aw, Maggie. I was just having a little fun."

The girl, however, was now ignoring Sammy. "You know her?" she said to Kay.

Kay gave Gerta a dark glance, scowled. "No."

Gerta felt wind blow past her face; it was cold.

Maggie looked at Gerta, then to Kay, said nothing. Instead, she walked slowly around Gerta, arms across her chest, looking at her.

"Scared little mouse," Maggie said.

Sammy had started talking to himself. As the old man tottered away, Gerta said, "Thank you for your help. I didn't know what to do."

"Sammy's harmless," said Maggie, the scorn in her voice clear.

"Look at her necklace, Mags," one of the boys said. "Could be real gold."

The girl leaned forward, her short-cropped curls almost brushing Gerta's cheek. "Is it? Real gold?" she asked. "And what's that stone hanging off it?"

"It's a ruby," Gerta said. "And yes, it's real gold. My grandmother gave it to me." Her glance moved to Kay. He met her gaze; offered nothing but silence in return. His anger, like the wind, was cold.

Maggie nodded in satisfaction. "Give it to me." She held her hand out, waiting.

Gerta stared at her. The necklace felt suddenly heavy against her neck, exposed.

"Now." The girl's voice had an edge.

Gerta could feel the anticipation of the others, a slight jostling as some of the boys moved closer. Kay stood absolutely still, a statue carved of ice and shadow.

Oh, Kay, Gerta thought. Out loud, she said, "No."

A moment of disbelief. Maggie found her voice. "What did you say?"

Gerta swallowed, hard. "I said no, you can't have my necklace. It—it means a lot to me." And to her grandmother. It had been a gift, from the great-uncle who had disappeared from family history; tenuous proof of his existence.

I never asked him, her grandmother said, hand outstretched, chain glittering in the kitchen light, *where he got it. How he could afford it. He gave it to me. I—never asked.* Gerta heard what her grandmother couldn't say: that they had been so poor. That things had been such a struggle. That he could not have paid for it with any coin she could accept.

It's all I have of him. You keep it for me.

The girl froze, her hand still outstretched. She drew it slowly back, a smile stretching across her elfin features. "So," she said. "The mouse has a backbone after all."

She threw her head back and laughed, but no one else did. Gerta started to let herself relax when one of Maggie's hands suddenly shot out and grabbed a handful of her hair, yanking her head closer. Gerta cried out in pain.

Maggie paused for a moment, her mouth close to Gerta's ear.

"I like you, so I'm only taking the necklace," she whispered. With her free hand, Maggie took hold of the necklace around Gerta's neck and tugged sharply, breaking the fragile chain.

Gerta stumbled to her knees as Maggie tucked the necklace into a pocket.

"I'd hurry home if I were you," she said. "It's not safe to be in this area after dark. Kay, escort her out of the park."

Kay opened his mouth as if to protest, but then shut it again.

After leaving the others, Gerta and Kay walked in silence. Kay took long strides, forcing Gerta to half-jog to keep up with him.

There were so many things that Gerta wanted to say, but she had trouble finding the words. By the time she found any, she and Kay were nearly at the edge of the park. She meant to ask Kay why he wasn't coming to classes, why he had let the girl take her grandmother's necklace, why he had chosen this group of friends over her.

But when Gerta opened her mouth, the words came out all wrong.

"I missed you," she said.

"Yeah, well, I didn't miss you."

They had stopped walking; they had reached the townhouse complex closest to school. Kay turned to her, took her by the shoulders.

"Don't come looking for me again," he said. "It's not safe for you."

"But Kay . . ."

His eyes closed briefly. When they opened, there was no light in their depths, no warmth. Only ice. "Aren't you listening?" His voice was harsh. "Leave me alone. I don't want you around."

And then he was gone, running, a small shadow of a boy melting into the deeper shadows of the park.

Cat is restless. Wind is restless.

In the City, they mark seasons by numbers, fitting them into flat paper boxes. So much of this life is in boxes.

The woman is singing. Her voice breaks on syllables; it is not a pleasant sound. She does not sing when the man is home. She does not sing when she is happy.

Cat looks up the stairs. The lights are out; they will not come on again unless the man changes the glass that holds them. Boy is in his room, and the room has become too small too contain him.

The woman hears him. Cat hears him. They both wait, in different places, in different ways. When boy comes down the stairs, his hand touches rail; his shoulders are heavy with straps; he is laden now by the past. Cat wonders if he will set it down, or if he will find it; it is hard to see the things that are on your back.

Boy pauses by the mirror room, the broken mirror, and presses his forehead into the closed door. His cheeks are flushed, but his lips are a thin, white line; they will not open. He touches the handle, and then his hand falls away.

He has done this twice before, and each time, he has opened the door and walked through it.

But the third time is different. He walks past. He will not listen. He will not look.

Her song is for him. Boy knows, but he does not join it. Instead, he walks to the door, stepping lightly over cat and gazing down.

Cat looks up at boy's face.

Boy is lost now. Lost.

Gerta knocked at the door. Once. She counted to ten, and knocked again.

Something about the way it opened was wrong, and she knew why when she saw Kay's mother, shrunken in the frame. Her lips were as red as her eyes, thick and unpleasant.

"H'lo, Gertie."

Gerta had no words.

But Kay's mother didn't seem to notice. "Kay's gone," she said.

"G–gone?"

"Gone."

"Gone where?"

The woman shrugged. "Someplace better, y'know? Someplace better than this." And then her eyes teared, and the taint of her breath filled the air. "Don't you go botherin' him, 'kay?"

She said nothing. Her tongue was frozen.

"Oh, hell. Bother him if you want. When you find him, tell him to write. Tell him I'm sorry."

Kay was gone.

Gerta paced the length of her room, finding it small. She watched her shadow cross the length of the floor, glimpsed her ghost in the window.

Her parents were speaking in the distance. Their voices were not raised in anger. Her mother's laughter was short, her father's longer, lower. She heard no words, but the current of their amusement was strong.

She wondered who laughed in Kay's house now, and why. If anyone did.

She could tell her parents that Kay had run away from home. She almost had. But to tell them was to make a decision, and until she made it, she couldn't say a word.

Because if they knew, she couldn't leave them.

Grandma, she thought, lifting her hand to her throat. The necklace was gone.

But she didn't need the necklace to remember her grandmother's words. Lost children, she had said.

What did it take, to be lost?

A promise? A promise to a dying man?

She looked at her bedroom door. At her closet door.

And then, quietly, she made a decision and chose one of the two.

Menlo Park was empty save for the old man, Sammy, who told her that Maggie and the others had gone to Cosmo's.

Cosmo's is closed, she'd told him. *It's been closed for almost two years now.*

He snorted. *Nothing is closed to Maggie.*

She didn't need maps or guides; she knew her way to Cosmo's. Her grandmother used to take Gerta and Kay there every summer. She wondered if, had it still been open, Kay would go with them now, but she didn't wonder long. She knew the answer, and hated it.

Stripped of its crowds and noisy rides, Cosmo's Amusement Park was like their childhood: empty. It had passed beyond her, and she had no way of holding it. Until now, she hadn't even realized that she wanted to.

Despite the sun, a chill breeze raised gooseflesh on Gerta's arms and bare legs as she wandered through the deserted fairgrounds. She shivered and hugged herself.

Echoing laughter near the old arcade caught her attention. Walking closer, she recognized some of the boys from Maggie's gang. They were throwing rocks at bulbs on a string of lights draped along the roof.

Heart pounding, she searched among their faces.

"He's not here."

Gerta turned to see Maggie behind her. The thin girl leaned against a picnic table, her hands covering the letters engraved their by pen-knife. She watched Gerta with narrowed eyes, arms folded across her chest.

"You're looking for Kay, aren't you?"

Gerta nodded, the movement minimal. Guarded. She had hoped to find Kay here, with this strange girl. He wasn't. She didn't want to expose the weakness of ignorance; Maggie had already made clear what that cost.

But she had to find Kay. Soon. She knew it. Swallowing pride—and anger—she asked, "Do you know where he is?"

Another shout. They turned. One of the boys had found a long stick and pulled down the string of lights. He and another stomped hard, the glass crunching beneath their feet, pieces skittering across the pavement like ice.

Maggie shook her head in tired amusement, turning back to Gerta.

"What makes you think he wants to be found? Especially by *you*?"

The boys had had bored with the lights and were starting to drift away, kicking at discarded pop cans, muttering to each other.

"Hey, Mags, whatcha doing? Who's that?"

"The tooth fairy," Maggie shouted back. "Who the hell does it look like?"

She sounded angry; the boy took a half-step back and then changed the subject. "Going to get some food. Are you coming?"

Maggie waved in his direction. "Later. I'll meet you back at the Ferris wheel." They milled a moment around the corpses of light-strings, and she frowned. "I said, *later*."

Maggie was in charge, here. Proof: Gerta watched until the pack of boys disappeared around a building.

"What will you do when you find him?" Maggie said, turning back to Gerta.

"I'll bring him home."

A pause.

"And what if he doesn't want to come home?"

Gerta had no answer.

Maggie glared at her for a long moment, then looked away. "He told me about you. Not a lot, mind you. But with Kay, it's more about what he doesn't say, isn't it?" A different expression crossed her face, one that Gerta almost recognized.

"You want him back," she said.

Maggie frowned. "I've got more where he came from. I don't need him." She shrugged. "He let me take your bauble. He didn't say a thing. He didn't lift a hand to help you. Why the hell do you care?"

Gerta shrugged. It was easier than talking, and Maggie seemed to appreciate it more.

"Yeah," Maggie said, when the shrug had disappeared and the silence became uncomfortable. "Whatever. You think you can get him back?" She spit. "Well, then. Follow me."

Gerta had to half-jog to keep up with Maggie's quick stride. Past the arcade, past the boarded-up refreshment booths, to a familiar-looking building.

The paint on the front doors was faded, but Gerta could still read the letters across their warped and dented surface: THE MIRROR HOUSE. This place was Kay's favorite, she remembered. They would run up and down the mirrored corridors, laughing. Sometimes, though, Kay would sit and stare at his reflection for what seemed like hours, not saying anything. She was never brave enough to ask him what he saw.

Maggie pushed, and wooden doors gave way with a creak of old hinges. Cool air rushed out as Gerta followed, shivering.

"It's funny, y'know?" Maggie said. "That this old place has been boarded up and closed down for so long. 'Cause look." She reached out and pushed something on the shadowed wall, and lights came on, one at a time.

"There's—there's electricity here."

"Good guess." Maggie's snort was derisive, but it was a half-hearted derision. "Yeah. Power. Lights. But it's funny. It's only here."

"Kay is in this place?" A hundred Gertas whispered. Endless reflections stretched out before them in different directions, but she could see Kay in none of them.

"No."

"Then why—"

"Just shut up."

Maggie led. Gerta followed. They walked through an area of the maze that Gerta had never seen before. Here, the floor sloped downward and their reflections were blurred by condensation on the silvered glass.

"I don't remember this."

"No," Maggie said. Scorn had peeled off the surface of words like old paint; what was beneath them was worse. "No, you wouldn't. Why would an uptown girl like you know anything about a place like this?"

Gerta's teeth snapped. "Kay lives two blocks away," she snapped. "He's not exactly a downtown boy."

"He knows the drill. Who does he have, eh? You go home. I bet your parents are still married and still speaking to each other. I bet they don't—" She spit. "Hell with you, anyway." She stopped; shoved her hands into her pockets. Jeans peeled down the smooth skin of belly, revealing navel.

Gerta swallowed anger. Hard. "I'm sorry. I didn't choose my parents. I didn't choose Kay's. Or yours." She looked at the passage that lay beyond them; at their reflections, bright and angry. "Where—where does this lead?"

"A tunnel," said Maggie. She started to walk, hands now fists beneath denim. Gerta caught up. "You should've dressed for cold."

The mirrors vanished, one by one; silver lay across the floor in shards. Gerta wondered if Maggie's gang had done the damage; it was so quiet, she couldn't imagine them here.

"Here," Maggie said. "What do you see?"

In the darkness, Gerta saw tiles on the floor, tiles on the wall beyond the mirrors. Something about them seemed familiar, but it took her a moment to cross the threshold between amusement park and train platform.

"It's a—it's a station."

"Yeah. A station." She noticed Gerta shivering, shrugged off her denim jacket, tossed it the distance between them. "You're going to need this, where you're going."

A faint rumbling in the distance.

"I don't understand," Gerta said.

"Neither did I," said Maggie. "Not until you actually showed up, that day in the park. Then I saw how it was with you two."

Maggie's jaw tightened, eyes grew too bright. "I'm not part of that. Can never be part of it."

The rumbling grew louder, and Gerta could see a faint light in the blackness of the tunnel.

The next moment was filled with train and screeching brakes and the hiss of a subway car door opening.

Then a silence, except for the mechanical hum of the waiting subway car, and a dripping of water from the metal sides.

The air smelled of winter.

"You'd better get going," Maggie said. "Trains here don't come on any schedule; you take 'em or you don't." She started to turn away, but Gerta put a hand on her arm.

"Please come," Gerta said. "You're his friend, too. Help me find him."

Maggie suddenly whirled, her face contorted. She pulled something out of her pocket and thrust it at Gerta's chest so hard that Gerta had to grab at Maggie's hand for support to keep from falling back. When Maggie yanked her arm back, Gerta found herself holding a slender chain.

Her grandmother's necklace.

"I don't owe you anything," Maggie said, her voice thick.

"It's not for me. It's for Kay." She struggled with words. "Because you're right. He did let you take this." She lifted the necklace; saw ruby light against her palm. "He did what you told him. He—"

"You don't get it. You've never been alone. Learn how, learn quick."

"Hey, Mags, you coming?"

Maggie swore. Her invective was as colorful as she was, and anatomically a good deal less probable.

A hundred faces were reflected in the distant mirrors. A boy. Two boys. Gerta was far enough away that she couldn't see them clearly—but she could hear something strange in their voices. Fear.

"I told you, I'd meet you by the damn wheel—what the hell are you doing following me here?"

Silence.

Maggie spit. "They are so stupid they couldn't live without someone telling 'em what to do." She spit again. "You understand, now?" She looked at Gerta. Looked hard. "No. You're pretty stupid, too. That train—it's only got room for one. You. Or me." She looked back at the waiting faces; the boys hadn't moved; they lingered like frightened children. "But only you, or me. Not you *and* me. And not me *and* them." She shoved her hands deeper into her pockets.

"You bring him back, and I'll do whatever I can to make him one of mine." She walked back up the slope, swearing as if curses were a song.

Gerta turned back to the open door of the subway car. It wasn't small; there was certainly room enough for all of them, and then some. But she had no sense that Maggie had lied. Maybe that would have been comforting, somehow.

She looked down at the necklace. Maggie had repaired the chain.

Room for one. "Maggie!"

At the edge of the mirrors, Maggie turned.

"Kay got on?"

"Yeah," Maggie said, the word so quiet it was almost a whisper. "Yeah, the bastard got on the train."

Winter, at last. The wind howls along the sides of the tunnel between train's body and earth's. Lost in the howl is a whisper, a hint of swirling snow, of form-

ing ice. Boy's breath clouds the windows; there is no
heat here that he does not bring with him.

Cat is gathered in his lap, and beside him is his
pack, the hastily gathered belongings of an old life.
Cat sees them clearly through the faded leather of an
old man's satchel: glass, watch, bread that will mold
with the passage of time. Two of these belong to a
dead man. It doesn't matter. Boy will forget them
when he leaves the train.

Beyond the windows, unfolding like story's gradual
middle, twilit sky; the condensation blurs stars and
moon's bright face. It is not the last bright thing boy
will see, but it is the last of the light he will suffer;
the dark is kinder, in the place that is coming. The
place that swallows this train, its lone passenger, its
cat.

Cat grows heavy as the train hurtles on. It loses
color; browns and golds give way to gray of flickering,
round lights. The train is old, but it is not older than
the city; it is an artifact of the gathering places of men,
a dream, a thing that cannot be—quite—forgotten.

Boy's hands entwine in fur.

In another life, cat would shrug them free, but in
this place, boy is newborn. What he does, he does by
instinct, and cat can afford kindness.

The kindness cat knows.

The train does not stop. Boy speaks, but the words
are lost to the screech of wheel against track, the lack
of oil, the sense of history. Here, boy will see his life,
the life he has left. He will shed his tears, as if they
were old skin. He will begin to understand what it
means to be lost.

If he is brave, he will never be found.

Cat is content, for the moment. The test will follow,
but each minute that passes brings boy and train
closer together.

Ice forms on the seats; ice gleams on the poles that
are meant for floundering hands. No one is here to

witness the fall of Winter, save boy, and he is almost beyond it. His face, his pale face, grows red with cold. Soon the red will leave his cheeks, and the pale, pale blue of frozen water will descend like curtain.

Cat's voice is mute, but as the train freezes, as the cold breaks the surface of skin and the shudder replaces the beat of heart, cat's voice will return.

Because that is the nature of this place: the mute are mute by desire and choice, and not by nature.

Cat has no urge to speak. Cat has watched the shards fall; has heard the words that pierce things, beneath skin, that boys hold sacred. Not even the blows and the bruises linger as long as the words, but they echo in this place.

Cat purrs. Cat purrs loudly, speaking like wheeled beasts but absolved of the responsibility of words.

The train slows. The windows are beautiful now, glass buried beneath the skin of frost's swirl, the design of heat and cold, of cold and cold.

Boy passes beyond shivering, and beyond tears; his eyes are blue as pale sky, where horizon meets land. And his hair is gold, bowed like willow fronds, a curtain across his unseen eyes.

White now, cat lifts head from lap.

"Come, boy," cat says, as the train glides into the station.

Boy nods and lifts cat; cat is the only thing he carries with him when he makes his way to the open doors and crosses the threshold.

The City of Lost Children is a dark place.

It was not made in darkness, but only in darkness does it rest and sleep; night is eternal in this land. There are no skies here, no watchful moon, no pale twinkling of stars in moving air. There is wind; the train brings that, over and over, and the cold lingers like the breath of winter serpent.

The City is not empty, but there are no tribes here.

There are no kings, no generals, no politicians or soldiers; there are no businessmen, no craftsmen, no tradesmen. There are songs, but they are silent for the moment; the voices that give rise to them are shaky with disuse, and the songs themselves are often wordless.

It is the words that are best forgotten, here.

But there is no time to mark the passage of words, the decay of memory; things have claws that are hidden, and not even the land itself can quickly remove them.

It is peaceful, this silence, this isolation.

Boy carries cat, as if boy were a messenger.

From the pockets of shadows that loom like buildings, that have shape and texture only when the eye has lingered long enough in darkness, the denizens of this silence peer out. Curiosity is not a crime here: they are children, after all.

They understand what the train means. They have all arrived through its doors, they have all chosen to winter here, denying the inevitability of spring.

They see cat, and they bow their heads, and they do not speak. Perhaps they will, when the boy no longer carries his white burden. But when that happens, the language they use will be a language that knows no nationality. Children are universal.

There are streets. Boy walks them, searching.

Cat climbs over his hands when the time is right, but it is difficult; the hands are stiff with cold, and boy will not surrender this last of his burdens with grace. Cat does not clip him with claws; does not hiss; does not draw blood. That has happened enough, and it is not for punishment that cat has brought boy to this place.

"Boy," cat says.

Boy's eyes are wide, luminous circles. Like targets, white, iris, pupil at their center.

"Boy, you let me live in your house for many years. This is my house. This is where I live. Will you stay with me?"

Boy says nothing. But his hands grow slack and cat climbs down, regretting—for just a moment—their growing lack of warmth.

"Come, boy," cat says. "Come see the bright place. Come sit in my Winter garden."

Kay.

Gerta couldn't stop shivering; the cold permeated Maggie's jacket, chilling her limbs, slowing her blood. There was no heat in the train, and the lights were a pale flicker of amber that cut out and returned without warning. She heard the wind; wondered if one of the windows was broken. It wouldn't have surprised her.

She stood, stumbled, and stood again; caught the metal poles that existed between the seats and held fast as she looked for the map above the train's closed, rattling doors.

There wasn't one.

She had no idea where she was going.

To keep the cold from getting worse, she kept moving; pole by pole she made her way to the small compartment which housed the driver. The door was closed.

She was afraid to open it.

But she did, and when she did, she closed her eyes for a moment as the wind howled. She wasn't surprised, wasn't numb; fear settled about her, bowing her shoulders as much as the cold had.

The compartment, of course, was empty.

Gerta hesitated for a minute, and then she lowered herself into the driver's seat; it was wider and softer than the seats the passengers were expected to share, but more important, she thought it would be easier to keep the small compartment *warm*. She closed the door quickly and the noise of the wind, the cold of it, seemed to ease.

Gerta forced herself to sit, to rub warmth back into her cheeks. She took her grandmother's necklace out of her pocket and put it around her neck. The slender chain was still warm from her body heat.

She held the pendant in the curve of furled palm as if to absorb this scant warmth—or protect it. And she watched as the tunnel continued without end in the darkness.

Kay had taken this train. He had taken this train and gone to wherever it was that the lost children went. Her grandmother hadn't come this far, and Gerta almost understood why; Maggie couldn't either. People needed Grandma. People needed Maggie.

The only person who needed Gerta was Kay.

The train began to slow; brakes spoke in the hiss and screech of air and metal.

Gerta opened the driver's door and stepped back into the car; was surprised to see the windows covered in the patina of frost.

The train gave a shudder and stopped.

Doors opened onto a platform that was so poorly lit, Gerta couldn't see the walls clearly. She had the feeling that they wouldn't stay open long, and she also had the feeling that, like trains in the real world, this one would simply reverse itself and retrace the tracks until it arrived in the place she had left behind.

Before she lost her nerve, she stepped out.

Although there was no moon, no stars, in the surface of rounded tunnel above the platform, she felt their light, saw by it: it was night, in this strange land.

She began to walk; her breath came out in a mist as she drew the jacket of the robber girl more tightly around her shoulders. The platform and the tunnels vanished at her back, but there was no station wall to guide her to the exit; instead, the gray, flat ground beneath her feet seemed to stretch out before her like an asphalt prairie.

Across it, rising in ones and twos, shadows that looked like distant buildings. She began to walk toward them, but stopped an hour later when she realized that they hadn't gotten any closer.

It wasn't the only thing she realized.

Scattered across the gray, twilight plain were people. They were always distant—but not as distant as the buildings—and they were also always alone. She had navigated school halls that were about as friendly as this, and she began to make her way toward one of them.

He was a boy—a boy two years younger than Kay, and with hair that was dark, black, a mass of curls. His eyes were dark as well, but his skin was the color of snow.

He did not look at her. He did not move at all.

She only knew he was real because at the last moment she reached out to touch him. He didn't pull back; he didn't respond—but he was solid; the fabric of his shirt was crisp and chilly beneath the tips of her shaking hands.

They were a forest.

They were the lost children. She navigated between them, speaking in their deaf ears, waving hands in front of their sightless eyes, touching their exposed cheeks. When she was frustrated, she shouted; when she had reached the limits of endurance, she kicked and slapped.

But they might have been stone; they had nothing to offer her, and she—obviously—nothing to offer them.

Terror kept her warm. Terror: This was where Kay had come. This place. These were what Kay would be.

But some treacherous part of her whispered, *Isn't that what he is now? You talk, you shout, you cry, and he does nothing. Go home, Gerta.*

Not without Kay.

She could not say when she found the boy. She wore a watch, and the hands moved, but the numbers seemed to have no relevance. The skies above—if they were skies—didn't change. Night didn't descend; morning didn't follow. She knew that she was hungry, but she had brought things that would ease hunger, at least for a little while, and she ate while she walked to keep warm.

And while she walked, she realized that she was casting a shadow, and when she turned, she realized that it *wasn't* her shadow. Silent, almost catlike, a boy had joined her desperate trek, and he walked ten feet to her right, hoarding all sound.

She almost shrieked with relief.

But his silence demanded hers; she looked at his profile, and if he had not been in motion, if his steps had not matched hers, she would have seen no difference from the rest of the children in this desolate place.

She stopped walking. He paused slowly, and then, as if walking were a great effort, he turned back, toward her. She saw him through the cloud of breath that hovered in the stillness beyond her lips: uncertain, barefoot, clad only in a ragged memory of long pants and a shirt.

She thought of wild deer, of easily startled animals; she remained standing as still as the children she had cursed or kicked, but her eyes covered the terrain of his face, seeking any change of expression, any motion of lip or eye.

After a while, she was rewarded.

His gaze fell from her eyes—the eyes he had met

without meeting—to the hollow of her throat. He frowned for a long time, as if his face was slow to thaw.

"Irene?" he said.

She lifted a hand slowly until she touched the hanging ruby that rested against her skin. His eyes watched that hand.

Her own widened.

"I'm . . . not Irene," she said, speaking softly. "But she's my—my friend."

He stilled.

"My name is Gerta," she said, too quickly. The stillness was bad. "And I—"

"You don't belong here," he said.

"I've come looking for someone."

"You don't belong here."

"Neither does he."

The boy shrugged. Turned away. And then turned back, eyes caught by ruby and movement of pendant. She was breathing too quickly.

"His name is Kay."

The boy shrugged. Gerta wondered why she hadn't once asked her grandmother what her great-uncle's name had been. Maybe because it didn't matter, here.

"I have to go there," she told him, and she lifted a hand, pointing to the distant building.

"The Snow Queen," the boy said quietly, his lips turning up in the pale, minute mimicry of smile. Memory, in its curve.

"The . . . Snow Queen. Is Kay with her?"

The boy didn't answer.

Gerta reached out and caught his hand; it was ice, in hers. His eyes widened.

She let go; he lifted his hand a moment, and then he said, again, "Irene. I can't come home."

She nodded. "I know."

He turned and began to walk.

She took a breath; the cold filled her lungs, scraped

her throat. The hand that had touched the boy was shaking wildly.

"Wait! Wait!"

He turned. "You don't belong here," he said. "But I do. Follow."

The boy stopped in front of an arch of ice, peaked in the center, that rose into the darkness above, illuminating it. Light flickered at its center, drawn from the ground as if it were the roots of this place. Winter light, and cold.

Gerta took a step forward and then paused; the boy was silent now. He did not move, and as she took another step, the distance between them grew.

On impulse, she turned back to look at his pale, un-lined face, its features familiar in the shadows cast by ice light. She lifted shaking hands to her neck, and un-clasped the thin chain of gold that had brought her this far.

She ran back to the boy, palms shaking in the chill that he didn't seem to notice. "Here," she told him, and before he could move, she draped the chain around his slender neck. In the real world, shaking hands would have dropped that chain before the deli-cate clasp could be fastened; in this one, as if by some ancient law of barter, they were just steady enough.

Her eyes met his.

He lifted his hand to touch the gold, and stared at her as if he knew her.

And then he turned and he ran.

Gerta stood alone, as she was meant to stand, the open doors of this strange, lost palace no invitation.

Beyond the doors was a great hall. The floors, smooth as glass, were cold; the soles of Gerta's shoes found little purchase there, and she slid across it, way-ward, her knees folding.

To fall here was death; she knew it. Knew it without knowing why, and without questioning the knowledge.

But she had crossed ice before, and although her shoes had no blades beneath them and she struggled with each step, she began to glide, awkward now, the memory of huge and comforting hands her companion and guide.

The stairs were worse.

They waited her at the end of the hall, and they were shiny and clear; there was no rail to grasp, nothing to help her through the long, twisting climb.

Kay had ascended these stairs. And if Kay had done it, she would do it. But it was hard; she placed foot against something that seemed solid, and she could see, with each hesitant step, the distance between the hall and the heights grow; they hid nothing. She could not afford to close her eyes, and she could not afford to look away; she saw the fall every time her toes and her heels touched ice.

But she had not come to fail.

Her breath was a white cloud, a wreath, some hint of warmth. It passed about her like a crown and she carried it as she went.

Hours later, days later, she touched the last stair, and it flattened into a plane of glass. Now each step was an act of faith, for the ice was so perfect she might be stepping out onto air.

Even this, she did. Thinking of hospitals, of dying men, of living boys.

She felt smaller and smaller as she walked through this last hall; felt insignificant as the hall widened out into a great room. Here, ice had color and light, and crystals born of cold grew from the ground in a mockery of gardens that she had walked at her grandmother's side. She touched nothing except the floor, navigating the leaves and petals of these odd growths. The path grew narrow in places, and she had to stop to catch breath, to find bearing, before she continued.

But Kay had come here, and if Kay had come here, she would.

*   *   *

The garden gave way; ice waited, and the first of the snows lay upon the ground in an unbroken, perfect layer. It was dusty snow; it flew in clouds around her feet as she crossed it, disturbing its perfection.

She trusted her feet no better in this place than she had in the hall; her steps were small, but they were firm. She walked forward at last into the throne room of the Winter palace, and there she stopped.

For there was a throne of ice in the center of the room, and upon it, clothed now in snow and white fur, skin translucent as ice, and eyes pale blue beneath a fringe of fallen, white hair, a woman.

And by the woman's feet, hands playing with cubes of ice, hair fringed with snow but golden in snow's light, sat Kay.

Cat looks up from boy; the throne is cold.

Girl is here. Girl, hair a shade of yellow brown, eyes murky, face red with warmth. Cat lifts a hand.

"Girl," cat says, "you do not belong here."

"Kay's here," girl says.

"Yes. Kay is finally here. But Kay belongs. Go home, girl."

"Kay *does not* belong here."

"Kay is lost."

"No," girl says, stepping forward, her breath heavy in the air, her hands shaking. "I found him."

"Finding him is not difficult."

Girl frowns, brows rippling. "Kay. Kay!"

"Boy," cat says, and turns her head to watch. Cat has set a task for boy, and boy is absorbed by it: the blocks are tumbling in his blue fingers. His breath is invisible now. His cheeks are white.

Boy looks up at cat's voice. His eyes and cat's are almost the same shade of blue; it is a Winter color.

"Boy," cat says. "Have you solved the puzzle?"

Boy frowns. Hands on blocks, he lifts his head and

looks at the red face of girl. She is too colorful in this Winter landscape.

Boy does not speak. But his frown changes.

"Kay?"

"I told you to leave me alone."

Girl flinches. Words have the power to hurt her. But they do not have the power to force her to go. "I heard you," girl says, abrupt now. Her hands form fists. She strides forward, and the snow almost takes her.

Almost.

But there is something of cat in girl; she finds her footing and she crosses the distance—the obvious distance—between them.

Cat frowns now. "Girl," cat says, "why have you come?"

"I've come for Kay."

"And what will you do with him?"

Girl is silent. Girl is . . . a girl. A child, like all lost children.

"You have no power, girl. Not here, and not in your own world. You cannot protect boy—"

"Don't call him that. He's *Kay*."

"He is boy. He has always been boy."

"He is *a* boy, but he won't always be a boy."

"This is the place where lost children live," cat says, "and they live here in peace and in safety. There are no angry voices. There are no harsh words. There is no pain. There is no pain, and the absence of pain lasts forever. I can promise boy that, and he desires it.

"What can *you* give boy?"

"I can love him," girl says.

"What does that mean, girl? You can follow him like shadow. You can wait at his door. But you cannot go beyond it. You cannot take him from the woman and her angry man. You cannot stop the bruises. You cannot stop the glass from breaking. You cannot protect him."

"Why do you want him?" girl shouts back.

Playing games with words, as the boy does, his hands on the ice, on the blocks. Their surface is changing as he touches them. Cat can see the letters finally break the smooth flatness of their surface. When the word is complete, the boy will be safe. At last.

"I do not *want* him," cat replies. "I offer him what I have: peace and safety. Want is not for this place; here, in the end, he will want nothing. And girl," cat adds, in a gentle voice, in a voice girl will understand, "You have not answered the question."

As if girl is a mouse, cat watches her, waiting, the ghost of a tail flicking this way and that in the shadows cast by throne.

The blocks spill from boy's hands; they are letters now, children's toys. He has come this far. Letters on the ice, letters before the throne.

What can you do?

Gerta closed her eyes. Opened them as tears broke the rim of lids and slid down her face. She *hated* them. Hated to cry in front of this strange woman. But she had no way of stopping.

Because what the Snow Queen said was true. She couldn't take Kay from his mother, even if she wanted to. She couldn't take him from his home. She couldn't protect him. She had never been able to protect him.

She didn't even know how to talk to him anymore; she could call his name a hundred times, a thousand times, and she knew, as clearly as she knew she need breathe, that he wouldn't answer.

"No," she said. "I can't protect him. I'm not his mother. I'm only his friend." The tears broke her words in all the wrong places. They tightened her throat; they choked off her breath, the comforting sight of cloud in the cold, cold clarity of the Winter garden.

She stumbled. Her knees bent. She couldn't see. And blind, she took a step forward.

The world slid out from beneath her; the step, small and desperate, was too wild in this icy place.

But she didn't fall. Hands caught her. Hands hauled her roughly up. Cold hands, pale hands; hands that she did not recognize.

Just as she couldn't recognize the face inches from hers, although she had come chasing it all the way from—from wherever it was. Kay's.

Before he could pull away, she threw her arms around him. She did not want to look at his face, at his eyes, at the terrible distance there; instead, she buried her face in his chest. Easier to cry there. Her tears burned.

Muffled, her voice carried through the cloth of a familiar shirt. "She's right," Gerta said. "I can't protect you. I can't—I don't—" She shook her head. "I don't have the right to make you come home. You—" She tried again. And again. Words were hard; she was colder now than she had ever been. "But I don't have to leave you here alone either. If you won't come with me, I'll stay. I found my way here. I've earned the right."

"You can't stay here," Kay said. Kay.

She looked up. Saw the pale shadow of bruise across his eyes, and beneath them, and in the hollows of his cheeks. "I can."

"You *can't*."

"You're here. I won't leave you."

"You'll die here, you idiot! You can't even walk—"
She shook her head. "I can learn."

His face twisted. He was angry now. The first real expression to cross his face, and it had to be anger. But it was better than nothing.

"I *want* to be here," he said, speaking slowly, forcing anger into the container words provided. "You don't."

"I came, didn't I?"

"Because you're stupid."

She swallowed. "Yes. Stupid. But that's my decision."

Kay tried to shake himself free, but Gerta would not let go—and he didn't try too hard. But he was sure-footed here, and she was not; he twisted them both around. To the throne. To her.

"Can she stay?"

"She cannot stay," the woman on the throne said. "Unless she can solve the problem of the blocks, Boy, she will age and wither. She will starve or freeze."

"Give her the blocks."

"She cannot touch them; they will melt in her hands. There is only death here, for her."

He looked at his feet, then.

At his feet, at the blocks there. Gerta saw his lips moving; his hands were still.

"What do you see in the blocks, boy? What is the word there?"

Gerta held her breath. Because she could see the blocks, even if she couldn't touch them.

"Gerta," Kay said, speaking her name for the first time since she had entered the room, "I think I will hate you forever, you are such an idiot."

"Boy?"

But Kay shook his head and closed his eyes. "I don't know," he said. "I can't see them clearly enough." He reached for Gerta's shoulders and forced her face away from his chest; his shirt was wet, but the water there was already freezing.

"Come on," he said, voice rough.

"But—"

"We're going now."

"Kay—"

"Now."

Cat slowly leaves the throne. Boy is gone; girl is gone with him. Cat nudges the blocks with nose and paw; the word is there. Boy could see it. Boy was lying.

Cat knows; cat has listened to his voice for many, many years.

Girl will take boy home, to pain. Boy will cry. Boy will rage. But boy will never be lost again because he will be afraid of the cost of being lost.

And boy will become man, and what manner of man, Cat cannot say. Cat's paw touches the letters.

E. T. E. R. N. I. T. Y.

It is dark, in the City of lost children, and cat grieves.

But there are other mirrors, and other stories, and perhaps in time, cat will find another boy—or girl—to save.

THE DEVIL'S BRIDGE

Edward Carmien

"The Devil's Bridge" is Edward Carmien's tenth short story to see print. In addition to being a writer, Edward teaches college writing, literature, and creative writing at Westminster Choir College of Rider University, where he is surrounded and enriched by the finest voices in the world. He lives with his spouse (ten great years!) and kids (two of the finest!) in New Jersey (joke all you want: William Carlos Williams lived here, too!)

On a spring morning like any other, the old woman found her cow on the wrong side of the Mynach. It was her bad luck the river was in flood, noisy and angry from the drop down five falls stretching above the cottage into a stewing cauldron. The waters collected there in a frothy boil before flowing down the valley.

I'd given her the weather for the day as usual, and as usual she'd ignored it. I licked my paws to show sun in the morn, then cleaned my ears to show rain in the afternoon. She wheezed her way out upon the porch to stare into the morning and proclaimed, "Looks a fine day!" This of course was only half true, but there's no teaching some people.

"Damn cow!" yelled the old woman at the beast, which cropped dewy grass in the cool air. Dog yapped in agreement. "How did that creature get to the other side?" she asked the brown mutt, who raised a curly-tufted ear at being addressed but said nothing.

He rarely spoke, being dim in the usual way of canines, and she didn't think to ask me. I could have told her the Mynach had risen late during the night from rain falling upriver. Cow had plenty of time to wander across shallow water to greener grass before the Mynach rose. Retrieving Cow would require a hike down the valley to cross the ford, then a hike up the valley on the other side. The long walk home wouldn't be pleasant with a grass-greedy cow in tow. There was no point waiting on the water: this was the spring flood. The Mynach, full of rain and melting snow, would be boisterous until high summer. Once the smell of new green was thick in the air, the river was sure to be busy until summer tamed it.

Over the sound of the Mynach rushing by, I heard goat hooves on the path, but a strange goat it was. Dog heard it, too, and growled: he's good enough at that sort of thing. I turned to look and saw a man, grinning and red-faced from the climb to the nape of the valley where the old woman kept her cottage. I looked behind him, but saw no goat.

Dog growled again, and the old woman took notice of the stranger.

"Has this cow offended, madam?" said the man. His long brown robes reminded me of the monks who paraded once each year through the village below.

"I need that cow," said the old woman with a glint in her eye. "But my old bones won't make the walk it takes to get her back. Mayhap you could fetch her for me? There'd be a fine meal in it for you, young man."

The stranger chuckled, a deep rumble that shivered

my tail and made each of my claws twitch. Dog whined for a moment, then fell silent.

"I can do better, widow woman. I can build a stout stone bridge, and you can cross to fetch your cow. On days to come, your cow can graze where she wishes."

The wind shifted, and I smelled sulfur. Just a whiff, but enough for Dog and the old woman to catch the scent, too. I saw her eyes shift to the stranger's feet, so I knew she also guessed there were legs ending in hooves and a barbed tail lurking beneath his brown robe.

"What's the cost to me of this fine bridge you offer?" she said then, eyes narrow and hands perched on her bony hips.

"My fee? I'm a simple man with simple needs. Take a few of your favorite treasures, simple though they be, when you fetch your cow. When you cross, I'll select one thing, just one, to keep as my own. Agreed?" The stranger's smile was thin and cunning, and the red of his blushing face grew more ruddy though he labored not.

The old woman considered for a moment, stroking her pointed chin. In the silence, the roar of the falls and the hiss of water churning in the stony cauldron seemed louder than before. She shifted her gaze down to Dog, then to me. I wanted to fold my ears down low but did not. Some trick boiled around in her, I could see it plain as moonlight.

The old woman smiled her own thin, cunning smile. "So all you wish is one thing first carried across the bridge?" Her twisty thinking was plain: she'd toss one of us across, and pay the hoofed one with one of our souls in place of her own. Waiting for the stranger's answer, she fixed her eye on me. So I was to pay the fee, was I? I'd see about that, or I wasn't a well-traveled cat enjoying a seventh life, with the promise of two more to come.

"That is all I wish. We have an agreement, then! If you would be so kind as to let me work in peace, you shall have your bridge before the sun gives way to rain."

"Rain?" she quavered, as if I hadn't told her the weather myself just minutes before.

"Indeed rain, following hard on the sun's course. I'd best be at work. If you please?" He gestured at the cottage.

Inside, the old woman gave me the last of yesterday's milk and rinsed the pail with the last of the water. She fretted and fussed about the tidy place, but something kept her from the window. I slipped out the back and climbed over the top of the woodpile, first my right forefoot carefully then my hind stepped onto the thatched roof. I mounted to the peak and stopped in the pleasant sun.

There he was, down on the bank. I regretted what I must do, for there were stories enough about cats and *that* fellow, and I didn't care to add to them if I could help it. Those of us with brindled fur are hard put to lead a peaceful life without my stirring the pot.

"Hoofed one," I said quietly, and proof enough of whom he was, his ears heard me despite the Mynach's roar and hiss. He turned and peered at me, then gestured. Down I came, quickly and lightly, first to the rain barrel's lip, then to the packed ground in front of the cottage. He held his tongue until I approached.

"What is it?" he rasped in his true voice. He knew full well the old woman couldn't hear a word.

"The old woman knows you, hoofed one. She twisted the words of your deal."

His eyes narrowed, for to him there is no such thing as a gift without troublesome strings.

"Of course she did. Why do you tell me this?" He knelt down, and his robe hitched up. A stench like rancid tallow candles and sick goat wrinkled my nose and almost made me sneeze.

"I live well here. If you take her soul, her life will be shorter than it might be." That was only half the truth, but I trusted him to guess the rest.

"Care you so for the leavings of milk and the occasional table scrap?" he sneered. His teeth were yellow. I remained silent and merely stared at him. His gaze felt like fire in my bones, but I held my gaze longer than he, who looked away to the river with a smile.

"What of it?"

Purpose done, I merely blinked and said "Leave her be. One of the village lads will fetch Cow back to her." He'd divined my meaning well enough, that she meant for me to cross the bridge first, and I came to him to save my skin, not hers. While he'd be pleased to get his fingers on my nine-fold soul, he'd rather have the old woman's if he could get it.

Apparently unconcerned, he grinned and bade me leave him. Tail high, I picked my way across the ground to the cottage. I heard rocks crack and split and stumble about as the hoofed man made the bridge, the work of months done in a minute. Inside, the old woman held Dog, stroking him for comfort. When she spied me, she put him aside and grabbed me by the scruff. I suffered this indignity and spoke to Dog.

"You know, Cow swears she'll kick your puny brains out next time you nip her flanks." Surely this would make him charge right across the bridge to get at Cow when he got the chance, and the hoofed one could take Dog's puny soul for all I cared.

Dog smiled the best he could. "I ain't crossin'," he growled under his breath. "And I'll be chasin' Cow f'years after goatfeet takes ye." I blinked in surprise and dismay.

"Hush now," said the old woman, misunderstanding as always.

I lashed my tail and thought of fleeing, but the old woman held me tight. All had gone awry. Dog would not run across the bridge as I'd planned. I'd hoped to draw the hoofed one's attention to the old woman so Dog could do so unnoticed. Now I needed a new trick, for if the old woman succeeded, I would pay the price, and if not, her soul would be forfeit. It was enough to make a grown cat urrrrrrrrrr.

"Widow woman!" called the hoofed man from outside the cottage. "Your bridge is done. Come cross it so I may select my fee!" There was a smile in his voice I could hear even through the rough-hewn door. The old woman lifted the latch and carried me out tucked under her arm, as if she were holding me close for a short walk in the sun.

"Hello, puss," he said silkily, and chucked me under the chin. I refrained from biting him, for his skin was hard as flint, and I doubted I'd like the taste of him on my tongue.

"She means to toss me over the bridge, simpleton. The old woman will cheat you and have her bridge for my soul, valuable enough but not what you wish." I hissed the words at him, and his face didn't change, though his eyes flicked from me to the old woman's face.

"Come, then," he said, features wreathed in a hard-edged smile. He waved the way forward and clenched his fist. My ears twitched, for there was power in the air. The sky darkened. Clear skies filled with rolling clouds, the afternoon rain called early by his casual wave. Lightning cracked at the head of Mynach Falls, and a crashing boom struck at us. The old woman staggered, and I tensed to flee, but she held me close. My whiskers twitched with a premonition. The hoofed one was one trick ahead of the old woman, I was sure of it.

The rains came before she'd taken a step, and rain I can't abide unless I must. With claw and tooth I forced my way free, fighting through the old woman's shriek of dismay down to the ground and away to the shadow of the cottage door where I could stand out of the rain. His hollow, cutting laugh at my flight was the laugh of a cheat winning a toss of dice with weighted bones.

"Come along!" the hoofed man shouted, face red as fresh blood in the gloom. "Let us fetch your cow, widow woman, and have the end of our bargain!" His voice carried a sneering gloat, for he'd gotten me out of the old woman's arms neatly enough, and now she'd have to pay his fee when she crossed.

"Nice work," growled Dog, who was standing even farther back in the cottage, peering out the door. "I still ain't crossin'."

"Fool," I spat. "If he forces her across, he'll have her soul, and she'll not live the day. What then, cur? Where will we sleep? What will we eat?"

"Go yourself, Cat," he said with a whine. I looked out into the driving rain. My plan had come to nothing, as both Dog and the hoofed one had proved cannier than I guessed.

From another life the answer came, a kitten memory of a temple courtyard and a flower-bedecked cow. Wide-eyed, I'd watched from a nearby ledge as gaily-robed women with bright red-and-yellow jugs of water had danced around the cow four times, wetting its tail each time round before finally kissing the placid beast and speaking quietly in its ear. "The Gospastami," my mother had whispered to me, sensing my confusion. "The cow-festival. They know a truth forgotten or never learned most other places. Cows walk where they will in this land, small one, and no one raises a hand against them." Cow, cud-chewing, Dog-tolerant, milk-giving *Cow* was the answer, and I hissed at myself for not thinking of it sooner.

"The shed!" I yowled at Dog, who had slunk farther back into the cottage. The hoofed one was leading the old woman on. She walked with him, but slowly, casting her eyes this way and that, hoping beyond hope for rescue from her folly.

"What? Why?" yapped Dog, barking loud over the rain.

"Go!" I commanded. He stood stock still, so I charged him. He pulled his lips into a snarl and bent low, ready to bite, as I knew he would. With a twisting leap I landed upon his back. Digging in, I yowled, "To the shed!"

Half-mad with pain and panic he yelped and cried his way out the door, bucking and leaping this way and that. Grimly I hung on and grimly I endured the rain because I must. Despite his pain and panic he made for the shed.

"Jump! Jump!" I shouted over the sound of the rain. He stopped and shook instead, so I bit through his ear with a quick motion and pulled. Dog froze, quivering. "Jump," I mumbled, half choked on his dirty wet hair, and he jumped, just right for once, as high as he'd ever jumped. I released his ear and waited, waited for the proper moment, then leaped straight up to the cowbell hanging on a rope from the eave of the shed.

Catching the rain-slick rope with my forepaws, I kicked the bell with my rear legs and out tolled the bell, dong, dong, dong. I kicked again, and again it rang.

Across the Mynach, Cow raised her head from where she'd been hiding it from the rain. It did not bother her that a bridge now stood above the torrent where there was once only spray. She ambled toward it, thinking of her dry shed.

With a curse that sizzled the rain striking his head, the hoofed man grabbed the old woman by the arm and tried to race Cow to the bridge. Seeing this, I kicked again to ring the bell, dong, dong, dong. Cow raised her head and stepped faster. All reached the span together, and met in the middle.

"Go back!" shouted the hoofed one, lifting his free hand as if to strike. But Cow knew he could not and would not hurt her, she being what she was and he being who he was. Instead, she pushed her broad head between the hoofed one and his captive, and the old woman broke his grip and dashed back to the near shore.

I clawed and struggled onto the roof, rain or no rain. The hoofed one screamed with rage but pulled back from Cow. She followed him close, and became the first one to cross the bridge. Once his feet were on the bank he cursed and steamed, then vanished in a billowing cloud of yellow smoke, for he could take nothing from Cow.

The rain stopped, and in the sudden quiet I heard the old woman mutter, "Fire and brimstone!"

"Get me down from here, old woman!" I caterwauled, and for once she seemed to understand.

"Clever puss," she cooed as she stood on a bucket to pluck me off the shed's roof.

Later, with half the village up to see the Devil's Bridge and hear the old woman's tale, it was she who'd outwitted the hoofed one by calling Cow across the span. All the while I sat in the shed and enjoyed dry fur and the feeling of warm milk in my stomach.

"And the devil, well, he's got no use for a cow, has he?" said the old woman as she finished telling her story for the third time. Yet again I pondered the mystery of people, how often they were right without knowing why. Luck of the two-legs, I guess.

"So, Cow," I said quietly. "How is it you're beyond the hoofed one's reach?" People in places I'd been had said as much, but they didn't know why, any more than they understood what they'd heard about the nine lives of a cat. Luck, death defying, indeed. Cow chewed her cud next to me, quiet, serene and warm to be near, as always.

"Maybe," Cow drawled in between slup-slupping chews of her cud, "maybe one is what one understands, Cat."

That was all she ever told me, no matter how cleverly I asked, or how often. This time it was enough to know, as any well-traveled cat knows, that the hoofed one can't touch cattle. One of the village girls, tired of hearing the tale, poked her head into the shed and ooooed when she saw me. I rolled onto my back to accept a good tummy rub.

It was no less than what I deserved, for no matter how the tale was told this day, cats would always know who had called Cow and cheated the hoofed one of his fee.

PHARAOH'S CAT

Lisanne Norman

Born in Glasgow, Scotland, Lisanne Norman started writing at the age of eight in order to find more of the books she liked to read. In 1980, two years after joining The Vikings! (the largest British reenactment society in Britain), she moved to Norfolk, England. There she ran her own specialist archery display team. Personal experience has always provided inspiration for her writing, no more so than with this short story, which shows the long-time fascination she has for the ancient cultures of Egypt and Crete. In fact, the background for the Sholan Alliance novels is based on the Cretan culture and climate which she visited in 1994. Now a full-time author, she has created words where warriors, magic, and science all coexist. Her latest novel from DAW in the series is *Stronghold Rising*.

It had been a long two days, distinguishable only from the ones before by two migraines yesterday and an incipient one now—and the blank page in front of me on the monitor screen.

Out of the corner of my right eye, I caught sight of a svelte black shape leaping up onto the back of the new easy chair that sat beside my desk.

"You shouldn't be up there," I said automatically, assuming it was Shadow.

Svelte? Not even the most doting of cat owners could call my Siamese/Burmese cross that—try big, burly, or, in the vet's words, not mine, a black panther, the veritable Beast of Bodmin Moor.

"Is that any way to greet an old friend?" a plaintive voice asked as I glanced round to see my visitor settle himself on his haunches.

"Tal?" I asked incredulously, swinging my chair round to face him.

"The one and only," he said, stretching out in the luxurious way only a cat can along the narrow chair back. "I see nothing much has changed in the last twelve years."

"Uh." I glanced round the room. "Actually, a lot has," I said, looking back at him. "You, for one."

"I meant the blank page," he said, ears flicking as his tail tip gently rose and fell in faint annoyance.

"And I meant you're . . . not really here, are you? How could you be?" I muttered to myself, turning back to my screen. "You passed on twelve years ago." Damned migraines, I hated 'em, but the visual disturbances and the odd hallucinations they gave me weren't usually this vivid, nor did they speak.

"Why don't you say it like it is?" he purred, stretching his paws out toward me. "I'm dead, pushing up roses and bluebells on the other side of this window. Nice choice of flowers, by the way, but did those double glazing cowboys have to squash them when they put the new windows in?"

"You're not here. It's the headache. I can't see you," I muttered to myself like a mantra, reaching for the tobacco tin and lighter on my desk.

From the side of my eye, as I rolled a cigarette, I watched him inch himself forward, paw at a time, just the way he used to do when he was . . .

"I still am," he said as his damp nose touched the back of my hand and made me jump.

"Geez, Tal! Don't do that!" I said, clutching for the cigarette before it rolled off my lap onto the floor. "You haven't changed, have you?" I demanded, grabbing my lighter and lighting my smoke to steady my nerves. "Never did like me sitting down doing anything that didn't involve stroking you."

He wrinkled his nose, whiskers twitching as he pulled his head back a little. "Good job I was disturbed. I always gave you your best ideas, didn't I?"

Swiveling round again, I stared at him. We'd gone through a lot together, he and I: several disastrous relationships and a move of five hundred miles.

"And most of that first book of yours," he added, blinking at me.

"You were the inspiration for it," I agreed gently. *Ah, what the hell,* I thought, reaching out to scritch the sides of his head. If he was a hallucination, he was a damned good one, and right now a dose of Tal was what I needed. I wasn't too grand to have a conversation with him!

"Yes, it is good to see you again," I said, relieved to find the head that reached up to meet me was warm and soft. I don't know what I'd expected, but very much alive was fine by me. "What brings you here now?"

"Your need for a story, obviously," he said, head butting against my hand as he tried to angle the scritches where he wanted them. "The left ear," he purred urgently, cocking his head on that side. "Just behind it . . . a little more to the right . . . Now a whisker to the left . . . Ah . . . !" He dissolved, going so limp he began to slide off the chair back.

In a flurry of black limbs, he scrabbled his way back onto his perch and sat there staring at me accusingly, as if it were all my fault.

I smothered a chuckle as he sniffed and lifted a front paw, beginning to lick it in a very dignified manner.

"So what's the topic of this story you're trying to write?" he asked, wiping his paw across his whiskers. "Must be something about us felines again, or I wouldn't have been drawn back to you."

"It is," I said, stubbing the cigarette out in my ashtray. "I'm trying to write a fairy tale."

"Ah, now, that I can help you with," he said, settling down again now that his dignity had been reestablished. "I know a lot of good tales. Many's the time I used to sneak out and listen to the storyteller down in the bazaar . . ."

"What bazaar?" I interrupted. "We've never been near one!"

He lifted his nose slightly, putting on the superior air that he'd always been so good at using. "You and I haven't, but there were other lives before the one we shared. Eight to be precise. Now do you want my help or not?"

"Carry on," I said, reaching for my coffee mug. "I'm all ears."

He sniffed, whiskers twitching as he delicately crossed his front paws and rested his chin on them.

"It was 1352 BC in Egypt of the eighteenth dynasty and a time of great turbulence. When the heretic Pharaoh Akhenaten had died, he'd left his young daughter Ankhesenamun and her nine-year-old husband as his heirs. Their regent was Ankhesenamun's grandfather Aya, an old man who'd been vizier to Akhenaten. He'd wielded great power while Tutankhamun was only a boy, but now, the young King was eighteen and wanted to rule in his own right, and that didn't suit Aya. One morning, Queen Ankhesenamun was awakened by the wailing of her servants to be told that her husband was feared dead. She rushed to his chamber to find Tutankhamun lying in bed unconscious, a thin trickle of blood coming from his nose and one ear."

Although I knew the popular history of the fabled boy king, I hadn't heard this.

"Don't stop," I said. "You've got me interested."

Have you ever seen a cat smile? I swear they can. Such a self-satisfied look was on Tal's face now.

"The young Pharaoh hovered between life and death for two months. Nothing the priests or surgeons could do helped. The Queen was distraught. Finally, Tutankhamun died without ever regaining consciousness."

"What had happened to him?"

"No one could, or would, say. When Pharaoh dies, Egypt is without a king until the period of mourning is over. The whole country came to a standstill. The men were forbidden to shave, and the women were unable to put their hair up. Her grandfather, as the only male relative, naturally took over all the funeral arrangements. Ankhesenamun, too distraught to care, was content to leave him once more in charge. Then, on the evening before the funeral, she went to her grandfather's apartment in the palace to speak to him. Hearing voices, rather than disturb him, she waited outside. But what she heard brought fear into her heart."

Tears coursing unchecked down her cheeks, she fled through the shadowy palace corridors with no idea of where she was going so long as it took her far from her grandparents' apartments. The strap of one flimsy sandal broke, almost tripping her. Sobbing, she stopped her flight only long enough to pick it up and remove the other; they must never know she'd been near their rooms, that she'd heard them plotting.

Catching the sound of marching feet, she ducked into a darkened doorway, pressing her hand over her mouth, terrified, but it was only the guard changing for the night shift. Something as natural as that, which scant minutes ago would never have bothered her, now had her hiding like a thief in her own palace. The few lamps that were all that graced the corridors in this time of mourning wavered and guttered briefly as she stood there shaking like a leaf, trying to still her labored breathing in case the guards came her way.

Gradually the tramping of the heavily-soled feet began to fade into the distance and she was able to breathe again. Her enforced stop had brought her to her senses, made her realize she couldn't just keep running. She had to go somewhere, but where? Where in Thebes could she be safe now that she knew the breadth of the treachery her grandfather planned? Stifling a sob, she thought of her husband's mummified body lying alone in the Hall of Purification in the temple complex at nearby Karnak. Then it came to her—her husband's temple! All services to the Gods had ceased because of his death. No one would be in the small sanctuary he'd built next to the palace.

Looking around, she tried to get her bearings. From the wall decorations, she realized she'd headed instinctively back toward the royal apartments. Sandals in one hand, she ran. Keeping to the shadows this time, she headed for the hall of pillars that opened out into the main courtyard gardens.

The jewel-bright colors of the lavish murals decorating the white walls and pillars glowed gently in the dim light reflected from the few lamps that were still alight. Darting between the forest of columns, she made her way quickly to the doorway. Though the moon was hidden behind clouds, a quick glance told her the garden was empty. Cautiously she stepped out into the cool night air, shivering slightly as her bare feet touched the damp grass. Pressing herself against the outer wall of the palace, she inched her way round the perimeter to the gateway. Hearing the laughter of the guards on duty there, she stopped just short, body huddled against the wall, ears straining to hear what they were saying.

"Stop scratching your face! Tomorrow, after the funeral, you can get that beard shaved off at the barber's," chuckled one.

"Aye, and so I shall. The wife won't let me near her—says I feel like a sanding sheet!"

More laughter from the first one, and some comments that made her face flush hot with embarrassment even in the darkness.

"D'you think the general's going to move against the regent?" asked the second speaker once the laughter of his companion had died down.

"If he does, he'll have to move tomorrow evening," said the first, lowering his voice. "You know the regent—doesn't like to lose anything he considers his."

"True enough. The way Aya acted even before the King's death, you'd have thought he was Pharaoh, not the regent. That one's got too many airs and graces! Wouldn't put it past that wily old dog to try marrying the little queen himself, even though he's her grandfather."

"Not if the general can help it!" laughed the first. "At least with him she'd have a man capable of giving her sons, not a dried-up ancient past his best!"

Hot tears scalded her face again as she tried to press herself even flatter against the wall. Was there no pity in this world? Would none of them let her mourn her husband in peace? First her grandfather, now the general of her armies wanted her in marriage!

"I think the regent'll get her," said the second, his voice sounding more distant. The tone dropped even further. "The way Pharaoh died, it wasn't natural. No one goes to bed and doesn't wake up like he did. I heard from one of the servants his cheek was bruised, and there was blood on his face. I've seen head wounds that do that after battles, haven't you? Sounds to me like someone visited him in the night, and I don't mean the queen."

Silence, followed by the scraping of shod feet and the creaking of leather armor.

"I'd be careful where you repeat that story if I were you," muttered the first. "The general wasn't in Thebes at the time."

"I'm not talking about the general, I meant the regent, Aya. It was a damned shame, I say. He was only a boy. Had the makings of a good king. Looked real promising, especially after that criminal we had last time."

"You're saying too much, just watch your tongue lest you lose that head of yours! Then you won't need no barber! Time we checked the causeway."

The footsteps moved off slowly, leaving her standing there in shock. Was this what the common folk were saying happened? There had been a bruise on his cheek, but her grandfather had said it was only because her husband had hit his face on the bed when the illness had struck him down. Could he have been . . . murdered . . . by her grandfather, just to get the throne? Though he'd tried to hide it, he hadn't been pleased when Tutankhamun had told him he wanted to rule alone. Many little incidents now came to mind, like the times her grandfather had answered the foreign nobles visiting their court before her husband could.

Could the man she'd trusted to protect her and her husband have betrayed them so completely? Suddenly light-headed, with a moan of fear she slumped against the wall. Would she be next?

"Did you hear that?" demanded one of the guards, his voice just audible.

She shrank farther from the gateway into the deep shadows, forcing the thoughts aside.

"Hear what?" asked the other sharply.

"Forget it. Probably just the wind."

Rubbing her hand across her eyes, after a minute or two she peered round the gate into the causeway. The two guards, dwarfed by the huge seated statues of the Goddess Sekhmet, were now halfway along the statue-lined avenue. If she stayed behind them, they couldn't see her until they turned round; then all she needed to do was hide in the shadows till they passed.

"Goddess Mut, Queen of heaven, protector of Pharaoh, protect me now," she muttered before slowly easing herself through the open gateway and disappearing behind the first statue.

When the guards drew closer to her on their way back to the gate, she clutched the back of the statue, heart pounding surely loudly enough for them to hear.

"Sekhmet, be my shield," she whispered to herself, holding her breath until they'd passed her and the immediate danger was over.

She remained where she was, face pressed against the cool stone. Memories of hearing her grandfather telling his wife how he intended to become the new Pharaoh by marrying her immediately after the funeral chased thoughts of him sneaking into her husband's chamber to murder him.

They ran round inside her head until, whimpering, she pushed herself away and turned toward the sanctuary. It was so close now. She ran, her feet barely touching the cobbles, not stopping till she'd entered the outer courtyard.

It was dark and quiet, just as she'd expected. Hesitantly, she walked toward the doorway into the inner court. Fear of a different sort filled her now as she slowly approached the first hall.

Once again, few lamps had been left lit. In the dim, flickering light, the temple looked and felt eerie. Her steps getting slower, she had to force herself to walk onward to the even more dimly illuminated inner room. Beyond there was the sealed shrine where the gods lived in their wooden caskets. The scent of orange-and-cedar incense filled the air, reminding her of the festivals at Karnak over which she and her husband Tutankhamun had presided. Her eyes began to fill with tears she rapidly blinked away as, her footsteps growing ever more hesitant, she approached the shadowed doorway.

She stopped, shocked to see the impossible had happened—someone was in the inner sanctuary! The double doors, supposed to be closed with a seal of clay that could be broken only by the head priest or Pharaoh himself, stood open wide. Light began to glow from the shrine room, spilling out suddenly into the chamber she was in, blinding her with its intensity.

Blinking in the radiance, terrified, she clutched the door frame. Something drew her onward against her will even though her heart was filled with dread.

"Welcome, child," said a low, feminine voice.

Relief flooded through her as a woman suddenly appeared in the doorway. It was only one of the priestesses!

"What troubles you, Queen Ankhesenamun? Why did you call me?" the woman asked

Puzzled, she stepped closer, unable to see the face of the priestess because of the intensity of the light.

"I didn't call you," Ankhesenamun said, then stopped as the priestess' head turned slightly and her features became visible—only to blur briefly into those of the lioness Sekhmet before returning to those of a woman.

"I heard your prayers while you were on the causeway," the priestess said. "Why have you need of my protection, Queen of Kemet?"

She whimpered, taking a step backward in terror.

"You have nothing to fear, Ankhesenamun," the woman smiled, holding out her hand. "You need my help else you wouldn't have called on me. Which have you need of—Sekhmet the avenger, or Bast the protector?"

"Protection," she stammered, falling to her knees. "My husband is dead . . . my grandfather Aya wishes to marry me as his first wife . . . and my servants believe he has killed my husband. If I don't have Aya, then the general of my armies will take me so he can become Pharaoh!"

Ankhesenamun watched as Mut—for it could be no other than the Mother since this was her shrine—frowned, her features blurring again into those of stern Sekhmet.

"If Aya did kill your husband, this is a serious crime that cannot go unpunished. As Protector and Defender of Pharaoh, I must avenge him. The Rule of Ma'at must be served or Kemet cannot prosper."

"No, Mother! I want only protection for myself," Ankhesenamun wept, her hand reaching instinctively for the goddess'. "I've no wish to be queen. The husband I loved is dead. Please, let me join your temple and retire from the court and its plots. I don't want to marry my grandfather or the general—I fear for my life!"

The stern face softened as the goddess took Ankhesenamun's hand and drew her to her feet.

"My poor child, you have no choice but to marry one of them. Only through Kemet's queens can the throne be inherited by a Pharaoh."

Her broken sandals falling to the floor, Ankhesenamun tried to stem the tears with her free hand.

"There may yet be a way, if you have faith in me," said Mut thoughtfully. "It's not without danger," she warned, her hand gently squeezing the young queen's.

"What must I do?"

"As queen, you're the incarnation of Isis and have a role to play tomorrow in the mortuary rituals for your husband's resurrection, so his soul, which is wandering loose now, can return to his body."

Guilt flooded through her. In her fears for her own safety, she'd forgotten her final responsibilities to her husband.

"Hush, child. Your fears were natural in the circumstances. Take this and wear it openly," she said, handing her a small winged scarab talisman on a chain of gold. "It will show that you are under my protection. Submit to the wedding ceremony, then call on me in the form of Sekhmet-Bast."

Ankhesenamun took the talisman. "But how will . . ."

"Have faith," smiled Mut, letting her hand go and bending down to retrieve the fallen sandals. "I will make you one of my own, a cat of stone, to be placed in this temple. Statue by day but alive on the nights of the full moon, you will be free of both the Regent Aya and the general."

Bewildered, she took the sandals Mut held out to her.

"If your faith is strong, child, your husband will be resurrected—and you will find each other again. Then, my spell will end and you will be reunited to live the rest of your lives in peace. Now put on your sandals and return to your palace. You are under my protection, none will see you or come near you to do you harm as you return. Should they try, I *will* be there."

Mut changed and showed herself in her full glory as Sekhmet the Sorceress, the Wrathful, the Destroyer of Evil.

"Be not afraid, child," she said as Ankhesenamun shrank back. "Only he who killed your husband need fear me. His reign will be short and not prosper."

When she risked looking at the goddess again, once more the gentle Mut stood before her.

"Thank you, Mother," she whispered, slipping on her now repaired sandals and getting slowly to her feet. She bowed deeply, fixing the talisman round her neck, then turned and walked from the sanctuary.

The next day passed as if she were in a dream. Sure enough, at the funeral, Aya was wearing the leopard skin of the heir and performed the most holy ceremony of Opening-the-Mouth for her husband, designating himself as the heir and future Pharaoh.

Once the funeral feast was over, he took her aside to speak to her.

"Egypt needs a king, a mature Pharaoh at her head, Ankhesenamun. You will marry me today."

When she said nothing, he smiled at her, and she shivered seeing the naked desire on his face. "You've no need to worry, child, you'll not lose your standing in the court. Have I ever failed you in my years as regent? I'll name you first of my wives, the Great Royal Wife. You'll rule by my side."

She drew herself to her full height. "I rule in my own right, Grandfather," she said formally, trying not to show the revulsion she felt. "I don't accept the need for me to marry you, but if it must be, I will do it for the good of Kemet."

"Don't give me that attitude, girl," he snapped, frowning. "It's thanks to me that you and your young husband kept the throne at all after that criminal, your father, died! There were many who thought they could take it from a mere boy of nine, but not me." He grasped her by the wrist. "Tutankhamun's dead now. Do you really think I'm going to step aside this time? Kemet needs heirs—my heirs—and you'll give them to me."

Up to this moment, she'd hoped against hope she'd been wrong and that her grandfather was an honorable man. That hope had just died.

"Bring your priest, Grandfather," she said quietly. "I've said I'll marry you for the good of our land."

Aya smiled and released her. "You're beginning to see sense," he said, gesturing to one of the servants.

Because, technically, the court was still in mourning, the ceremony was simple and witnessed only by those few present at the funeral feast.

As Aya leaned toward her to claim his first kiss as her husband, she moved away from him. It was now or never.

"Sekhmet-Bast, give me the strength to do what I must," she said, clutching the amulet with a shaking hand.

A coldness was starting to spread throughout her limbs. Cries of shock and terror rang in her ears as the world around her began to shrink and everyone began to recoil away from her. Then her vision faded, as did her hearing, and she knew nothing more.

Her senses awakened one by one. First was hearing, then sight. She felt stiff, and began to stretch languorously, stopping in surprise when she saw the paws of a cat where her arms should have been. The weight of the amulet round her neck reminded her of Mut's promise.

Taking a few moments to examine her new body, she found it pleasing. Then she turned her attention to her surroundings. The room was almost in darkness, yet she could see very clearly. She wasn't in the temple as she'd expected, but in the palace, in the throne room. Surprised, she jumped down from the pedestal on which she sat and padded round to see what changes had taken place.

The room had been redecorated with scenes of Aya's coronation, and there she was, in the place of his First Wife, beside him. Angrily she paced in front of the mural. How dare he put her in the scene when she hadn't been there!

Her rage burned hot and fierce. Raising herself up

on her haunches, she raked the wall furiously and repeatedly with her claws until she'd obliterated as much of the paintings of herself and Aya as she could reach. Then she padded over to the royal throne and, making sure her claws first punctured its skin of gold, she shredded that. Aya might now be Pharaoh, but she would remind him of her presence.

A grumbling in her belly finally distracted her and she realized she was hungry. Her last meal had been some of the leg of the sacrificial calf at her husband's funeral. Since that had been at least a month ago, it was no wonder she was famished. But where would she find food at night in the palace? Sitting down behind the throne, she began to plan her next moves and was startled to find herself automatically beginning to lick her paws and claws clean of the traces of paint, wood, and gold.

Jumping up, she skittered off toward the doorway and out into the corridor. Her nose, now far more sensitive, caught the whiff of something that smelled deliciously edible. With no more thought than her overwhelming hunger, she began to follow the smell and soon found herself in the courtyard and at the doorway to the kitchens.

The noise of low chattering and the banging of pots and dishes sounded from inside. Sticking her nose round the corner she saw several servants busily clearing up the remains of the night's meal and washing the dishes. Sniffing again, she knew the wonderful aroma definitely came from here. Pangs of hunger gripped her and once again, her belly rumbled. Venturing in, she tried to locate the source of the smell. It came from a table, the one at the back of the room, farthest from the cooking fires and oven.

Salivating with hunger, she sized up where the servants were and, belly low to the floor, began to creep round the edge of the room. A few steps, then she'd freeze, then a few more.

"Aiiee! A cat!" The woman's shriek almost deafened her.

Plastering herself to the floor, ears flattened against her skull, she stared in equal terror at the servant.

"Where?" demanded a young male voice as she heard the sound of his bare feet running in her direction. "Where is it?"

Instincts she didn't know she possessed kicked in as she propelled herself forward under the table and darted for the other side of the room.

"A cat? You're afraid of a cat?" an older male voice laughed.

"It's the queen, come back to punish us!" wailed the woman, her voice rising in pitch. "Mut save us from her!"

Ankhesenamun cowered there, backing into the corner as she listened to what they were saying.

"Be silent, Meryt," ordered the older man, his voice growing closer. "You'll have the guard in here if you carry on like that. It's only a cat."

"We don't have a cat here, and you know the story of what happened to the queen . . ." began the youth.

"Nakht, if you got nothing sensible to say, then keep it to yourself! A cat's a blessing to any house, they keep the vermin away. Where did you see her?"

The voice came closer and suddenly the man's face bobbed into view as he bent down to look along the floor.

"I see it! Over in the corner," he said, grinning. "Go cut the tail and a bit of flesh off that fish on the table up there, Nakht. Put it on a plate and bring it here. Likely that's what drew her in here in the first place."

Meryt began to wail again, and the older man's head disappeared along with his legs as he went over to her. The sound of a sharp slap followed and the wailing abruptly stopped.

"And stay quiet," he ordered. "I don't want you frightening her away!"

Nakht's feet hurried over to where the delicious food smell was coming from, and her attention momentarily diverted by the suddenly increased aroma, she failed to notice that the older man had crept closer. A whiff of his stale sweat made her look back then cower, hissing and spitting, even closer into the corner.

"Here's the fish, Khnum," said the youth, passing the plate down to him.

"Now fetch her a small bowl of water," he said, waving it enticingly. "Here, *miut,*" he said gently. "You must be hungry."

She was, but she wasn't stupid enough to let him get close to her yet.

"Block that doorway, Meryt," he said, sighing and putting the plate down. "I don't want her to escape."

Nakht came back and a bowl of water joined the plate on the floor. Hunger pangs were making her feel ill now and that fish—*Ugh,* another part of her mind was saying, *Raw fish!*—smelled so good.

Both men backed off to the other side of the room, joining the woman. Slowly she relaxed enough to creep forward a few paces, neck stretched out, sniffing. Oh, it smelled so good! Pace by pace she grew closer until she finally reached the dish. Swallowing her pride, she took a delicate nibble, keeping her eyes still on the servants. It was as good as any feast dish she'd tasted. In no time at all it was finished and she was lapping the water to quench her thirst.

"Good girl, good little *miut,*" said Khnum, edging closer again.

Looking warily up, she saw he had another dish in his hand.

"Like some more, girl?" he asked, getting down

onto his hands and knees and sliding the bowl toward her. "Try this."

She waited for him to push it closer to her, but both he and the bowl stayed where they were. Obviously, he wanted her to go to him. Cautiously, she came closer, skittering back when one of the others knocked something over on the table where they stood.

"Will you two stand still!" he said over his shoulder to them. "I want her to trust me! We could do with a cat round here; there are too many rats getting into the store room."

He sounded friendly, and he could be a permanent source of food for her. Even though she'd only be a cat for three days each month, she'd need to eat if tonight was any gauge.

Trusting the goddess to be as good as her word on the matter of her safety as she had been so far, Ankhesenamun crept closer to investigate the new bowl of meat scraps. Before long, Khnum was stroking her as she tucked into food that appealed more to the human inside her.

"We'll call you Miut, shall we, girl?" he said, scritching her behind the ears.

She stopped eating with surprise as she felt her body begin to vibrate.

A nervous laugh came from Nakht as he ventured closer. "She's purring. Sounds like she likes her name."

"You can't call her 'cat,' " objected Meryt from her place by the door.

Purring. Why should that surprise her, she thought as she finished off the scraps of roasted duck.

"She likes it," said Khnum, reaching out to pick her up.

Ankhesenamun voiced a protest, surprising herself at the mew that came out. It made Khnum laugh.

"I wouldn't laugh," said Nakht, grabbing the older man's arm. "Look at the talisman she's got round her neck!" .

"I told you it was the queen! The stone cat had one round its neck, too!" wailed Meryt, clutching the rag she held to her face in fear.

"Be quiet, woman!" said Khnum, settling Ankhesenamun against his chest with one arm and using his free hand to examine her amulet. "It's a talisman from Mut, right enough," he said, letting the winged scarab fall back gently against her fur. "If it is the queen, even more reason we take care of her." He turned to look at Nakht and Meryt. "You'll say nothing of this, hear me?" he said quietly. "She's got the Mother's protection, it's not for us to interfere. We'll feed her, hide her if necessary. Let the gods see to their own business."

"But what about Pharaoh?" asked Nakht.

Khnum gave him a long look. "You want to argue with Sekhmet?"

"How'd they know Sekhmet was involved?" I asked Tal.

"Who else could turn a person into a cat?" he asked disdainfully.

"Fair enough. What happened when Aya saw that the paintings of him in his throne room had been scratched by a cat they didn't have?"

"Aya was furious. He had the palace searched and all the staff questioned, but Khnum, Nakht, and Meryt said nothing about the cat they called Miut. Of course, they couldn't find her because at dawn's first light, she became a stone statue on her plinth again."

"Did she actually go back to the throne room, or was she magically transported there at dawn?"

Tal stretched his forelimbs and frowned at me. "You're rushing me," he said sternly. "She was magically transported there. When the search proved fruitless, Aya called in the workmen to repair the paintings and the throne, but it was a task that took more than one day. You can imagine how he felt when the next day dawned showing all the work had been undone again during the night."

I chuckled, imagining the queen sharpening her claws on the wall and the throne. A small revenge, maybe, but one calculated to drive the Pharaoh mad with rage.

"Why didn't he just destroy the statue?"

"He didn't dare because it wore the amulet of Mut, remember?" said Tal. "When the fourth day dawned and there was no damage to the wall or to the throne, Aya began to relax. However, that day, the priests from the temple of Amun came to speak to him about the matter. All of Thebes was talking about how Pharaoh's stone cat came to life and shredded not only his royal throne, but the painting of his coronation. This threatened the stability of his reign, the priests said. They began to ask him awkward questions."

"I'll bet they did! Was that the revenge Sekhmet had in mind all along?"

"Possibly," he said. "Aya reassured them and they finally left. That night, however, when everyone was asleep, he took the statue to the small temple of Mut and placed it in a niche there, telling the priests that he was giving it to them as an offering to the goddess. They had to accept it because it had the talisman of Mut round its neck."

"So what did Ankhesenamun do when the next full moon came? Did she manage to get into the kitchens and get fed? Did she go back to the throne room?"

"Good job patience goes with being a cat," sniffed Tal archly. "By the time Ankhesenamun had visited the throne room for the third time, Aya decided enough was enough and moved his court and his capital to the city of Memphis."

"So what happened to Ankhesenamun? Aya would have closed down the palace in Thebes, obviously."

"Not completely. He left a skeleton staff there, including the kitchen servants, so Ankhesenamun was still able to eat there for the next few years. Needless to say, she did scratch the mural again, but it was never repaired. Time passed, and when the palace was finally closed down, Khnum came to the temple on the first night of the full moon to take her to his own home and feed her there even though by now the priests were well aware of her and left food out, too. When Khnum died, she mourned him, but as she'd already put in a good word for him with Mut, she knew his afterlife was assured."

"So how does this story end?" I asked. "Does she find her Prince again?"

"Pharaoh," he corrected me. "Whose tale is this? Let me tell it my way! Gradually the temple fell into disuse, and even the townsfolk who lived nearby began to forget the story of how a queen had become a Pharaoh's stone cat. Ankhesenamun now had to wander farther afield to find her food, but her amulet still served her well, until one night nearly fifty years later. A new Pharaoh was about to be crowned, one called Ramesses II."

As soon as she woke, Ankhesenamun jumped down from her niche and picked her way out through the rubble of her temple until she was where the outer courtyards had been. Turning round, she saw that in the intervening days even more of the building had been taken apart to be reused elsewhere, likely to finish off the mortuary temple for King Seti, Ramesses' father. The outer walls had long since gone, as had the earthly presences of the gods Amun, Mut, and Khonsu from their inner shrine.

On the wind, she could smell the scents of rich food and hear the voices of happiness and laughter. The late Pharaoh Seti had obviously been buried and the time of mourning was now over. Following the noises and the smells, she headed into the narrow streets, keeping always to the deepest shadows. She'd witnessed many funerals now—all Pharaohs came to Thebes to make their final journey to the West and their tombs in the Valley of the Kings. Though food would be plentiful for many days now, as was the custom, the city would also be full of all the court officials come from Memphis, including the soon-to-be-crowned new Pharaoh. That meant she had to be doubly careful since after the long period of national mourning, the people were ready to celebrate to the full on the free beer donated by their next ruler.

She was in the sector she knew best, that closest to the temple complex of Karnak, main home to the gods to whom her small temple had been dedicated. There was an inn there where sympathetic drudges would often feed her scraps, and a small bowl of milk if she was very lucky.

Staying close to the walls, she kept her eyes on the groups of singing and dancing revelers. Snatches of songs floated after one such group of young men, obviously from the court by the richness of their clothes and jewelry, and she smiled to herself remembering Khnum and the others from the palace kitchens. On feast days they had always sung as they worked. Compared with her necessary trips into the city now, those days seemed uncomplicated and almost happy. She tried not to think that before many hours had passed, some of these young men would be reeling drunk and likely to come to blows with each other, and the life of a cat, even one wearing Mut's talisman, would mean little to them.

Hurrying now, she wound her way past the shops, newly opened after the seventy days of mourning, their goods spilling out into the street. Shopkeepers stood in brightly lit doorways, calling to the revelers, enticing them to come and inspect their wares. All was noise and bustle, the air filled with the scents of the perfumed courtiers and the sweat of the common people, all overlaid by the smell of roasting meats.

The inn was just ahead, and hunger had gripped her belly in a tight fist of pain—it was the first night of the full moon and she was starving. The inn was just ahead, thankfully, because the smell of food was more than she could resist. Outside the entrance, several men of various ages stood arguing. She stopped, crouching against the wall watching them as their discussion grew more heated. Creeping closer, she tried to make out what was happening.

"You got no right coming down here and acting the Memphis lordlings over us!" one burly commoner said angrily. "Where are you when we need help from the court? At Memphis, that's where! We're only good enough for you when you come here at festival times!"

"Let's go elsewhere, Merire," said one of the young nobles. "It isn't worth the trouble."

"That's it, go back to the palace!" jeered the commoner's companion. "Drink your own beer and leave us ours. That's right, isn't it, Didia?"

"We're not looking for trouble," said Merire in a reasonable tone. "We just want to buy a meal, that's all."

Ankhesenamun froze. His voice . . . there was something about it that drew her a few steps closer.

"The court's still too somber after the funeral," said the third courtier. "We wanted to get out and relax, where's the harm in that?"

"Where's the harm?" demanded Didia belligerently, reaching out to push Merire farther into the street by prodding his chest. "I'll tell you where the harm is! You people with your fancy clothes," he said, his look raking the young man up and down, taking in his fine pleated linen kilt and the beadwork collar he wore. "You come down here and make for our women, talking sweet to them, taking them off to your lodgings until you go back to Memphis. Then you just throw them aside like used toys!''

"Like used toys," his companion agreed, crowding Merire. "Leave our women alone."

"I assure you, we're not interested in your women," began Merire.

"And I said leave!" bellowed Didia, reaching again to push him.

Merire caught his hand, forcing it back against the wrist, making the man cry out in pain.

"And I said we're not looking for trouble, or your women," said Merire softly as his friends stepped forward to back him up. "Now step out of the way unless you want to make an issue of this. I'm sure the city guards would be interested." He let Didia go, standing with his body held ready for trouble.

The second commoner stepped back hurriedly, realizing the three young men were all well muscled and not soft-living courtiers.

"Maybe we were a little hasty," said Didia sullenly, rubbing his wrist as he slouched aside.

"You were," said Merire, stepping past him and into the inn, followed by his two friends.

Silent as a shadow, Ankhesenamun followed them in, hiding under a table as she watched the owner catch sight of his noble customers and rush to greet them. Then they were shown to a small alcove and seated at the best table in the inn.

While they ordered, she darted through the forests of legs to their table and crouched beneath it for a moment before carefully sniffing at each of them in turn. Once again, there was something about the scent of the one called Merire that was vaguely familiar. It drew her to him.

"That could have been nasty back there," said one of his companions. "We should have just left it, Merire."

"You worry too much, Hori," said Merire. "We've

every right to come into the town and eat here if we wish. I can see his point, though," he conceded. "He isn't to know that we aren't looking for entertainment with local women."

"Speak for yourself!" laughed the other one. "Personally, if I see a comely young girl . . ."

"You'll leave her alone, Simontu," said Merire sternly. "What you do in Memphis is one thing, but coming here and womanizing when we know we're leaving in a few days is not right."

"Your beer, sirs," said a female voice she recognized.

She heard the thump as the three cups were placed on the table. "I see you've found an admirer already."

"Excuse me?" said Merire, obviously confused.

"Miut's found you," she said. "She's under your table. Shall I bring her food here with yours?"

A head bobbed down to look at her. Startled, her back automatically arched and her fur began to bristle.

"A cat!" he exclaimed, reaching a hand toward her.

"Our Miut isn't just any cat," the girl said. "She's protected by Mut."

Ankhesenamun relaxed her stance, recognizing him and stretched her neck forward to sniff his fingers.

"So I see," said Merire, letting her sniff. "Yes, bring her some food."

"Don't encourage it," said Simontu. "These city cats, bags of bones the lot of them. You never know where they've been."

"This one looks quite respectable," said Merire, growing bold enough to stroke her head. "And she's wearing an amulet, an expensive one from the looks of it."

Ankhesenamun ventured closer. Every sense she had was saying she could trust this man.

Another head bobbed down to look at her.

"She certainly looks well fed," said Hopi. "If she eats here, then the food must be good!"

Merire chuckled. Ankhesenamun moved closer still, butting his hand with her head as she began to purr.

"How do you know she's a female?" he asked.

"All cats are," said Hopi easily, sitting up. "Pick her up, let's have a look at the amulet she's wearing."

Merire reached down with his other hand and scooped her up. The surprise of it made her mew and struggle at first, but as he held her close and told Simontu to move up on the bench, she grew still. His scent was strangely familiar. There was definitely something about this man that she liked, she decided as he set her down on the end of the bench beside him.

"So you're Miut, are you?" he asked, scratching her under her chin.

She purred happily, lifting her head up so he could reach her throat more easily.

"Mut's talisman," said Hopi, leaning across the table. "No commoner could afford a piece of jewelry as expensive as that."

"She might be a temple cat," Merire said, bending forward for a closer look. "We're not far from the main one at Karnak."

The whole amulet was shorter than the length of his thumb with the scarab itself made of a beautifully carved lapis lazuli set in gold, with a solar disk of red carnelian at its head. The minute feathers on the upward curving wings were formed of inlays of turquoise, lapis, and red carnelian separated by thin strips of gold. Falcon's legs, separated by the bird's spread tail feathers, gripped the sacred *shen* symbols of eternity. It was a talisman fit to grace the throat of any Pharaoh, or his queen.

"It's *kheper*—a symbol of transformation," he said thoughtfully as he continued to tickle Miut under the chin. "Such a talisman ensures the protection of the wearer and is a spell to make her heart receptive to a divine judgment."

"If she were a temple cat, they'd feed her," said Simontu, leaning back against the wall behind him. "More likely she belongs to some minor Theban noble and is just slumming it down here."

"I doubt that," said Merire, caressing her head as she butted his hand again. "You're a real mystery cat, eh, Miut?"

The serving girl came back with their meals and bowls of food and water for her.

"I see you've made friends," she grinned, putting the bowls on the bench beside Ankhesenamun.

"Yes. Do you know where's she from?"

"I don't rightly know for sure. Local talk has it she lives in the ruins of the temple where the old palace was in the days of Tutankhamun."

Startled, Ankhesenamun looked up at Merire just as he looked down at her. Their eyes locked only briefly, but it was long enough to send a surge of joy through her heart. It was her husband, born once more into the world of the living!

"How did she come by the amulet?" he asked.

"I don't know. My father would have it that she's a queen turned into a stone cat by Mut when Aya became Pharaoh after Tutankhamun died," she laughed. "Full of strange tales, my father is."

"Can you ask your father to come and tell us the story?" he asked.

"I'll ask," she said, glancing round the room, "but you may have to wait until we're less busy."

"We'll wait," Merire assured her.

Simontu groaned. "Merire, you're not going to keep us sitting here all evening just to hear some tale about a magical cat are you?"

"I'd like to hear it, too," said Hopi.

"I *have* to hear the story," said Merire, a strange look crossing his face as he looked back at Miut. "I don't know why, but it's important to me."

Ankhesenamun's heart began to beat faster. He

knew she was important to him! As she ate, she began to pray to Mut that he'd remember who he was and recognize her.

"I know you're interested in entering the priesthood, but isn't this carrying it a bit too far?" said Simontu. "We're supposed to be celebrating tonight!"

Merire gave her head a last scritch then turned to eat his meal. "If you don't want to stay, you can go back without me," he said. "I don't mind."

"Not after what happened outside," said Simontu. "We stay together."

As they ate, Ankhesenamun studied Merire's face. Now she knew what to look for, she could see the resemblance to her late husband. This new face he bore was as handsome as his last one had been. His own dark hair, worn shoulder length, framed an oval face. The nose was slim, and like her husband, his almond-shaped eyes were outlined in dark eye paint. His full lips spread in a smile as he noticed her studying him.

He bent his head toward her. "Like what you see, Miut?" he whispered, a faint chuckle underscoring his words.

Indeed she did, and she mewed her appreciation.

Laughing, he sat up and continued eating.

The owner of the inn came over not long after they'd finished and Ankhesenamun, ears pricked wide, sat and listened to the story as eagerly as Merire and Hopi. The innkeeper knew all the main facts, but he' did embroider the tale, saying she had been the avenging spirit of Sekhmet as well as Queen Ankhesenamun taking revenge on her grandfather Aya for killing her husband, King Tutankhamun. He didn't, however, know the final part of the story, that she was waiting only for her lost love to be reborn so they could be reunited.

When the innkeeper had gone, Simontu laughed. "You two were really taken in by his story, weren't you?"

"How would you explain the amulet?" asked Hopi.

"Some child probably found it in the palace ruins and put it round her neck."

"A child would more likely give it to his mother to sell," said Merire thoughtfully, moving the empty bowls onto the table to give Miut more room. "And the story would explain why no one has tried to steal it from her."

Simontu shrugged. "I don't really care one way or the other," he said.

"What a terrible fate, though," said Hopi, shaking his head. "To be condemned to a life as a stone cat except for the nights of the full moon."

"Better than marrying your grandfather," said Merire, picking Miut up. "There's something about the story that rings true. Are we ready to leave?"

"You're not taking her back, are you?" asked Simontu, exasperated.

Merire hesitated. He'd automatically picked her up because he knew he couldn't leave her behind. "Yes," he said unequivocally.

"Cats are worshipped in the north, Simontu," said Hopi as they all rose. "Either as Sekhmet or Bast."

"Well, keep her away from me! She's probably covered in fleas. And don't blame me if you wake up and find her straddling your chest, fangs bared as she did to Aya in the story!" said Simontu.

That's not true! I only scratched the wall and the throne! she thought frantically. What if he believed the story and left her behind? Her blood ran cold as something else occurred to her. How could she possibly tell him who she was? When dawn came, would she become stone again? How *was* Mut's spell to be broken? She let out a wail of anguish as she realized she had no way to tell Merire anything.

"Sounds like she's not too happy to be leaving," said Hopi as they stepped out into the night.

Head turned to answer his friend, Merire didn't see Didia and the flash of his knife as it sliced toward him, but Ankhesenamun did.

How dare he threaten the life of her beloved, she thought as, throwing caution to the wind, she kicked back against Merire's chest and launched herself at Didia's face, turning in mid-leap into a spitting ball of feral rage.

Instantly alerted to their danger, the three friends turned to face their attacker. Didia's knife clattered to the ground as he screamed in pain, desperately trying to dislodge the cat that was savaging his throat and face.

A circle of jostling, curious passersby was already beginning to gather. Merire hesitated, torn between rescuing the cat and making sure Didia didn't harm any of them.

"Get the knife," he said to Hopi, making a dive for Didia just as the man tore Miut loose and flung her aside.

Still screeching, Didia was holding his hands over his face and backing away, blood pouring from between his fingers. Merire grabbed the wounded man by the arm, looking around to make sure no one else was waiting to attack them.

"Fetch the guard," he ordered the nearest man. "He tried to stab us. Hopi, where's Miut?" he asked anxiously, knowing that Didia was no threat to them now.

"She's hurt, Merire," said Hopi from behind him. "When he threw her off, she hit the wall."

Dread filled him as he glanced over his shoulder to

where the cat lay crumpled on the ground at the foot of the wall.

"It's only a cat, Merire," said Simontu.

"It's a cat that just saved my life!" he said angrily, thrusting Didia at him and running over to Hopi.

Oblivious to everything else, he knelt in the dirt beside her small, crumpled body. She was still alive, but her breathing was ragged and a thin trickle of blood from her mouth was pooling onto the ground beside her.

Ankhesenamun lay there panting. The pain was so great it filled her completely. She couldn't understand why this had happened. Wasn't she protected by Mut? The goddess had said no harm could come to her, and despite many brushes with trouble, she'd been safe, until now. To be so close to her love and then for this to happen! Then a calmness settled over her. He was still alive and that was what mattered most. She'd seen him again, been held in his arms, and if that was all the goddess could give her, it was enough. Her senses dimmed and darkness claimed her.

"I think she's dead," said Hopi quietly.

"She can't be!" said Merire, tears springing to his eyes as his hand gently stroked her head. "I won't let her die!"

"There's nothing we can do for her," Hopi said regretfully. "It was a brave thing she did, risking her life to save yours."

"I can take her to the Karnak temple," he said, reaching forward to pick her up. "There's a physician there. She wears Mut's amulet—they'll have to help her! King Seti believed them to be manifestations of the goddess!"

"The guard's here," said Simontu, his shadow falling over them. "I'm really sorry she's dying, Merire," he began.

"You tell them what happened," said Hopi, giving him Didia's knife. "I'm going with Merire to the temple."

Cradling her carefully in his arms, Merire pushed the curious townsfolk aside and ran like one possessed, not knowing why the small form whose life was slowly ebbing away was so important to him, just knowing that it was.

At the temple, now the funeral was over, the elaborate preparations for Ramesses' coronation were underway. The priests were none too pleased to be disturbed by a couple of distraught young men, one of them bloodstained and carrying an unconscious cat. Then they saw the amulet and recognized Merire as the son of one of the prominent court nobles and suddenly, Merire and his friend had the attention they needed.

"There's little I can do for her," admitted the physician after examining her. "She's gravely injured."

"What about the goddess? Mut gave her the amulet, surely she can cure her?" Merire demanded.

"But the sanctuary is sealed," objected the physician. "It can't be opened until morning, and then only by the head priest."

"Then get him! Cats are sacred to Sekhmet as well as Mut! Pharaoh Seti believed they were divine! She saved my life, I can't let her die!" he said angrily, carefully picking up her limp and unconscious body.

Sighing, the physician gestured to one of the acolytes, who rushed off to find the head priest.

It took several minutes, but at last the head priest of Amun arrived. "This is most irregular," he began.

"Look at the amulet," said Merire, pointing to the bloodstained winged *kheper* still round Miut's neck. "Isn't that enough to tell you she's beloved by Mut?"

The priest paled and turned on the physician. "Why wasn't I told of this?" he demanded.

"Is it important?" asked the physician, puzzled. "Agreed it's an expensive winged scarab . . ."

"That amulet is unique," said the priest as he ushered Merire out into the corridor. "Especially when worn by no ordinary cat! Don't you know the story of Ankhesenamun, Tutankhamun's Queen?"

"Wait here, Hopi," ordered Merire as they left the room.

Merire held her close as he and the acolyte hurried after the priest through successively smaller and darker chambers until they reached the innermost sanctuary of Karnak. He suddenly knew without doubt that Miut was more than she seemed, that the tale of the Pharaoh's stone cat was indeed true, and this was Queen Ankhesenamun.

"Mut, please don't take her from me," he whispered, holding her close as the priest broke the clay seal on the cord fastening the double doors leading to the inner shrines of Amun, Mut, and their son, Khonsu.

The head priest flung the doors wide, and by the light of the sanctuary's single lamp, Merire watched him hurry over to the wooden shrine housing the image of the goddess Mut. As the priest bowed his head and began intoning a hymn to the goddess, he was filled with a sense of déjà vu. He recognized the room, and the images of the gods and the goddess!

His common sense told him it was impossible. This was the holy of holies in the temple, no one but Pharaoh or the head priest was allowed to enter here. The knowledge was little comfort as he stepped hesitantly into the room. Suddenly light-headed, the room seemed to swirl around him—he was the one intoning the hymn as he reverently washed the statues in water from the sacred lake, he was drying them, then anointing them with sweet smelling oils.

The room seemed to lurch once more, and he was back, listening to the priest.

"Hail to thee, Sekhmet-Bast-Rê, Mother of the gods, Bearer of Wings, Mistress of the Two Crowns . . ."

Merire could feel the small heart beating against his bare chest beginning to slow. "Don't give up!" he whispered frantically, bending down to touch his lips to the small furred head. "Please, Ankhesenamun, you must live!" For a brief moment, wisps of half-remembered memories tugged at his conscious mind.

"Great one of magic in the Boat of Millions, Holy one . . ." intoned the priest.

Her heartbeat faltered, then strengthened, but the rhythm was different. Now it matched the beat of his own heart. Even as he was wondering about this, Merire felt Miut become heavier in his arms. Her breathing slowed till it also matched his. Surprised, he adjusted her in his arms, watching her as she grew heavier yet. Suddenly her form seemed to blur and lengthen. He blinked, then let out a cry of shock as he found himself no longer holding a cat, but a young woman—an extremely beautiful one.

The priest faltered in his prayer and looked round, then fell to his knees before the image of Mut.

"Praise to thee, O daughter of Rê, Mother in the horizon of heaven!" the priest said fervently. "Thy justice has been done!"

Ankhesenamun stirred, moaning softly as she opened her eyes.

They all heard the gentle voice that filled the chamber. "Did I not tell you that your faith would be rewarded, child?"

"It *is* you," Merire whispered, looking down at a face he now remembered well, a face of delicate features framed by a fall of rich, dark hair. Her deep brown eyes gazed lovingly back at him.

"Are you still hurt?" he asked anxiously, feeling such joy fill his heart that he wondered it didn't burst.

"I'm well, now we're together again," she smiled, reaching a delicate hand up to touch his face in wonder. Her eyes filled with tears. "I missed you so much," she whispered.

"I remember very little," he confessed, turning his head to kiss her hand. "Only our love for each other."

"That's as it should be. Thanks to Mut, we have a new life together now," she said, her hand curling round his neck and drawing his head down to kiss him.

The priest scrambled to his feet and slipped out of the sanctuary. Outside, they could hear him sending the acolyte for a robe for her.

Reluctantly, Merire broke the kiss to look over to the statue of Mut. "Thank you, Mut," he said. "I had intended to enter the priesthood before this, but for the gift of my love returned to me, I will serve you."

"You returned the true faith to Kemet, Merire-Tutankhamun. Ma'at has been served well. Balance and order have finally been restored," whispered the goddess.

Dipping his head in homage to the goddess, he turned to carry Ankhesenamun out of the shrine room. "What shall I call you?" he asked he gently. "I need to know what name to tell the priest if we're to be married again."

"I'll keep the name Miut," she said with the ghost of a smile. "I've grown rather fond of it and it has served me well."

Merire laughed and hugged her close. "Miut, my own little cat," he teased, touching his lips to her forehead.

"That's a great story, Tal," I said, as I finished typing. Getting no answer, I glanced over to the chair back. It was empty.

"Tal?" I called softly, looking round the room.

Where was he? Then I noticed daylight showing through the curtains. I began to wonder if I had been hallucinating after all, but when I looked more closely at the chair, on the velvet cushion on which he'd been sitting, he'd left the imprint of his body—and the story I've just written.

CAT-FRIEND

Josepha Sherman

Josepha Sherman is a fantasy novelist and folklorist whose latest titles include *Son of Darkness, The Captive Soul,* the folklore title, *Merlin's Kin,* and, together with Susan Shwartz, two STAR TREK novels, *Vulcan's Forge* and *Vulcan's Heart.* She is also a fan of the New York Mets, horses, aviation, and space science. Visit her at www.sff.net/people/Josepha.Sherman.

Now, I had never had it in my mind to be a witch or indeed any other sort of magic worker, certainly not with what people said was happening over in Salem and surrounding towns. Even without those warnings, there I was, nothing much to the eye, a skinny girl with the plain name of Mari—which was short for the too-ornate Damaris, I was told. I lived a catch-as-catch-can life in a backwoods New England village near to the edge of exploration, with no one to take my part. But yes, unlikely though it might seem and though I wasn't sure of it yet, there was some small magic stirring in me.

Still, as far as I was thinking about it at all, magic was useless so far since it could grant me neither friend nor steady source of food and shelter. In fact,

most of my problems came not so much from being
an orphan as from being the orphan of folks who were
considered just a little too close to witchy ways for
comfort.

Magic draws magic, they say. However, before some
good-hearted soul, witch or wizard, not afraid of what
the more saintly might say, could find and shield me,
train me in what skills might grow in me, it was my
Aunt Dorcas who found me. Aunt, that is, or at least
so she claimed to be, since I never remembered my
poor parents mentioning any kinfolk. Of course, I had
been a small child then, back before the carriage accident that took them both, so for all I knew, they
maybe *had* mentioned her before I was old enough to
know. But no kin had showed up at the funeral—
not that I would have known, being so sorrowful and
bewildered at the time.

Not that any of that mattered. I was still a girl, years
yet from adulthood, and she was a big, strong, broad
woman with eyes like gray stone and a face and manner showing few signs of age and many signs of getting
her own way with one and all. Including me. Not that
anyone in the village truly bothered to stand against
her, not when it meant getting rid of the orphan they'd
all been more or less ignoring. Didn't have to have
their consciences troubled by that either, since it
wasn't as if I were being thrown out with nowhere
to go.

So off we went, Aunt Dorcas and I, to her ram-
shackle house in the middle of nowhere much: weeds,
bushes, a more-or-less-tended vegetable-and-herb garden, and trees all around. The house, outside and in,
dated to maybe a hundred years back, old for that
part of the wilderness, one of those good, solid wood-
plank buildings, originally stained a dark brown but
already weathered to a nondescript color. The sloping
roof was still fully shingled but looked as though a
good wind would change that fact. In other words, the

place showed money had once been there, and wasn't
there now. The hearth was worn with time but still
lined with good New England marble, and while there
was not very much furniture to fill the great downstairs room, what was left, a table and some benches,
was well-made, even though badly in need of polish.

It seemed pretty evident from my first clear-eyed
look at the place that Aunt Dorcas wanted me with
her not out of any kindness toward kin, but because
I would make a handy servant—one who needed no
wages.

By that place in my young life, to be honest, I
hadn't expected anything other. I had seen little charity in others so far, after all. But to be even more
honest, I had harbored the tiniest of hopes that life
here would be otherwise. It would have been nice, so
very nice, to have a kind word, a sense that someone
wanted me.

This could have been worse, I reminded myself
sternly after a few days had passed. I could have been
out on the roads like the poor starvelings I'd seen,
some of them younger still than me. Maybe I wasn't
getting any scraps of kindness from the woman who'd
taken me in, but I was getting food, plain but filling
stuff, and a straw pallet on which to sleep. For the
first time in my life I had a homespun dress that fitted
and didn't have mended patches. And if the room in
which that pallet lay was tiny, a corner up near the
rafters, barely more than a closet with a sliver of a
window in one wall, well, at least it *was* a room, with
a door I could close. I usually was tired out enough
from the day's work, chopping wood or pulling weeds
or mending clothes or sweeping out the hearth's ashes,
to sleep well, hardly even stirring till the first gray
light of morning.

Sleeping, that is, except for when I had the unex-
pected visit from a cat or two. Aunt Dorcas would
have screeched like a horny-owl if she'd known they

were visiting me, sliding through that narrow window or stealing through cracks in the walls. She hated cats, said that they were nasty, dirty, flea-ridden creatures, bits of old Mischief, and not worth the drowning.

The cats clearly didn't care what she thought. They snuck into my room every now and again, as I say, late at night, one or two at a time, calico or gray, black or striped, purring and soft-furred and willing to be cuddled by a lonely girl. Once there was even a visit from a pretty dove-gray mom-cat with three gray kittens. I'd lain awake for hours that one night, stifling my giggles, watching with much delight as the three tiny balls of silly fur pounced on each other and, occasionally, on my toes.

Why was this happening? Was I drawing them to me by some sudden magic? Or did they simply have some feline reason all their own? No matter. The cats liked me, loved me, where no one else did.

And so the days slid by, and I grew toward the edge of womanhood. Never did I guess what the truth might be about my aunt, what she truly was or why she'd taken me in. Naïve, yes, I was that, but in my own defense, what else could I be? I'd had no experience in the world other than the village and the villagers turning their backs on me.

Then one night, a sharp nip on my nose from a black-and-white tom brought me to a jarring awakening. For a dazed moment I stared blankly into the cat's green-glinting eyes, wondering why he'd nipped me. And then I heard voices . . . voices coming from downstairs. We'd never had visitors before, and certainly not in the dark night.

Suddenly as overwhelmed by curiosity as any cat, I tiptoed after the tom to where, if I crouched, I could peek through the balcony's rails without being noticed and just about make out the main room.

Aunt Dorcas was there, and with her was a tall, cloak-shrouded figure. A man, I guessed, by his height—yes, and by his grim, cold, deep voice.

"Is it ready?"

It?

"Not yet, not yet." That, to my astonishment, was my aunt, using a sweeter, more wheedling tone than ever I thought possible for her. "These matters take time. First there must be a testing."

"See that there is. And see that it does not take over-long."

The unspoken menace behind those words chilled me so suddenly and thoroughly that I didn't wait to hear more. I scrambled up and hurried back to my pallet, hugging a friendly calico cat to me like a doll. But no one came after me, and at last my pounding heart returned to its normal beat. The cat's rhythmic purring lulled me back to sleep.

The next day, I was uncertain of what, exactly, I had overheard. It? Testing? Did it have anything at all to do with me? After all, my aunt's business was surely her own.

But that night, when I had finished scrubbing down the room and was just about to bank the fire for the night and head to bed, Aunt Dorcas said, "Wait. Come here."

Puzzled, I went to her.

"Stand up straight, girl."

In itself, that wasn't alarming; she almost never called me by my name. I obediently stood up straight. My aunt circled me, studying me with her piercing gaze, but I determinedly refused to wince.

"Gawky thing still," she muttered. "No beauty, and no dowry. You had best hope I can successfully find some other role for you than the traditional ones." Aunt Dorcas glared. "That is, of course, if you have been chaste. You *are* still a maiden?"

In her voice was an edge that warned, I'd better be.

How, I thought, remembering my lonely life, could I be aught else? "Yes, ma'am."

"Have you ever heard of scrying? Don't gawk at me like that! This is nothing devilish, nor are you about to be turned over to witch-finders. Now, have you heard of scrying?"

"Yes, ma'am."

She nodded. "Go get the good bowl. The one with the silver plating. And fill it with rainwater. Nothing else, mind! It must be clear rainwater."

Of course I knew what she wanted. She meant for me to look into the mirror that the water in the bowl would form, and beyond it at whatever visions I might happen to see.

Testing? Or was I drawing conclusions where there were none?

But no sooner had I begun staring into the water, intently and not a little scared, what with my aunt all but breathing down my neck, than I straightened in alarm.

"What?" Aunt Dorcas snapped. "What is it, girl?"

"The cats!" I cried. "Did you not hear them screeching?"

She snorted. "Flighty girl. I heard nothing. Now, get back to work!"

But I could not concentrate. Every time I tried to stare into the water, I heard the cats screeching, almost as though they were warning me, *no*!

At last my aunt gave up. With a snarl of "Useless lout!" she hurled the water at me and stalked off.

I finished my chores without a word from her, ate my meal without a word from her, and went to my bed without a word from her.

I lay awake for a time, troubled without knowing why I was so bothered. Scrying . . . there were those who'd say it was against the laws sent down from heaven. I wasn't sure if that had been one of the reasons those in Salem had been hanged. But was scrying really sinful? It hadn't felt like that. Still, it had felt very strangely wrong. And the cats . . . I'd heard them as if they'd been warning me, I knew I had.

Aunt Dorcas tried to use me in other forms of scrying in following nights, but I saw nothing in the hearth flames but cat faces mewling warnings, and read nothing in the scattered ashes but cat fur raised in alarm. I felt nothing but ever-increasing fear. I failed again and yet again to be of any use, and at last Aunt Dorcas slapped me across the face in sheer frustration. As I blinked away startled tears, she snapped, "You are a useless waste of time! A failure!"

What did that mean? In panic, I wondered if she was going to throw me out. *Testing*, I kept thinking, and wondering what happened now. But when I tried desperately, almost weeping, to ask her, Aunt Dorcas simply repeated angrily that I wasn't worth her trouble, and refused to say anything more.

I finished that day's work in chill fear. What if she really did mean to get rid of me? I kept hearing the stranger's deep, cold voice. I kept picturing those poor folks out on the road, begging or starving. Even if I ran away this night, what could I do, with no money, no skills other than those of a rough servant? Still with the cold weight of fear in the pit of my stomach, I went to my pallet and lay shivering until at last I drifted into exhausted sleep.

The cats woke me, nipping at me till I woke, my shriek stifled by fur. They backed off enough to let me breathe, but there was no doubt that they meant to warn me. There were more cats crowded into the little room than ever before, a living carpet of nervously stirring fur. *Get up*, they urged me, and I took the warning, getting to my feet and slipping into my dress. But when I tried the door, it wouldn't open. At first I thought it was merely stuck. But then I knew:

"It's bolted!" I whispered to the cats.

They shoved against it, but all their massed strength and mine together still wasn't enough to open it. Panic surged up within me: Why should Aunt Dorcas lock me in unless she meant me harm? The cats prodded and nipped at me. They wanted me to do something, but what?

"What do you want?" I whispered. "I don't understand!"

They only continued their desperate proddings and nippings till I drew back in alarm, about to strike back at these who had been my only friends. But there was something else growing in me, more than fear, stronger than anger, something burning up and blazing free—

Magic. My magic. I had no idea how I did it, but I was suddenly a cat among the cats, and slipping easily with them through the narrow window out into the free world outside. I was an odd, pale cat, rough-furred and not particularly pretty, but it was so amazing to have this shift in senses, this sharpening of scent and sound, this change in how I moved, to have a tail to lash and whiskers to twitch—oh, I cared not how I looked in that first wild moment.

But I was a human as well as a cat, and the two natures were too overwhelmingly curious. I *had* to know what Aunt Dorcas had been planning to do with me.

That was when I discovered that not only had I become a cat, I had gained the feline language as well. It is not one simply of vocal sounds, like the human tongues, but one of sight and whisker-twitches and scent as well. The black-and-white tom swaggered over to me, now larger than I was. And if I had not been human as well as cat, I would, no doubt, have been intimidated by him.

"You make a nice little cat," he told me. "A pity it is not your mating time."

I reacted not as a cat but as an outraged woman might, slapping him across the face with a paw—fortunately for him recalling at the last instant to keep my claws sheathed.

"I am *not* your kind!" I told him sharply.

"Yes and no," he replied, smiling as cats do. "We shall see what happens when your time does come."

I all but slapped him again. I would not be cat at that time, I resolved. Assuming that I could become human again . . . ?

I could. I would. "But now I will find out what she does in there."

"Foulness," a plump gray queen cat snapped.

"Ugly scented," a small black cat agreed.

"Things not right," a second queen, calico, agreed.

But they were truly cats, after all, and they could not think as humans. There was no useful information to be gained from them. So I slipped easily back into the house, and many of the cats, including the arrogant black-and-white tom, followed me.

In that instant, I knew that the cats were right. With my altered senses, I could smell the foulness, and with my human mind I knew: Aunt Dorcas was working in the Black Arts. A second wary sniff told me another truth. She was not my aunt, not my kin at all.

She wanted me for my magic, yes, and because I was still a maiden. For one wild, purely feline instant, I thought shamefully of the black-and-white tom, and how I could rob her of that last matter.

No. I would conquer her as honest woman, not sly girl.

I concentrated on my humanity, trying to rouse the same fierce power that had made me cat. Nothing was coming, nothing . . .

Then the door flew open. The cloaked figure was a darker form against the night, dramatic as something out of a play. And now, with a cat's altered senses, I knew what it was that stood in the guise of a man. Dorcas had reached deep, indeed, in her search for power.

I dove into hiding with the other cats, scenting their fear, feeling my own fur rise.

"Is it ready?" the Evil asked.

"Uh . . . yes, yes, in a way," Dorcas all but dithered. "I have the girl locked up even now."

"You do *not*!"

It was the first time I had seen Dorcas actually blanch. "But—I—"

"It is not locked up. Where has it gone?"

It! I was the "it!"

Dorcas was clearly panic-stricken. "She couldn't have gotten out! The door is still bolted!"

"You are a fool. Clearly, it has discovered its power. And without control over it, you have failed me!"

"No! She's here, she has to be!"

"You waste our time."

He—it—them—the Evil Thing was about to attack, I knew it, and attack to kill. Should I let Dorcas die? Wouldn't the Evil go away then?

But I couldn't do it. She was a cold, harsh woman, yes, but was that reason enough for her to die? I remembered those poor folks who had been hanged in Salem for no proof other than hysteria. And I sprang forward, power blazing up within me, not cat nor woman but both in one, thrusting out a paw, a hand at Dorcas. The power flamed from me to her. She screamed and the scream changed as she shrank, changed to a cat's mewling as she became a dark gray queen that darted up the chimney and was gone.

The Evil turned to me, and I saw blood-red eyes and jet-black pupils. Nothing human, nothing but Evil, indeed. But before it could strike or even speak, I shouted in my cat and human voice: "End this!"

Again, I felt power blaze within me. And it was answered. Cats swarmed from out of corners, leaped through windows, sprang at the Evil. It cried out once, but even Evil could not fight against that burying force of fur, that savagery of claw and fang. It fell, and when the cats backed off, spitting and hissing, there was nothing of it but a stench, quickly dispelling, and a spot of burning on the floor where it had fallen.

What, then? Dorcas the cat never returned. I took over her house, and lived in comfort, my cats all around me. Human when it pleases me, cat when it pleases me, I have the black-and-white tom in cat or human form as well. No one from the Salem witch-fearing fools dares come here, though I will help those who dare my feline entourage.

Oh, yes. I have no doubt I was meant to be a sacrifice of magic power to the Evil. But I am now much more than that. Have you not heard the old tale of the cat who cried, "Now I am King of the Cats!"?

I am Queen of the Cats.

THE BEDTIME STORY

Edward Serken

Edward Serken is a Long Island resident who enjoys reading, playing with his children, Jessica and Andrew, and, of course, writing. He has been married to an eternally cheerful lady named Jodi for ten years and counting. Mr. Serken has appeared in *Night Terrors*, *Midnight Mind Magazine*, and is curently at work on a horror novel, about the near-death experience.

Maureen came into the playroom, smiling. "I know you're having fun with Daddy, Amy, but it's time for bed."

Amy was sprawled on the carpet in the midst of her baker's dozen of Barbies.

"I'm sure that Mommy will tell you a story," David offered from the floor beside the little girl.

"I will," Maureen said, putting hands on her slender hips. "But only if you get off your tush this minute and come with me to brush your teeth."

"Come on, sugar," David urged. "Go with the nice lady."

As Amy pushed herself up from the floor, David was once again struck with the sense of her. Their little girl. People tell you to savor every moment, they grow so fast, pay careful attention. Solid advice, and he wasn't one to argue the point. But to see your daughter with your own eyes, feel your throat bulge with a mixture of hope and dread and consuming love. It could hit at any moment, even when your little girl in her yellow Tweety pajamas follows your wife out of the room.

David put the dolls in the pink toy chest that sat beneath the playroom's window. Cleaning done, he sneaked upstairs to Amy's bedroom door.

It was ajar. David crouched down beside the door, listening to the familiar sounds of Maureen getting their daughter ready for bed. She fluffed and tucked the blanket according to Amy's directions. The pat-pat-pat of a pillow being fluffed. Then came the magic words:

"Who shall we read from tonight? Narnia? Harry Potter, maybe?"

"No," piped Amy. "No. Tell me a story, Mommy."

"Oh?" Maureen's amusement came through in her tone. "What story should I tell you?"

"You know," Amy said and David could picture the sly smile on her face. "Tell me a Sleepy story."

"All right."

David took the slight noise he heard to be his wife settling down next to their daughter on the bed.

He'd never told Maureen about his spying. The first time he heard his wife telling the stories, he'd thought she was reading from a book. Going into Amy's room and finding nothing that came close to the colorful creatures that populated the land she spoke of, David came to a surprising conclusion. She had made it up. This woman, who taught advanced mathematics, who read only nonfiction, someone who treated their child's affection for fantasy with tolerance, was creating a world filled with magical cats.

Cats with soft golden fur, large almond-shaped eyes, and tails that curved into question marks pranced through the Land of Dreams. They visited Earth to usher children into dreamland. Two to each boy or girl in the world: one to help the good dreams in, one to keep the bad dreams out.

"Remember their dos and don'ts?" Maureen asked, a little of the schoolteacher leaking into her voice.

Amy nearly shrieked, "Yes!"

"Recite, please."

And Amy did:

"Do like ice cream. Don't like spinach. Do like nice boys. Don't like bad boys."

"And?"

"Do like nice girls. Don't like bad girls. Do like sunny days. Don't like rainy days. Do like sand. Don't like mud."

So he listened and thought it wonderful that Maureen had kept her secret from him, this wild streak of imagination that she shared in pieces only with their daughter. It could only strengthen their bond. If dad was left out? Well, this dad was willing to take the hit to his ego.

He closed his eyes and drifted along with the flow of the tale.

When David came to get Amy from school the next day, the teacher said she'd been in a fight.

"Nothing serious. Nothing to get worked up about at all. Just a squabble between two girls," Mrs. Karn explained. She was a plump woman, somewhere in her fifties, with a nest of dense gray hair and black-framed glasses. "They wanted the same toy, you see. Janny pulled Amy's hair on the playground. Amy pushed her. They made up before the class was done. I just thought you should know."

"Thanks, Mrs. Karn. We'll talk to her about it tonight."

"Yes, that will be good," the teacher said, clearly

sounding doubtful, maybe wondering if she should have spoken in the first place.

David looked past her, beyond the doorway of the office and to the school's front steps where he glimpsed Amy waiting for him. Perhaps it was the way Amy was sitting—it looked as though she was holding something on her knees.

"Usually your wife gets Amy. Is anything wrong?"

"No. No. She has to sub all week for a later class at the college, and my agency is a lot closer."

"I see," Mrs. Karn replied.

"Thanks," David said and got out of the small chair, happy to do so because he felt himself cramped, somehow reduced. That was the effect of the classroom, of course. The chairs and tables were smaller for the kids.

He went to fetch his daughter and found her holding a schoolbook. Certainly nothing she would have been stroking with care.

On the way to the car he asked Amy if she had a nice day.

"Yes."

"Oh? Did anything happen? Anything you want to tell me about?" He opened the back door and escorted her into the child safety seat.

"No," Amy said, not meeting his eyes.

"You sure?"

This time she only nodded.

David didn't press the issue and had actually forgotten the incident by the time Amy's bedtime came.

He was busy drafting notes for the next day. The PowerBook sat open on the kitchen table before him while Maureen played with Amy in the next room. He was writing some key strategic points for a video that went out to divisional sales reps for a large electronics chain.

He rubbed a cramp in his wrist when he heard Maureen tell Amy it was bedtime. He followed their voices into the downstairs bathroom. Amy stood on the plastic purple chair so her head nearly cleared the sink. Maureen stood to the side.

"Hey, guys."

Amy turned, mouth dribbling foam, brush held daintily in her hand. She grinned at David through the froth.

"Don't stop brushing," Maureen admonished. "How's it going, David?"

"Okay," he said. "There's only so many ways you can say sell more or you're out of the picture."

"Nice," Amy said.

David nodded as he reached for a towel and began to pat Amy's face, clearing her of toothpaste and its cloying scent.

"How good for her teeth can that stuff be when it smells so sweet?"

"It's fine."

"It tastes good, Daddy."

"I'm sure." He laid the towel on the sink's basin. "Give me a good night kiss, sweetie."

On his cheek, soft, quick, but not the perfunctory kind older wiser parents assured would come. He had buried his own parents in his early 20s: Dad from stroke and Mom by cancer.

"G'night," he said, waved a hand, suddenly felt silly for bringing more importance to the moment than it warranted. He started away, back to the PowerBook and its dull words.

"Mommy, can we have a story now?"

David stopped and waited for the answer.

"Yes, of course. Finish up here and we'll see what happens next to our furry friends."

David returned to the kitchen table. He cracked his knuckles, tipped back on the brown cane chair, made a few experimental stabs at the keys, and frowned at the monitor as though it were to blame for his block.

He leaned forward. The chair's front legs returned to kitchen tile; he stood, turning his back on the table. He eyed the garbage can, saw it was near its limit. Not altogether full, but close enough for an excuse to get some air, walk off the walls building inside his head. He tied the trash bag closed and pulled it from the can.

David toed the sliding door open and stepped out onto the back porch. Leaning over the wooden railing, he dropped the bag in one of the three bins that were aligned with the porch. Stepping away, David looked toward his daughter's lit window and caught more than he bargained for.

It was a clear evening, just a hint of January in the air. A fat moon hung in the black sky. Against it, at the top of the Strather house was something moving independently of night's backdrop. Pacing, really, for that was what David took its back and forth movements to be. As quick as he spotted it, the thing darted off the roof and scampered away, meshing completely with the shadows at the side of the house.

No doubt just a squirrel out late. Part of his mind was adamant that the animal had been bigger than the ones who made their residence in the branches of the front yard's tree. If it was a cat? Could that fact even be considered a coincidence? He shook his head at his own foolishness, returned to the house not even caring what had seemed to stand sharp and straight as a weathervane at the roof's tip. Was it a cat? What was the big deal? Where was the harm.

"She can't bring pets to school."

This meeting wasn't going well. Around David's neck his tie felt too tight, a knot at his throat that he wanted to wrench away. His cell phone had beeped in the middle of a discussion on the finer points of turning his script into an *essential selling tool*. Mark Grost, his supe, kept hitting the manuscript with an open palm, giving David the impression he wasn't exactly wowed by his work. The call had been a nuisance and a relief. He excused himself and took the call in the next room.

"I'm sorry?"

"Well," said the teacher. "It should not be a surprise that children *cannot* bring their pets to school. Last year I had a child sneak his turtle into class. One girl got deathly ill from touching the thing's shell. Allergies, you know," she said sagely.

"Mrs. Karn, I'm afraid I'm not following this conversation. Amy brought an animal to class?" David turned his head away from the glass-walled office he'd excused himself from a minute ago. Frankly, he didn't want to meet his supe's stare: the gaze drilling holes into the back of his neck was enough.

"Yes, and I hope you won't mind my suggesting you declaw him . . . or is it her? Jannie got quite a scare when the cat tried to scratch her."

"We don't have cats," David blurted.

"Oh," Mrs. Karn said softly. There was a second of silence before her voice sounded again in the mouthpiece. "Perhaps it was a stray then . . . or lost. It had a collar."

He had to convince the teacher there was no cat, there couldn't be any cat. He tried to push words at her, but they refused to come. There was a brushing around his legs. Something soft.

"Mr. Strather?"

"Yes?"

"Did you hear me, Mr. Strather?"

"We don't have any pets." David forced his eyes down to the beige-carpeted floor.

"Well," Mrs. Karn began, and there was a definite

tone of humor now. "You may have one by the end of the day."

"I'm sorry, Mrs. Karn. I'm in the middle of a meeting and I need to go."

"Of course. I did try to call Mrs. Strather, you know. She wasn't in."

"I understand. All right. Sorry. Gotta go." He thumbed END and slipped the cell into its waist holder. He opened the door and returned to Mark's den.

"I apologize for that."

"No need," Mark said, though his eyes told a different story.

The rest of the day passed in a blur. Revisions went fast. Grost was happy with the final product and the outline. After a few rounds going through server traffic, it was e-mailed to the client. David returned to his desk to entertain the thought of calling back Amy's teacher. He nixed it, opting to call Maureen. He was startled when she picked up on the fourth ring.

"They actually decided to give you a break?"

She laughed. "To what do I owe this pleasant surprise?"

"Like I never call you? Hey, how about going to dinner tonight? Maybe the new Japanese place that just opened?"

"What? We don't—"

"I won't listen to excuses and I will not take no, got it?"

"And Amy?"

"Your mother can watch her."

"Who is this and what have you done with my husband?"

"Come on."

"Okay. Okay. I'm not saying no or anything close. Let me call Mom and see if she can do it. It's short notice, so don't be too disappointed."

"I'll call. I insist," he said, struck with inspiration. Before Maureen could speak again, he jumped in: "I'll give you a ring in five minutes. If I don't get you, I'll leave a message."

"Sure," she said.

"Great."

He hung up briefly, then snatched back the receiver and punched more numbers. He got his mother-in-law on the line.

"Hey."

"Hey, yourself," Kristen Marling said.

"I have a favor to ask."

"So ask."

"Can you mind the young one tonight? We want to grab some dinner, maybe a movie."

"Let me check my social calendar," Kristen said, a laugh behind her words. He pictured her. Kristen was an older, shorter version of Maureen. "Nope, I'm open," she returned.

"This isn't Bingo Night, then?"

"Don't push your luck, David."

"Fine. Let's say seven?"

"Sure, sure. No need to shlepp my granddaughter. I'll come to your house."

"Even better. Let me ask you something else."

"Yes?"

"You used to tell Maureen bedtime stories?"

"What?"

"Fairy tales about cats," David suddenly felt foolish and anxious simultaneously. "They help children get to sleep. Does any of this sound familiar?"

"Oh, wow. You could knock me over with a feather. The Sleepies, huh?"

"Yes." It was close to a shout. "That's right. This may sound odd, but where did you get the idea for them?"

"What do you mean?"

"Well, did they come from a . . . a book? Did you

make it up yourself?" Could she hear the desperate note he was hitting? Should he mask it with a chuckle? He did so. "Maureen's telling Amy those tales now," he said. "They're really wild."

"They can be," Kristen said. "To be honest, I have no idea. They're just stories, David. Family stories. My mom told them to me, and her mom told her, and so on and so forth. Do you mind me asking why the interest?"

"Not at all," David said, picking up a BIC pen and turning it over in his fingers. "Just curious. I mean, Maureen's never been one for that sort of thing, and all of a sudden she's making up rules for Dreamland. It struck me funny, is all."

Kristen said, "Been around as long as I can remember, our family guardian angels. One time I thought one of my great-aunts tried to write them down, but nothing came of it. I don't know why. She was supposed to be a writer, that one. Would have made a great book, if she had. Would have been something. You know, my mother used to claim she could see them. Went through this whole act about the Sleepies being our family secret. How they protect us from harm, stick around to see us not just into sleep but all the time. Isn't that funny?"

"Hysterical," David said.

Maureen got Amy from school, so that left David a clean exit from work. His wife had sounded thrilled with the prospect of their "date" when he told her it was a go. He was even excited with the possibility of some quiet time with Maureen. He'd already shuffled much of the conversation with his mother-in-law to the back of his head and was busy forgetting the rest when he left the office and took the elevator down to the garage.

It all came back when he saw the marks on the driver's side door.

They looked exactly like scratches, deep grooves in the Chevy's paintwork that started below the door handle then hooked down.

He bent to give them a closer look, traced the clawed path, and gritted his teeth.

Standing, David scouted the rows of parked cars as though a clue might be hiding there. He turned back to the marks that looked nothing like a sideswipe from another vehicle or even a deliberate scarring by somebody's key or knife.

Scratches.

He pulled in and saw the cats.

One standing on either side of the driveway, stiff sentries with eyes shining in the dark. As quick as he spotted them, quicker was their exit. Leaping onto the car's hood with perfect grace, they bounded forward—for a moment he thought it possible they could break through the windshield. They jumped the roof instead and landed on the back with an audible thump that gave David just a flash of orange-yellow in the rearview before they disappeared from sight.

David took his hands off the wheel, put the car in park and turned off the engine. It took a little bit before he had it together enough to get out of the car. He walked around to the house on legs that felt stiff and unsure. Getting inside didn't help much.

The house was quiet. Amy should have rushed to greet him, Maureen close behind with a smile and kiss. He shoved his jacket off, threw it on the couch.

"Maureen?"

There should have been an answer. His wife should have called down to tell him they were upstairs. They were in Amy's room playing and everything was okay, the way they should be.

He walked to the stairs and peered.

"Amy?"

He put a hand on the railing and started up.

A cat sat on the top landing. Fine orange-yellow fur, large odd eyes, and a luxurious tail wrapped around its frame. Nothing in the creature's posture said it was in the slightest disturbed by David's presence. As he crept closer, the cat started to clean itself, starting on the wide pad of one paw.

David got to the top landing.

The cat purred loudly.

David stepped gingerly over the animal, fully expecting its claws to rip his leg clean through to the bone.

Stepping away, he turned once to see what the feline was doing. The cat extended its body, flexing itself to the limit, allowing its claws to flash once. David saw that the nails were patterned with strange terrible red spirals.

"Maureen?"

Nothing.

"Amy?"

The only response came from the cat, its purr getting louder as it paced toward him. It moved slowly, with alarming casualness.

What could he say? Nice kitty. Please don't kill me.

David said, "I'm Amy's dad. I would never want to hurt her. I love her. I love her very much, so if you think that I would want to hurt her, you're wrong. I would never. Never."

The animal stopped a foot away. It sat back and regarded him with bright eyes that were larger, wider than a cat's eyes had any right to be.

David backed along the landing.

It tracked David but didn't spring on him. He edged into his daughter's bedroom and found Amy sitting in the middle of her bed, thin blue-jeaned legs dangling over the edge, her bare toes just inches from the floor. She had her arms crossed over the white sweater Maureen had knitted for her last Christmas; her head was down, chin nearly resting on the breastbone.

Maureen sat beside her, also with her head fallen forward, still dressed in one of her smart teacher outfits.

"Maureen? Amy? Why didn't you answer me?" The cat followed him into the room.

Purring its soft hypnotic rhythm, the sound winding around father, daughter, and mother.

"Look at me, please," David said and stepped toward his daughter.

Amy's head sprang up, as though she was roughly awakened from a dream. Her eyes opened, and with one trembling finger she pointed to her window.

David crossed the room and opened the curtain.

"Look," Amy said in a trembling voice that sounded strangely adult.

The front lawn was covered in the odd cats. There had to be more than a dozen there, sitting, rolling, watching. All of them watching his daughter's window with hungry interest.

All purring.

"Two to each boy and girl in the world," Amy said.

A slam turned David's attention back to the room—to the cat, which had presumably risen on its two backpaws to fling the door closed.

"But there are special boys and special girls," Maureen said, raising her head slowly as though a string attached to the back of her had been pulled. "And those are the children they *especially* care for."

"Oh, my God."

They were all over the room.

The cats.

Climbing into the laps of Maureen and Amy, sitting on the chair by his little girl's desk, somehow clinging to the walls. They stepped along the ceiling with unearthly skill, upside-down eyes striking him with hard stares as they sauntered across in perfect symmetry.

"Amy? Listen to me now. You have to listen to me."

Maureen stroked under the chin of the cat sitting on her legs. It was a bit larger than the one near the door. "The special ones help their story be told," Maureen said in a lifeless tone. "They make their story live."

Amy said, "We need Grandma, Daddy. We need Grandma to help them."

And wasn't there a gleam in Maureen's eye, something that said she had been excited about her mother coming over for all the *wrong* reasons? Not Maureen but whatever was tugging at that invisible string. Whatever helped her spin out the stories.

"You have to go now," his wife told him in that peculiar voice. "You have to go. You won't be hurt. You have to go now."

Because the Sleepies wanted to be real, David thought. Had they been real at one point and over time, as the stories were forgotten, did that weaken them? Could they be going extinct from lack of belief? Had their birth been in tales spun by Maureen's bloodline or were they, as he suspected, far older? A living story fossilized by indifference, now roaring back to reality, resurrected by the dreams of a child and her mother.

"Fairy tales," David said, out loud, in a dry whisper. "None of this is real."

The doorbell rang downstairs.

"Let her in and then you have to go," Maureen said. The cat in her lap raised its head and actually grinned at David, a smile full of sharp teeth.

The cats parted—a living river of orange, yellow and white, their tails waving—so he could walk through to put a shaking hand on the doorknob. He turned it and walked out. Heartbeat thundering in his ears, he moved past the purring shapes gathered on the landing. A large one perched on the newel banister like an ornament, its tail sweeping near the bottom of the wooden post. So many. So insistent.

The doorbell rang again.

His eyes fluttered. The bell's harsh call opened something inside his mind. If it was magic the cats were using against him, then the doorbell's clang had ripped through it. Not enough to jar him into action, but it did halt his progress, one hand on the railing, one foot poised for the next stair.

What must his mother-in-law think? She knew David was always punctual and her daughter was the same. He really *should* let her in. He really ought to. Realization swam in, weak at first but gaining momentum that carried through his thoughts and finally translated into movement.

David began going back upstairs with a slow drugged gait that gained speed as he ascended.

Like coming out of a dream, a long terrible dream that he was able now to see through.

You should open the door and let her in, David.

Not his own. Not this silken voice that droned in his ear, a purring mantra urging him to return, retrace his steps to the front door.

He would not be swayed.

He bolted the remaining stairs, jumping them to the landing and then bulleting up the rest into his daughter's room.

"Amy, Maureen, I want you to wake up now. Wake up this instant!"

Maureen said, "What are their dos and don'ts, daughter?"

"Amy, I don't care what your mother says. I want you to wake up, Amy! Do it now!"

The cats were forming around him, tails whipping at the air; their purrs forming a new sound. A threatening sound. Churning, the howl that came from within their alien hearts and minds reaching into David's head. They had every intention of squeezing his brain into goop. Cats dropped from the ceiling, swooping down on David like bats. He batted them away with his arms and hands.

"Amy, Maureen, wake up!" he shouted.

"Do like good girls," Maureen said dreamily. "What are some more?"

Downstairs the doorbell rang continuously.

"Please help me," David pleaded. He fell to his knees. As the animals circled, his vision blurred; their eyes loomed monstrously huge in their narrow faces. The large cat joined them, leaping from Maureen's lap to the floor. Strutting through the throng. It shoved its tail against his ankles. The appendage was surprisingly strong. It tripped David to the carpet on all fours.

They fell upon him in a rush of fur, teeth, and claws. Amy shrieked, "Daddy!"

His head hit the floor, yowling searching out the tender spots behind his eyes and deep inside his ears.

"I'm sorry, Daddy. I'm so sorry," Amy cried, rushing to him, putting her small hands on his back as the Sleepies continued their assault. He felt the heat of her hands on his cold skin through his shirt.

"End their story," David muttered past the blurring orange-yellow frenzy.

"Daddy, I didn't mean to hurt you. Mommy said that—"

"Never. Mind. Nevermind. Just . . . end their story, Amy." End it as it began, David thought at her. *Once upon a time . . .* Where is the matching bookend to that sentence? Come on, Amy. Come on!

David forced his head to turn some, squinted one eye open, he saw that his wife was kneeling beside his daughter. Maureen's eyes weren't glassy or fixed, thank God. But she wasn't fully "awake" either. It was the large cat not being near Maureen that allowed her to regain some sense.

David seized his chance, hoping whatever gap had

been left by the creatures leaving their hosts could be torn wide.

"End it," David whispered. There wouldn't be many more chances if Amy didn't. Not the way his head felt. Not the way pain speared through his skull. "Go ahead. Go . . . ahead."

"Can Mommy help?"

"I don't . . . know, Amy. Ask . . . her."

"Mommy?"

The cats jumped him, sending him back down to the floor with a harsh thump, claws raking at his back, in his hair, his legs. Their discontent thundered in his mind. His sense quailed, shrank. He closed his eyes.

"Let's wish them a happily ever after," Maureen said, voice showing her fear. Her tone proved to David the hold of the cats was slipping. He rallied, calling his remaining strength to support his wife and daughter for the final assault.

"Ready?" Maureen asked Amy.

He forced his arms over his head to protect his vulnerable neck from raking claws. *Come on, Amy, Maureen. Come on!*

"On three."

"One . . ."

Furious banging sounded downstairs. Hell hath no fury like a mother-in-law scorned . . . or ignored, he guessed in the small region of his brain still beyond the cats' fevered howling.

"Two . . ."

Maureen batted at the cats, trying to get them away from David. None of her blows were effectual. They swarmed over him, biting now. He couldn't help crying out as one locked onto the webbing of his left hand.

"Three!"

Could he hear Kristen yelling? Screaming in a voice that reminded him of those police dramas where the detectives kick down doors?

"They lived," Maureen and Amy said in perfect unison, "happily ever after."

And again; louder.

"Happily ever after."

The noise in his head lessened, hummed now. The howling changed to a whine of dissatisfaction. It hurt to move. David tried anyway, and forced his eyes open.

The effect of Maureen's and Amy's sentence was immediate. David thought again of magic. He embraced the word as he watched the Sleepics lose definition. Merging into one another, becoming a blanket of orange-yellow and white that faded, faded to the same cream of the carpet.

How long did the three of them sit there staring as the cats dissolved into shadows, transfixed by the changes as their power dissipated. Finally, nothing but themselves and their memories were left.

They waited until the only sounds in the house were the panicked chiming of the doorbell and the flurry of fists on the door.

Exhausted, bleeding from countless scratches and a dozen bites, David reached out for his wife and child. Gathering them into his arms was its own form of magic. He was reluctant to let go, even if that was inevitable.

At last, he looked down at his daughter, touching her cheek. "Amy, I think you can let your grandma in now."

BARGAINS

Richard Lee Byers

Richard Lee Byers holds a B.A. and M.A. in Psychology. He worked in an emergency psychiatric facility for over a decade, then left the mental health field to become a writer. He is the author of over twenty fantasy and horror novels, including, most recently, *Dissolution, The Black Bouquet,* and The Dead God Trilogy (*Forsaken, Forsworn,* and *Forbidden.*) His short fiction has appeared in numerous magazines and anthologies. A resident of the Tampa Bay area, the setting for a good deal of his contemporary fiction, he spends much of his free time with fencing foil, epee, and saber.

T he word went round, and those cats who were able yowled for Waspwatcher through the night, while the humans cursed them for spoiling their sleep. But no one professed to know his whereabouts, because none of the local felines knew him by that name.

Nor did he proclaim himself. In his time, he'd prowled down many paths, lived with a human child until a fever killed her, taken to the streets and alleyways thereafter, fought in the wars against the scuttling Whisperers few Big Folk ever glimpsed, and tried to counsel a queen. Now he was a barn cat, beholden to no one, living on the mice he caught. It was a decent sort of existence so long as you took care the horses didn't kick you, and he was content.

As it turned out, his reticence availed him nothing. Bronze appeared with the morning, pacing through the rectangle of yellow sunlight that fell through the open door, pausing for an instant to drink in the smells of hay, equine droppings, and, Waspwatcher supposed, himself. He wished it were someone else. He couldn't deny his identity to a friend, nor find it in himself to chase her away either. He descended the steps that connected the loft with the floor, and then he and she circled, looking one another over.

"How did you find me?" he asked.

"I'm clever," Bronze replied. "Why didn't you answer the call?"

"I figured whoever had come was here as her messenger."

Bronze snorted. "Still angry, and so proud. She's the queen, Waspwatcher. It was your place to advise, but hers to decide."

"And my right to leave if I wanted. We're cats, not Bigs."

"She knows that, just as she knows she can't order you back. But she needs you."

"With twenties of others eager to be her knights?"

"Not so many anymore."

He cocked his head. "Is she in disgrace? Are they going to depose her? It would serve her right."

"I've heard talk. It's unfair. She's been a good queen overall. The bargain benefited everyone, yourself included."

Bronze was right, but, disgruntled, the black tom with his notched ear was averse to admitting it. "Then everyone should be happy."

"Well, they're not, because it turns out you were right to worry. Perhaps we shouldn't have traded. The witch is misusing what we gave him."

"Sharing? I wouldn't be surprised. No Big can keep a secret."

Bronze twitched her whiskers in laughter, though the gesture had little genuine humor in it. "This one can. He has the opposite problem. He's decided he doesn't want to share the Greatest City with us. He's killed many, and driven out more. Those few who remain do so because they can't *get* out, I imagine."

"How can he threaten so many?"

"We aren't sure, except he's made a pact with the dogs, or bound them to his will."

Waspwatcher bared his fangs in a sneer. "Why not, they're eager enough to be bound. But why does the witch even care about chasing us away?"

"We thought he'd use what we bartered to obtain a bigger house and more servants. The things other humans want. Maybe he did, but he's also hunting his own kind. It's ugly, and perhaps he feared we'd stop it."

"I can tell you want to. A royal herald should be wiser. Killing each other is just something Big Folk do."

"This is different. Strange enough that other humans have taken special notice and grown afraid, and the Queen wonders if he's just getting started. How much harm will he cause before he's done?"

"Good questions, which I can't answer."

"The answer is for someone to track him down and stop him."

"Good luck to 'someone,' whoever he may be."

Bronze spat. "Don't play stupid! You know what the Queen asks, and you know why. Who accomplished more against the Whisperers?"

"I'm older and slower now. Another will fare better."

"I doubt it, and I hoped you'd want to go. Once, when we were on an errand together, you told me you fought on behalf of humans and felines both, and we're all in trouble now. Besides, this plea means everyone at court, even the queen herself, admits you were right. Doesn't that smooth your ruffled fur?"

"What it doesn't do is explain how I'm to prevail when Her Beauty has already given my every advantage away. I'll bet I'm not the first knight she's asked. Her own pride would have prevented her seeking me at the start, and the others just didn't come back, did they?"

"No," said Bronze, "and I don't know how to win. I just hoped we'd find a way together, as in the old days. But I'll go alone if I must."

"That's a witless thing to say." Certainly if the messenger hoped to manipulate Waspwatcher thereby, for though cats knew every sensible emotion, they were essentially free of guilt.

Bronze bristled. "Witless? I have plenty of tricks. I'll think of something." She wheeled and stalked away.

To his surprise, the abrupt departure pulled at Waspwatcher as if his little human girl had come back to life, dangled a length of string for him to catch in his claws, and now was tugging on the other end. He wondered if he'd been lonely, and never realized.

But he didn't wonder long. He wasn't inclined to examine his own feelings. That was more Bronze's way, to the extent it was any feline's. Waspwatcher was what he was, and acted as he chose, which at this moment, was to bound through the door and catch up with his old comrade a few yards farther on. Bronze gave him an arch glance.

"Don't say anything," Waspwatcher growled.

"Certainly not."

Traveling, they crossed a land girt with railroads, the steam locomotives smelling of smoke and hot metal, roaring, clattering, and screaming across the low green hills and through the little towns. No living cat could remember a time when Bigs hadn't built such things, but their stories did. Waspwatcher thought it must have been more pleasant. Humans, deaf as they were, had no conception how painfully loud their machines could be.

The two cats killed, scavenged, or stole their food, and rested as needed. When Waspwatcher slept, the dreams were sweet and vivid, for that was what the witch had bartered, delicious phantasmata for every feline on the island. It had proved an irresistible enticement for a species that spent more time in slumber than awake, or at any rate, the queen had proved unable to resist, and upon opening his eyes and realizing how his own dreams had delighted him, her onetime champion felt refreshed and vexed simultaneously.

It wasn't long after sighting the Greatest City, a jumble of towers shrouded in dirty air, that he and Bronze came upon the first festering body. The smell of furious dog still clung to it, although the cats didn't need scent help to tell what had killed their brother. They recognized the tooth marks, and the manner in which the calico's slayer had mauled and tossed him.

Waspwatcher turned to his companion. "We're still a long way out," he said. "Either the dogs are spread thin, or the witch has a lot of them."

Bronze said, "I think he has a lot."

Waspwatcher bared his fangs in annoyance and, if he was honest, a touch of fear. "We'll have to walk softly, then."

"Let me try something." She murmured one of the charms messengers and storytellers learned. "That may help us hide."

"I'll still go warily, if it's all the same to you."

They spotted a canine an hour later, as they were skulking through shadow in a thicket. It was a terrier, its red leather collar indicating it had a home with humans, but its dirty, matted fur suggesting it hadn't been there for a while. The felines could tell from its smell it wasn't rabid, though it moved as if it were. They hunkered down, and the dog passed by.

Bronze stretched, preening with satisfaction at the efficacy of her magic. Waspwatcher wasn't as impressed. They'd been downwind of their foe, and the real test would come when it was the other way around. For as every kitten learned at its mother's teat, cat nose sharp, but dog nose sharper.

"I don't think the witch made a pact with them," the black tom said. "That terrier looked like someone had claws hooked inside its head. I know it's only a dog, but that's . . . wrong."

"I told you," Bronze replied. "I do wonder if the human witch was always sick on the inside. He didn't seem to be when he came to see Her Beauty."

"No," Waspwatcher admitted, "not even to me. I just opposed the trade—I would have been against making that bargain with any Big."

"Then you don't think the Queen and I were completely foolish."

Waspwatcher snorted. "Let's keep moving."

Soon after, they found a weed-choked culvert that didn't smell of dog. They laid up for the rest of the afternoon, prowling on when darkness fell. A wheel-rutted road led them into another group of houses, where they sniffed out odors of cooking and garbage to find their supper.

Then a four-legged shape stalked stiffly from the alley ahead. Waspwatcher bared his fangs. He'd imagined the area might be safe, for wouldn't the Bigs take alarm at a dog acting strangely and kill or drive it out? The answer was evidently no. Perhaps in their blindness, they hadn't noticed.

The cats slipped under a wheelbarrow and crouched motionless in the shadow beneath. A breeze sprang up, whispering in precisely the wrong direction. Maybe it wouldn't matter. Maybe Bronze's charm would hold. Or perhaps the witch's power had dulled the dog's senses.

No. The canine, a towering mutt that looked as if it had some mastiff in it, abruptly lurched around, following its nose. It loped forward, eyes and teeth shining in the gloom.

The cats wheeled to run. Another dog, a spaniel, was slinking up behind them. They tried to dart around it, but it cut them off.

Waspwatcher whirled back around to confront the mongrel. He arched, bristled, glared, and hissed. Unfazed, the mutt drove in.

It was several times larger than its intended prey, and plainly eager to kill. The tom knew he'd have to strike hard and at the proper moment to survive. It was difficult not to lash out too soon, but he made himself wait as the mutt hurtled at him. Its jaws opened to bite, and now it was time. He pounced and clawed. At his back, a man's voice shouted, "No! Bad dog! Bad dog!" Likely it was a trick Bronze had conjured to confuse her opponent.

Waspwatcher's talons missed the mutt's eyes, but slashed the soft wet nose and furry muzzle. It balked, which gave him the chance to renew the attack. This time, he did scratch an eye. The dog ran away whimpering.

Waspwatcher whirled. Bronze was bleeding at the shoulder, where the spaniel had bit before she tore herself free. Despite the distraction of the disembodied voice, the dog still pressed her hard. The tom rushed in on the canine's flank. Together, he and the herald gashed the slavering beast and put it to flight.

"Are you all right?" Waspwatcher asked.

"So far," Bronze said, an edge of pain in her voice, "but look!"

More dogs loped from the darkness. The travelers had attracted an entire pack of the possessed animals.

Waspwatcher knew they had no hope of fighting so many. They'd been lucky to fend off the first two.

At least they weren't boxed in anymore. "Run!" he said, and they did, sprinting all out to stay ahead of the hunters with their longer legs.

The chase made a commotion. Waspwatcher heard the Bigs in their houses stirring. Unfortunately, they all seemed sluggish and dull-witted. Even if one eventually moved to intervene, it would likely be too late. The tom looked for a refuge cramped enough that a dog could do no more than poke its nose inside. Or a means of getting off the ground.

It was the latter he discovered, a crooked runt of an oak standing beside a cottage. "Come on!" he called. He sprang up into the lower branches and onward, then glanced back. Bronze had never been as able or fearless a climber as he. Still, she scrambled high enough quickly enough to keep herself out of the jaws of the dogs jumping after her.

"Keep coming!" Waspwatcher called, fearful she'd freeze where she was. For a moment, it looked as if she had. Then a maddened dog charged the tree and did its scrabbling utmost to run up the trunk. It got as high as a man's head before falling down. The assault jarred the messenger into motion.

Waspwatcher led her onto the sloping cottage roof. "So much for you fixing it so they wouldn't notice us," he said. He'd rather have her annoyed with him than thinking about her mistrust of heights.

She spat. "The charm worked for a while! My shoulder hurts!"

He looked at the bloody punctures, more in loose skin, fortunately, than the muscle underneath. "Is it bad?"

"I guess not. But what do we do now?"

"Run away over the rooftops until we shake the dogs off our track."

She stared at him. "I don't know if I can."

"Unless you know a better trick, I think it's the only way. I've seen you do that kind of thing before."

"I'm older, too. Perhaps my legs aren't strong enough anymore. I'll falter if I try."

"Don't be stupid. You don't seem any older to me. Besides, I only agreed to this foolishness because of you, so you can't quit on me." He bumped her head with his own.

"All right," she said. "Let's go, fast, before I lose my nerve."

He studied the roofscape, picking out an escape route. Generally speaking, the houses didn't stand too far apart. Variations in height posed more of a problem, but he and Bronze would simply have to cope. He backed away from the brink for a running start, then charged forward.

A few jumps, he made only by a whisker. He feared Bronze wouldn't do as well. She did, though. Perhaps she knew a charm to bear her up. At odd moments, he knew a wild exhilaration that reminded him why he'd taken to the streets and subsequently become Her Beauty's knight in the first place.

Alas, excitement was his only reward. The dogs kept pace with their prey. If anything, the chase attracted more of them. Waspwatcher had no idea what to do next. Then a whistle blew, and brakes ground. A train was coming, and, by the sound of it, stopping.

"This way!" He and Bronze raced straight for the gas-lit platform at the edge of town, dogs in their wake.

Waspwatcher couldn't see a way to descend to the ground by degrees. He and Bronze simply flung themselves off the edge of a roof two stories up. Their feline craft cushioned the fall, though the impact jarred his joints.

The cats ran on, now nearly in reach of the pack coursing just behind them. They darted beneath the train. The maneuver gained them a moment, since their larger pursuers couldn't scramble under as easily. Waspwatcher found a place where brick had crumbled, providing an ascent a feline could use to swarm onto the platform.

Bigs milled about, boarding and exiting the train, carrying valises or pushing loads of them on carts. Waspwatcher pivoted toward the open door into one of the cars. Then hesitated. He'd never ridden in such a conveyance. He'd known cats who claimed they had, but it was difficult to believe anyone could survive being trapped inside a bizarre contraption hurtling at such speeds.

"It's just like your barn," said Bronze, "only with wheels. Keep going!"

They bounded inside. As far as they could tell, no Big noticed. The humans could scarcely miss the abundance of maddened dogs rushing onto the platform, however. Cursing, they broke the momentum of the pursuit with kicks and swinging canes. One of the men in the matching coats and caps slammed the door, making sure no hound darted into the car. The bang gave Waspwatcher a twinge of fear. Still, he climbed up on the seat beside Bronze, reared up on his hind legs to look out the window, and laughed at the canines' frustration.

"This was a good idea," said Bronze. "Can you stand it for a while?"

"What are you asking?"

"The train's pointed south. If we ride it to the Greatest City, we'll avoid a lot of dogs."

Waspwatcher reminded himself that knights didn't cringe. "I can bear it if you can."

At first, it *was* terrifying, the noise, vibration, and rocking, the accelerations and decelerations that always caught the cats by surprise. Still, riding inside didn't make them feel as if they were streaking along at such an insane speed, and gradually they relaxed, until their chief concern was simply remaining unseen.

Hiding became more difficult as, over the course of a number of stops, the car grew increasingly crowded, but they found refuge in a floor-level niche with sharp-smelling rags and bottles stored inside.

It kept them safe until the train rolled to a stop, and, chattering and jostling one another, nearly all the Bigs got off. The cats followed. A man in a cap did spot them then, and grunted in surprise, but they slipped out before he had the chance to take exception to their riding where, he might think, they didn't belong.

Beyond the door, they found themselves in a space larger than several barns, where the walls climbed up and up to a glass ceiling. A number of trains stood sighing and grumbling. Despite their proximity and countless hurrying human feet, Waspwatcher felt a flicker of pleasure, because while he'd never ventured onto the platforms before, he knew this station from scavenging years before. For a moment, he felt he'd come home.

This nostalgic feeling didn't last. A cat couldn't spend time in the teeming streets without noticing the absence of his fellows, and the mood of the Bigs as well. Waspwatcher had seen them upset before, when sickness gripped the town, or they heard word of some defeat in one of their own faraway wars. This was different, shakier and shriller.

"It's as if they feel helpless," Bronze observed. "They're just afraid to admit it."

Waspwatcher twitched his whiskers. "Well, thanks to us, they *are* helpless. It only remains to be seen whether we are, too. Where does the witch lair?"

"We don't know. He left his old quarters before the trouble started."

"Then all we can do is hunt him where he hunts others."

The cats set out for the proper district, Waspwatcher still grappling with the odd feeling that this was the same city he'd abandoned, but different. As always, it bustled, and he had to watch out for wagons and carriages rolling everywhere. Yet now men were digging up the streets, impeding traffic and making things more dangerous than ever. He asked why, but Bronze didn't know.

"Murder!" a boy cried, brandishing a newspaper. "Murder number six!"

Both cats comprehended something of human speech, even when they didn't grasp its full, often irrational, implications. They looked at each other, then, seized by a common urgency, broke into a run, defying wagons and lurking dogs to do their worst.

Rushing recklessly, they finally reached the right district, one of the dirtiest and most crowded parts of the city. Some wearing helmets and carrying nightsticks, others not, the Bigs who dealt with such things still picked around the body. A uniformed "copper" held a pair of bloodhounds on leashes. Manifestly in the witch's sway like all other dogs, the canines started to stalk toward the felines, but their keeper yanked them back. Resisting an impulse to taunt the wretched beasts, slaves twice over, Waspwatcher scrambled up a heap of trash and onto the top of a fence. Bronze followed.

They had a good view. Suddenly the tom no longer felt playful in the least. It wasn't the careful cutting, precisely, nor that he could tell the witch had let the woman run away a few times, making her think she might escape before catching her once more. Waspwatcher had done that, many cats had, but with prey. A Big had no business doing it, certainly not to a female of his own species with whom, if the smell could be trusted, he'd mated first.

"You see," Bronze growled, "it's unnatural."

"I warned you," Waspwatcher replied, although he

hadn't, for who could have anticipated this? "We'll wait until the humans clear out, then try to pick up the trail."

A cart came after a while. Some of the men wrapped the bloody corpse in a sheet and shoved it in the back. The wagon departed, followed by that particular group of Bigs. Others kept coming to gawk and exclaim at the site. After a time, the cats realized they'd just have to put up with it.

The travelers jumped down and prowled over the ground, much as the police had done before them. Waspwatcher caught another odor, one he'd never smelled before, a musky, unnatural combination of feline and human swiped against a wall. "He marked the site," he said.

"If he left a string of them—"

"We can follow. I doubt he was so careless, but we'll try."

"Damn filthy cats!" a human shouted. "They want the blood!" A stone flew over Waspwatcher's head. He and Bronze fled before other missiles followed. He reckoned they'd learned all the site had to teach them anyway.

As he'd half expected, it wasn't enough. The murderer had left scent signs here and there throughout the slum, at street level and on rooftops, but never in a way that allowed his hunters to track him. In the weeks that followed, the cats prowled by night, watching and listening, and the witch killed three more women. Waspwatcher felt blind and deaf as a human. The Bigs grew more frazzled and frantic, and sometimes mobs pursued some hapless soul through the streets. The whole city felt as if, any second, everyone might start screeching and scratching at once.

"Can't you find the witch with a charm?" the tom asked, as once again, darkness gathered the city in its claws.

It wasn't the first time he'd posed the question, and

Bronze twitched her tail in annoyance. Still, she deigned to give her usual answer. "How? He knows all our tricks and how to counter them, for that was what we traded him. He has his own human arts, too."

"As I pointed out back in my nice warm, cozy barn."

Frustration made her as quarrelsome as Waspwatcher himself was feeling. Glaring, she drew herself up for either a harsh retort or a paw swipe. Then, however, she faltered, and her yellow eyes narrowed.

"What?" he asked.

"He knows the secrets of the Two Peoples, and accordingly, no cat nor Big can find him. But does he know the secrets of the Whisperers?"

"I don't know. Does it matter?"

"It might, if they agree to help us."

Waspwatcher stared at her. "That's mad."

"Maybe not. We can ask."

"Meanwhile hoping they've decided to love cats in general, and have forgotten the two of us, who killed so many of them?"

"Who knows how they think? In any case, I'm the Queen's messenger, so it's my place to talk to them. You don't have to come, and perhaps you shouldn't. That way, whatever happens to me—"

He spat. "If you go, so do I. We do have to try something, no matter how idiotic."

The cats knew a good many things the average human would have difficulty believing. One was the existence of places in the Greatest City where even the ubiquitous rats wouldn't go, and when Bronze and Waspwatcher entered a crooked lane unblemished by the rodents' droppings and gnawed holes, the tom knew they were getting close.

He glimpsed the first Whisperer only moments later. It was hiding inside the remains of a broken crate, but he could still make out the glistening, almost jellylike flesh and portions of the pulsing organs that should be on the inside, yet stuck through the skin nonetheless. Roughly the size of a cat itself, the sentry, realizing Waspwatcher had spotted it, bolted in its lopsided way, yammering almost inaudibly.

The mutter had more complexity to it than a dog's bark or a stoat's squeal. Like Bigs and felines, Whisperers truly spoke, and on a perverse whim, Waspwatcher had once argued it qualified them as a People. Wiser cats, however, had long maintained that the extraordinary differences between one Whisperer and the next, and the lack of symmetry displayed in each individual, disqualified them, which perhaps was just a fancy way of saying the creatures were too disgusting for such a classification.

Waspwatcher and Bronze charged after the Whisperer. They needed to trap the imp and explain they wanted a parley before it roused a horde of its fellows to attack.

The Whisperer disappeared around the corner of a tenement. Waspwatcher found the strength to sprint faster, made the turn, raced within reach of his quarry, and sprang. With a breathless little sigh of a shriek, the creature collapsed beneath his weight.

The soft, slimy feel and rotten smell of the wriggling thing made Waspwatcher yearn to shred it. He struggled to hold it immobile instead. Then metal groaned, and he looked up.

Two more Whisperers had crept from hiding, carrying a rusty old revolver with them. One held the barrel out of the dirt, supporting and stabilizing the weapon. The other strained to cock the hammer, using the hands that were its species's principal advantage in their struggle with cat-kind. Waspwatcher wondered fleetingly if the imps had recognized him and Bronze. It would explain why they were so quick to expend the hoarded treasure a bullet represented.

He jumped off his captive and rushed the gun. One Whisperer finished dragging the hammer back, then shifted its hands to the trigger. Its partner pivoted the muzzle, aiming. Waspwatcher bounded sideways. The revolver spat flame and roared. The cat felt the projectile streak past his flank. He lunged into a cloud of sulfurous smoke and lashed out savagely. No mercy for these Whisperers. The firearm was too dangerous.

One imp collapsed. The other reeled back with its twisted monkey face in tatters. Unsupported, the revolver fell. Additional Whisperers shambled in the gloom.

Then Waspwatcher's fur stood on end. The instant after, sparks flared and popped on the imps' bodies. The charm didn't generally kill Whisperers. They feared and hated it, though, and the present lot proved no exception. They fled deeper into the shadows.

Waspwatcher looked around. In addition to working the magic, Bronze had taken over the task of holding the prisoner down. "They'll be back soon," she said.

"I know." Now that it was over, Waspwatcher felt shaky from charging the revolver, and hid it as best he could.

Bronze glared down at the captive. "We speak your tongue." Waspwatcher didn't, but he did when his friend shared the gift with him. "So don't pretend you can't understand me. You vermin always do that, and I'm not in the mood." She dug her claws deeper.

"Fine," the Whisperer replied, voice charged with hate despite its faintness, "I'll talk, and I'll say, run away, before my brothers come with many, many guns!"

"We can't do that," she said. "Waspwatcher and I need to talk to your king. Take us in to see him and we'll let you go."

The Whisperer sneered. "No cat sees the king."

"Die, then." Bronze tore at the imp.

"Wait! Wait! If I take you, you let me go as soon as you're in."

"Agreed," Bronze said. That made sense to Waspwatcher, insofar as anything about this idea did. Whisperers were fundamentally vicious, even in relation to one another. If they decided to kill the cats, concern for one hostage wouldn't balk them.

The messenger let the captive up. It led the felines toward a door and cheeped out a password. Nothing happened. It cried a second time. Finally, the latch clicked. The portal swung ajar, revealing the unquiet darkness inside.

Waspwatcher bared his fangs and bristled himself bigger, then he and his companions entered the tenement. He barely had time to glimpse the rope-and-pulley system the Whisperers used to control the door before imps lunged from the shadows ahead. He assumed he and Bronze would have to fight or flee, most likely to no avail. But their guide leaped forward. Shoving and pummeling at the attackers in the lead, it screamed, "No, no! The king decides! The king decides how they die!"

Waspwatcher had heard more reassuring declarations, but to his surprise, it deterred those who wished to assault him and Bronze. Muttering, they crowded toward the walls, clearing a path deeper into their domain.

It was a narrow path, and Waspwatcher's fur perforce brushed the almost liquid vileness of them as he moved. He bore it as best he could until the entrance hallway became a room, and the press diminished.

That scarcely made his situation any less unsettling. Not with the Whisperers shifting to seal the entryway behind him, not with so many creeping in the shadows and the whole ruinous house asigh with their muted babble. Still, he kept sneering as the erstwhile captive led them on, attracting more of its curious and malevolent fellows in the process, past jumbled heaps of human-made stuff the imps had stolen and scavenged.

Some of the items, like knives and needles, were of obvious utility to Whisperers. Others, such as torn, filthy playing cards and empty cans of pomade, were not, and a few articles, including a cherrywood coffin with brass handles, were so big and unwieldy it was difficult to imagine the imps hauling them here. Perhaps they used it all to manufacture the talismans of spite, insanity, and misfortune they loved to hide in human habitations. Even now, some of the makers were sewing and gluing away, so intent on their work they didn't even glance up when the felines passed.

Finally the cats reached a big, high-ceilinged room that, for all its ugliness and menace, had an odd familiarity about it. Waspwatcher recognized the attitudes of supplicants, functionaries, and bodyguards, all focused on the needs and orders of the monarch ensconced at the center of it all. This was the court of the Whisperer king.

To make the creature a throne, his subjects had found a round little table to serve as a dais, and atop that set a smiling gilt Buddha from "the Orient," what or wherever that was. On a stained silk pillow in the statue's lap sprawled a Whisperer with a sly, squashed-looking face. The tip of one lung and an extra arm with too many joints protruded from its left flank.

The cats' guide drew a breath. "Your Hatred," he said.

"Shut up," the king replied. "Get out of the way." The guide made haste to obey, and the monarch glowered down at the felines. "Why?" he said at last. "Why come of your own free will? Are you crazy?"

"No," Bronze replied. Waspwatcher was impressed. She addressed the imp as calmly as she would her own queen, without any show of fear. "I know it's unusual—"

"Unusual!' You two are the enemy, you most of all. We'll relish your deaths as we'd delight in killing your lady herself!" The crowd snarled its agreement.

Bronze had no difficulty making herself heard above

the clamor. That, Waspwatcher supposed, was the one advantage to palavering with Whisperers. "Yes," she said, "my friend and I have bested, hurt, and mocked you, time after time. So you know we're clever, which means it's worth listening to what we have to say. If you like, you can always try to kill us afterward."

The king grunted. "Talk, then. I'll use the time to plan your torture."

"Thank you," she said. "You speak as if Waspwatcher and I are your greatest foes, and we've always rejoiced in that. But it isn't true anymore. A new thing has come into the world threatening Whisperers and cats alike."

The imp smirked. "That's a puny, desperate lie. I know the witch endangers you human-lovers. We laughed to see him kill and chase you out. But he hasn't done anything to us, or should I say, he hasn't done us anything but good. With you gone, we thrive, and play with the Bigs however we like."

"I'm glad you know who I mean," said Bronze. "That saves us time. But I jeer at your decline! I remember when Whisperers delighted to fight their own battles. You used the war with us cats to weed out the weaklings among you and strengthen your race. I guess you finally lost the stomach for it."

The king glared. "Do you think to turn our own teachings against us?"

"I think," she replied, "that too many Whisperers will pilfer too much food, and make themselves too conspicuous in general. The Bigs will finally notice you, and they won't like you much."

"We're not afraid of humans or anything else."

"Including the witch? Do you think he's not aware of you already? Rest assured, he is, if only because we are, and the knowledge is part of what we traded him. Aren't you worried he'll drive *you* out when he gets around to it?"

"Why would he?"

"For the same reason he turned on us. He simply doesn't want anyone about who knows him for who and what he is."

"He also delights in tormenting other humans," Waspwatcher said. "Why, then, should he share the sport with you?"

"Whatever he wants," the king replied, "he doesn't know our tricks. *We* aren't fools enough to barter them away."

"Still," said Bronze, "by now, he may have tricks enough."

"We . . ." The Whisperer hesitated, then spat like a human, expelling thick, dark saliva. "You think you can make me jump at bumps and squeals. You're nowhere near subtle enough for that."

"Your people understand human speech," she replied. "I've heard a few can even read their writing. Since the witch has drawn the Bigs' attention to your domain, have you bothered to heed what they're saying on the street and in newspapers? Or have you been too busy celebrating because one of them drove out the cats as you never could, thereby proving himself your better?"

Waspwatcher realized the crowd had fallen into true silence, as opposed to the *nearly* inaudible but busy rustling of before. The cats' arguments were affecting them somehow, though precisely how, he couldn't say. It was possible they'd grown so angry it choked off speech in their crooked throats.

"What are they saying?" asked the King.

"That these old streets are full of poverty, misery, and vice," Bronze replied. Waspwatcher had only a murky idea what "poverty" was, and none at all what "vice" signified, but perhaps his friend and the imps understood. "That the only way to improve them is to pull down the decrepit tenements and build anew. Can the Whisperers stay hidden if that happens? Even if you can, you'll lose your homes."

"They wouldn't do all that work."

"Have you watched them digging up the streets?" the black tom asked. "I don't understand the reason, but it shows they'll go to any amount of trouble, re-arrange anything, if the notion takes them. That's what makes them Bigs."

"What do you want, then?" asked the king. "Whisperers to fight alongside you?" His vassals cried out in protest.

"Sun and moon forbid," said Bronze. "We couldn't bear it anymore than you. Just find the witch for us. We'll fight him by ourselves, and you'll have the consolation of knowing that if we lose, he'll likely kill us as painfully as you would have yourselves."

"A carnival," said the king.

"What?" she replied.

"That's my price. Three nights each year when Whisperers can do as we like, and no cat will interfere. Swear it in your lady's name."

Diplomat though she was, Bronze bared her fangs in anger. But she said, "With the understanding you won't use the time to molest any felines, I swear it in Her Beauty's name."

"Then it's a bargain," the imp lord said. "Kissmatch can help you find your witch." He waved his hand, and a small Whisperer, much of its body covered with burn scars and oozing blisters, limped from the crowd.

The king's sudden acquiescence left Waspwatcher feeling incredulous. Until he and Bronze actually exited the nest, he suspected a cruel joke at their expense, and afterward was unsure which of their arguments had swayed the monarch. Perhaps the king had already been worried about the witch. Maybe the cats hadn't even needed to agree to the "carnival," and the tom bristled at the idea the enemy might have gotten the better of them. But he forgot about it once Kissmatch pointed out the witch's lodgings, and, lurking in hiding after weeks of fruitless seeking and dog-dodging, Waspwatcher finally saw his quarry.

At first glance, the witch appeared no different than when the tom had seen him at Her Beauty's court two years before. He was plump, young, and neatly dressed, with gingery sidewhiskers, and a bitter tang of human magic clinging to him. Yet now, in an unobtrusive way, he *prowled,* and his face looked thin as a wet white paper mask clinging to something toothy and fierce underneath. He reeked of the melding of cat and man, so much so it was hard to believe other Bigs didn't notice.

Waspwatcher stayed absolutely still. It wasn't just because he reckoned the witch had at least as good a chance of spotting him as any dog. In truth, his heart raced with terror, although he didn't entirely know why.

After the witch passed by, Bronze quavered, "Mad or sick. I told you."

Waspwatcher stretched, trying to make a show of confidence. "Well, we're making progress. We found him, and proved we can spy without him noticing we're near." Or maybe they'd simply been lucky this time. "If we pounce and catch him by surprise, clawing for his eyes and the arteries in his neck . . ."

She snorted. "Now that you've seen him, do you really think that could work?"

"No." The unfortunate truth was, sick, deranged, or whatever, the Big stank of cunning and power. "I don't. So I suppose we'd better follow him and see what else we learn. We'll keep our distance and go carefully."

It was nerve-racking work. Despite the darkness and all the cover and distractions the teeming city provided, Waspwatcher repeatedly balked, fearing the witch was on the brink of whirling and glaring into his eyes. Still, perhaps because he and Bronze struggled to keep their heads and stalk with every iota of their craft, it didn't happen. They tailed their quarry into the slum which was his hunting ground.

The witch led a drunken, dirty woman into a lightless cul-de-sac. Evidently he didn't care about mating with his victims anymore. The tiger-striped fur sprouted at once, and claws slid from his fingertips. Despite the latter, he still carried a large knife. He used it for the bulk of the stabbing and cutting. After he finally permitted the "whore" to die, he opened her still further. Some of what he extracted, he ate on the spot. Other morsels he wrapped to carry away.

Waspwatcher shivered. The witch was horribly feline, and at the same time, utterly unlike any cat that ever was.

The murderer slipped away across the rooftops. Some other Big discovered the body almost immediately, and whistles shrilled. Waspwatcher prayed someone would take notice of the witch, but nobody did. Even after he descended to street level, the killer sneaked along with consummate stealth and cunning. He probably didn't even need the fealty of the police dogs to keep him safe. He knew it, too. Contemptuous of the frantic searchers casting about, he lured a second woman and mutilated her even more thoroughly than the first.

That was when the cats abandoned the trail. Waspwatcher had seen all the horror he could bear, at least for one night, and Bronze agreed.

"Do you know," said the messenger after a while, "he hid and crept so well that sometimes I thought we'd lost him. Then I feared he was circling around to take us from behind."

"Well, he didn't," Waspwatcher snapped, and, noticing his own irritation, was somewhat cheered thereby. He was getting angry that he and Bronze, champions of their people, felt so cowed, and that was as it should be. "What did you observe that might be *helpful*?"

She hissed. "What did you, if you're so clever?"

"Nothing, and that's why I look to you. You're the wise one, at least that's what you always told me."

"Yes." She gave her head a shake, as if to dislodge some of the ugliness she'd witnessed. "When his eyes and nails changed . . . we undertook to teach him what a cat knows, but it's almost as if we *made* him a cat, or rather, a mockery of one."

Relieved his friend was shaking off her funk, Waspwatcher stretched. "I like humans, but cats are more beautiful. Our secrets are grander, so why wouldn't they overwhelm a Big's mind?"

"You should have made that argument when you urged the queen to turn him away."

"I would have if I'd thought of it. So. Maybe we understand what happened to him. Does it lead us anywhere?"

"Let me think." Bronze pondered for a long while. Finally: "Throughout the hunt, he used feline charms and never his own."

The tom cocked his head. "He smelled of human magic. I thought perhaps it helped him a time or two. Certainly he still commands the dogs."

"Yes, but those are old charms. Human ones last longer than ours. While we were watching, he didn't cast any new ones."

"If he's losing his hold on being a true Big, maybe it doesn't occur to him to use his old magic anymore. That would make him weaker."

"Perhaps, but if it leaves him a better cat than we are—"

Waspwatcher spat. "Nobody's a better cat than I am! Certainly not a dog-loving half-thing!"

Bronze flinched at his vehemence. "Fair enough. Do you have a plan?"

"What do you know about human charms?"

"Not much. Why would I? They come out of books sometimes, and they take forever to make, like Whisperer magic." She snorted at such a cumbersome system.

"Do Bigs bind the power up in trinkets like the imps do?"

"Perhaps," she answered slowly. "Maybe that's why it lasts longer."

"Then, maybe I do have an idea."

They lurked to catch the witch venturing out again, but this time didn't follow. Once certain he was truly gone, they found an open window and slipped into his lair.

Waspwatcher immediately recognized the place as a boarding house. It was less filthy and crammed with transients than the ones in the killer's hunting ground, but nothing special either. The tom had little grasp of how humans managed "money." Still, he reckoned a witch could have done better for himself. Evidently deranged ones didn't care.

The rooms and hallways ahead, echoing with footsteps and conversation, redolent of cooking, cigarettes, and human sweat, smelled of dog as well. Creeping softly, the cats eventually spotted a retriever dozing beside a piano, but made sure it didn't notice them. Almost as wary of Bigs, they followed the witch's scent up a staircase. Here at last in these cramped confines, the hybrid was easy to track.

He'd closed the door to his room. Waspwatcher pushed, but the latch wouldn't give. Bronze, who couldn't be held in or kept out by any such contrivance, trilled a coaxing little charm. The door clicked and swung ajar.

The space on the other side was unremarkable except for the leather trunk beside the narrow bed. That fouled the stale air with stinks of raw flesh going rotten and human magic. Waspwatcher reared on his hind legs and tried to raise the lid with his front paws. It wouldn't lift.

"Let me," said Bronze. She attempted the same charm she'd employed a moment before.

Something long and hot leaped from the brass lock, streaking past Waspwatcher to attack his friend. It snatched her up somehow, and she shrieked in shock and pain.

The tom ripped at its flank. The thing wouldn't leave off savaging Bronze to strike back at him in any normal way. But every touch of its hot, scaly flesh and blistering blood seared and punished him.

Bronze finally succeeded in fighting free of the spirit's grasp. Smelling of burned fur and blistered skin, she bounded beyond its reach. The sentinel rounded on Waspwatcher, and he, too, scurried back. At a distance, it was easier to make out the red, shining serpentine body rooted in the keyhole, and the ruff of bone beneath the beaked head.

The tom hurried to Bronze's side. "Are you all right?" he asked.

"No," she hissed. "Maybe. I'll heal. What about you?"

"I'm fine." The guardian struck at them so viciously that the heavy trunk lurched an inch. Bronze cringed, and Waspwatcher nearly did, too. "What can we do?"

"Run."

He glared. "I know it hurt you. But you can banish a hostile spirit."

"Not one bound by the witch, not quickly, not before it calls its master back to it. It's crying for him now. We have to flee before he finds us."

The burning spirit's aggression made it hard to think. Waspwatcher strained to do so anyway. "Say we do just run away. What happens after? The witch will know cats have slipped past the dogs and found his den. He'll have our scent. He can hide from us anew, lay traps, and guard his magic even better. We can't give him the opportunity, so here's what we'll do instead." He explained his plan.

She stared at him in dismay. "You don't know you can do that. Or that I can accomplish my part in time for it to help you. You're just guessing—"

"Stop!" he snarled. "The queen picked us to do this, you and me. She thought that of all her champions, we had the best chance. Well, this *is* our chance, and we're taking it. If we're wrong, we'll die, that's all. That's no different than it's ever been."

"I . . . you're right."

He nuzzled her. "Do we have at least a couple of minutes before the witch comes back?"

Her eyes narrowed. "I think so."

"Then help me make a mess."

They clawed and scattered everything they could and still keep out of the fiery spirit's reach. Waspwatcher pissed and shat on the Big's bed, and Bronze charmed open the window behind it. She gave her friend a look of mingled concern and encouragement, then slipped from the room.

She'd nearly waited too long. A moment later, Waspwatcher heard the retriever's nails clicking on the stairs. Likely the witch was climbing them with the dog, his tread so cat-light the risers didn't groan.

Sure enough, man and canine both appeared in the doorway. The hybrid still resembled an ordinary Big but was no less terrifying for that. Resisting the urge to bolt, Waspwatcher bristled and spat. If the witch thought himself a feline, with a cat's pride and temper, then let him react to the insult of the knight's contempt, the fouled bed, and the spoiled possessions with a spasm of rage. Let him give chase at once, without noticing the scent of a second intruder hanging in the room.

Hissing, teeth lengthening into fangs, the murderer slunk forward. Leery of the lashing guardian spirit, the retriever hesitated, then followed its master. Wasp-

watcher wheeled toward the open window. The sash
fell, impelled either by some human magic or a feline
charm of opening turned on its head.

The cat spun. The killer swiped at him. The tom
twitched out of range, then leaped to the floor between the guardian and dog.

The red spirit struck. Waspwatcher jumped aside.
The guardian's beak snapped shut on the retriever's
foreleg. The canine screamed.

Together the two creatures made a thrashing confusion, tangling with the witch's legs just long enough
for Waspwatcher to break for the door. It started
swinging shut, but he sprang and cleared the narrowing gap. In spite of his desperation, he knew a
split second of mocking glee. His pursuer's trick would
actually lengthen his lead by an instant.

The wind knew, he needed it. He had to get out
and lure his foes away from the boarding house and
Bronze. He cast about, while windows banged down
and doors slammed.

He raced downstairs. As he reached the ground
floor, something plummeted to land beside him. The
witch had swung himself over the banister and
dropped. Waspwatcher twisted away from a snatching
hand. The retriever charged down the risers.

Waspwatcher ran on, scrambling into a parlor. Here,
workmen lounged and waited for supper, providing
him a feeble sort of protection. The witch couldn't
show his fangs and claws, nor pounce with quite the
same agility, while other Bigs looked on. Some of the
humans even tried to restrain the snarling, frenzied
retriever.

Unfortunately, some of them tried to catch Waspwatcher, too, and the chase soon penned him in a
corner. Meanwhile, doors and windows closed.

Then someone got hold of the retriever and dragged
it backward. Waspwatcher darted through the opening
thus created, under an ottoman, and back out of the

room. Just as he reached the front hall, the exterior door opened partway. The lodger who strove to enter exclaimed in puzzlement as he shoved against the unseen resistance of the witch's magic. The tom scrambled over the tops of the workman's muddy boots and out into the streets.

At least now the witch wouldn't be able to shut any more doors and windows in his face, and Waspwatcher hoped that if he kept among the crowds, his pursuer wouldn't be able to use the rest of his magic to best effect either. For a minute, it seemed to work that way. Then several dogs loped into view. Evidently, the murderer was calling his minions in to cut Waspwatcher off. This contingent spotted the feline and charged, knocking humans off balance with their avidity for the kill.

Waspwatcher no longer had anywhere to go. Not at ground level, anyway. He avoided the dogs' first rush by leaping into a window. He looked for the next step, and saw no possibility other than a fat man lumbering by. He sprang onto the Big's shoulder, staggering and astounding him, dug in his claws to keep from slipping off, then bounded onto a roof.

A knife flashed at him. He flung himself aside. The blade sliced back, and he dodged again. Leaping, he put a little distance between himself and the witch.

The hybrid had cast off his mask of conventional humanity for glaring slit-pupiled eyes, pointed ears, and tiger stripes. He crouched on a ledge just above the heads of the crowd, where any of the Bigs could have looked up and seen him. Still, Waspwatcher reckoned not even the portly man who'd served as his stair step would do so. His enemy's magic prevented it, that and the distraction of all the dogs suddenly coursing through the streets.

"I remember you," said the witch in feline speech. "It makes sense that of all of your queen's agents, you got the closest. Perhaps if I send her your skin, she'll know better than to dispatch any more."

"You can't go on like this," the tom snarled. He didn't actually think he could convince the murderer of anything. But if the human wanted to palaver and give him a chance to catch his breath, good. "Are you so mad you don't see what you've become? Renounce what Her Beauty gave you!"

"I paid well for it, and made no promises concerning what might happen after." Without warning, the hybrid lunged. Plainly, he'd hoped the moment of conversation would lull Waspwatcher into dropping his guard.

The tom wrenched himself aside, then reflexively lashed out with his claws. He nicked the wrist of the witch's knife arm, but at the same instant, the talons of the Big's other hand slashed down at him. Waspwatcher dodged and twisted. It saved his life, although one of the hybrid's claws snagged in his fur before ripping free.

The cat wheeled and ran. He needed to remember his present task was to flee, not attack. For the moment, the latter was simply too dangerous. The witch gave chase.

Over the course of the next few minutes, the complexity of the Greatest City's roofscape alternately aided Waspwatcher and proved a peril. He seldom ran out of places to dash or jump. But at the same time, the hybrid had plenty of cover.

And when headlong pursuit became a stalking game, the witch invoked his subtler magic. Shadows danced and moaned, ruffling Waspwatcher's mind with feelings of panic and disorientation. The cat recognized some of the charms from having seen Bronze employ them. They were supposed to scare, distract, or confuse him into making the wrong move, or no move at all until it was too late.

He understood, but comprehension only helped a little. Time and again, he only avoided a pounce and a sweep of the knife by a whisker. Perhaps that was only because the hybrid was playing with him. The witch had already shown he loved a game of cat-and-mouse. Now Waspwatcher filled the latter role.

Unfortunately, all such games ended the same way, and the tom reckoned the conclusion of this one was fast approaching. He felt it in the pounding of his heart and the labored gasping of his lungs. He didn't know if Bronze had succeeded at the task he'd given her. That was one of the unfortunate aspects of his scheme. But he'd have to assume she had. Otherwise, he was doomed.

He began to fight back. He clawed and bit, risking an additional stroke from the witch's knife or talons before he turned and bolted. His first effort caught his pursuer by surprise, and cut deeply. The hybrid screeched.

Waspwatcher started choosing his way over crumbling cornices, rotten shingles, and arched, grimy skylights. Despite the witch's feline craft, he still possessed a human's weight. He shouldn't be able to traverse the same path without it collapsing.

Somehow he did, and without any reduction in speed. He merely cast the knife away, dropped to all fours, and, by dint of a charm, dissolved the shoes and socks from feet that were now hind paws, clawed and furry as his hands. Then he snarled and raced on, his longer stride relentlessly closing the distance. He was ready for the kill.

Waspwatcher tried to use his smaller size to help him outmaneuver the witch as if the latter were a dog. To no avail. Perhaps Bronze had been correct. The hybrid was a better cat than any born in nature.

The killer chased him to the brink of a drop-off. The next roof was too far away for jumping. The witch had cornered him. He laughed.

Waspwatcher spat back at him, "Let's finish it.

You're ugly, clumsy, and stupid, no cat at all! I pissed
and shat in your bed, human! I pissed and shat in
your bed!"

The witch snarled and lunged. Waspwatcher faked
a leap in one direction, then dodged the other. The
hybrid wasn't fooled. He seized the true feline and
dug his claws in.

Squirming madly, Waspwatcher sank his fangs into
the base of the witch's thumb. Startled, the hybrid
loosened his grip. The cat burst free. He scratched the
witch's face. Spun. Leaped.

He landed in the middle of the street and the host
of dogs wandering there. A dozen canine noses swung
his direction. Then the witch sprang down after him
and into striking range. He lifted a clawed hand.

A hound's jaws snapped shut on the wrist. An instant later, at least one snarling dog worried every
limb.

Did they recognize the creature who'd enslaved
them? Did they resent him? Perhaps they were simply
reacting to the biggest, strangest cat they'd ever seen.
Either way, by distracting the witch and leading him
on a chase, Waspwatcher had given Bronze the opportunity to dismiss the guardian spirit, open the hybrid's
trunk, and dissolve whatever charms she found there.
Plainly she'd succeeded, freeing the dogs to attack.

They were equally free to molest Waspwatcher, but
at least he realized it. It enabled him to dodge the
few that were still interested in him and scramble beyond their reach. Afterward, he perched atop a gable
and watched the witch die, enjoying the fact that it
took so long.

Bronze demanded a full account. "Our people will
expect me to tell the story," she said peevishly, her
burns obviously still paining her, "and I missed the
climax!"

"What's the difference?" Waspwatcher replied.
"Your tales are always full of lies anyway."

She showed him her fangs. "Are you coming back to court?"

"Yes," he said. It would be good to see the queen he'd loved as no one else in his life, except for Bronze and his little girl. "If only to make sure this folly never recurs. Cats need to stop talking to any Bigs, witches included, stop altogether."

"Aren't you afraid they'll forget we're a People, too?"

Waspwatcher snorted. "Even humans aren't so blind as that."

ALL THE PIGS' HOUSES

Mickey Zucker Reichert

Mickey Zucker Reichert is a pediatrician whose science fiction and fantasy novels include *The Legend of Nightfall, The Unknown Soldier,* and several books and trilogies about the Renshai. Her short fiction has appeared in numerous anthologies, including *Battle Magic, Apprentice Fantastic,* and *Knight Fantastic.* Her claims to fame: she *has* performed brain surgery, and her parents *really are* rocket scientists.

Elliot Pig curled up on the cloth-covered ticking of his padded divan, a tattered copy of *The Tales of Tom Kitten* clutched in his cloven hoof and a crock of fresh creek water on the table to his left. A gentle rain clicked softly against the roof, held at bay by finely woven sheaves of straw. *Not a drop of leakage.* Elliot smiled, a flush of warm satisfaction suffusing him. He had built the cottage with his own hooves, along with its sparse furnishings, and he reveled in the results. His two brothers had admonished him to use more enduring materials, to enlist the assistance of the town's carpenter and builders. Ezra's teaching job brought in enough money that he could afford such luxuries, as well as the wood to build his modest log cabin. Elijah had a similar home, temporarily, while he waited for the builders to finish the fancy brick mansion his doctor's income had bought him.

Elliot hefted his water and took a mouthful. It tasted sweet and clean, and he savored its simple purity with the same joy as he had his house. He did not begrudge his brothers their luxuries or their successes, though he did sometimes wish his mother had had more experience with money. When the fairies had come to the human world, offering its animals the choice of remaining as they were or beginning a world of their own, his mother had leaped at the opportunity. Only three of her litter of nine had made the same choice: Elliot and his two brothers. His mother had divided the coins the fairies provided into three, intending to educate each of her sons in the human world. The smartest, Elijah, moved ahead; and his share took him all the way through medical school. By Ezra's turn, much of his money had gone for living expenses for which Mother had not thought to budget. By the time he finished, there was not enough left to educate Elliot past high school.

As they made their livings, the older two had provided for Mother and Elliot until her natural death. Both had offered Elliot the money to build himself a finer home, but he had refused. He preferred the fulfillment that came with his achievement: materials purchased through his own efforts, a series of sweaty odd jobs, a project completed by his own calloused hooves. He had even built every stick of furniture, and he celebrated his labors and achievements every time he looked at or used them. Had he not earned those things, they would not mean so very much to him. Now, as he sat in great contentment, he wondered idly how so many of his ilk could have chosen the cold comfort of a sameness that meant a short life of barely intelligent grunts and squeals, of wallowing in mud holes, and a trough filled with pig chow and table scraps. He, his brothers, and his mother had chosen a life of effort and uncertainty, of wonder and stress, yet it came with glorious moments such as this one that he would not trade for anything.

A knock at the door interrupted Elliot's thoughts. Hoping one of his brothers had come to call, he set aside the creek water and the book, heaved himself from the comfort of the divan, and headed toward the door. "Who's there?" he called out in a happy singsong.

A gruff voice wafted through the straw. "Little pig. Little pig, let me come in."

Elliot froze at the lintel, hoof halfway to the latch, and terror raised beads of sweat on his upper lip. It was a cold voice, a wolfy voice, and it sounded hungry. Most of the animals of the Fairy World had formed a camaraderie, but a few had espoused the worst characteristics of the humans whose societies they emulated. The dirtiest animals had embraced sanitation, even the shyest had learned their common language, and they all wore clothes to cover the parts that some had come to see as vulgar. Nearly all of the carnivores had embraced vegetarianism, aside from the richest who could afford to buy their meat prepackaged from the human world where animals now bore only some physical resemblance to their fairy counterparts. Yet, a few, mostly wolves, preyed on their neighbors.

Apparently mistaking Elliot's silence for a problem hearing, the wolf shouted. "I said, 'Little pig, little pig, let me come in!'"

All of the pink drained from Elliot, skin ashy white beneath bristles of hair. He managed to pry his rigid left hoof from his open mouth, and it sank down his face to pull at the stiff hairs sprouting from his chin. "No!" He spoke in a terrified squeak, before he could think. *Shouldn't let him know I'm afraid.* He shook his head, ears flapping, trying to clear it. *Too late for a pretend dog.* It was a long shot anyone. A pig rich enough to own a human-world pet would live in a finer home. *If I sound brave, maybe he'll think I have some way of protecting myself.* He looked at his hoof and tried to fill his tone with courage. "Not by my . . . chin hair . . ." It reminded him of a parlor game, and he switched to song to buoy his courage. "Not by the hair of my chinny-chin-chin."

A hushed moment followed, during which Elliot wondered if the wolf had simply left. Just as he considered a careful peek through a partially opened door, the wolf spoke again. "Then I'll huff."

"Huff?"

"And I'll puff . . ."

"What?"

"And I'll *blow your house down*!"

Despite his fear, Elliot could not hold back a chuckle. "You'll what? Are you mad?" It was a silly question. Wolves who chatted with pigs one day, then ate them another could hardly be considered of sound mind.

The whoosh of rushing air filled the next several seconds, followed by a massive, howling exhale that rattled the house down to its timber frame. Straw shuddered, then peeled from walls and roof in sheets and braids that unraveled under the hurricane force. While Elliot stared in stunned amazement, his house collapsed around him, straw spewing in all directions, churning through the dying air currents. A moment later, he stood among the devastation. Bits of straw clung to his skin and clothing, swirled through his water, and sprinkled down like rain. He looked up to a lanky, sharp-fanged wolf wearing jeans, a T-shirt, and a battered top hat.

Seized by a hot surge of panic, Elliot ran.

The wolf pursued at a swift and wild gallop that ate up the gap between them. Screaming in terror, Elliot quickened his pace. His breath caught in his throat. He had never moved so fast in his life. His legs ached, and he knew he could not keep up the breakneck pace much longer.

Where am I going? The thought managed to seep through the swirl of desperate alarm that usurped all logic. He forced himself to think past the grim certainty of death, the anticipated agony of knifelike teeth sinking into his flesh. *Town! He wouldn't dare eat me in the streets.* He made a sudden turn on the woodland path that left the wolf scrambling to follow. For an instant, they came nearly eye to eye. Desire glazed the wolf's dark orbs, and saliva dribbled from his muzzle. His breath rasped, louder than the pig's own rapid panting. At first, that made little sense. Lean and long-legged, the wolf should endure the race far longer than any squat, fat pig. Apparently, the lung work required to blow down an entire house had tired him.

Every minute dragged, and it seemed like hours before Elliot's pudgy legs carried him, aching, to the line of cottages and shops that made up the town proper. A few looked up as Elliot trotted through the street, the wolf at his heels. Elliot dared not waste his breath on a scream. Already, their pace had slowed to little more than a fast walk, and no one seemed to recognize his distress. He skittered through a familiar alley, the abrupt turn gaining him another few inches. He threw himself against the door to his brother's wooden cottage, pounding wildly with his hooves. "Ezra!"

Though the cry emerged hoarse, Ezra must have read the panic in it. The door wrenched open, and Elliot hurled himself inside. "Close it! Close it!" he managed to gasp, sprawled across the planked floor. "Close . . . the . . . damned . . . door!"

Ezra slammed the heavy panel in the wolf's face and threw the bolt home. The slam of a body against wood thundered through the cottage, followed by a volley of fistfalls.

Ezra turned to his panting brother. "Big bad wolf?"

he guessed, using the slang for one of the animals who succumbs to the meat madness.

Elliot nodded, saving his voice.

After several moments, the pounding stopped, and the wolf growled a warning. "This isn't over yet, piggies."

Elliot curled into a ball on the floor, moaning.

Hours later, the brothers discussed the situation over plates of buttered potatoes and mugs of apple juice at a table purchased, with four matching chairs, at the furniture store in the market. Neat cupboards lined the walls, stocked with drying herbs, flour, and crockery. Pots lay stacked in the corner, though Ezra, like Elliot, confined his cooking to the outside. The log cabin had inner walls dividing it into four rooms: kitchen, meeting room, bedroom, and study. Slightly broader of face and longer in the tail, Ezra had the same pink-all-over coloring as his brother.

"So," Ezra said, for at least the third time. "He just blew your house to pieces."

"To pieces." Elliot made a grand gesture to simulate straw flying in all directions.

"With his breath."

"With his breath," Elliot confirmed around a mouthful of potatoes. Nervousness always increased his appetite.

Ezra examined his own plate. "Strong lungs."

Elliot stared at his brother. "I was too busy running for my life to admire that."

Ezra smiled. "No doubt. And mourning months of hard work."

Elliot refused to consider that yet. No matter how difficult or long the effort, he could replace things. For now, all that mattered was his life.

Ezra's voice turned almost scolding. "You should have let me loan you the money—"

"Stop." Elliot refused to listen to the tired argument. No one could have predicted a long-winded, animal-eating wolf would topple a house with his breath. A thought came to Elliot suddenly, and his eyes widened with terror. "You don't think he could blow your house down, too." The image of those wicked teeth filled his mind's eye, and he quivered in his seat, a chunk of potato shaking off his spoon.

Ezra patted the mud-chinked logs. "Solid as the trees it's made of."

Elliot loosed a pent-up breath, accepting his brother's reassurance, though doubts whittled at his confidence. Though not as dense and strong as wood, woven straw had a toughness that had weathered it through many storms. His house should not have fallen either. "Has Elijah moved into his new house?" he asked, trying to sound casual so as not to suggest he did not trust his middle brother.

"The brick one?"

Elliot nodded.

"I'm not sure." Ezra put aside his spoon, swallowed, and rubbed his forehooves. Clearly, he understood the implications of Elliot's question, yet he took no clear offense. "It might not hurt to ask him."

Glancing wildly in all directions, Elliot slipped from the wooden house at Ezra's side and glided into the night. Most of the village cottages had gone dark, but cook fires and candles flickered through a few windows. Warm orange flames lit the modest wooden cottage that currently served as Elijah's home. Elliot sighed, pleased and disappointed by the sight. He appreciated the closeness of his oldest, wisest brother, and the fact that he was still awake; but it bothered him to realize that Elijah had not yet moved into the brick mansion that seemed certain to foil the airy wolf.

As the pigs glided to the front door, they glanced nervously at one another. Elliot hated to bother his busiest brother at any time, but especially after so many had already chosen to sleep. A competent, kind-hearted doctor, Elijah worked hard for his money and for long hours. "The curse of the competent," Ezra called it. Capable work garnered more clients, who demanded more time. Every business strived for it, but those that succeeded could find themselves overwhelmed. It seemed worse for doctors, since accidents and illnesses could happen at any time; and, in their worst moments of crisis, everyone wanted the best.

Elliot could not bring himself to disturb their eldest brother. Finally, Ezra raised a hoof and knocked.

No immediate answer came, and the pigs stood in silence for several moments. Just as Ezra raised a hoof for another strike, a voice wafted to them. "Who's there?"

"It's Ezra and Elliot," Ezra said. "May we come in?"

The door flew open, and Elijah stood framed in the doorway. He wore red pajamas with white stars and squiggles, and a hat of the same material covered his ears. He was pink, like his brothers, with a few black spots on his body and neck. "Good evening, brothers. Come in, come in."

Now more concerned for who might lurk outside than for bothering his industrious brother, Elliot accepted the invitation eagerly. Ezra also scrambled inside, making certain to shut the door behind him and throw the bolt.

His caution did not escape Elijah. "What's wrong? Are you all right?" When both brothers nodded, he waddled toward the kitchen. "Tell me all about it over a cup of tea."

Reassured by Elijah's manner, Elliot glanced around. The entryway opened onto two sparsely furnished rooms, then continued as a hallway that led into the large kitchen and a gathering room. Unlike Ezra's home, Elijah's also had a spacious loft that served as a bedroom for him and any guests.

Elliot and Ezra followed him down the hall to the doorway of the kitchen. Elijah waved over his shoulder toward the gathering room. "Sit. Get comfortable. I'll bring the tea."

Elliot and Ezra obeyed, arranging themselves on a pillowed sofa. The room also contained a sturdy coffee table, a cabinet, a fireplace, and a cozy chair. A textbook lay on its cushion, and a small calico cat lay curled on the open pages. A half-filled mug balanced on one plushy arm. The mantle held framed family photographs, a large one of their mother in the center, and a smattering of small awards and knickknacks.

As the two pigs chose their resting places, the cat rose and stretched luxuriously, tongue unrolling like a miniature pink carpet, and its fangs exposed. It leaped from the chair and strolled leisurely toward the pair on the couch.

Elliot stared at the little animal. "That's a human world cat," he whispered.

Ezra nodded, crossing his stout legs with effort. He glanced at the approaching animal with lips tightly pursed and eyes narrowed, as if he feared it carried the plague.

Though not rare, pets were a luxury item, especially since they usually required a would-be owner to accept whatever creature happened to come his way. Very few Fairy World animals made the potentially dangerous journey to the Old World, and they usually brought back more practical items with a marketable certainty. Humans tended to mistake them for hallucinations or for their unintelligent counterparts.

"Keep it away from me." Ezra did not take his eyes from the approaching animal. "Human world critters give me the creeps."

Apparently taking the words as a welcome, the cat leaped into Ezra's covered lap, nestling between one blocking leg and his stiffly crossed arms.

Elliot smiled for the first time since his ordeal. "Apparently, she doesn't have the same reaction to you." Though entertained by the irony, he secretly wished the cat would come to him. He had petted a cat once and loved the soothing feel of the soft fur beneath his hoof, the happy rubbing of its body against him. He thought he understood why pigs did not make good human pets. Not only would they not fit comfortably in a lap, but stroking one felt more like petting a toothbrush.

Elijah entered, juggling three steaming mugs and a stack of pastries. Ezra rose, dumping the cat from his lap and taking two of the mugs, while Elijah took a more secure grip on the remaining one and the treats. "Luckily, I already had the water on." They set everything down on the table. "Lady Larcha's cinnamon chamomile. Delightful."

The cinnamon did smell good, but Elliot could not help teasing. "You'd compliment Larcha if she made you a plate full of cow dung biscuits."

"True. True." Elijah took his mug in one hoof and a pastry in the other. "And I'd eat them, every one."

Ezra had long speculated to Elliot that the building of the brick house had much to do with winning the heart of the fair lady Larcha. They would need security and room for their own crop of little piggies. Though he wanted to ask about Elijah's intentions, Elliot held his tongue. Now did not seem the time. Instead, he accepted a mug of tea and a pastry. A full belly would go a long way toward alleviating his discomfort.

Ezra picked up his own mug and pastry, then took his seat. Almost immediately, the cat leaped back into his lap. "Hey!" He wiggled his legs to discourage the cat, who seemed barely to notice the rockiness of its perch. "What's with this critter?"

Elijah took a bite of pastry. "Cats know who doesn't want them around."

"But—"

"And gravitate *toward* them."

"Oh." That seemed to satisfy Ezra, who ceased his efforts to dislodge the cat, perhaps with the notion that, if he stopped showing his displeasure, the cat would move on.

Elliot wanted to talk about his brother's new acquisition, but the events of earlier that evening kept cycling through his head. He had exhausted his ability for casual conversation. Instead, he squeaked out the story of his ruined straw house and the wolf, his desperate run for town, and the wolf's final threat.

Throughout the story, Elijah listened intently, saying nothing, pausing to take a bite of cookie or sip his tea. Only after Elliot had clearly finished did he speak.

"I'm sorry. That must have been horrible." Elijah's tone held a sweet note of commiseration that added deep sincerity to his words.

Elliot nodded, appreciating his brother's sympathy.

"A wolf, you say. With a good set of lungs and a hankering for pork."

Elliot nodded. "He'd have eaten me alive if he'd caught me." Describing the scene brought it all back in terrifying detail. Resisting the urge to hide beneath the couch, he set aside his mug, worried his trembling hooves might spill it all over the partially carpeted floorboards.

"You know," Ezra said thoughtfully, one hoof casually stroking the calico as if of its own accord. "I'm beginning to think maybe Peter's right about the need for some kind of human-type government. So long as we have a *herbivore* for a leader."

Elliot did not have a strong opinion on that matter. He could see both sides. Government meant taxes and regulation, whether of the monarchical, dictatorial, or democratic variety. Many also voiced the concern that, no matter how it started, the strongest and fiercest would end up in charge once they paved the way for obedience to any commander. To enforce laws would require a strong militia or police force, which could become corrupted. On the other hand, many parts of the human world seemed to manage those problems and keep their societies comfortably lawful.

Not that any of it mattered now. The Fairy World had no laws to enforce and no one to enforce them if they did. Though clearly immoral, the big bad wolf's pursuit did not violate any formal decree.

Elijah shrugged. He had long ago made his view on the matter clear, and he already sided with structure. "Can you describe this wolf?"

"Well . . ." Elliot considered. "He was . . . a wolf. Big ears, long snout, sharp teeth, wicked-looking eyes."

Ezra loosed a strained laugh. "That's like differentiating between us by saying pink and fat with a curly tail." He smiled to show he meant no offense. "I'm sure Elijah believed you when you said it was a wolf."

Elijah gave his middle brother a reproachful look but followed up on his comment. "Was there anything different or special about this particular wolf that you remember?"

Elliot swirled his tongue around his mouth, reawakening the taste of cinnamon. "I was mostly focused on the teeth. And running." He closed his eyes, wracking his memory.

"Understandable," Elijah encouraged.

Elliot stalled with another sip of tea, which he swirled around his mouth. It did taste good, the cinnamon leeching the bitterness from the chamomile. "Brown fur, perhaps a shade darker than average for a wolf. Thin and rangy. Dressed casually, even a bit shabby, though he had a hat." That was all he could remember, and he let out a sigh. "Does that help?"

"Help what?" Ezra shoved a whole pastry in his mouth, and cherry juice oozed from the corners of his mouth. "What good does it do to know what he looks like? I won't be going near *any* wolves for the rest

of my life, and I'm certainly not going to try to talk
to him."

Elijah lowered his head to his hooves, remaining
calm. "Well, I've got a few wolves in my practice,
and most are normal, decent sorts willing to listen
to reason."

"Not this one." Elliot put down his mug. "Do you
think you might actually know this big bad?"

Elijah shrugged without looking up. "If I did, I
couldn't tell you. Professional ethics forbid it."

Elliot knew better than to argue. No laws constrained them, but Elijah subscribed to one of the few
professions that constrained itself. "So what do we
do?"

Elijah gave both brothers an encouraging look. "If
the wolf could do the same damage to Ezra's house
as yours, he would have." He finished the last bite of
pastry, then scratched at his snout with his now-free
hoof. "At least we know he can't handle blowing
down two houses in the same evening, and I doubt
he'll act in broad daylight, law or no law. You're safe
tonight. If anything happens tomorrow, come straight
here. I'll make certain I'm home."

Elliot took some comfort from his brother's promise
of assistance, but he still suffered from cold prickles
of worry. "And the next night?"

"The next night?" Elijah considered. "That's jazz
night at the club. Wouldn't think of missing that."

When Elliot looked stricken, Elijah added, "Why
don't you both come with me? My treat."

Months had passed since they had done anything
together as brothers. Elliot appreciated the invitation,
and he could tell by the broadening look on Ezra's
face that he did, too. "It's a date," the middle brother
said.

The following evening, Elliot paced the floors of
Ezra's wooden cottage, unable to sit still. Tired of

teasing his wildly nervous brother, Ezra sat at the kitchen table, reading. Crazed movement accomplished nothing. They both knew it; yet Elliot found himself incapable of controlling the incessant drive to pace.

Though Elliot anticipated and worried for it, the pounding on the front door still caught him off-guard. Licking his lips furiously, he looked at Ezra.

"Who is it?" the middle brother called, his tone revealing a trace of fear as well.

The cold, wolf voice carried through the chinking. "Little pigs, little pigs, let me come in."

Elliot wrung his hooves. Ezra seemed at a loss for words, so he borrowed the ones Elliot had used. "Not by the hair on our chinny-chin-chins."

Elliot skittered toward the back of the house while Ezra studied the wolf through the parlor window.

"Then I'll huff, and I'll puff, and I'll—"

"Attempt to blow my house down?" Ezra supplied with a confidence Elliot did not share. It was bluster, he knew, yet he envied his brother's ability to demonstrate even a false composure under lethal pressure.

"As you wish," the wolf said, as though the idea had originally come from Ezra. Without further explanation, he sucked in an enormous breath of air that seemed to pull the cottage toward him, then released it in a frenzied whirlwind that battered the little cottage hard enough to shudder it.

To Elliot's relief, the structure held. He let out his own miniscule breath, edging toward a rear window despite the respite. Somehow, he knew the wolf would not give up so easily.

"As I said . . ." Ezra started over the sounds of the wolf gathering a second lungful, ". . . attempt to—"

A gale force of air struck the house a second time, louder than thunder. It rattled every timber to its core, sending the house into a rollicking dance, accompanied by the horrible screech of splintering wood. Like a live thing, the cottage seemed to scream, then wood shattered, flinging debris in a tornado volley that spewed in every direction. Elliot flung himself to the floor as furniture funneled over him and the construction of the house toppled into a splattered arrangement of logs and sticks.

Ezra caught Elliot's arm. "Run!"

Elliot stumbled to his feet in time to see a toothy, grinning face flying toward him. Wailing, he ran, too panicked to think clearly. Luckily, Ezra acted for both of them, hauling his hapless brother around his neighbor's to Elijah's cottage. They both pounded on the door. The oldest brother whipped it opened, shoved them inside, and slammed the panel closed in the face of the howling wolf. He threw the bolt home.

"W–w–w–wolf," Elliot stammered out, without bothering to rise from the floor.

The little calico sniffed at the figures on the floor, demonstrating none of their urgency.

The wolf hammered his paws on the door, and the latch rattled as he apparently tried in vain to work against the bolt. "I'll have you yet," he shouted. "You'll run out of places to hide!"

Elliot swallowed hard. In his mind, they already had. He clambered to shaky legs, glancing between his brothers. "What do we do now?"

Elijah stared out the window, nodding slightly. "Did you get a better look at him?"

Elliot shook his head, but Ezra replied, "Tall and thin. Brown eyes, and a white tip on the end of his bushy tail."

"A white tip, that's unusual." Elijah finally moved from the window. "Yes, I see it." After a moment's silence, he added, "He's gone."

"Gone?" Elliot drew a bit of solace from his brothers' calm exchange, though he did not share their composure. "For how long?" He clambered to his feet.

"The night, at least, I'd wager." Elijah gave Elliot an encouraging smile. "Hungry?"

"Not yet." For the first time in his life, Elliot felt too terrified to eat. "Your brick house. How soon till it's done?"

Elijah gestured his brothers to the gathering room. "A couple of months."

"Months?" Elliot repeated in a moan.

"At least."

They headed toward down the hallway, Ezra scrambling to his feet to follow. The little calico zipped ahead, claiming a seat on the sofa moments before the brothers did the same. The calico lay between them, purring contentedly.

Ezra spoke first. "He'll be back tomorrow night."

"That's all right." Elijah tossed himself into his chair, readjusting books and papers to sprawl casually across the arms and seat. "We won't be here."

Elliot gave his oldest brother a puzzled stare. "What do you mean?"

"Jazz night," Elijah reminded.

Ezra's eyes went as large as pancakes. "Jazz night? With a wolf hunting us? Are you mad?"

Elijah shrugged. "We're at least as safe at the club as here."

Elliot had to agree with Ezra. "I'm afraid I'm too worried to enjoy a performance."

"Trust me," Elijah said. "Getting out will be good for all of us."

Tables filled the enormous common room, crammed full of animals of all varieties, shapes, and sizes. Cook smoke swirled around the customers, dancing through the hearth and candlelight like ghostly vapors. Rousing music slammed Elliot's ears, making conversation impossible, to his relief. The music helped to clear his head, but his thoughts remained grounded on the big bad wolf.

Ezra nudged Elliot suddenly, nearly unseating him.

Elliot scrambled back into place, rounding on his brother. "What did you do that—?"

"Look." Ezra jabbed a hoof toward the stage.

Elliot studied the figures in the band. A brown-and-white cow tapped out a beat, a saxophone hanging from a strap around her neck. Beside her, a dog clutching a trombone waved his head. A rooster flung his comb and wattles around as he slammed a ricky-ticky beat on his drum set. In the center, a dark wolf blew a trumpet solo that incorporated some of the highest notes Elliot had ever heard. Each time the wolf blasted out a shrieking pitch, the audience cheered wildly. "What . . . ?" Elliot started, then noticed the wolf's tail. A white tip bobbed with every movement. "Is that . . . ?"

"It might be," Ezra shouted back. "Elijah?"

The oldest brother snapped his fingers and rocked his head to the rhythm.

Elliot hunched down in his chair and hoped the wolf would not notice them.

Elliot spent the next day pacing the confines of Elijah's house and worrying. He could barely remember his last comfortable night of sleep, the last time food tasted good in his mouth. He saw no sign of the little calico and wondered where it spent the day while he and Ezra ate and took their fitful naps. He broached the subject only once. "Ezra, do you think that jazz trumpeting wolf . . . ?"

"It would explain a lot."

Elliot imagined it would take a great amount of wind and control to play jazz trumpet with such ferocity and talent . . . as well as to blow down houses.

Elijah returned home at dusk to a dinner of toast and jam surrounded by a huge pile of vegetables. He walked into the house with the cat tucked under his arm and dumped her onto the chair before greeting his brothers.

Elliot could not help staring. "You bring your cat to work?"

"Just today." Elijah flopped into his chair and scooped his plate from the table. "She had a special assignment."

The calico hopped to the floor, then sprang nearly into Ezra's plate. Only a quick and sudden shift of weight rescued his food.

"What could a pet cat possibly do at—"

A hammering paw at the door cut Elliot off with a startled gasp. All three pigs put aside their food to listen.

"Little pigs, little pigs, let me come in!"

Elijah raised his hooves as if conducting a band, and they all said in unison, "Not by the hairs of our chinny-chin-chins."

"Then I'll huff—"

"What are we going to do?" Elliot whispered, breaking out in a cold sweat.

"And I'll puff—"

Sweat beaded Ezra's brow as well, but Elijah looked the picture of calm. The cat sprang from Ezra's lap and trotted toward the door. Elliot craned his neck around the corner to watch her.

"And I'll blow your house down!"

The cat stretched up the door until her paws tapped the bolt.

"Do you want out?" Elijah asked.

Horror stole over Elliot. "Don't open that door!" He leapt from the sofa to chase after his brother.

The wolf began sucking in a deep lungful of air, then stopped, coughing.

Elijah scooped up the cat.

Elliot grabbed Elijah's arm. "Are you crazy?"

Elijah turned, finding Elliot directly in his face. "I'm not going to open the door," he promised.

The wolf sucked in another noisy burst of air, only to lose it in an enormous sneeze.

Elliot stepped aside, and Elijah galloped past him back to the gathering room. He opened a window and dumped the cat outside. The animal raced toward the front, drawn like a magnet to the one who could least tolerate her presence.

The wolf huffed again, the sound a vast and whistling wheeze. He lapsed into a fit of staccato coughs. "I'm gonna—" He coughed. "I'm gonna—" A fit of coughing stole his words, swiftly declining to a breathless, gasping hack.

The wolf turned and staggered into the darkness, while the pigs danced and laughed in Elijah's log cottage.

Elijah Pig finished examining his patient, a dark-furred, brown-eyed wolf with a white tip on his bushy tail, and replaced his stethoscope around his shoulders. "You have wheezes and crackles in your lungs. Your face is blotchy, and your nose has a ton of mucus in it. I'd say you had another allergic reaction, Sylvester."

"I thought so." Sylvester sat up on the table, refastening his vest. "The allergy shots always worked before. What do you think happened?"

Elijah looked thoughtful. "I don't know." He pulled at the stiff hairs on his chin.

"I was fine the previous night. Had a great set down at the club."

"I know. I heard you. You're talented."

"Thanks." Frustration gruffened the wolf's voice. "But I can't play like this." He sneezed hard enough to send papers tacked to the wall awash.

Elijah continued to stroke his chinny-chin-chin. "Have you changed your diet lately? Have you been eating anything strange like . . ." His eyes went dark. ". . . meat?"

Sylvester studied the doctor. "I . . . I mean I haven't . . . actually . . ."

"Because meat of any kind deactivates your allergy shots." Elijah shook a vial tainted with cat dander. "I guarantee, if you so much as . . . pursue a piece of meat, you'll never play trumpet again."

"I . . . understand," Sylvester said. "Consider me the strictest of vegetarians from this day forth."

Elijah nodded, setting down the vial. "Nurse, get me a vial of batch 1."

"I'm sorry," Sylvester said softly. "I . . . didn't know. From now on, I'll save my blowing for my jazz."

The doctor smiled. "See that you do, Sylvester Wolf. See that you do."

EVER SO MUCH

Bruce Holland Rogers

Bruce Holland Rogers lives with three cats—Osha, Sitka, and Trillium—and one wife in Eugene, Oregon. Bruce's stories have won two Nebula Awards, a Stoker, and a Pushcart Prize. Some of his short-short stories can be found online at shortshortshort.com. He is also the author of a book for writers called *Word Work: Surviving and Thriving as a Writer*. As we write this, Bruce is working on a novel that has one lamentable defect: so far, it hasn't got any cats in it.

Once upon a time in a fishing village along the windy shore there lived a boy with neither mother nor father. His name was Duncan, but the villagers called him Small Catch, which described his usual haul. When he might have been mending his nets in his tiny hut, he was as likely to be gazing into the fire while thinking of the grand palaces of kings. When he was out upon the sea, he watched the horizon and dreamed of distant shores and other countries, forgetting to lower his nets until half the day was gone. Even on his best days, he caught hardly enough to feed himself.

Duncan's boat leaked. One day, as he was pounding

bits of old rope into the very worst gaps, he looked up to see one of the village men striding over the rocks toward the sea with a burlap sack in his hand. Something inside the sack squirmed and mewled. Duncan put down his mallet and followed the man. "What do you have there?"

The man stopped and looked at Duncan. Then he held up the sack. "A wee cat," he said. "Runt of the litter, and bound to die anyway."

"Ah," Duncan said, for he understood that the man mean to throw sack and all into the sea. "Will you let me have it, then?"

The man considered a moment, then laughed. "Aye, by rights the runt *should* belong to Small Catch." And that is how Duncan came to own a cat.

II

From then on, Duncan's fishing was worse than ever. To any other villager, a kitten was useless until it was a cat, and as a cat it was good for nothing more than catching rats. But Duncan took great pleasure in playing with his kitten as it grew up, and just as much pleasure in watching it when it was grown, even though the cat—like most cats—spent much of its day sleeping. Duncan took to the sea just often enough to see that he and his cat did not starve, and it was a near thing at that. Some days he caught only one silverling. Other days he landed only a pin fish, which he had to prepare carefully to avoid the poison in its liver.

A kind of loyalty grew between the boy and his cat, though it was hard to say whether it was the cat that was loyal to Duncan or the other way around. They were always together except when Duncan put out to sea. On the narrow village paths or along the rocky shore, the cat followed Duncan or Duncan followed the cat. Villagers joked that it was a good match, that each was as industrious as the other.

On one rare sunny day, Duncan sat with his cat among the rocks. Duncan was on one side of a tide pool, and the cat was on the other side. Duncan watched the light glittering on the sea, then closed his eyes. He sighed. "Oh, my little cat," he said. "What is to become of me? The thing that I do best is dream, but there is no fortune in dreaming."

A high, little voice, just like a cat's voice, said, "There is ever so much to see."

Duncan opened his eyes wide and looked at his cat. The cat calmly returned his gaze. Duncan looked to the left and to the right. He looked behind. No one else was near. "Little cat, little cat!" he said. "What did you say?"

But the cat only peered down into the tide pool, as if it knew full well that Duncan had heard and remembered the words. Duncan peered into the pool, too. At first he saw only water, rocks, and sand. Then he noticed the tiny motions of an itsy bitsy crab creeping along a crack. He saw a minnow dart from one shadow to another. The longer he watched, the more he saw. An urchin waved the little arms that grew between its spines. A starfish crossed the sandy bottom no faster than the sun crosses the sky.

This was not the first time that Duncan had stared into a tide pool. This was not the first time that he had noticed more and more tiny creatures the longer he looked. But this was the first time that he had taken into his heart the truth that there was, indeed, ever so much to see. And not only in the pool, but on the rocks, along the shoreline, in the bird-filled air above and the in the clouds far beyond, there was ever so much to see.

III

Now Duncan the dreamer was Duncan the watcher as well. He was yet more idle than before, for when he would begin to mend his nets he would notice how each knot had its own shape, how captured bits of kelp were of different kinds, how the salt drifted from net to the earthen floor, dusting it white. Like his cat, he would sit for a long time with his eyes half-closed, considering the wood grain in the walls of his hut.

One day when all of the other boats were out, and Duncan sat on the rocks watching the waves with his cat, a great procession of men and horses came along the shore. Duncan and the cat watched them, and there was ever so much to see. In advance of the procession rode two helmeted soldiers wearing the king's colors of red and gold. They scowled at Duncan as they drew near. Then came a boy no older than Duncan, dressed in silken leggings and a quilted tunic. His face was pale, his arms were thin, and he seemed barely able to hold himself erect in the saddle. A red-bearded man dressed much the same rode close beside him, as if to catch the boy if he fell. Behind these came two worried looking men dressed in black. The thin one clutched a holy book, gazed heavenward, and moved his lips in prayer. The fat one glanced warily at the surf that lapped the horses' hooves and at the waves farther out from shore, as if he did not trust the sea to stay in its place. Behind these came solemn men in the quilted, ruffed, and silken clothes of court, followed by more soldiers. There was ever so much to see!

Duncan scrambled over the rocks, the cat following behind him, to keep up and to see what more there might be to see. So he was near enough to see the pale boy's head loll with sleepiness. He was near enough to see the red-bearded man shake the boy as if to wake him and keep him in the saddle. And Duncan was near enough to see something golden fall from the boy's hand and into a crack in the rocks, just before the boy himself toppled and landed in a heap on the sand.

The fat man in black urged his horse forward, dismounted, and unstopped a vial that he held beneath the boy's nose. The thin man in black prayed all the harder. The rest of the procession waited. At last the physician had roused the boy, who was helped back into his saddle. The boy's hands trembled as he tried to hold the reins, but he smiled bravely as he spoke to those around him. Duncan felt sorry for him and also admired his determination.

The riders continued. Duncan raised his hand to wave "Ahoy!" to a soldier, but the soldier touched the hilt of his sword and glowered so darkly that Duncan dared not tell him that the boy had dropped something. Duncan waited. When the procession was gone from sight, he sought the fallen treasure.

"A box," he said, showing it to the cat. The outside was beaten gold, decorated with the shapes of birds and flowers. But when Duncan opened it, and saw the pages, he realized that it wasn't a box at all. It was a little book. Priests and learned men could read these words. "I wonder what it says?"

IV

The king's messengers brought word to all the villages on the coast that the prince, who had recently taken the sea air, had lost a treasured possession—a little golden book. Whoever presented himself at court with the book would receive a reward befitting the prince's gratitude. The whole village, from children to fathers to grandmothers, was soon searching the shoreline for the prince's book. Duncan sat next to his overturned boat and watched them, feeling uneasy. His cat lay on top of the boat, eyes closed. Nearby, two young men of the village leaned against their own boats to watch the searchers.

"Oh, my little cat," Duncan said, "shall I tell them that they search in vain?"

A high little voice, just like a cat's voice, answered him: "There is ever so much to hear."

Duncan turned to look at his cat, but the cat's eyes were closed. "Little cat, little cat, what did you say?"

The cat opened its eyes, then stretched and yawned a yawn from the end of its tail to the tip of its tongue. It sat, closed its eyes again, and twitched its ears. It listened. Duncan closed his eyes, too. He heard the rush of the surf, the crying of gulls, the voices of children as they searched and called to their searching parents. Wind rolled in Duncan's ears. The more he listened, the more he heard. And though the two young men were some distance from him, he heard a boat creak as one of them leaned against it, and he heard the man say to his companion, "And why aren't you looking for it?"

"Because I've seen gulls snatching fish from other birds. It takes one kind to catch a fish, and another kind to eat it," the other man said. Then they both laughed. Whether this man was in earnest or not Duncan knew that what he said of gulls was true. Some gulls and some men found it easier to steal from others than to seek their own fortune. As soon as word got out that the prince's book had been found, no road between the village and the palace would be safe.

Duncan went inside his hut, wrapped some dried fish in a cloth, hid the golden book beneath his hat, and set out for the palace. His cat followed along. Every so often, they stopped by the side of the road to listen. When they drew near to the palace, Duncan heard a horse nicker softly in the woods where he thought no horse should be. He and the cat waited for nightfall, and then for midnight, and then for the moon to go down. Then they heard the conversations of a band of robbers who built a fire and cooked their dinner only now, when it was too dark for anyone to travel. Only then, when the robbers' thoughts were on the stewpot and their eyes were on the fire, did Duncan and his cat creep by in the dark.

V

Morning found them outside the palace. Duncan presented himself at the gate to claim his reward, and the cat darted in ahead of him, as cats will sometimes do at an open door. Where the cat had gone, Duncan did not know. Meanwhile, soldiers ushered Duncan into the throne room where the aged king sat on his throne and the ailing prince lay upon a litter. Beside the prince stood the priest, the physician, and the man with the red beard, who seemed not at all pleased to see so low a commoner in court. The prince, however, seemed not to notice the ragged state of Duncan's clothes. He was delighted to have his book returned to him. It was a book of poems, and he read one aloud before clutching the little book to his breast.

"Name your reward," said the prince, "and as it is in my power to grant, you shall have it."

And the king, who was pleased to see his ailing son so happy, added, "And as it is in *my* power, you shall have it."

Duncan looked at the high ceiling, the tapestries on the walls, the courtiers in their fine clothes. "I have often dreamed of being inside a palace," he said. "I ask for my reward only that I be permitted to stay a while at court."

"So shall it be," said the old king. To the red-bearded man, he said, "Brother, see to it that he is made suitable."

"My king," the man said, "I do not wish to leave my prince's side."

"I thank you for your devotion," the king said, "but

you serve your nephew best by making this boy fit to be among us for a while."

The red-bearded man bowed, then he bade two guards and Duncan to follow him. As soon as they were out of the throne room, the king's brother said a word and the guards seized Duncan by the elbows and hurried him so briskly through the halls that he thought surely they meant him harm. Even at a time such as this, Duncan remembered that there was ever so much to hear. The guards' boots clomped and echoed in the long hallways. Pots rattled and knives chopped, so that Duncan knew they were taking him to the kitchen even before the door was opened to the warmth and cooking smells. The king's brother dismissed the guards and summoned the cook. "Wash this," he said, waving his hand at Duncan. "It is to be made presentable at court."

"Him?" said the cook. "Him at court? Better to have one of my pots-and-pan boys before the king!"

"Indeed. But His Royal Highness commands it. Clothes will be sent. Burn the rags he's wearing." Then, as he turned to go, the king's brother muttered softly to himself, "No such follies when *I* am king."

There was ever so much for Duncan to hear.

"Right, then," said the cook. She called to her kitchen boys to bring a cauldron and water both hot and cold. "Clean him up," she commanded, "and don't spare the scouring brush out of kindness!" The boys made a bath of the cauldron, and they peeled and scrubbed Duncan as if he were a turnip. They kneaded him dry with rough towels and dressed him in the clothes that were brought.

Duncan's skin was sore, and the clothes itched against his skin, but when he was led up to the dining hall and saw the feast, he was glad that he had asked for this reward. There was ever so much to see: the honeyed meats, the fruits, the breads, the pastries. There was ever so much to hear: the worried conversations of the court, the tunes of the royal musicians. Duncan watched and listened and kept his peace. He learned how the courtiers feared for the prince's life. No effort had been spared for him. His priest was the holiest of men. The physician who attended him was most learned, the court physician from an allied kingdom in the mountains, but even he could not cure the mysterious illness that had come upon the prince of a sudden. All through the feast, the prince lay upon his litter, eating no bite of food and tasting no wine. Duncan saw how the prince tried to smile and be of good cheer, and again Duncan admired his courage. All through the dinner, the king's brother sat at his nephew's side and encouraged him to eat.

When the last bones had been thrown to the dogs, the king summoned Duncan. "Now you have been at court one day. What have you learned?"

Duncan said, "I have learned that the king's brother expects to sit upon the throne."

At that, the court grew still and silent. The king's brother glared at Duncan. The king's face reddened. "It is treason to speak such words of the royal family!"

The prince struggled to sit up and said, "Please, father . . ."

But the king did not wait to hear what the prince had to say. "This boy shall yet be our guest at court," the king said, "but I have different quarters in mind for him now." And Duncan was thrown into the dungeon.

VI

Duncan sat in the driest corner of the cell, which was not very dry at all. He shivered and wished he had his former clothes, for though tattered, they had been warm.

As Duncan despaired, his cat stepped through the

iron bars of the door. In its jaws, the cat carried a mouse so fat that it could only have come from the royal kitchen. The cat lifted each paw in turn to shake off the damp, then set to eating dinner.

Duncan rested his forehead on his knees and said, "Oh, my little cat, what am I to do? I dreamed of seeing the palace, but not this part of it!"

A voice answered, "There is ever so much to smell."

Duncan raised his head. Who else but the cat could have spoken? Duncan said, "Little cat, little cat, what did you say?" But the cat did not look up. It crunched mouse bones as if it knew very well that Duncan had heard. When the cat had eaten the very last morsel, it sniffed the moist floor where the meal had been, then sniffed the air.

"What is there to smell but the damp and rot?" Duncan asked. But he breathed in through his nose. He smelled the wet stones of his cell, and also the rusty smell of the iron door and its lock. He smelled mold and mildew and the stench of royal sewers. When his cat drew near, he smelled a trace of mouse flesh on its breath. None of these smells pleased Duncan, but it was true even here in the dungeon: There was ever so much to smell.

VII

After Duncan had been three days in the dungeon, the king sent for him to see what he had to say for himself now. Duncan bowed before the throne, bowed again to the prince on his litter, and bowed even to the king's brother. "I meant no treason," he said. "Your Highness asked me a question, and I spoke only the truth."

The king frowned, but the prince said, "Is it not as I said? This boy is a simple fisherman, and when he speaks, it is with the simple truth. There is no treason

in his words if my uncle does in truth expect to be
king, and who at court does not expect that? If I am
not made well, father, it seems that I shall die before you."

At these words, the king grew pale. The uncle assured the prince that he would surely recover and one
day take the throne. But the prince's gaze never left
Duncan. "Come forward," he said. When Duncan
drew near, he could smell the powders that perfumed
the prince's clothes, as well as the mustiness of the
prince's sickbed. "We have treated you ill," said the
prince, "for you have given us only kindness and hon-
esty. If my father will grant permission, I restore your
presence at court."

The king's jaw was set, but he nodded.

Duncan bowed again, and as he did so, he smelled
the faintest hint of something both fishy and bitter on
the prince's breath.

"My Prince," Duncan said, "you are being
poisoned."

The king's brother laughed, perhaps a bit nervously.
"The prince is served by a learned physician who
knows more than a fisherman knows of poisons."

"Your Highness," said Duncan. "I do not doubt
that the physician is a learned man, but is he not a
man of the mountains? The poison given to the prince
is a poison of the sea."

Now the king's brother grew pale. The king gave
Duncan leave to make a search, and two guards to
go with him, and they went straightaway to the royal
kitchens. Duncan wasted no time as he lifted lids from
jars and sniffed at shelves as a cat might do. The cook
protested this intrusion, but her protest changed to
weeping when Duncan's nose led him to a scrap of
burlap inside a flour bin. Wrapped in the burlap was
a black bit of dried fish liver, roughened on all sides as
it had been nicked and shaved away a little at a time.

When she was brought before the king, the cook confessed and accused the king's brother who had, of a sudden, made himself scarce. The palace was searched, and then the forest around the palace, and then the entire kingdom. But the king's red-bearded brother was nowhere to be found, and it was supposed that he had chosen exile before justice. It is sad to say that the cook alone was given the reward that she and the king's brother had earned together. If you know anything of kings, you can well imagine how she suffered, and if you know nothing of kings, then it is a mercy not to tell you.

VIII

The prince, once he was no longer given poison, recovered his usual vigor. Duncan, for his service to the court, was made a courtier for life and given a little room—much drier and pleasanter than his first one. His cat shared the room and also had the freedom of the palace.

In time, the king died and the prince became the new king. Duncan was the man whose eyes and ears and even nose the new king trusted most, and he trusted Duncan to tell the truth when asked for it.

With the passing of years, the cat grew old and fat, but it never spoke again . . . unless it was the cat who Duncan heard one night long after a royal feast. Duncan had fallen asleep at the table. No one woke him when the king and courtiers all left the great hall. The dishes and table scraps were left for morning, and the lights were put out. Duncan woke in darkness. He heard what might have been the sound of cat feet alighting on the table. He heard a familiar little voice that might have been a cat's voice. It said: "There is ever so much to taste!"

"Little cat, little cat," said Duncan. "What did you say?"

But there came no reply other than the crunch of a chicken bone.

SUEDE THIS TIME

Jean Rabe

Jean Rabe is the author of fifteen fantasy novels and more than three dozen short stories. Among the former are two DragonLance trilogies, and among the latter are tales published in the DAW anthologies *Warrior Fantastic, Creature Fantastic, Knight Fantastic,* and *Guardians of Tomorrow.* She is the editor of three DAW collections, including *Sol's Children* and *Historical Hauntings,* and a Lone Wolf Publications CD anthology: *Carnival.* When she's not writing or editing (which isn't very often), she plays war games and role-playing games, visits museums, pretends to garden, tugs on old socks with her two dogs, and attempts to put a dent in her towering "to-be-read" stack of books

Prince wasn't charming.

Not as far as I was concerned.

He stood in the middle of the castle drawbridge, his wheat-blond hair a mass of tangles, his jowls sagging, and his vacuous black eyes fixed unblinkingly on me. As I returned his stare, a thick strand of drool spilled over his lower lip and stretched down to pool between his front paws. A threatening growl rumbled up from his barrel-shaped chest, and he tipped his snout to display his sharp teeth.

No, Prince wasn't charming at all.

Though I was several yards away, on the far bank of the moat, I could smell him. The early morning breeze pummeled me with the redolence of whatever long-dead thing he'd found to roll in. I could well imagine he had fleas—a burgeoning colony of them— as when he wasn't watching me, he was usually scratching at himself with his hind legs or vigorously rubbing his rump against a post. He probably had mange, too.

It was my master who named the wretch "Prince," just three weeks past—the day he spied the grubby mongrel looking so apparently hungry and forlorn and whimpering so damn theatrically.

How my master could find this creature even remotely "adorable and oh-so-cute" was a mystery.

How he could take this insidious cur into our magnificent castle . . .

How he could let this filthy animal sleep at the foot of his bed . . .

How he could feed this . . . *thing* . . . choice bits from the table . . .

And how he could fashion a collar of the finest leather and the most exquisite sapphires for the beast's thick neck (the jewels being the only princely aspect of the fiend) . . .

. . . was well and truly beyond the scope of my considerable intelligence to grasp.

The worst of it—Prince wasn't even a dog.

Oh, he certainly looked like a dog, even to my keenly perceptive eyes, a wavy-coated retriever of some sort or an overgrown water spaniel with a fanciful plumy tail. He could bark with the best of them, shake "hands," roll over, even play "fetch" when the mood struck him. And he was quite practiced at passing wind under the dining room table when guests were present, and hiking his leg against the castle's walls when none of the guards were watching.

But to call him a dog would be an insult to lowly canines everywhere.

"Prince" was an ogre.

I accidentally discovered his dark secret late last night. And mere minutes later—before I could reveal him for the monster he is—he chased me out of the castle just as the drawbridge was raising, forcing me to spend the night beyond the moat on this chill, damp ground. When the bridge was lowered just an hour ago to greet the dawn, he immediately sidled out, no doubt to keep me from getting back in and warning my master about him. You see, I can speak the human tongue when I've a wont to. And the moment I tell my master the truth about his dear "Prince," he will order the ogre captured and slain.

I would attend to the killing myself. Unfortunately, "Prince" is a tad smarter than his departed brother was. I dealt with that particular ogre a few years ago.

I suppose I should explain.

I am Minew Milakye, a chartreux of some distinction. For those of you regrettably unknowledgeable about the finer points of cats, the chartreux is an ancient and esteemed breed that originated in France and was raised into numbers by a sect of Carthusian monks. All of my kind are known for our splendid and wooly slate-blue coats, bright orange eyes, even temperaments, and sharp wits. My wit is sharper than most.

It was my dear mother who named me Minew.

It was my master who drolly and fondly dubbed me Puss, as in "Puss 'n Boots." My good friend Charles Perrault reasonably accurately penned the story of how I came into my master's company—a far better telling, I might say, than he rendered of the sagas of that cinder girl and the child who looked quite silly in the vermilion riding hood.

The curtailed version of my story: I "belonged" to

a miller who died. The miller's will made provisions
for his eldest son to receive the mill, his middle son
to acquire the donkey, and his youngest son to be
given me.

The youngest son struck off, saddened by his lot
and unappreciative of my company until I revealed
that I could speak his simple language. I took pity on
him, and so I promised that I would make him rich—
if he would buy me a fine cloak, a velvet hat, a small
bag, and a pair of shiny black leather boots for my
back paws (on occasion I enjoy walking on two legs).
He was reasonably quick to attend to my requests,
and I was quick about my schemes.

Decked out quite nicely, I presented the nearest
king with various sundries, claiming them all to be
gifts from my master the handsome and noble Marquis
de Carabas. (What a grandiose title I created for the
lad!) When the king's curiosity was suitably piqued,
and when he began toying with the notion of arranging a marriage between his beautiful daughter and the
mysterious Marquis de Carabas, I invited the royal
family to visit my master in his castle.

Now my master didn't have a castle, but I'd heard
tell of an ogre who owned a magnificent one. All I
had to do was take the castle away from the brute.
So I paid a visit to the ogre, a quite magical if dim-
witted creature, and I told him that I'd heard he had
great arcane powers.

"Yep, I sure do," the ogre replied. "I can change
into things . . . a lion . . . an elephant . . . ya know,
things."

"That's wonderful!" I played along. "But you're so
tall! I bet you can't turn into something tiny." I fur-
rowed my brow. "Say . . . a blackbird. Or even more
difficult . . . a mouse. That would be impossible even
for one of your magical talent, wouldn't it?"

"Nope. Not impossible," he shot back. "I can do a
mouse. Watch this."

On the spot the fool cast a spell and transformed himself into a little gray one, which I snapped up, chomped its head off, and swallowed.

Before the hapless beast had a chance to give me indigestion, the "marquis" had a magnificent castle to show off to the king and the princess. And, soon after, the "marquis" had a beautiful royal wife, and was able to attract a staff of servants and two dozen well armed and armored guards.

It looked like the lot of us would live happily ever after.

That is until three weeks past when my master brought "Prince" into the castle, and until late last night when I accidentally caught "Prince" prowling through the kitchen for a late-night snack. "Prince" was walking on two olive-tinged legs the size of tree trunks and had shed all of his doggy hair in favor of his natural warty ogre hide. No wonder the dog had smelled odd, not like other canines I'd been downwind of. Unfortunately, "Prince" spotted me, and because of that I'm standing here on this chill, damp ground rather than lounging on a pillow high in the castle waiting for breakfast to be served.

How was I to know the ogre whose head I bit off had a brother?

How was I to anticipate that said brother would use magic to show up at the castle looking like some overgrown, sad-eyed water spaniel? And that he would be standing guard on the drawbridge at this very moment, turning the pool of drool at his feet into a veritable lake?

How was I to know?

Quick-witted though I am, do not expect me to be omniscient. So of course I couldn't have known about "Prince." Still, I felt some responsibility to warn the marquis about the detestable creature. I had put the Marquis de Carabas in the castle after all.

I glided closer to the drawbridge, trying to gauge

whether I might be able to race past "Prince" and into the castle proper before he could catch me. The beast's eyes lost their empty look and glimmered darkly.

"Ya ain't comin' in, cat," he whispered just loud enough for me to hear. His voice sounded like bits of gravel jostling around inside a bucket. "I heard whatcha did to my brother. Word gets 'round, ya know. So ya ain't never comin' back in. This's my castle now." He punctuated the sentiment with a loud dog-belch that added to the evil smells assaulting me.

"Your castle?"

"Yeah. I inherited it. From my brother who you killed."

"Inherited. Big word for an ogre."

He growled and scratched at a plank.

"Fine. Your castle," I hissed. "Then I suppose I have no alternative but to leave." I turned tail and sauntered into the bushes. To myself, I added: "But it is *not* your castle. There is no way you're claiming the place with the marquis, his royal wife, and all those guards traipsing around. Ogres are powerful. But not powerful enough to deal with that many people." Still . . . ogres live a very long time. Perhaps the lout was going to remain a dog for the next several decades, waiting until my master grew old and died and the castle was abandoned—provided the princess did not produce an heir to pass the castle along to. Or perhaps the ogre intended to remain a dog forever. Maybe he found the ghastly form an improvement over his natural one. Maybe he liked sleeping at my master's feet. Maybe he liked the princess cooing over him and scratching his ears, maybe he liked hiking his . . .

Maybe he had something sinister planned.

I needed to get inside and talk to the marquis. I knew the marquis' brother was coming to visit today—the middle son who had inherited the donkey. Perhaps

I could sneak in with him, hop into a pack or something. But he might not arrive until the afternoon, and I didn't want to wait that long.

Neither did I want to wait out the ogre-dog, hoping he'd grow bored of standing on the drawbridge and go elsewhere, giving me an easy way in.

No, I couldn't afford to wait. And so I decided to make an arduous sacrifice. I drifted deeper into the foliage and began circling the castle wall, paralleling the moat. I breathed deep and steadied myself for what I had to do. I located a suitable spreading fern, and beneath it I carefully placed my boots, cloak, hat, and bag for safekeeping. Then I continued on my route until I was behind the castle, where "Prince" couldn't see me.

I padded to the moat's edge. The breeze sent faint ripples across the water, making my reflection shimmer and dance and seem somehow mystical on this early morning. Water—the thought of it made my throat instantly dry. A shiver raced down my spine as I urged myself into it. Some say the part of the cat that hesitates is the paws. Especially over the prospect of getting wet. But I know it is essentially the whole of the cat. Every inch of me wanted to stay on this dry, chill ground. Every inch except one very small and persistent part that made me again pity the young man I'd turned into a marquis. And it made me want to warn him.

"No recourse," I said as I somehow found the water lapping over my toes, then against my stomach, as I somehow found myself practically submerged and swimming oh-so-quietly toward the rear of the wall that circled the castle. I felt something brush against my side, and for an instant I wondered if there were foul beasts lairing in this foul water. But nothing grabbed me, no toothed snout appeared, and no carnivorous fish dared to strike at my churning legs. And so moments later I found myself on the opposite bank, wet, cold, wet, thoroughly miserable, and thoroughly drenched. I started to rub against the tall grass that grew against the castle wall, then quickly stopped myself when I recalled where "Prince" tended to relieve himself. I most certainly would rather be wet and miserable than . . .

I glanced up at the crenellated wall. Though I'd lived inside the place for the past few years, I'd never appreciated just how imposing that wall was. Thick and impossibly tall, ogre-sized naturally—likely constructed to keep out whatever huge creatures might threaten ogres (never mind keeping out small clever cats).

"No recourse," I repeated, as I stretched against the wall and began climbing, claws digging into the hardened mud mortar between the blocks of stone. My muscles were screaming in protest before I'd reached the halfway point, and my chest felt like a fire being stoked. The small part of me that had urged me into the moat was delighting in this. For too long I'd been sedentary, enjoying the pampering of the marquis and the princess and the servants. My walks were brief ones, my lounging considerable, and my food heavy on the tasty aspect and light on nutrition. Often someone carried me up and down the stairs.

I should be carried up and down the stairs, I told myself. *I should be pampered.* "Why ever am I doing this? Why? Why? Why?" I hesitated, clinging fast and working hard to catch my breath. *I'm doing this so I can be carried up and down the stairs,* I decided. *I'm doing this to oust "Prince."*

I don't know how long I hung there, waiting for the fire within my chest to die down just a bit. It seemed like an eternity, my paws aching fiercely, but I knew it was only minutes. By the time I resumed my climb, and by the time I'd made it to the top, my fur was still dripping.

The small part of me that had impelled me up the wall rejoiced in the exertion. The rest of me simply rejoiced in the view. It was all so amazing from the top of the wall, the lush greens of the woods and meadows spreading away in all directions, the water of the moat looking like a silver ribbon festooned with beads of sunlight. The breeze carried the scent of wildflowers, the small fragrant ones that hung on at the close of summer, and I could hear the faint twitter-song of swallows. Turning inward, I could see the castle and the service buildings around it—the stable, blacksmith's stall, and the barracks. Workers busied themselves scurrying about while the guards stood like statues—two on either side of the archway that led to the moat, two on either side of the castle door, two more on parapets. The castle itself stood in the midst of it all, made of white granite shot through with glistening veins of black, a turret rising above this wall with a pointed conical roof looking like a spear jutting into the cloudless sky. There was a window high in the turret, and I'd never thought to perch in it before and absorb the view.

I would now, after "Prince" was dealt with and I'd retrieved my clothes and boots. I'd make that windowsill my favorite spot, and from it I would survey this glorious countryside—after I climbed the stairs to reach it, of course, making sure that small part of me was satisfied that I'd gotten some exercise. An ogre did not deserve such a magnificent place, and could not appreciate the beauty of the land. An ogre would not enjoy the view. So the ogre had to go . . . now.

The castle was trimmed around the windows and balconies in pale blue, the marquis' favorite color. But the trim had been burnt orange and was chipping dreadfully when I'd acquired the place from "Prince's" brother. The ogre hadn't done much to keep the place up. His brother would do no better job. I felt bile rising in my throat as I continued to think of the ogre-dog that was likely still on the drawbridge.

I started down the other side of the wall, using the cover of the castle to hide my presence. It was a little easier climbing down, and easier still to rush across the ground and dart inside the kitchen door that was timely being opened by a cook.

"Puss!" she said, as I shot past. She'd made a motion to pet me, but I hadn't the time for such pleasantries. "Where's your hat and . . ."

I was well beyond her and her trivial prattle, through the dining room and into the gallery before I came to a stop behind a suit of decorative plate armor. Here I listened for the beat of the place. Every castle has a heart; sometimes it's a strong one—like those great ancient edifices belonging to important kings. Sometimes it's a small and feeble one, like a few places I'd slipped into during my kitten days, pretentious castles built for men who have titles but lack the miens and brains for leadership. This castle, I'd learned shortly after its previous owner's demise, had a dark heart. Its beat was hard to hear, but if you were a chartreux and if you listened for it, you could manage.

Its steady thrum spoke of its long decades on this land, of its deep foundation filled with dungeons and treasure chambers, of the bloodstained floors in its secret rooms. It beat with the brush strokes of paintings stolen from merchant caravans, with the stitches of great tapestries fashioned by human slaves, with the last gasps of the lives lost to the ogre who once held sway here. And it pulsed with the presence of the damnable ogre-dog.

Why couldn't he have stayed on the drawbridge?

I could hear the beast in the room beyond, nails clicking rhythmically over the stone floor, breath coming short and even. He must have come in from the drawbridge shortly after I'd given up that route, and was now patrolling the main room and the winding stairway that led up to the chambers where the marquis was most likely to be found.

His ogre-heart beat in time with the castle's, not as strong, but darker, I sensed. The marquis would deal with the monster today, I vowed. Then perhaps the beat of the castle's dark heart would be silenced and a new heart would replace it—one that beat in time with mine.

I slipped back into the kitchen and made my way up the narrow stairs that lead to the cook's room. Faintly, from below, I heard the clacking of the ogre-dog's nails. Could he sense me as I sensed him? Could he smell my pleasant musky odor as I was forced to stomach the stench of him?

I moved faster, darting beneath the cook's bed while I listened more carefully. The clacking was coming up the stairs.

Faster still and I was out of the meager room and into the hall beyond, rushing toward a wider staircase that would lead to the sitting room the young marquis and his princess favored. My sides were aching from the exertion of the swim across the moat, from climbing the wall, from now climbing these stairs. The small part of me that was oh-so-proud at my efforts would be prouder still when the ogre met his demise.

Faster.

"Puss!" the princess exclaimed as I slipped into the massive sitting room filled with stolen paintings and slave-made tapestries, scented tapers, and the soft glow spilling in from high narrow windows. "Puss, you're wet! And you've lost your cloak and boots!"

The clacking was louder, the beast closing.

I glanced about for the marquis-I'd-made. I'd never spoken to the princess, only to my young master. Speaking to her now—and about a horrid ogre—would yield nothing but a shocked look on her pretty face. She'd hear my words, but she wouldn't listen to what I had to say.

The clacking and . . .

Humming! The young marquis was humming in the room beyond, the music room he called it, a polished marble place filled with poorly strung harps and ill-tuned lyres. I was a blue-gray streak past the princess and into the next room, a chartreux blur heading straight toward my master sitting on a plush velvet chair, a skidding mass of fur as I scrambled to come to a stop.

"Puss!" he exclaimed. "You've been out all night! You're wet!" His tone became playfully scolding. "You've lost your cloak and boots. I'll have to buy you new and . . ."

"No." It was the only word I could manage at the moment, and it wasn't in reference to his offer of new attire. "No." The word was directed at what was swirling around his feet. There were puppies, eight of them—writhing balls of golden hair and shiny black noses, wagging plumy tails and merry yappings. "No. No. No."

"So you don't want to wear clothes anymore?" He reached down and picked up one of the pups, cradled it in his lap and twirled his long fingers around its ears.

They weren't puppies. I could sense it as I could sense the castle's heartbeat. Ogres, all of them.

"They're not puppies," I started. The words were coming fast now. "I never told you the whole story of how I got this castle for you. There was an ogre. . . ."

"Yes, yes," he said. "I remember. You somehow managed to slay the vile monster after a fierce battle."

I inwardly groaned. I never told the Marquis de Carabas the truth, that I'd tricked the brute into transforming himself into a mouse. The slay-the-vile-creature-after-a-fierce-battle-story seemed much more glamorous at the time. The marquis didn't know that ogres could magically assume different shapes. Didn't know about the mouse. Didn't know about the true nature of the dog he'd brought into the castle. I'd only told the true story to Charles Perrault and a few stray cats, all good friends.

"Ogres are magical creatures," I began, deciding there wasn't time to explain everything. I was listening for the clacking of Prince's nails, but I couldn't hear it anymore. My heart was pounding too loudly.

"Not so magical as you," he kindly returned.

Much more magical, actually, I thought. Aloud, I said: "They can turn into things."

He cocked his head in polite curiosity and reached down to pick up a second pup.

"Things like dogs and puppies," I continued. "Those aren't real puppies. They're ogres. All eight of them. And Prince is an ogre, too. Last night . . ."

The marquis laughed then, loud and long, throwing back his head and cackling upward so his voice bounced off the ceiling. When the mirthful cacophony finally subsided, he fixed his eyes on mine. "You're clever, Puss, trying to make me think these delightful creatures are ogres. You probably want me to toss them out of the castle."

"That wouldn't be good enough," I said. "They'd come back. How'd they get here to begin with?"

"The pups? They came in yesterday late in a farm er's cart. He was as surprised as the cooks that they were hiding behind the bushels of potatoes. Aren't they . . . charming?"

"They're ogres," I repeated. "You'll need to drown them. Or behead them. Skewer them with a long spear and . . ."

He laughed again, but curtly this time. "I know cats don't care for dogs, Puss, but you're being a little ridiculous." One of the pups stretched up and licked his chin. Another, between his legs and where he couldn't see, raised its lip in a silent snarl directed at me.

I snorted. "Ridiculous? I'm being realistic. They're ogres, the pups *and* Prince—warty, green-skinned, smelly monsters that will find a way to . . ."

He drew his eyebrows together and studied me.

"That will find a way to . . ." I so hated to talk in front of the ogres, but what alternative did I have? ". . . to get rid of the guards and deal with the servants, chase you out of this wonderful castle. Kill you, maybe. Probably. Ogres kill people." The heart of the castle beat with the last gasps of dozens of humans the previous ogre-owner had slain. Perhaps the heart was too dark to change.

"They're puppies, Puss, charming, adorable puppies." He offered me a slight smile. "And they're staying. The princess and I discussed it, and we've agreed to keep them all."

"You can't, you . . ."

"And you'll have to accept them."

I shook my head, droplets of moat water flying away from me. "I can't. I won't. They're ogres and . . ."

"Then you'll have to leave."

What? I stared at him incredulously. *What did he say?*

"If you can't accept the pups and Prince, you'll just have to find a home elsewhere."

I heard the clacking again, glanced over my shoulder and saw "Prince" standing in the doorway behind me. He was looking at the marquis, tail wagging a greeting.

"There's my good boy," the marquis gushed. "Prince" trotted over and settled in next to his chair.

I needed time. I had to think. There must be a way to get the marquis alone. Perhaps I could again catch "Prince" prowling in the pantry late at night, get my master to see the monster for its true self. But there were nine ogres now, a formidable force. Nine ogres would be more than enough to handle the servants. But nine ogres might not be enough to tackle the marquis' armed and armored guards. There was still time to deal with this threat, especially if the ogres were attacked while in pup form. Kill them as I had swallowed the mouse. Still time and . . .

"Dear!" The lilting voice of the princess carried in from the sitting room. "One of the maids says she's found more puppies—a half dozen. Isn't that wonderful!"

"No." I had to think. I whirled and bolted from the room, a blur of blue-gray that was in an instant beyond the princess and out onto the landing, was racing up steep stone steps that added to the ache in my sides.

"Puss?" the princess called.

"Leave him be." This from the marquis. Though I was putting distance between myself and the lot of them, my hearing was acute enough to pick up the conversation. "Puss doesn't like the pups. But he'll get used to them. He'll have to."

"He'll have to if he wants to stay here," the princess finished. "The pups are . . . charming."

Charming. The word rattled around inside my head. *Charming.* Perhaps that was it! Perhaps the oh-so-magical ogres had cast a charm spell on the marquis and the princess. Perhaps that was why my master wouldn't listen to reason, *he couldn't listen to reason,* couldn't see the pups for what they really are.

How could I get my master alone? Or at least catch him when none of the ogres were around. Six more of them! Fifteen in all. I skidded to a stop on a higher landing. Fifteen ogres could defeat my master's armed and armored guards. Fifteen ogres would be enough to take back this castle. To wipe out the servants. To kill the marquis and the princess.

I sensed the castle's dark heart beating more strongly, even as my own heart hammered wildly in my chest. It was no longer a matter of dealing with the ogres. It was a matter of getting my master and his wife and as many others as possible out of the castle before the ogres made their move. I turned to retrace my steps, deciding to make another attempt at reaching the marquis-I'd-made, when I saw a ball of golden fur bounding up the stairs toward me. The pup's expression was pure malevolence, and I wasted no time in heading back up the stairs.

How was I to know that the ogre whose head I bit off had a brother?

And that the brother had fourteen ogre-friends?

Before I reached the next landing, even the small part of me that had been delighting in all this exercise was complaining. My lungs burned, my chest heaved, my head pounded and my legs throbbed. I wanted desperately to stop, to lie down somewhere and rest. But I forced myself on, and at a faster pace still, as the ogre-pup that chased me was far from winded.

The stairs were narrowing now, as we were in the narrowing turret, and they were becoming increasingly steeper. While at first I considered that an advantage, as my agile cat legs could better handle them than awkward pup feet, a look behind sent my head to pounding more. The pup had cast a spell and transformed itself into a dog, one similar to "Prince," though even uglier. Within moments, I suspected it would be on me. It would chomp my head off and devour me. It would reclaim this castle before my body had a chance to give the monster indigestion.

"Faster!" I shouted, and somehow my legs complied. "Move!"

Then I was at the highest landing, through a narrow door, and up on that very high windowsill that provided a glorious view of the countryside. I had no time to absorb the splendor, however, as the ogre-dog burst into the small, round room, snarling and snapping and dribbling saliva on the floor.

Though the sill was oddly high, he could perhaps reach it—barely—if he stretched up on his hind legs.

I would go out the window, climb down the stone. In fact, I started to do just that—until I spied three sleek-coated pointers far beneath me. I couldn't smell them, but I was certain they were ogres, too. I spun and looked about the room. There was an iron chandelier hanging from the ceiling, and if I sprang just right I could catch it, pull myself up and get beyond the ogre-dog's . . .

I bunched my leg muscles and prepared to leap, then I stopped myself when his ugly eyes caught and held mine.

"Ya talk too much, cat," the dog said. Twin strands of drool spilled from his mouth. "Ya shouldn't've went blathering like ya did to the marquis. Shouldn't've exposed our secret, not that he believed ya. Shouldn't've suggested he drown us. Wasn't polite, cat. An' here I surmised that you were a critter with some brains."

Blathering. Surmised. Big words for an ogre, I thought. Perhaps they weren't all so stupid as the one whose head I . . .

"Them stray cats we caught a month or so back, they seemed pretty smart—and real tasty.'Fore we ate 'em they talked to us 'bout how you killed the ogre what used to live here. Ya shouldn't've told them cats 'bout it."

No, I shouldn't have, I agreed. I risked another glance at the chandelier. It was higher than I'd ever jumped before, but perhaps I could . . .

"If ya had kept your mouth shut, we wouldn't've known. Grizwald wouldn't've learned ya ate his brother, my second cousin once removed and Rati-gan's and Zebedee's best friend. Griz wouldn't've got us all together and had us come here. Should've kept your mouth shut, cat. 'Cause now I'm gonna see if you're tasty, too."

"I guarantee you I'm all gristle," I replied. If I missed the chandelier, I'd fall right in front of him. There had to be another way out. . . .

The dog sat back on his haunches, watching me. "Should've kept your mouth shut," he repeated. "At least the marquis didn't swallow a word ya said. At least . . ."

"What are you going to do to him?" Despite my master's unwillingness to believe me, I held a fondness for him.

The dog made a gesture that approximated a shrug. "Griz . . . Prince . . . likes the marquis well enough. So we probably won't kill him. Probably keep the human tied up in the dungeon. Bring him out and set him to waving at merchant wagons to lure 'em in."

"And everyone else?"

Another shrug. "Once upon a time we ogres was peaceable sorts."

Not any longer, I knew.

"So I 'spose we'll kill 'em. Maybe we'll keep the princess and one or two others around to cook for us. Maybe we won't. Ratigan can cook when he puts his mind to it."

The dog's tongue lolled out and his eyes took on a hungry gleam. As I contemplated my options—either the chandelier or climbing out of the window, both bad options—I saw him change. The fur melted off him like butter, seeping into the cracks of the stone floor and disappearing. The skin beneath was a pale green, dotted with warts and festering boils. There were muscles, and they were growing as I gaped. The entire dog was growing, and its limbs were changing, becoming manlike and thick and long. Arms extended and front paws turned into massive hands with fingers ending in ugly, cracked nails. The chest became defined and impressive, and the head became hideous. The ogre's face was shaped like an egg, hairless save for a dozen uneven strands that jutted from the top. His eyes were crooked, the right being slightly higher and larger than the left, and the nose was wide and puglike, looking as if it might have been broken a few times. The lips were large and bulbous, licked by a wide black tongue.

"I like gristle," he said in a sonorous voice that echoed off the walls.

He gave a chuckle then and reached for me, and in that instant I abandoned the chandelier notion and leaped from the windowsill and into the room. In a heartbeat I was through his legs, speeding across the floor and out the door, scrambling over the landing and down the stairs. I was a blue-gray blur heading toward the music room, intent on trying one final time to get the marquis to listen.

"Puss!" the princess exclaimed as I ran past her. She was still ensconced in the sitting room, a half-dozen golden-furred ogre-puppies around her dainty slippered feet. "Dear kitty, have you . . . ?"

I barreled into the next room, my clawed feet skittering over the polished floor and taking me to my master.

"Father's cat!" A sneeze. "You still have father's cat."

My master had company, the new voice belonging to the middle brother. The man was sitting several feet away from the marquis, leaning against an enormous harp and sniffling into a handkerchief.

"Yes, Puss is still with me, and . . ."

"Listen," I blurted, eyes darting from one pup to the next to "Prince," who had taken a discreet position behind the marquis. "You have to listen to me!"

"Father's cat talks?" Another sneeze. And another.

"Yes, brother, and sometimes he—"

"Listen!" I broke in. "They're ogres. All of the pups are ogres. And if you and the princess and your brother and the servants and the armed and armored guards don't leave, you all could be dead by nightfall."

The marquis didn't laugh this time, and for a moment I thought I'd reached him. That notion vanished, however, when his eyes narrowed to thin slits.

"You listen to me, Puss."

The brother sneezed quite loudly this time.

"And you listen good. I like these pups. I like Prince. I like them better than you."

What? His words were daggers, and I heard them well, just as I heard the castle's dark heart beat faster and stronger, just as I smelled the stench of the ogre-pups. I was reeling from all of it.

"I never liked you, Puss. I only tolerated you because my father liked you. Then I tolerated you because you got me this castle and the princess."

The brother sneezed again and again.

"I don't like *any* cats, Puss. Never did. In fact, I hate cats. They're too aloof. They're too independent. Can't stand the hairballs and the finicky behavior. Dogs, Puss. I like dogs. No. I *love* dogs. All of these pups and Prince are staying, and . . ."

"Ahhhhhhhhh-chooooooooooooooo!" The brother was caught up in a sneezing fit.

". . . and you're leaving, Puss," the marquis continued, raising his voice. "You're leaving right this very instant."

"I'm leaving, too, I'm afraid." The brother stood, handkerchief over his nose. "I can't sit here another moment. I am so allergic to dog fur." His eyes watered as if he'd been to his best friend's funeral. "I can take the cat with me if you'd like. I rather fancy the notion of having a talking cat."

"The pups," I tried one final time, catching the angry gaze of the marquis. "They're ogres. They're going to—" Then I felt myself being lifted and held beneath the middle brother's arm. He stuffed the handkerchief in his pocket, sneezed again, and petted me with his free hand.

"You're damp," he said to me, as he carried me out of the music room and paused in the sitting room to bow to the Princess. "However did you get so damp?" he continued, as he started down the stairs.

"And you're out of breath. I bet those pups were chasing you."

"Yes, chasing," I said.

"No pups will chase you in my house," he returned. "It's a good house, sturdy and small, nothing like this castle. But you'll like it."

"No dogs," I said.

"No. No dogs. I'm so terribly allergic to them. I've a donkey, though. He doesn't talk, but you'll like him."

"I'm sure I will," I replied, as he carried me out of the castle's front door, strode to the stables, and deposited me on the donkey's saddle.

"Your paws!" he exclaimed, taking note of the rest of my condition. "You've got a few broken claws, and your pads are bleeding."

All the running, I thought, the climbing up and down the wall, the scrabbling up the stairs. I wasn't used to it, and my paws were paying the price.

"Perhaps I should buy you some boots," he continued, as he led the donkey across the drawbridge.

Behind us I could hear the playful yip of the fourteen puppies and the loud bark of "Prince." Fifteen ogres. Eighteen if the three pointers outside the window were ogres, too. A veritable force of monsters! The marquis' guards couldn't possibly . . .

Then my breath caught, as on the grounds beyond the moat I saw seven more dogs, a motley looking crew—terriers, shepherds, and a one-eared shaggy sheepdog. They smelled just like "Prince." Thankfully, they waited until we were over the drawbridge and headed away from the marquis' lands before they scampered across and hurried to join the other ogres. The marquis would be going to the dogs, all right. I fervently hoped at least some of the people within the castle walls could find their way free before . . .

"Did you hear me, Puss?"

"Minew, my name's Minew Milakye."

"Would you like some boots, sweet Minew?"

My eyes took on a faraway look as I thought of the fine cloak and hat, bag, and boots I'd lost beneath the spreading fern.

"Yes," I answered with fervor. "I indeed would fancy a new pair of boots. Suede this time."

THE COBWEBBED PRINCESS

Andre Norton

In a literary career spanning more than six decades, Andre Norton (1912–2005) wrote over one hundred novels in a number of popular genres, including juvenile, Gothic, and historical stories. Her best-known work, however, was in the fields of science fiction (the "Beastmaster" saga) and fantasy (the "Witch World" series). She received numerous awards for imaginative writing and in 1984 was accorded the status of Grand Master.

For *Magic Tails* she offers a heretofore-undiscovered version of "The Sleeping Beauty" by the feline author Purrault; its hero is based on her Lynx-Point Siamese, Cobweb, one of ten cats who really run the Norton household.

I t was going to be a good day—a couple of sniffs of such breeze as managed to find its way through the narrow windows of the princess' chamber told me that. I jumped to the floor, rattling through the drift of parchment-dry leaves that had blown in last fall, and paid my respects properly to the Lady Bast with forelegs extended to the limit and head bowed.

The large chamber was dim; three of the windows

bore a double curtaining of rich brocade within and tapestry-tight overgrowth of vines without, while the fourth had been sealed with a branch that had been driven into it by a winter storm. However, I had no difficulty in making my morning inspection.

Maid Mafray still snuggled atop the pile of linens she had been carrying when the magic had struck so long ago. Under a veiling of dust and more leaves she had grown no older, of course; that was part of the spell. Diona, Lady of the Wardrobe, had not moved either. Her head still rested on the folds of the gown she had been about to present for the princess' approval at the moment the curse had cast its word-web over the castle.

I padded back to the huge curtained bed and leaped up onto it. My charge lay there as comfortably as I had been able to dispose her, the covers made as smooth as I could arrange them, with patting paws and cloth-tugging teeth, under her chin. Her silver-fair hair fanned out to form a net, living but motionless, over the satin-covered pillow. Yet, even as I watched, her eyelids flickered.

Tensing, I crept closer with the same care I took to hunt one of the skittish wildfowl that landed in the courtyard below. A line appeared between my lady's arched brows, and I began to purr; turning on the soothing rumble I hoped would banish what could only be an evil dream. Now her head turned and, with the movement, swung one of the strands of hair across the chain of the amulet she had ever worn about her neck and snagged the lock so that it was pulled painfully.

Crowding against the girl, I touched her lips with the very tip of my tongue. I knew of both the bitter spell that had reduced her to this state and the sweet kiss that would revive her from it, and I had long ago begun to wonder whether perhaps it were up to me and not some dream-born stranger to perform that act. I had tried it twice before when her night was troubled but had met with no success; never had the sleeping shape shown that it was more than an effigy of the Princess Charlita of Fallona—

—until now. Was the third time, indeed, the charm?

The princess' lids fluttered, then opened, and her eyes stared into mine, recognition at once evident in their violet-blue depths. I retreated as she sat up. Dust puffed forth from both the pillows and the heavily embroidered coverlet as she pushed them away; she sneezed vigorously and shook her head, and with the gesture caught sight of Mafray. My lady frowned and, lifting a hand, brushed it across her eyes before glancing at her maid-in-waiting again. Charlita might have just returned from the ensorcelment of decades a-dream, but her wits were perfectly clear.

"The curse—" Her voice, loud in the silence, broke off suddenly. She was shivering. I crept forward and stretched my neck so I could lick at her arm, but I did not gain her attention by that small gesture of comfort. Instead, she rolled halfway over, then sat on the edge of the bed, which was raised on a dais two steps above the floor. More dust rose, and she coughed and waved her hands before her to fan it away.

"Mafray?" The princess slid down from the bed. She nearly fell as her long-unused feet skidded on the platform, but at last she stood on the stone flags. A few more steps, each increasingly sure, brought her to the side of the sleeping girl; Charlita's death-in-life might have ended, but her serving maid's had not.

Jumping from the bed, I padded over to her. To be sure, I have certain talents, and they have been well proven; however, I could not communicate directly with my charge, and this restriction would, I feared, cause difficulties. The girl looked at me and frowned, and I strove to reach her, mind to mind. If she possessed any Gift, it was limited; yet it was not wholly absent, for she sensed the intensity of my focus and stooped swiftly to gather me up into her arms. She knew how to properly lift a cat, placing one hand under my front legs and supporting my hindquarters with the other.

"You were there when—" Charlita hesitated, then began again. "Urgal wielded the rod—the Silver Rod—"

I stiffened and must have put out my claws in my surprise, for my charge gave a little cry, and I hastened to sheathe them again. What had she just said—how could she know? The Sleep should have held her too deeply to dream of—*that*!

The princess shifted her hold on me so that our eyes met, and she said firmly, as though by forceful utterance she could make her telling a truth, "You are Cobweb, my birthday-fairing from Granddam Foreby—but you are more than any mere cat." She gathered me closer so that my head was again near to her chin, and once more I gave her a quick touch-of-tongue.

Still carrying me, Charlita moved across the floor, carefully avoiding Maid Mafray, and headed for the nearest window. There she lowered me to the wide sill while she herself wriggled forward to peer through an opening in the curtain of vine.

Her gasp was almost a cry. What lay below was enough to shock anyone whose last memory was of a castle filled with life and light, not a gigantic mausoleum where time itself was held in check by a spell set working by evil witchery. The girl retreated from the view, her face pale.

"It is true, then, Cobweb—the curse has indeed fallen upon me, and through me upon all these innocent folk—" She paused and turned her head to gaze first at Mafray and then to Diona. "Yet I am now awake, so why not they also? Why not they?" Her chin quivered.

I knew as well as she the conditions of the curse, its why and wherefore, and its birth from the jealous spite of the Great One who had come late to Charlita's christening. The princess appeared to be reviewing those terms, as well, for now she studied the forefinger of her right hand.

"No sign remains, Cobweb," she murmured, then lifted her eyes to me once more. "I remember, dear furred one—you tried to stop my taking up that spindle!"

I bowed my head, for I, too, remembered. Like all my kind, I was proud of my quickness of movement, deft play-of-paw; but in that far and fateful hour, that skill had either failed me—or *I* had failed. My mistress had taken up that tool of labor she had found lying on her bed, and it had turned in her grasp as a serpent might writhe, so that its point had struck deep into the first finger of her right hand. Then the dire enchantment had fallen on her, and on every being beneath this roof save myself. And not only had sleep overwhelmed those within the castle, but forgetfulness of the Kingdom of Fallona itself had spread like a poisoned mist throughout the adjoining lands. It was as though the most potent Older One had wiped the very memory of our realm from the world.

"Yet do all indeed still dream?" Charlita queried of the air as she stepped towards the nearest of three tall wardrobes. "Perhaps not all; let us see!"

The girl had taken the Sleep in her chemise and her belaced underskirts, for she had been about to try on the dress which Diona held ready just as she sighted the spindle protruding from beneath a pillow on the bed. Now she tugged open the door of the wardrobe before her and pulled out the nearest of the gowns within.

Thus Princess Charlita and I went searching throughout the castle for some sign of waking life, though I knew she was as certain as I that our quest would be fruitless. She hailed sleepers, sometimes going so far as to pat a face, pull gently on a shoulder, an arm. Nowhere did her touch evoke a response—a lack that grew from the merely frustrating to the nearly unbearable when we reached the palace library. There my mistress beheld her mother, resting not ungracefully against her embroidery frame, and her father seated at his desk, his head pillowed on a pile of parchments. Charlita did not intrude upon the king and queen but instead subsided into a high-backed chair placed just inside the door and sat twisting her hands together, fighting sobs. I jumped into her lap, and again she hugged me. Slowly her weeping quieted; then she spoke.

"Everyone but you, Cobweb. How did *you* escape?"

How I longed for the gift of speech, or at least mind-touch, so that I might tell her! The answer was that I had fought then with the full strength of that talent which was my birth-gift from Bast. Soul to soul I cried to Her, the patroness of home and hearth: *Let me not fall into slumber, Lady, but remain awake to watch and ward, for this human one was mine to cherish, and I did not succeed in keeping her from harm.* My recollection of that plea was interrupted as the girl tightened her embrace.

"There was to be a prince, Cobweb, who was to awaken me with a kiss. Goodness knows, the curse and its cure were told me over and over from the time Nurse Ardith thought I was able to understand words. So—where is my royal rescuer?" She laughed harshly, then hiccuped as though holding back further tears.

Perhaps would-be saviors *had* visited throughout the years. However, the hedge of thorny brush that was the outward sign of the curse had grown dark and dense around the castle until it was more forbidding than a barrier of stone. Had any high-minded youth come seeking my mistress, perhaps in an attempt to prove a legend true, he had neither found nor fought a way through that living wall.

The belief grew within me that I had failed once more in my duty—that what I had done, if I were indeed responsible for the princess' waking (as I grew ever more certain I was), had been wrong.

Once again the girl's hands tightened grip on me, lifting me up until I was eye to eye with her.

"What do I do now, friend-in-fur? We alone are awake—we . . . alone! Do I play 'hunt-the-spindle' again—return to sleep? *Tell* me, Cobweb!"

Charlita's voice held a near-hysterical edge I did not like, and I cared even less for the way she shook me as she posed her questions. I wanted to strike out with a claw-spread paw but, knowing that fear and not cruelty caused her to handle me roughly, I contented myself with hissing.

All at once I caught movement at the desk where the sleeping King Ludoff dreamed on his parchment pillow. The library windows, which were the only ones in the palace to contain glass, could admit no breeze to stir the papers that lay there, yet a small cloud of dust had just risen. Now I distinctly saw the topmost sheet of parchment quiver, then one corner roll up.

We cats depend upon sight to hunt, whereas dogs rely upon scent or hearing. Thus it did not surprise me that the great warhound, Briser, still lay behind the king's chair as deep in slumber as his master, for, whatever its nature, this intruder moved in utter silence.

The page beneath the king's fingers set to wriggling like a living thing, working its way to freedom. I heard the princess gasp, felt her move to rise. However, I could spare her no attention, for at that moment I only wanted to know what creature, hidden from my sight, was making itself free of this room. I leaped to the floor, crouched, and launched myself upward, aiming for the top of the desk. Claws came to my aid, and I scrambled over the edge safely, to see the paper floating above me, motionless. I heard a snort like a suppressed laugh. Briser moved his head, and the spikes on his thick collar rasped against the stone flooring. I expected him to awaken, but he did not.

To my amazement, Charlita was the one who acted. Two strides brought her to the desk. Her hand was already out, and now it shot forward and her fingers closed firmly about the edge of the parchment. However, the sheet did not yield to this persuasion but strove to wrench itself free; plainly whatever—or whoever—held it would not surrender its prize without a struggle.

Once more I crouched and sprang, and it came as no surprise when one of my forepaws raked on cloth I could not see, tearing it, while my claws caught in flesh and a smell of blood followed. I strove to turn my body as it hung in the air and strengthen my hold. The long years of keeping life in my body by stalking the wildfowl that invaded the courtyard stood me in good stead now.

The limb to which I had attached myself was now flailing up and down, and I would surely have been dislodged in another moment; fortunately, though, another warrior had joined the fray. Past my head flew a massive inkwell of malachite, but its flight was a brief one, for it thudded home only inches from my own struggle. The sound of its meeting with a very solid surface was followed by an exclamation as that portion of the invisible opponent to which I clung swung suddenly downward. I was raked off on the rim of the desk and landed on the stone flags, my head so awhirl that for a moment I could only lie, limp and asprawl, coughing with body-shaking expulsions of air as a gout of dust billowed up to envelop me.

When I had blinked my eyes clear, I could make

out a dark blot hovering in the air. That there was substance to what I had attacked I knew, and now, though the invader remained unseen, the splatters of ink betrayed both its presence and position.

Briser—I knew the strength of the great war-dog. Never before had I wanted him to rouse, as I found myself wishing; neither had I ever done what I did in the next moment. Moving belly-down so that I could see the hound's response, I raised my voice in such a caterwaul as should have brought all the castle awake and to arms.

The blotch of ink turned, dipping toward me, but it did not attack again. My princess leaned forward, too, and, in what seemed a single movement, she both seized the floating foolscap and straight-armed the space of air that was empty of all but the airborne stain. The edge of the paper snapped taut, but she got both hands on the disputed sheet. Her body tensed as she resisted the contending force, and her wide skirts swirled as she kicked out, meeting, as I had done, solid opposition.

The page came suddenly free, as whatever was facing us backed against the king's hound and fell. A hard crash followed, suggesting that a body of sizable proportions had made close acquaintance, unexpectedly, with the floor; the sound of the impact was followed by a moan.

Charlita thrust the parchment roughly down the neckline of her gown, then turned and caught me up while I was still ridding myself of the dust. Not turning her back on the dark spot, which lay almost at our feet, she began to retreat.

I was already considering what defense we might employ if we were to be matched fairly against this menace. Though it could not be seen without aid (or additions), we had, at least, managed to make its presence known. Now to its nothingness must be added a something that would render it completely visible. Had my charge heard my thought? No—surely not; her mind must merely be especially keen after its long rest. Yet this whisper reached me as she held me tight:

"More ink—or wine, perhaps." Then we were at the door.

Abruptly Queen Symma's embroidery frame shook. The stain rose upwards once more into the air and moved away from man, dog, and desk. My mistress waited no longer but hastened from the library, brushing as she did so against one of the pair of door-guards who drowsed at their post. However, Charlita had taken only a quick brace of steps into the hall when she paused. Evidently she was not yet minded to leave the battlefield, for she turned back to the door, though she did not reenter. Loosing my claws from the now-battered lace of her bodice, she placed me upon the floor; then she moved to the nearer of the two sleeping soldiers.

"Guard you are, Sergeant Flors," she declared, "so guard you must."

With a push, she destroyed his balance, and down he went; a moment later, his comrade joined him. The two now lay against each other and across the open doorway, where their bodies formed a considerable obstruction. Stooping, the princess made sure that the armsmen lay face up and as easy as they might.

"Flors and Winster. Be sure I shall remember this service."

She returned to me and made as if to scoop me up again, but I moved away on my own four feet, having had enough for the moment of floating aloft like What-Is-Its-Face.

"Kitchen!" Charlita spoke the word aloud, no whisper this time but an order for us both. Once more, my thought was in tandem with hers.

We had visited that part of the castle before in our search for waking life, and I recalled with amusement the sleeping cook and her cat, who had both been snoring lustily at the time.

Cook and Cat remained deeply a-dream when we returned. Pastry Cook still lay over the marble slab where he had evidently been at work. Various scullery maids and pot-boys lay slumped about the cavernous room where they had been stricken down at their labors for, though Head Cook might have been taking her ease when the sorcery struck, her underlings had been busily employed. But of actual foodstuffs none were to be seen.

And food we must have ere long. I felt the pinch of hunger, and I was sure that the princess did also, now that she was conscious and calling upon the strength of her body. But while I might quiet my belly by a stalk in the courtyard, whether any viands suitable for a human still remained in this place was another matter. Charlita was of the same mind, for she stood beside the cook's chair, surveying intently the appointments of the room. In a moment her attention had centered on the array of cabinets set against the walls.

Some time later, I sat on the broad expanse of a large table, cleansing a paw that I might employ it to remove some of the dust which had turned my cream fur a grimy gray. My charge had pulled up a stool and was seated at the opposite side of the board. Before her stood three small pots; the thick stoppers of wax that had sealed the vessels for so long now lay beside them on the polished wood. Having sniffed once and then again, Charlita inserted a spoon into the first pot and brought out a dollop of thick paste. She gave this lump a cautious lick, then waited. One hand still held the heaped spoon; the other was tightened into a near-

fist around the amulet that had never left her neck
since the morning of the fateful birthday whose close
had seen her and all her world spelled asleep.

Having sensed no taint in what she had sampled,
the princess nodded and opened her mouth wide for
the whole of the spoon's contents. I wondered whether
she thought of the nursery-verse about the queen who
had gone to her own kitchen in search of honey when
I smelled the sweetness of berries from her find. I was
pleased that she had found such sustenance and hoped
that I might shortly slip away to my own private
larder.

Between raids on the preserve pots, Charlita drew
forth from her bodice the creased parchment from the
library and spread it as flat as she could in a square
of sunlight that reached the table from an upper window. Now curiosity, runs the proverb, is a bane to my
kind, rather than a blessing. I myself hold that, without
questions, answers cannot be found. But when the answers arrive *before* the questions . . .

My dampened paw shot out but did not come down
upon that crumpled sheet. The girl was viewing it up-
side down but had not tried to shift it, which must
mean she did *not* know—

My movement, though quickly aborted, had drawn
her attention. She stared at me and then, to my astonishment, opened her fist so that the amulet it
guarded could be fully seen. The talisman was not new
to me, nor was it a recent arrival in this world. Such
charms had been worn by the women of a royal house
that lay so far back in time its very name was lost;
even the land where that house held sway had been
broken by a hammering sea and blasted by fire from
the earth until it, too, had been forsaken and forgotten.

I stood. Though I knew that my gesture revealed a
sacred and secret feline ritual (or did it? Cats, after
all, *do* stretch upon occasion), I made the deepest

obeisance my body could render, raising a purr of homage loud enough for the princess to hear—and an even more royal Lady.

"Great Bast, I, your kit, await your will. You have given into my paws the fate of this two-footed one— and I say that, though she may not sing in Your temple, she is yet worthy of Your care." Thus did my purr-prayer rise.

I saw the lavender of Charlita's eyes darken, her lips part as if she would answer me, but she made no sound. However, the amulet, which had been dangling from her fingers by its chain as she watched me, suddenly swung forward and touched my head between my ears.

"I . . . dreamed," she murmured, gazing into the distance. I believed she was speaking to me; then, when her eyes met mine in full focus, I was sure of it. "A dark enchantment was laid upon me—that I accept as a truth beyond denying. Now I also acknowledge that, having escaped its hold alone, I must act to aid those still ensorcelled."

My mistress fastened the chain about her throat and tugged her talisman forward so that it lay openly upon her breast. Then she glanced down at the parchment.

"And this writing contains the truth to guide us, Cobweb—is that not so?"

Was her action the answer I sought from Lady Bast? That I believed. Our patroness was a dealer in deep mysteries; indeed, neither the Daughter-of-Dark who had invoked the curse nor the Dweller-in-Light who, at the last moment of its pronouncing, had changed death for its gentle mimic, sleep, would dare raise eyes in Her presence.

Setting a forepaw on the foolscap sheet, I dipped my head in the accepted gesture of agreement used by the princess' own kind—a nod—and together we went forth from the kitchen.

The light had grown noticeably dimmer when we

emerged into the hall that had brought us here; the patches of sun that penetrated the narrow, high-set windows were nearly gone. I could almost believe that the Dark Itself was rising against us. An odd stirring troubled the air at the other end of the corridor, but I could make out no shape distinctly in this half-light. If the intruder who bore the blazon of ink had come in search of us, it was still far behind.

We paused before an ironbound door that, strangely, had not had its bar-lock set. The portal groaned dolefully as the princess pushed it open, revealing the head of a staircase. The darkness grew denser as we descended, yet it never completely obscured our sight; perhaps my Protectress aided our vision and warded off blindness.

We traversed a lower hall onto which storerooms opened, then started down yet another flight of stairs. I heard Charlita's breath catch.

"Do we go into the center of the earth?" she asked in a near-whisper. I answered with a soft chirp, and she stooped to pick me up, then rested her cheek for a moment against my head.

Twice I caught the sound of footsteps, faint but steady, from behind—perhaps the creature we had already faced was indeed in pursuit. Yet I held to my hope of protection by the Lady Who carried the symbol of Life Everlasting in Her hand. Curiously, within me, and perhaps within Charlita also, the conviction grew that we were truly guarded by sure wards. The feeling persisted until the way we followed, which had been gradually narrowing, ended in an unbroken wall. I, however, had dealt with that barrier before, though the first time I had challenged it I thought I had failed, until—

I shifted in the princess' arms, and she understood and placed me on my feet before that blank surface. Its stones were a pale gray, a hue that seemed leached of all life. If despair could take a color, that chill hue would be its choice.

I set my paw to the wall. My claws scratched against the rough surface, though whether they left any record there I could not tell. Push thus, said my memory—and thus—and *thus!*

The door in the upper reaches of the castle had protested when we used it, but no sound came now. Before us, an opening expanded, its air illumined only by a dull gleam as of twilight. Silent ourselves, we passed within.

There was resistance—a power-ward of some sort had certainly been set here. My charge hesitated, but I caught the hem of her now-bedraggled gown between my teeth and used a force she could not resist to draw her on. She raised her chin determinedly and gathered her strength to advance.

It was a strange place we had entered. What we had reached was a bowl of stone held deep in the earth, but at first glance it seemed that we stood in a night-drowned forest. Trunks of trees arose on either side of a path leading forward, their branches interlaced to form a roof well above the princess's head. Strange rock formations with the look of plants ordered the trail; yet even they showed no color but the unbroken dusk gray—

—until my mistress moved forward. As she stepped through the futile defense of the ward, an awakening began around us. A spotting of rainbow-hued dots came alive on tree trunks, and on bone-pale branches and dead-looking leaves on ground-growth. Faintly at first, but swiftly becoming stronger, sound followed—a flowing chant, both solemn and inspiring. We were surely approaching a shrine of power. As we set feet (and paws) on the path, the disks of rainbow radiance on the trees began to run together, melding into each other until they became so dazzlingly bright that we dared no longer raise our eyes to watch.

Time ceased to have meaning, and distance did the same; we seemed to cross a wide plain and to patiently keep to the track for a very long time. The end came suddenly as we halted at the foot of a second barrier that framed another stair—one so narrow that any castle dwellers who sought to use it must needs go in single file. Our eyes had adjusted to the light by then, for we could clearly make out the head of that staircase. But at the sight of what was displayed there, Charlita stood still, her hands braced rigidly right and left against the stone that walled the climb.

"The Scepter of Margalee," she said.

So—some portion of what was now legend but had once been history *did* remain. The House of Lud had given kings to Fallona, ten of them in direct descent. However, before those had come (it was rumored) rulers of a different bloodline, each of whom had, in turn, been greater than the humans over whom he or she had reigned.

But with the passing of years both the power and knowledge of the First Lineage had declined, and at length the House of Lud had triumphed after a red slaughter. The talents of the Firstborn had dwindled, then began to be viewed with suspicion. Archives were looted, and any information that might have restored tales to the status of truths was sought out and destroyed.

The handful of seers who had stood against the last Ludish ruler had withdrawn—

—until the casting of the Sleep-Spell! I had guessed that more than one of the old Great Ones had come forth again when I had been made the tool of good Lady Ulava, whose quick action had softened the malison against Charlita; now I knew my suspicion to be true. When is a curse *not* a curse . . .

A small bead of blood appeared on the princess' lower lip as she spoke, and her words, too, were bitten and spat out in anger:

"So—are we still to be pieces in a game played against our wills? We shall see!" Her body taut with rage, she began to climb the stairs, keeping her arms braced against the walls to move her upward the more swiftly. I followed as closely as I could.

And I in turn was pursued. The ink my charge had hurled at the library interloper had dried upon it but not faded. Whoever—or whatever—wore the sinlike stain was coming after us slowly; it did not begin its own ascent until we were near the head of the steps.

The princess used the momentum from her push against the walls to propel herself onto a platform that spread across a landing much wider than the stairs. At mid-point of that level space rested a block of un-worked stone over whose surface curled thick lines of some pure metal. Thrust deep into the rock by its point was the ancient symbol of the rulers of Fallona: the Scepter of Margalee.

Charlita stood gazing up at the length of chased and bejeweled silver; and, as she contemplated the rod that bespoke authority over her kind, I was aware of the presence of my own queen. With a leap, I sprang past the princess, voicing the claim-cry of the cat, and landed atop the stone that held the Scepter. Lowering my head, I set my mouth around a section of the rod where the wood was exposed, bit down hard, and held on.

Charlita reached forward to grasp the huge rock, intending to climb it, but a moment later she backed away with a gasp to stare upward. Immediately over-head, the Golden Key of Bast, by men called the Ankh, had sprung into being and now hung in midair above the scepter-bearing stone. In that moment, we were all frozen into place as surely as if chains had been cast about our limbs.

"NO!"

In the space of a single breath, the same word was shouted by three different voices; at the same moment, two different Powers struck at me. No, the attacking wills belonged neither to the princess nor to the one who appeared to be shaping himself from the very air as he stepped up next to her, his tattered left sleeve fluttering in crude pennons from the standard of his arm.

I could feel the air to both sides of me curdling into other shapes, but the blaze of the Sacred Key so dazzled my eyes that I could see only the princess and the young man beside her. He stood arrow-straight, and his dark hair was cropped as though he were prepared to don a helm of war, yet his belt did not even hold the sheath for a sword. A prince, it would seem, had come at last— and doubtless when he was needed least.

The youth had been studying my mistress closely, and the frown that had earlier bent his brows was fading. When he saw that he had caught Charlita's attention, he swept her the bow of the finished courtier, his left hand held before his heart but not quite touching the betraying blot. He smiled, and as he did so I judged that, though he was young, he already knew the worth of the policy "wait and see."

My princess, however, was not so ready to agree to what was certainly an offer of truce. She returned his smile, but with a meaningful glance at the stain.

"Your Highness . . ." The ingathering of mist to the prince's left had become solid, and the voice that spoke belonged to the serene and stately figure now revealed. This was Ulava of Fallona, so mighty a servant of Light with the ancient Gifts once common in her land that her very name was a title. Now she looked beyond the youth to me, holding her hand forth in respect and welcome—

—as another also hailed me, but with clawed fingers that raked the air in a gesture of contempt and dismissal. "Cat!" cried Urgal of Morh, the Great One of Dark power who had been born from the mist to the prince's right. "Think not to hold *that*—" she indicated the scepter, "—which is for your betters."

I did not relinquish the rod of rule to the Shadow-wielder, nor did I, in any way, deign to acknowledge her presence. Her skin, which sagged with age, flushed. Whatever power she had gathered down the years, she had never gained the ability to stop the ravages of time on her person. Neither had the Lady on her other side—Ulava, who had once been both sorceress and queen; but time had enhanced and not diminished her.

The Dark One set palms together, and her fingers began to move as though she would weave something from the air. With that action she also moved her lips, though nothing she uttered could be heard.

Ulava spared Urgal not a glance as she stepped forward to join the princess and prince. Join them she did, in more than one way, for, placing a hand on the shoulder of each, she turned them so the youth faced the maid.

"Once done, ill done," she intoned, "twice done, well done. *Finished!*"

The pair might no longer have had any wills of their own. Prince No-Name-Nor-Nation and Princess Char-lita of Fallona made not a move toward one another, but their lips met as if they were dreaming.

All about, the massive stone walls seemed to draw a deep breath; the castle itself was waking, as well as the people and creatures it held.

The palace might indeed have shaken off its sorcerous sleep, but Urgal, she who had called down the curse, was not yet defeated. I rocked back and forth, holding onto the scepter with all the strength in me and striving to work it loose from its free-standing position. I obeyed no actual order from the Lady of the Key, but Her will was at work. The gemmed rod shifted in my mouth-grip, tilted, and pointed at the enemy.

Suddenly I became a channel, as power that was neither mine nor native to my kind coursed through me. Shooting through my body up the scepter, it poured out the head of the rod and down, rained in a molten-gold flood over the last Priestess of Night, puddled, and rose about her twitching body. Urgal's wrinkle-wrung mouth opened in a soundless scream. Still further I turn-mouthed the scepter until its heavy ornate head swung floorward; and then a Force I *did* know made Herself felt. Down from My Lady's Life-Promise above shot a beam of white light to touch the rod. I could not choke back a cry of pain as Her lightning blazed through me up the scepter's length. The blast struck Urgal full on, and the Dark One staggered, fell, and vanished in a pillar of fire.

Thus ended what has doubtless become an oft-told tale: the story of a princess placed under an evil enchantment of sleep until a kiss awakened her and her ensorcelled folk, of a reckoning between Darkness and Light such as will occur many times again.

It was not given to me to know what happened— to learn whether my princess wedded her prince, then reigned with him wisely and well until Fallona rose to greatness once more in a "happily ever after."

No, my destiny lay in another direction and a different realm; for so great had been the demand of both the Powers of Light on my body that it could no longer remain in the mortal plane. But as I still held, exhausted, to the Scepter of the Great Ones, my eyes, which were closing to this world, opened to another. Above me, the glowing ankh became the figure of a Lady robed in light, a human woman with the countenance of a cat. Bending down, She gathered me into Her arms, murmuring to me of a new land and new life to come in Her service. And together, in joyous anticipation, we passed through that door to which Her symbol was, indeed, the Key.

Lisanne Norman

The *Sholan Alliance* Series

"Will hold you spellbound" — *Romantic Times*

TURNING POINT	0-88677-575-2
FORTUNE'S WHEEL	0-88677-675-9
FIRE MARGINS	0-88677-718-6
RAZOR'S EDGE	0-88677-766-6
DARK NADIR	0-88677-829-6
STRONGHOLD RISING	0-88677-898-0
BETWEEN DARKNESS AND LIGHT	
	0-7564-0015-5

This new, seventh novel takes readers into the heart of a secret Prime base—where Kusac must make an alliance with an enemy general to save his son's life.

To Order Call: 1-800-788-6262

Irene Radford

"A mesmerizing storyteller." —*Romantic Times*

THE DRAGON NIMBUS

THE GLASS DRAGON
0-88677-634-1

THE PERFECT PRINCESS
0-88677-678-3

THE LONELIEST MAGICIAN
0-88677-709-7

THE WIZARD'S TREASURE
0-88677-913-8

THE DRAGON NIMBUS HISTORY

THE DRAGON'S TOUCHSTONE
0-88677-744-5

THE LAST BATTLEMAGE
0-88677-774-7

THE RENEGADE DRAGON
0-88677-855-7

THE STAR GODS

THE HIDDEN DRAGON
0-7564-0051-1

To Order Call: 1-800-788-6262

Irene Radford
Merlin's Descendants

"Entertaining blend of fantasy and history, which invites comparisons with Mary Stewart and Marion Zimmer Bradley" —*Publishers Weekly*

GUARDIAN OF THE PROMISE
This fourth novel in the series follows the children of Donovan and Griffin, in a magic-fueled struggle to protect Elizabethan England from enemies—both mortal and demonic.   0-7564-0108-9

*And don't miss the first three books
in this exciting series:*
GUARDIAN OF THE BALANCE
0-88677-875-1
GUARDIAN OF THE TRUST
0-88677-995-2
GUARDIAN OF THE VISION
0-7564-0071-6

To Order Call: 1-800-788-6262

DAW 32

JENNIFER
ROBERSON

To Order Call: 1-800-788-6262
www.dawbooks.com

Tanya Huff

Victory Nelson, Investigator:
Otherworldly Crimes a Specialty

"Smashing entertainment for a wide audience"
—*Romantic Times*

"One series that deserves to continue"
—*Science Fiction Chronicle*

BLOOD PRICE
0-88677-471-3

BLOOD TRAIL
0-88677-502-7

BLOOD LINES
0-88677-530-2

BLOOD PACT
0-88677-582-5

To Order Call: 1-800-788-6262

Tanya Huff

The Finest in Fantasy

SING THE FOUR QUARTERS   0-88677-628-7
FIFTH QUARTER   0-88677-651-1
NO QUARTER   0-88677-698-8
THE QUARTERED SEA   0-88677-839-5

The Keeper's Chronicles
SUMMON THE KEEPER   0-88677-784-4
THE SECOND SUMMONING   0-88677-975-8
LONG HOT SUMMONING   0-7564-0136-4

Omnibus Editions:
WIZARD OF THE GROVE   0-88677-819-0
(Child of the Grove & The Last Wizard)
OF DARKNESS, LIGHT & FIRE   0-7564-0038-4
(Gate of Darkness, Circle of Light & The Fire's Stone)

To Order Call: 1-800-788-6262

DAW 21